An excerpt from *Four Weeks to Forever* by Karen Booth

"I'm starting to feel like I can trust you."

"You can."

Colin stepped closer to Corryna, drawn to her in a way that he felt on a molecular level. "I hope you know that you can trust me, too."

"I think I know that."

"I want you, Corryna. One hundred times more than I wanted you that night, and I really, really wanted you."

Pink colored her cheeks, making her even more impossibly beautiful. "I'd be lying if I said I didn't want you, too, but this wouldn't be like that night. Neither of us had anything to lose then. Now we're working together on a wedding that is immensely important to our businesses. Sex will make everything more complicated."

He reached for a lock of her hair and twisted it in his fingers. "It's just you and me. Together in my bed isn't complicated. It sounds perfect."

An excerpt from *Make Believe Match* by Joanne Rock

Oliver Price followed the woman with his eyes all evening long.

Elbows resting on the rail of the patio overlooking an outdoor bar and firepit, he shook the last ice cubes in a glass that had been a scotch on the rocks half an hour ago. He easily spotted Jessica Lewis in the crowd below as she sidled around a lit fountain in the courtyard to deliver drinks to guests with a smile.

Even when he'd been engaged in party small talk with friends earlier in the evening, he found his attention veering back to the curvy waitress with eyes that shifted between blue and green, the color of a summer sea.

Just thinking of a set of irises that way—a summer freaking sea?—told him how unwise his reactions seemed when it came to the sexy server. It was also a bad idea. Because he'd felt her rapid heartbeat when her body had been pressed to his. Seen her cheeks pinken with awareness. And nothing about the way she'd reacted to him suggested she shared his views about purely recreational, no-strings sex.

No. His gut told him Jessica was the sort of woman who waited to indulge herself until after the third date. Or quite possibly until the chemistry was too irresistible to ignore.

Cursing himself for thoughts he had no business thinking, he pivoted away from the railing, telling himself he ought to leave the party. Before he seriously considered that drink with Jessica.

KAREN BOOTH

&

USA TODAY BESTSELLING AUTHOR
JOANNE ROCK

FOUR WEEKS TO FOREVER
&
MAKE BELIEVE MATCH

HARLEQUIN
DESIRE

Special thanks and acknowledgment are given to
Karen Booth and Joanne Rock for their contributions to the
Texas Cattleman's Club: The Wedding miniseries.

HARLEQUIN®
DESIRE™

Recycling programs
for this product may
not exist in your area.

ISBN-13: 978-1-335-45752-3

Four Weeks to Forever & Make Believe Match

Copyright © 2023 by Harlequin Enterprises ULC

Four Weeks to Forever
Copyright © 2023 by Harlequin Enterprises ULC

Make Believe Match
Copyright © 2023 by Harlequin Enterprises ULC

For questions and comments about the quality of this book,
please contact us at CustomerService@Harlequin.com.

Harlequin Enterprises ULC
22 Adelaide St. West, 41st Floor
Toronto, Ontario M5H 4E3, Canada
www.Harlequin.com

Printed in U.S.A.

CONTENTS

Karen Booth is a Midwestern girl transplanted in the South, raised on '80s music and repeated readings of *Forever...* by Judy Blume. When she takes a break from the art of romance, she's listening to music with her college-age kids or sweet-talking her husband into making her a cocktail. Learn more about Karen at karenbooth.net.

Books by Karen Booth

Harlequin Desire

Texas Cattleman's Club

Blue Collar Billionaire
Rancher After Midnight
Four Weeks to Forever

Little Black Book of Secrets

The Problem with Playboys
Black Tie Bachelor Bid
How to Fake a Wedding Date

The Sterling Wives

Once Forbidden, Twice Tempted
High Society Secrets
All He Wants for Christmas

Visit the Author Profile page
at Harlequin.com for more titles.

You can also find Karen Booth on Facebook,
along with other Harlequin Desire authors,
at Facebook.com/HarlequinDesireAuthors!

Dear Reader,

Welcome back to Royal, Texas! I'm so excited for you to read my contribution to the Texas Cattleman's Club: The Wedding series!

I found so much to love in this book as I was writing it. First off, I love writing florists, and Corryna, my heroine, owns a little flower shop right in the heart of downtown Royal. I so admire her determination and persistence as a small business owner and as a woman who's had to overcome a divorce. Then there's Colin, the Irish chef. I have quite the weakness for a rich Irish accent, especially when it's wrapped up in a package like Colin—tall and strong, brilliant, and more than a little sure of himself.

The conflict between these two is white-hot from the start, but I could see them together from that very first chapter. Some books are just like that—it feels like the characters are meant for each other. I hope you see some of that when you read it!

Drop me a line anytime at karen@karenbooth.net and let me know if you enjoyed *Four Weeks to Forever*. I love hearing from readers!

Karen

FOUR WEEKS TO FOREVER

Karen Booth

For Angela Anderson.
Thank you for being such a
stellar ambassador for romance!

One

Corryna Lawson was placing a perfect peony in a bouquet when everything around her went black. The music she was listening to abruptly cut out. The light from the decades-old overhead fixtures in her floral shop disappeared. "What the hell?" she asked no one, speaking into the dark cavern that was now the back room of Royal Blooms. Hannah Waters, her main counter clerk, had gone home hours ago. Corryna liked to stay and work late, listening to music and getting lost in her designs. Her love for flowers and the artistry of arranging them were not only the reasons she'd started this business, they were also the parts of her job she never questioned. Plus, it wasn't like she had anyone to go home to. Not anymore. Not since her divorce.

She grabbed her phone from the worktable and switched on the flashlight function, then wound her way past the buckets of blooms and into the front of her shop. The large picture windows facing downtown Royal were black as night. By the looks of it, the businesses across the street had also lost power. She unlocked the front door and stepped outside, momentarily blinded by the headlights of passing cars. Down the block, patrons were filtering out of The Royal Diner and onto the sidewalk, seemingly just as surprised as she was. In every direction, all she saw was darkness.

This was not good. Corryna had thousands of dollars of floral inventory sitting in the refrigerators in the back of her shop. She not only needed the blooms to fill upcoming orders, she needed them to work out the floral designs for the June nuptials of acclaimed bestselling author Xavier Noble and Hollywood actress/producer Ariana Ramos. Corryna had lived in Royal for nearly eight years, and the Nobles were long-standing pillars of the community. The wedding was more than three months away, but it was going to be the social event of the year, and Corryna was damn lucky to have such a prestigious job.

Morgan Grandin from The Rancher's Daughter, the upscale women's clothing boutique next door, stepped outside. "Oh, hey, Corryna." Morgan used a small flashlight in order to see while inserting a key into the dead bolt on her shop's front door. "This is a real pain in the butt, isn't it? I hate having to close early, but it was pretty slow."

Corryna flipped off the flashlight on her phone to save the battery. Luckily, there was enough ambient light from the moon to help her see some things, like Morgan's fair-complected face and striking red hair. "Any idea how long the power is going to be out?" Corryna asked.

Morgan shrugged and hooked her handbag in the crook of her elbow. "I just talked to my sister Chelsea. Her husband, Nolan, said the whole town is out. Who knows when it will be back on. I hope it's not days."

"Days? But…but… I don't have days." Corryna couldn't disguise the panic in her voice. She didn't have thousands of dollars to lose. Her shop was just barely breaking even, after she paid herself her pittance of a salary. She could not let her flowers go to waste. It would be a setback that would take months to recover from. "I have to save my flowers. They're all in my fridge which already doesn't work that well. It'll be a matter of hours before they start deteriorating. I have weddings this weekend. What do I do?"

Morgan stepped closer and eyed the front of Royal Blooms. "Well, shoot. I never thought about that."

"Seriously. I need you to help me think. Any ideas?"

"Uh… So you need another fridge, right?"

"Yes. A massive one." She so appreciated that

Morgan was calm because Corryna's anxiety was making her shoulders bind up and her stomach sour.

"Except the power is out everywhere. So you also need a place that has a generator."

Dammit. Corryna blew out an exasperated breath. "Yes. Of course."

"They have both of those at the TCC." Morgan was referring to the Texas Cattleman's Club, which was the hub of social life in Royal. "But I know for a fact that their generator isn't working. I guess they got a new one and it's faulty."

This mission was sounding more doomed at every turn. "Do you have any other ideas? I'm desperate."

"Who else has a fridge that big and a generator? It would have to be a restaurant."

As soon as Morgan said that, Corryna had her answer. The problem was she didn't like it. In fact, she hated it. What was that old saying about desperate times calling for desperate measures? She had a feeling she was about to put that to the test. "What about Sheen?"

Morgan reached out and grasped Corryna's arm. "Oh, my God. Yes. They have both."

Morgan had so much sheer enthusiasm in her voice that it broke Corryna's heart to think about what she was about to say. "The only problem is Colin Reynolds." She could hardly spit out his name, she disliked him so much. The owner and head chef of Sheen was an arrogant, bristly, penny-pinching jerk. "He doesn't like me. And the feeling is mutual."

"No. How is that possible? Everyone loves you."

"Not Colin." Corryna knocked her head to the side. "We had two unpleasant run-ins. This was a while ago, but they were both bad."

"Oh, really?" Morgan did like a bit of gossip, and there was always plenty to go around in Royal.

"Yes. The first was when he hit on me in The Silver Saddle at The Bellamy." She'd been sitting at the bar of the tapas restaurant at the luxury resort, trying to gain some intel on who Ariana and Xavier were hiring to do their wedding flowers. "I told him that I was a lost cause and he should go chat up someone else. I thought I was being self-deprecating, but by the look on his face, he took it as a massive insult."

"So you're not dating at all?"

"Not really. I mean, I'd like to, but it has to be the right situation. I definitely don't need a guy like Colin. Whenever he's romantically linked to someone, it doesn't last long."

"I hear he's quite the playboy."

Corryna had heard the same. Colin's reputation in Royal was notorious. Women fawned over him. They swooned. It was part of the reason it was impossible to get a reservation at Sheen. Frankly, it was embarrassing. Sure, he was far better than "good looking"—six foot five with messy, shaggy light brown hair, a square jaw and penetrating green eyes. But who wanted the arrogance that went along with the handsome exterior? "Two days later, he canceled Sheen's contract with my shop. I took a massive hit

to my bottom line. Plus, he was such an ass about it."
My customers care about my food, not your flowers.
Even now, she could hear echoes of his annoyingly
sexy Irish brogue. Corryna had a real weakness for
a man with an accent. "He was just being vindictive.
I think he figured out who I was and decided to get
back at me. I don't think his ego could handle it."

"I wish I could come up with another option, but
I can't. No one else has a big enough fridge for all
your flowers."

Corryna grumbled under her breath. "Yeah. Okay.
I guess I gotta do it, huh?"

"Are you going to call him first?"

Corryna shook her head emphatically. She was
certain Colin would tell her no straight away. "I need
the element of surprise. Plus, I figure if I show up
with a truck full of flowers, it'll be that much harder
for him to say no."

"What if he isn't there?"

"Oh, he'll be there. He's a total workaholic." *Sort
of like me.*

"It seems like you know a lot about this guy you
supposedly hate."

Corryna had done some research online the night
he'd canceled his account with her. She wanted to
know his weak spots. Unfortunately, she couldn't
find a single one. He'd had a meteoric rise in the
restaurant industry. Everyone thought he was brilliant. He made piles of money, to put on top of the

fortune he'd been born into. End of story. "People talk. I listen."

"Well, if you want, I can help you load up your flowers," Morgan said.

"Really? You'd do that for me?"

"Yeah. Of course. Let's do it."

Corryna led Morgan into her shop and grabbed the keys for the delivery truck, then they started ferrying buckets of flowers out into the back alley where the vehicle was parked. Twenty minutes later, the truck was full and Corryna needed to get on her way.

"Thank you so much, Morgan."

"Yeah. Of course. Good luck with Colin."

"Thanks. I don't just have a feeling I'm going to need it. I know I will." Corryna hopped in and started up the engine, then embarked on her trek to Sheen. With every traffic light in town out of commission, she had to drive with caution. Creeping down these familiar streets and roads at a snail's pace while everything was dark left her feeling like she'd landed on another planet. Once she got closer to Sheen, even that looked peculiar. The restaurant was built entirely of glass, so it was usually brightly lit and looking like a jewel box. Not tonight. A small soft glow from the center of the building was the only indication that Colin Reynolds's generator was indeed working.

She pulled into the parking lot and parked right next to Colin's ridiculously expensive show-off of a car—a black Jaguar SUV. One of the things she'd learned about Colin during her online sleuthing was that he came from incredible wealth and power. In his life, making a fortune from being a restaurateur was a family affair. As if he wasn't already intimidating enough.

This would have been an excellent time to chicken out, but she wasn't about to lose her business because of a blackout. She'd just have to face the handsome jerk, do her best to hold her own, then make a swift exit. Colin Reynolds was not the sort of man she needed to spend any time at all with.

With his feet on his desk, Colin Reynolds was savoring another sip of his Redbreast 27-year-old Irish whiskey when headlights beamed into his office from the parking lot of his restaurant, Sheen. He immediately dropped his feet to the floor. He wasn't expecting anyone in the middle of a blackout. Peering through the window, he saw a white delivery truck and immediately recognized the colorful Royal Blooms logo emblazoned on the side. The headlights switched off, and for a split second as the light faded, he saw Corryna Lawson climbing out of the vehicle. Was he seeing things? He *was* on his second glass of whiskey, and at forty-two, his eyesight wasn't what it once was. She was wearing a white top, which made it easier to study her as she ambled toward the entrance to the restaurant. How life was full of surprises.

He immediately headed to the front door and unlocked it. "If you're here for dinner, we're closed." Even through the darkness, Corryna's flawless complexion seemed to glow. Her sexy, radiant beauty had been the reason he'd asked her out at The Silver Saddle the first time he'd seen her. To his shock and dismay, she shot him down. He'd been turned down once or twice in his life, but Corryna's rejection had really stung. She'd given him some line about how she was a lost cause. Any man could take one look at her and know that couldn't be further from the truth.

"Not here to eat. I need your help." Her voice was icy and defensive, as if she was expecting him to say no.

He prided himself on being at least a little unpredictable. Plus, he needed to extend an olive branch. The last time he'd seen Corryna, he'd said a few unkind things about her business. He wasn't proud of it, but his ego was bruised and he'd lashed out. "Sure. Of course. What can I do?"

Corryna stepped closer and narrowed her eyes. She was wearing a pair of jeans that smartly followed every sumptuous curve of her body, and the white blouse he'd noticed moments ago skimmed the contours of her breasts perfectly. Her wavy brown hair went from dark to light in a sexy tumble. He'd seen countless gorgeous women in his life, and he'd taken more than a few of them to bed. But Corryna was an exceptional beauty, in part because she seemed oblivious to it. "What's the catch?" she asked.

"None. You said you need help. With what?"

"As you know, the power is out. Unlike you, I don't have a generator. And I had thousands of dollars of floral inventory in my cooler that I was about to lose."

"And you'd like to use my walk-in."

"If you don't mind. Yes."

"Sure. Absolutely."

"Really?" She still didn't seem convinced.

"Yes. Come on now. Get on with it." He marched past her to the rear of her truck and opened the doors. The interior light flickered on, revealing the volume of flowers she'd brought along. It was going to be tight in his fridge, but this was no time to go back on his promise.

Corryna joined him, standing at his side. "I'm begging you to be careful. I have two weddings this weekend. Many of these flowers are for that."

"What makes you think I'm not going to be careful?"

"Oh, I don't know. I seem to remember you telling me something about not caring about flowers."

"I didn't mean it like that." He grabbed several buckets and led the way into the restaurant. He trailed through the dining room then into the kitchen and back to the massive walk-in refrigerator. He set down the buckets and opened the door. A rush of frigid air hit his face. "Quickly. Can't keep the door open long. The generator can only do so much."

"Got it." She hustled into the cold room ahead of him.

"At the back, please. Just be careful of the beef. It's dry aging. A lot of money on those shelves." He followed her, stealing a glimpse of her ass as she bent over to set down several buckets. It was a real shame she'd turned him down. He knew for a fact they could have a whole lot of fun together.

"Of course I'll be careful," she snapped as she turned back to him.

"No need to be angry. It's only a suggestion."

She sighed and looked him in the eye. "I'm sorry. I'm a little stressed, okay?"

He felt bad. Of course she was under strain. Until a few minutes ago, she'd thought she was going to lose the most precious thing her business could have—her inventory. "You don't need to apologize. I'm sorry if I'm being an ass. Let's get on with it and save your flowers."

They rushed back outside, and made six or seven trips back and forth in order to load up the refrigerator. "Thank you, Colin," Corryna said when they were finished.

"Can I interest you in a whiskey?"

"I should go home."

"You just did all that work, and I know it's been a hard night. It's just a drink. We'll sit and talk and you can tell me why you don't like me."

Corryna let out a dismissive tut. "You're the one who doesn't like me."

"Did I or did I not make a pass at you at The Silver Saddle? I didn't do that merely for fun. I did it because I thought you were gorgeous. I did it because I *do* like you."

"You're a terrible liar."

"Which is why I don't do it. I am an open book. And I don't invite people I dislike for a drink."

"I don't know…" She cocked an eyebrow, but seemed like she was open to a bit more persuasion.

"It's delicious. The best you'll ever have."

"Okay. Fine. I'm game. What else do I have to do? Go home and sit in the dark?"

Colin did his best to hide his satisfied grin. "That's what I want to hear. Right this way." He led her back to his office, where the whiskey bottle was still sitting on his desk. This was one of his favorite spaces in the restaurant—a true retreat, with modern earth-toned furnishings. Needing order in his life whenever possible, he kept everything as tidy as could be.

"This is so nice." She ran her hand along the smooth tawny leather of one of two generous armchairs opposite his desk. "My office is about one quarter this size."

"Thank you. I like it, too. Which is a good thing because I spend so much time in here." He grabbed a match for his glass from the corner bar and poured them each a drink. He handed her one, then raised his glass in a toast. "To helping others."

She clinked her glass with his, then took a sip.

"Mmm." She rolled the glossy amber liquid in the glass, admiring it. "This is delicious."

"Just like everything that comes from Ireland." He bobbed his eyebrows up and down at her in an attempt to flirt. He'd suffered her rejection once, but it didn't mean he wasn't willing to try again.

"You're terrible."

"I'm also delicious."

Corryna laughed and shook her head, then sat on the edge of his desk. "Can you answer me honestly this time? Did you cancel my contract with Sheen because I turned you down at The Silver Saddle?"

"As I tried to explain before, I did not realize you were the same woman until you came into Sheen to yell at me. By then, it was too late. I'd already made my decision."

She took another sip. "Why am I still not sure I believe you?"

"You said it yourself. I'm a terrible liar. I'm no good at it."

"Okay. I guess that's good to know." She still didn't seem convinced.

"I've nothing to hide. Ask me anything."

"Why me that night at the bar? There were dozens of hot women there."

She wasn't wrong. "I just told you. You're gorgeous. Plus, something told me you were a challenge. I love that. It gets my blood pumping."

"Then why did you give up so easily?"

"Because you were trying to deflect. And there's usually a reason for that."

"But you still seemed disappointed."

This wasn't an easy topic for Colin to discuss. He didn't enjoy ruminating over his failures. That was territory his father liked to tread, pointing out every instance in which Colin had come up short. "Of course I was. It was brutal. The most stunning woman had turned me down. I thought I had a chance. I guess I was wrong."

She pressed her lips together tightly. "You weren't entirely wrong. If I had been in a better headspace, I probably would have said yes."

"That would've made me incredibly happy." He reached out and brushed the back of her hand with the tip of his finger. "And I know I could've done the same for you."

She watched his finger on her hand, then peered up at him with her remarkable pale green eyes. They swept back and forth in the softly lit room. She was still sitting on the edge of the desk and he was standing right before her. They were mere inches from each other, breathing in sync, electricity traveling across the tiny sliver of space between them. "You're a player, right? Never get serious with a woman?"

He shrugged, then dared to reach out and take a lock of her silky hair and twist it around his fingers. "I'm whatever you need me to be."

"Anything?" She bit down on her lower lip, and he sensed that he was getting somewhere.

He rubbed the side of her jaw with the back of his hand. "How long has it been since a man has made you feel good, Corryna?"

"It's been a while."

"I mean really, really good."

"So long. So very, very long."

He stepped closer, but with her sitting on the desk, he had to straddle her knee in order to get his legs against the edge. He pushed her hair back from her shoulder and leaned down to nuzzle the side of her neck with his nose. "Does this feel good?"

"Yes." Her voice was soft and yielding, yet full of desperation.

It made everything below his waist go tight. He could set her on fire. He knew he could. With an open mouth, he kissed her neck. She grasped his shoulder and moaned in delight, then raised her knee until it was right against his crotch. That bit of pressure nearly made him lose all ability to see. "Corryna, I want you just as much as I did that night at The Silver Saddle. Maybe more."

"Prove it to me."

He was lightning fast unbuttoning her blouse while he worked his lips up and down her neck. He tugged her sleeves down her arms, then reached back for the clasp of her bra. She wrapped both of her legs around one of his, pressing the top of her thigh against his length, which was heavy and hard.

He pulled her bra off and gathered her breasts in his hands, rubbing his thumbs across her nipples as he kissed her. She angled her head to the side and took the kiss deeper. She delivered so much raw, unbridled enthusiasm that he wondered where it came from. Was she like this all the time or had he brought it out of her?

Not that he cared to know the answer. Not now.

He wasted no time unbuttoning her jeans, and she slid off the desk to give him better access. Tugging them down her legs, and taking her panties with them, he dropped to his knees. He was still fully dressed, every inch of him longing to bury himself in her. But he'd made a promise about making her feel good, and he intended to deliver on that.

"Sit," he ordered. "In the chair."

She did exactly as he'd asked, leaning back and letting him drink in the vision of her naked body while he took off his shirt, then his jeans and his boxers. He was so primed for her, but he wanted to leave her with something memorable. He dropped to his knees again, took one of her legs and hitched it up over his shoulder, then grasped her hips and pulled them forward until her butt was at the very edge of the seat. He spread her folds apart with his fingers, then lowered his head and swirled his tongue around her apex. She instantly curled her fingers into his hair and gasped. He knew that he was on the right track. He continued with his ministrations and it only took moments before she was digging her heel into his back and crying out.

"Colin… Colin… I want more," Corryna muttered.

"Good. I do too."

He hardly got the words out before she did something he never expected. She lowered her leg, sat up and pushed back on his shoulders until he had no choice but to lie back on the floor. Next thing he knew, she was on her knees. Then straddling his hips. Then she took his length in her hands, which made it impossible to think. She guided him inside her. He didn't have time to ask about a condom. *She must be on the pill*, he thought.

She dropped her chest against his, grinding into him hard. He met every movement of hers with a thrust as he kissed her, and dug his fingers into the fleshiest parts of her bottom. It was hot and fast and reckless. He'd had plenty of wild sexual experiences, but this was one for the books. The pressure was coiling in his belly so tightly that he couldn't hold on much longer. He felt himself on the edge. About to go over the cliff. Then Corryna gave way again. She called out into his neck and he thrust once or twice more, the release slamming into him.

She collapsed against his chest, breathless. His hands squeezed her full hips. She was as luscious as a ripe summer peach. He wanted her again. And again. This blackout might turn out to be the best thing ever.

"That was fantastic," he said.

She pushed up on her arms and looked down at

him. "Um. Yeah." She rolled off of him, grabbed her underwear from the floor and stood up. "It was nice."

"Nice? I don't do nice." He rolled to his side, enjoying his chance to watch her step into her panties, even though it was unsettling to hear the way she stomped her feet when they hit the floor.

"It was ten minutes of fun in your office. Don't make it more than it was." She wrestled her bra on.

"Ten minutes? It was more like fifteen. You had two orgasms, Corryna. I'd say that seemed like more than fun."

"I wasn't keeping score." She put on her top, fumbling with the buttons. She seemed rattled, which was incredibly confusing.

Meanwhile, he felt great. Relaxed. Ready for more. And she was ruining it. "I wasn't saying you had to count. I was only feeling like I deserve some credit."

"Please stop talking."

He decided to stand up and put on his boxers. He couldn't recline naked on the floor forever. "I don't understand why you're in such a rush. Unless you want to go to my place. Or yours."

She stepped into her jeans. "No. Sorry. That's not happening."

"Why?"

"Because men are bad for me, and you are a man."

He stood there frozen, blinking as he took in her words. This was not the normal postsex response he got from a woman. Usually they were begging for more of him. It was often *his* job to say things like "that was nice, but it's time for me to leave." "Okay…"

She strode to the door, then turned back to look at him. "I'll come back for my flowers when the power comes back on. If you aren't here, can someone else help me with them?"

"I'm always here."

"Colin, that was my way of telling you that it'd be better for me if you weren't."

"Tell me how you really feel." He watched as she again turned back to the door. "Corryna."

"What?"

"You can avoid me for a few days, but you can't ignore me forever."

"Sure I can. You canceled your contract with me, remember?"

"I'm not talking about that. I'm talking about the Noble-Ramos wedding. We're both working on it."

"What? No. You're just trying to rattle my cage."

He shrugged and plucked his jeans from the floor. He didn't have the strength to argue with her anymore. "I guess we'll just have to see then, won't we?"

Two

One month later

Corryna arrived for her Monday morning meeting with Rylee Meadows, the wedding planner, a few minutes early. She didn't want to risk being late. The Noble-Ramos wedding could make or break her business. Do well, and she'd have countless opportunities to work for some of the most prestigious members of the Royal community. Fail, and she would continue to struggle financially. She couldn't allow that to happen. She had two employees, who she adored, counting on her. Plus, her ex-husband, Dan, was expecting her to fall flat on her face someday. He'd always said she had no business sense. Every day she kept her doors open, was another instance of him being dead wrong.

She parked her car in the main parking lot at the Texas Cattleman's Club, a sprawling single-story dark stone and wood building with a slate roof. The history of the TCC was woven into the fabric of Royal, as it had been the hub of social life for over one hundred years. If there was a big party in this town, it most often happened here.

Corryna had very mixed emotions about the TCC. It was her introduction to Royal eight years ago, when she and Dan had come here from Dallas for a wedding. Over the course of that weekend, they both fell in love with Royal. Corryna was working in a flower shop at the time and desperately wanted to open one of her own, but couldn't find an affordable space in the big city. She and Dan drove through downtown Royal one day that weekend and spotted the vacant storefront that would eventually become Royal Blooms. He'd never been one to indulge her dreams, but he did that day. He not only wanted to sign a lease on the space, he was willing to uproot his own career in real estate. He'd said he could sell houses anywhere. It had seemed desperately romantic at the time. Little did she know he was running to get away from the husband of one of his mistresses. His many betrayals were the reason why, even six years later, she did not trust men. But the Texas Cattleman's Club didn't only spark bad memories. Corryna also met her best friend, Jessica Lewis, who was serving at the wedding at the TCC, just as she did for all sorts of events now. Working with flowers, and her friendship with Jessica, had gotten Corryna through her divorce. And now she was so tied to Royal that she couldn't imagine ever leaving.

Corryna climbed out of her car and straightened her dress, a very professional off-white sheath with a wide dark brown leather belt and matching pumps. Not at all what she would normally wear on a weekday. Most days, she was in jeans, sneakers and a cute top, prepared for a day on her feet, arranging flowers and running her shop. As she was making her way across the parking lot, she spotted Rylee. Rylee was tall, blonde and absolutely stunning.

"Rylee!" Corryna called, hurrying to catch up to her. She and Rylee had met a month or so ago. Corryna had gifted her a gorgeous bouquet in an attempt to seal her spot as florist for the wedding. The next day, Ariana's best friend and maid of honor, Dionna Reed, had arrived at Royal Blooms with Rylee to see Corryna's talent on display. Luckily, Corryna's friend Tripp Noble, Xavier's cousin and best man, had given her a heads-up that they were coming so she had everything ready to knock their socks off. And she got the job.

"Corryna, hi." Rylee shook Corryna's hand. She looked every bit the part of wedding planner with a chic designer handbag hooked on her arm. "Thank you for meeting with me in person today. I'm really glad we're getting going on this. Xavier and Ariana were very clear. They want everything about the wedding to be seamless. I have to attend to every detail."

"Of course." Corryna had heard that the bride and groom had exacting tastes, and she was thrilled about having the chance to wow them with her designs. She and Rylee entered through the large central doors of the TCC and into the spacious lobby, with its soaring ceilings and an abundance of light from many windows.

"Two of the most important attractions at the reception, aside from our happy couple, will be the flowers and the food. Xavier and Ariana want their guests to feel something. They want it to be memorable. That's why the three of us are meeting today." Rylee opened the door of the main ballroom.

"Three of us?" Corryna followed her inside.

"Yes. You, me and the caterer."

Corryna took one more step and saw him—Colin—standing next to a table in dark jeans, a crisp white dress shirt without a tie, and a midnight blue tailored jacket that drew attention to the straight lines of his shoulders. He looked so damn sexy that she wanted to bite the heel of her hand. Memories of their one night—or more precisely, fifteen minutes—flooded her senses. His hands on her naked body. Kissing him. Her losing her mind. He'd said and done everything perfectly. And she nearly hated him for it.

"Hello. I'm Colin Reynolds." He held out his hand

to shake hers. The second their palms touched, she thought she might catch fire.

Corryna turned to Rylee. "We actually know each other. He's trying to be funny."

He shrugged. "Some people find me hilarious."

"Apparently, those people could not make our meeting," Corryna said.

"Uh, is there a problem here?" Rylee asked. "Because I've heard things about you two, and I'm sensing tension. That's why I asked you to meet me here, rather than at Sheen or Royal Blooms. We can't have tension for this wedding. No problems. No disagreements or personal problems. Everything has to be perfect."

"Understood," Colin said, then pointed to a bakery box on the table. "I brought chocolate croissants, freshly baked early this morning by my pastry chef, Elena. Can't have tension or problems when there's chocolate and baked goods."

"Oh. Wow. That was so thoughtful of you," Rylee said.

Corryna was too busy trying not to drool. Colin was enough of a temptation in his own right. Then he had the nerve to bring her absolute favorite pastry? How was she supposed to function right now?

"Let's go ahead and get started then." Rylee led them over to a round table and sat.

Corryna took a seat, leaving an empty chair between herself and Rylee. Colin, of course, sat right next to her. Now it was the heavenly smells at the table that were hard to ignore. This close to him, she picked up on warm cedar and citrus, which only served to remind her of the way he'd smelled when they'd had their tryst in his office. It was intoxicating.

"As I was saying to Corryna out in the lobby, Xavier and Ariana were very specific with their instructions," Rylee said. "After Dionna and Tripp's recommendations, they know you two are the best and are certainly up to the task. The theme is Hollywood glamor, and Ari and Ex want the entire wedding to be as cohesive with that theme as possible. An immersive experience for their guests. With Xavier being a writer and Ariana in the film business, they appreciate masterful creativity more than anyone. They feel that the food and flowers are a crucial part of the wedding weekend, so they want the floral designs and the menus developed together. Side by side. We want you to bring everything together in a symphony for the senses. I want you to think about colors, textures and smells. It should all marry perfectly."

With every word, Corryna felt her spine get a little stiffer. This was an exceptionally tall order. "We could exchange notes," she offered to Colin.

"I've already worked out the passed hors d'oeuvres with the best man and maid of honor," Colin said. "So, Corryna will have to work around me. I hope that's clear. The food can't follow the flowers. It will never work."

"Well, we need to talk about that," Rylee said, raising a finger before she returned her attention to Corryna. "Exchanging notes won't be enough. I need you two working in concert with each other." Her phone began to ring and she consulted the screen. "I am so sorry. You'll need to excuse me for one minute. I really have to take this." She answered her call, then rose from the table and wandered over to the other side of the room.

"Teacher's pet," Corryna said.

"I don't even know what that means."

"They don't have teachers' pets in Ireland?"

"I predominantly grew up in the US, actually. Boarding school. And I was attempting to make a joke."

"Your sense of humor could use some serious help."

He reached out and cupped her hand, which was resting on the table. "Excuse me. Do you mind telling me why you're being so rude? You're the one who ran out after we had sex."

Corryna's vision flew to Rylee. Thankfully Rylee was immersed in her conversation and had not heard Colin's string of unpleasant and highly personal comments. "It was *sex*, Colin. Nothing more. Surely you're familiar with that concept. Or at least that's what everyone in Royal says about you."

"Just because something is casual doesn't mean it can't be cordial."

She knew he was right, but it wasn't as simple as

that for her. She shouldn't have fallen prey to Colin that night, but he'd had the gall to tell her she was beautiful and a million other nice things, and well, it had been a lifetime since a man had said anything like that to her. Then he went and kissed her neck, which was her absolute biggest weakness. She could not resist a guy who did that to her, especially one as steaming hot as Colin. Of course, as soon as her second orgasm had faded away that night, she realized her mistake. Her ex-husband had destroyed her faith in men, but she'd always told herself that if she ever did get involved again, it would be with a nice guy, certainly not a man with a massive ego who was known for having women falling at his feet. She'd been cheated on. More than once. She couldn't retrace her steps. "I'm sorry. I will do my best to be nicer."

"I know you're capable of it. Everyone says that you're the best part of going into your shop."

"People say that?" She didn't want to sound so eager to hear more, but she was. It was nice to get a compliment.

"They do. You're known for excellent customer service. People always say you're so warm and welcoming." Under the table, he traced a line down her leg, filling her with ideas of what it might be like to have him take off her clothes again. The thought sent heat rushing over her.

"Thanks. That's nice to hear. You can stop touching my leg now."

He grimaced and pulled back his hand. "Your turn to say something nice about me."

She looked at him with as quizzical a look as she could manage. "Do you really want to know what people in town say about you?"

"As a chef, yes. Nothing personal, please. Then things will really get messy."

She laughed quietly and shook her head. Dammit, he was charming, as intent as she was of not being swayed by any of it. "Fine. People say that your food is exquisite. It's innovative, but not pretentious. It's perfectly balanced and always delicious."

He jutted out his lower lip and nodded. "Not bad. You could write a food column, you know."

"I actually haven't eaten your food."

His eyes grew comically large. He pressed his hand to the center of his chest and slumped back in his chair. "A dagger. Straight to my heart."

She swatted his arm. "I'm sure you're doing just fine. Every night at Sheen is sold out from what I hear."

"That's true. It is."

"See? You're fine."

"I still want to cook for you." Colin leaned in and pressed his nose right above Corryna's ear. "Actually. Scratch that. I *need* to cook for you."

She slugged him in the leg and grabbed a croissant. "Is this close enough? I hope so." She took a tiny bite, but it was too delicious to not let out a small moan.

"You like that?"

She didn't want to admit how much she did. Between the buttery flaky piece of heaven that was the croissant and his smooth voice, she was experiencing yet another true moment of weakness. She had to stop doing that around Colin, as soon as humanly possible. "It's good. Could use more chocolate."

Colin had never been so turned on, especially in a meeting. He didn't get haunted by women, but his one night with Corryna had stuck with him. Maybe it was because things between them had gotten so hot, so fast, and then was over just as quickly. It left him wondering what would happen if he had a real stretch of time with her, to savor every inch of her body and for her to do the same to him.

"I'll let my pastry chef know your comments," he said.

"Sorry about that," Rylee said, striding back to their table. "As I was saying earlier, your collaboration must be very hands-on."

Colin snickered. He couldn't help but laugh at the absurdity of their situation. Corryna crossed her legs in the opposite direction, away from him.

Rylee opened a large three-ring binder. "So, Colin, you're going to need to scrap everything you decided with Dionna and Tripp," Rylee said, referring to the wedding's maid of honor and best man. "The bride and groom changed their minds about that particular slate of hors d'oeuvres. They want you to push yourself. Start over."

Colin was not only no longer turned on, he found absolutely none of this to be amusing. "Excuse me?" He didn't think of himself as a man with a big ego, but he took immense pride in his food. "Push myself?"

"They want something different. They definitely do not want anything that has already been on the Sheen menu. Everything must be innovative. New. Exciting. Memorable," Rylee countered.

Corryna shifted in her seat and took another bite of her croissant. When Colin glanced at her, she was smiling, so either the pastry was pleasing her greatly or it was Colin's reversal of fortune that was making her so damn happy. Possibly both.

"My food is always all of those things," Colin said.

"Then you'll have no problem, right?" Rylee asked.

Colin cleared his throat. He wasn't about to reply with more protests, even though he was more than a little annoyed. This job was immensely important to him. "Of course."

"So back to your collaboration," Rylee said. "We want a truly immersive experience for our guests."

Colin couldn't begin to imagine how this was supposed to work. He and Corryna had a compelling dynamic, but it wasn't based on collaboration. It was more like a big argument swirling in the center of a tornado of sexual chemistry. They might be able to build a fire together, but what exactly would they burn down in the process?

"Colin? Will that timeline work for you?" Rylee asked.

He shook his head to clear his thoughts. He hadn't been listening. "I'm sorry. Can you go over that again?"

"Yes. You have one month to present the full menu and let me, and possibly Dionna, taste each new dish. At the same time, Corryna will bring in the proposed arrangements." Rylee pushed a piece of paper across the table to him. "This outlines everything I think we will need in terms of courses, as well as various dietary restrictions I'll need you to work around."

"That works." His words suggested complete confidence, when he was feeling nothing of the sort. He glanced over at Corryna, feeling more uncertain than he had in some time, but he was damned if he was going to let on to it. "We can do it. Together."

Rylee rose from the table. "Perfect. So we'll meet in four weeks, sample the food, look at the flowers, make any changes, and we should be good to go. Please keep me apprised of your progress as the month goes on. I'll check in with you once or twice. We'll see how my month goes. My schedule is pretty packed."

"Don't worry about us." Corryna popped up and offered her hand to Rylee. "The schedule will work just fine. Thank you so much for the opportunity. I'm thrilled to be working on this wedding."

"Xavier and Ariana are very happy to be working with local vendors." Rylee reached out to shake Colin's hand. "I'm really looking forward to tasting your creations."

"Thanks," Colin said. As soon as Rylee left, he pinched the bridge of his nose and stepped away from Corryna, doing his best to clear his head.

"Colin. Are you okay?" Corryna set her hand on his back.

He liked her touch. It did something to him. It sent a jolt of electricity through him. If everything else wasn't so messed up, he might take the time to enjoy it. "I'm annoyed. It's fine." He started for the door, his mind already running one million miles an hour. He needed to get to work right away. Start from scratch. Somehow be brilliant, on demand.

Corryna was right behind him. "Colin. Hold up. Talk to me. If we're supposed to be working together, then you need to tell me what's going on."

How did he explain this in a way that didn't make him sound as though he was too proud about his work? "I didn't enjoy hearing what Rylee had to say about my food. To be honest, it was a punch to the gut. But it's fine. I'll work harder. I'll push myself more."

"I don't understand why you're so upset. Do you really even need this job? Surely you're making more than enough money these days."

"Excuse me? What do you know about my business?"

She reared back her head, seeming put off by his response. "All I meant is that I'm sure you're doing fine. Every night at Sheen is sold out."

"That's true. It is."

"So, see? Don't stress about this wedding."

"It's a point of pride, Corryna. This isn't about money."

"You get plenty of high-profile jobs. Surely one more won't make or break you or the restaurant."

"No. It won't. But it will look bad if I don't have the job. If it goes to someone else, Sheen suddenly won't be the best restaurant in town. Which means it isn't one of the best in the state. Or in the country for that matter."

"Oh. Okay."

"What?"

"Nothing. You and I are just coming at this from very different perspectives."

"How exactly?"

"I'm worried about paying my employees and covering my mortgage, and you're worried about whether people will see you as being the best of the best."

It was then that Colin appreciated just how vulnerable a situation Corryna must be in. And she was dependent on him to make this work out, whether or not that made any sense to either of them. "Both of our businesses will benefit from this collaboration.

So, let's do our best to make it work. When do you want to meet? I suppose we should start as soon as possible. My days are tight, but my kitchen staff runs the kitchen most evenings. How about tomorrow?"

She looked up at the ceiling, flaunting her graceful neck. He was suddenly bombarded by memories of burying his face in it, of his lips skimming her soft skin and his nose inhaling her sweet scent. How was he supposed to work closely with her and resist her for an entire month? He didn't see that happening. "It's a Tuesday. That should work. Do you want to start with food or flowers?"

"Flowers. I don't know enough about them, aside from the edible ones like nasturtiums."

"I won't lie. I'm a little nervous about going first."

"You're going to have to get over that if we're going to work together."

She drew in a deep breath through her nose. "Okay. Tomorrow night at my shop? Six o'clock? That's right after we close."

How Colin relished the thought of being alone with her. "Would you like me to bring a bottle of wine?"

"Okay. But no more whiskey."

He hated hearing her say that. It created a knot in his belly. "Why not? I thought you liked it."

"I loved it. But it also got me into trouble. I couldn't think straight."

Colin dropped his head to one side and shook it, hoping to express his dismay. "Corryna, that's the best kind of trouble. I would love to get into that kind of trouble with you again."

She pressed a finger to the center of his chest. "Colin. We're working together. Absolutely not. You heard Rylee. She wants no tension between us."

"And that's the best way to get rid of it."

She cocked an eyebrow at him, admonishing him with a single look.

"I suppose you're right. But that doesn't mean I won't stop trying." He looked down at her hand, which was still touching him, sending a current right through his body. They were all alone in this big ballroom. The building was relatively quiet. The table they'd just been sitting at seemed sturdy enough. Or there was the wall. His mind was a torrent of sexy ideas—kissing her neck again, palming the silky skin of her bare thigh, pushing that dress up past her waist... "Can I walk you to your car?"

"I suppose." She turned back to the table where they'd just been sitting. "Hold on one second. We can't leave those croissants sitting there."

"Absolutely not. Go ahead. Take them." He stifled his grin. He took great pride in knowing at least part of the way to her heart. "There's more where that came from."

"Don't tell me that. It'll only make me feel like I have to be nice to you." She plucked the box from the table and held on to it tightly.

"Don't you want to be nice to me?"

"I'm thinking I'd like to stay closer to the word you used earlier. Cordial."

"Why only that?"

She pressed her lips together tightly, scanning his face. Was she thinking what he'd been thinking mere seconds ago? That their attraction was palpable and so worth giving in to? "I have a feeling it will help me stay out of trouble."

Three

Corryna needed something to keep her mind off her meeting with Colin, so she was thankful that her Tuesday at Royal Blooms had been unusually busy. They'd had dozens of deliveries to make, plus a potential new bride and groom came in for a wedding consultation, and sadly, local banker Winston Alderidge of Alderidge Bank had passed away, which meant there were quite a few new orders of condolence. Corryna loved that her work got to be a part of special moments in people's lives—new babies, weddings, graduations, and yes, funerals and memorials. Even those sad occasions could be honored and marked with an expression of beauty, and Corryna couldn't think of anything more suitable than flowers.

"Well, that's it for me today." Her delivery driver Mike hung up the keys for the Royal Blooms truck on the hook outside of Corryna's office, then stood in her doorway. He was tall and skinny as could be, with freckles and reddish-brown hair. "Can I do anything for you before I head home?"

Corryna looked up from her computer, where she'd been doing her least favorite activity—staring at spreadsheets. Staring was no exaggeration. When it came to numbers, she struggled for them to make sense. "You're more than good to leave for the day. Go home and kiss that sweet baby of yours." Mike and his wife, Serena, had a six-month-old baby girl named Penelope. Everyone who met this little girl instantly fell in love, but Corryna was especially smitten.

Mike grinned like the proud dad he was. "That's definitely the first thing on my schedule when I walk through the front door at the end of the day. It's so amazing to see the way her face lights up. It makes every little challenge worth it."

Corryna's heart squeezed tightly. There had been a time when she'd seen herself with a life like the one that Mike had, with a partner to love and a child of her own to care for and shower with affection. Unfortunately, her path had diverged wildly from that. "Say hi to Serena for me. And thank you for everything today. We have Winston Alderidge's funeral on Friday, so keep that in mind. It's only going to get busier this week."

"Got it."

Corryna glanced at the time on her computer. The shop was set to close in a half hour, which meant Colin would be arriving soon. She still wasn't sure how this was going to work. All she could think about were the words Rylee had used—things like "hands-on" and "working in concert with each other." Those were not simple asks. If she and Colin were going to collaborate creatively, they would need to get on the same wavelength and stay there. They would need to understand each other and establish a healthy give-and-take. How was she supposed to do that with a brilliant but stubborn chef who she had a proven weakness for?

The only answer was that she was going to have to stay strong. That was all there was to it. She was going to have to establish hard boundaries and keep them. The trouble with that plan was that she needed to let down her guard when she was creating. She needed to stay loose, open to possibilities, and most importantly, stay trusting of everyone and everything around her. She'd struggled to reach that state in the aftermath of her divorce. She trusted no one other than her best friend, Jessica. Dan had hurt her deeply, and the trauma from his betrayal had carved deep grooves into her heart. It quickly became her impulse to put up walls, and that was still a well-honed reflex, but she had learned to overcome it at times. She might have overcompensated that night with Colin, but he'd gotten to her with his words and handsome face, and perhaps a bit of whiskey.

Luckily, Corryna had the health and future of Royal Blooms to keep her on the straight-and-narrow path. The Noble-Ramos wedding was key to her success, and that meant she and Colin had to keep things as professional as possible. No more kisses. No more taking off clothes. No more sex. That was a onetime thing. It was not going to happen again.

She jumped when her phone rang, and she fumbled to answer, seeing on the caller ID that it was Jessica. "Hey, honey. What's up?"

"Can you do a quick hike tomorrow morning? It's my only time off for the foreseeable future, and I miss you. I miss seeing your face."

Corryna's schedule had gotten considerably more busy as of today, but she could not pass up time with her best friend. Plus, early April in Texas was prime time for wildflowers. "That's a great idea. I'd love to go. Can you come by the shop at nine tomorrow? I'll duck out for a few hours. I can come in early to make up for my time away."

"I don't want to put you out, Corryna. You already work so hard."

"You aren't putting me out. At all. And… Well… I have something I'd like to talk to you about."

"What kind of something?"

Really, her something was a *someone*. Corryna considered spilling the beans, but she was deathly afraid that Hannah, who was still working the front of the shop, might overhear her. "I'll tell you tomorrow if that's okay. It's a long story."

"Well, now I'm going to be wondering about it all night. I don't get even a tiny hint?"

Corryna sighed. She couldn't leave Jessica completely in the dark. Jess worked many catering jobs for Sheen and knew Colin. "Remember when I complained about Colin Reynolds after he canceled my contract with Sheen? Well, we've had a few more run-ins since then. It's messy. And complicated." Guilt weighed on Corryna for having kept her one-night stand a secret from Jessica, but she was embarrassed to admit that she'd lost control like that. "That's all I can tell you right now."

"Okay. I trust you. I'll just have to be patient."

There was that word again—trust. "See you tomorrow morning." Corryna ended the call and checked the time once more. There was now only five minutes until Colin was set to arrive. She bustled into the retail space, where Hannah was wiping down the long wood counters. Hannah had a bubbly personality, a quick smile, and had worked at the shop for four years, since she turned sixteen. Now she was a little less than two years out of high school. She was young and carefree—Corryna had been like that once, and she enjoyed seeing her old self in someone else. "Hey, Hannah. Where are we on closing up?"

Hannah tucked her rag into the pocket of her

apron, then took the broom down from the hook on the wall. "I just need to sweep. If you can close out the register, we'll be all set."

"Will do." Corryna tapped away at the touch screen of the point-of-sale system Dan had insisted they get when Royal Blooms first opened. Corryna knew it very well now, but there had been a steep learning curve at the beginning. Pen and paper had always made more sense to her, but this was pretty foolproof by now. She ran an end-of-day report every day, which told her the sales and remaining inventory. Once a week, the system told her what she was running low on, although Corryna knew her flower stock like the back of her hand.

The bell on the door chimed, and Corryna looked up. In walked Colin, holding a bottle of wine and looking like a male model with his tall stature and the devil-may-care glint in his eye. He was wearing dark jeans and a black T-shirt—a simple enough ensemble except for the fact that it showed off every hard contour of his arms. Memories of his hands on her body wound through her head like a cyclone. "Colin. Hi."

"Hello there." He strode in like the ultraconfident man he was, and set the bottle of wine down on the counter. "Ready to get to work?"

Corryna's vision flew to Hannah, who was blinking so much it was like she thought he was a mirage. "Colin, this is Hannah. She's not only one of my best employees, she's studying at Royal Community College to get her floral design certification. Hannah, this is Colin Reynolds. He's the owner and head chef of Sheen."

Bright crimson rose in Hannah's cheeks as she shook Colin's hand. Apparently his appeal extended to women of all ages. "It's nice to meet you."

"Nice to meet you, too. Tell me, Hannah, how do you like working for Corryna?"

"Ummm…" Hannah turned and looked at Corryna with wide eyes, like she wasn't sure what she was supposed to say.

"Go ahead," Corryna said. "Tell him."

Hannah returned her attention to Colin. "She's the best. It's super fun to work here. And she's paying for me to go to school. She always lets me go home early on Fridays, too. I've graduated, but I love going to my high school's football games. It's a big deal around here."

"Thanks for telling me about working at Royal Blooms, Hannah. Now I know where to come looking for a job if the restaurant doesn't work out," Colin joked as he studied Corryna with his mesmerizing green eyes.

Her pulse pounded in her ears as she couldn't bring herself to look away. His gaze made her feel so exposed, but in a way that made her want to give him everything. How did he do that? It was his superpower on full display. A warning shot across the bow. "You can head home, Hannah. I'll take it from here," Corryna said.

"Okay. I'll see you tomorrow. Bye, Mr. Reynolds." Hannah flitted into the hall that led to the office area. Moments later, the chime on the back door sounded, leaving Corryna and Colin all alone.

"This is quite a nice little shop you've got here, Corryna," he said.

"I know it's not fancy like Sheen, but I love it. I feel at home here."

"That's important." He picked the bottle of wine up. "Do you have any glasses? Then we can get to work."

Corryna was torn about whether wine was a good idea. She wanted to stay in control, but she appreciated the idea of taking the edge off her nervousness. "I'll have a small glass. That's it."

"Whatever you say."

Corryna went back to the tiny kitchenette next to her office where employees often took their break, and grabbed two glass tumblers. "This is the best I can offer."

"It works. And luckily, they now sell really good wine with a screw-top." He poured them each a glass, and handed one to her. "Now show me how you work."

Corryna led him to the back room, which wasn't a glamorous setting. It had old concrete floors and beat-up wood workbenches for designing arrangements. "Well, normally the first thing I do is look at what the customer wants. Then I bring that to life."

He pulled up a stool alongside her bench and sat

on it. "Other than the old Hollywood glamor theme, we don't know what the customer specifically wants, other than creativity and seamlessness and all of those other words Rylee threw out at us yesterday. Hmm."

"And we're supposed to be coordinating our two very different disciplines." Corryna leaned against her bench, thinking about the best way to approach this, while trying to ignore how tempting Colin looked when he was also deep in thought.

"I think the most important part is that we have to sort out how to work together."

"Yes. I agree." It was such a relief to hear him say that. "Until we figure that out, we can't get much done."

"And this is a trial run. So how about if I tell you about one of my dishes at Sheen, and we can talk about it, then you can pull out some flowers and put together an arrangement?"

"That makes sense."

"I mean, you haven't actually been to the restaurant, so you'll have to imagine what it tastes like."

"Very funny. Just tell me about one of your dishes.

"One of my signature appetizers is a warm Spanish goat cheese with white wine, lemon and thyme, served with grilled house-baked sourdough bread."

Funny how him uttering the names of a few ingredients in his buttery accent made her feel like she might faint. "Sounds delicious."

"Does that spark anything?"

She didn't want to tell him that what it really sparked was her attraction to him. "Yes. Several things. I'll be right back." She wandered into the cooler and grabbed lavender, white irises, branches of lemon leaf for filler, and one of her favorite flowers, a chartreuse green beauty with an unfortunate name given her audience. She dropped the stems into a bucket of water and walked out into her workroom. "I don't want you to think I'm pandering, but the green ones are called Bells of Ireland."

He grinned and admired the tall spiky stems with bell-shaped blooms. "Very pretty. What made you choose those?"

"The green made me think of thyme. I chose irises because they're architectural, but still delicate, and they grow well in arid climates like Spain. The Spanish goat cheese inspired that choice. The lemon leaf is self-explanatory. I was thinking lavender for its herbaceous smell, but I'm not sure it will work. I worry it's too fragrant. Might interfere with the guests' enjoyment of the meal."

"May I?" He stood and took one of the branches of lavender from the bucket and raised it to his nose. "It's heavenly," he said, closing his eyes and inhaling the scent.

Corryna's knees went wobbly at the sight. "But?"

"But I think you're right. Too strong a smell."

"Good. This is good." She nodded, her creative mind kicking into gear as what she wanted to create began to form before her eyes. She saw possibilities—shapes and compositions—and she wanted to explore them. For the first time, she felt as though a collaboration with Colin might actually be possible.

"Now I want to see your artistry in motion. Ignore me. Pretend like I'm not here. Do what you love to do."

That part about ignoring his presence was easier said than done. It would be nearly impossible to disregard him completely. He was that magnetic. Her attraction to him was that potent. But she needed this partnership with him to work. Her business depended on it. "Okay, then." She pushed the bucket to the side, pulled out a modern cylindrical vase and grabbed her floral scissors. They were cool and weighty in her hand. There was always something so comforting about holding them. Made of hand-forged steel, they were one of the first serious investments she'd made in her career as a floral designer. They were a reminder that despite everything, she still believed in her talents. As she stole a split-second glance at Colin, who was sipping wine and keeping his eyes glued to her expectantly, she realized how much she needed that sliver of confidence. One wrong word and he could shake her resolve to the ground.

Colin had not expected to be so mesmerized by the sight of Corryna arranging flowers, and yet here he was, sitting in her workroom, feeling a sensation that he hadn't experienced in quite some time—inspiration. He saw the fire of creativity in her. He

saw the miracle of a creator at work—shutting out
the world and focusing only on the medium. In his
best moments, when he could take his eyes off the
bottom line, and stop chasing things like prestige
and awards, he could be like that. He wanted to be
more like Corryna as she placed the flowers with
confidence, relying on instinct rather than analysis.
When he'd first started in the culinary arts, he was
like that—drawn to invention. Now it was all about
outrunning his family's legacy and making a name
for himself. It was a mission he was dedicated to.
He would not let his father win, even though it required a more exacting and ruthless approach than
he preferred.

When she was done, she stood back and took
a deep breath, scrutinizing her work. "Well?" she
asked.

He stood and rested his thumb and forefinger on
his chin, as if he was contemplating the meaning of
the universe. Eventually, he gave up the ruse. "It's
stunning." *You're stunning.* He couldn't get past his
frustration at their tryst in his office. He felt cheated.
He'd only had the tiniest taste of her, and he wanted
more. "This is something I could never do. You use
softness to create structure. You take nature's beauty,
which is already flawless, and somehow make it
more profound."

"Wow. Now who's ready to launch a writing career?"

He chuckled, giving in to her quick wit. "What

can I say? Watching you is like watching a painter at the canvas. I had no idea where you were going when you started. I certainly didn't envision something this amazing."

She shrugged. "Thank you. It's decent. It needs some work. Still not sure about the asymmetrical design. Sometimes I have to toy with things."

"That I can do. I tinker with food all the time. Taste it. Add a bit of this or that. Or sometimes I'll be stumped about how to fix a dish and then it will come to me later." He considered asking if she wanted to toy with *him*. He was completely open to the idea. But now wasn't the time. He did want to work well with her. This job, even though he didn't *need* the money, was important to him. He'd hustled to elevate Sheen's already sterling reputation. It would be irreparably damaged if he was fired.

"Yes. Exactly. You get it."

He poured them both another glass of wine, and she didn't protest even though she'd said she only wanted one. Wanting to spend more time with her, he grabbed another stool and pulled it over to the bench for her. "So. Tell me. Why haven't you been to the restaurant?"

"It's not exactly in my price range."

He took a sip of his wine. "Why not? You must do really well here. Don't you?"

She shook her head. "No."

"I don't understand. Why not?"

"The business barely breaks even. Which is partly

my fault. My costs have gone up, but I've been reluctant to raise my prices. I was constantly raising prices the first few years after I opened, just so that I could keep up. People complained."

"Corryna, prices have to follow costs. Always. It's part of how you make money."

"I know. But it's not that simple." She blew out a long frustrated breath.

"You're paying for Hannah to go to school. That's taking money out of your pocket, too."

"I guess I don't look at it that way. It's an investment in my future. She's going to graduate soon and then she'll be able to help me more, which could help me expand my business. So it's worth it to me, even if things are more than a little tight right now."

None of this made sense to Colin. He knew for a fact that flowers had very high margins, and the rent for her space had to be quite low. "Who does your books? Maybe you need someone new to take a look and give you some advice." He was the perfect person to do it, but he didn't want to stick his nose where it didn't belong.

"I do them. Reluctantly. But I do them." She swirled the wine in her glass and took another drink. "Numbers are not my strong suit. My husband was always responsible for that part."

He'd heard people talking around town about Corryna's ex-husband, but he wasn't sure if the stories were true. "I understand he didn't exactly treat you like a gentleman should."

A low ironic laugh escaped her lips, reminding him of how wonderful it was to kiss her. "Uh, no. I think six different mistresses puts him solidly in the category of not a gentleman."

Colin had known it was bad, but not that horrific. "I'm so sorry. That's bloody awful."

"And that's just the women I know about. I have a feeling there were more, but I really don't want to know."

"How did you find out about it? The cheating?"

"The husband of a woman he was sleeping with showed up at the shop, looking for him. He was screaming and yelling. It scared the crap out of me. It terrified my employees. And of course, that meant I had to confront Dan, who tried to deny it. But the husband knew a lot about him, and once I started presenting him with those facts, Dan eventually admitted it."

"I'm so sorry. What about the others?"

"That all came up during the divorce. My attorney hired a private investigator. He found out about the other women."

Colin felt his anger rising up inside him. He didn't even know her ex-husband and he already wanted to punch him square in the face. Resorting to violence was never the answer, but it would be a small measure of justice in the world. "I'm so sorry that happened." He reached out for her hand, and her vision was drawn to the sight of his touch. It was just like before. A current of raw attraction flowed so instantaneously between them. It felt vital, like water and air. And dangerous, like fire.

Corryna pulled back her hand, leaving him no choice but to follow her lead. "To make things worse, I'm pretty sure Dan was stealing from the business while we were married."

Colin was already infuriated by the misdeeds of her ex-husband, but hearing that he'd taken money from her struggling business? His blood went from a simmer to a hard boil. "Why do you say that?"

"It's pretty simple, really. When we were married, he did the accounting. And he always told me how tight money was. When we went through the divorce, all of that proved to be true. We were just barely breaking even. But then after the divorce and the settlement, I noticed that there was more money at the end of the month. Orders hadn't gone up dramatically. Nothing else had changed. That seems pretty suspicious, doesn't it?"

"It seems more than suspicious. It's sketchy as hell."

She frowned. "I was worried about that. My lawyer wanted to hire some special accountant to look into it, but the divorce was already getting so expensive and I just wanted it to be over, so I said no."

"A forensic accountant."

"That's it. I don't really even understand what they do."

Colin had lots of knowledge of forensic accountants, in part because his father was prone to hiring them when he had a dispute with a business partner. His father was always convinced others were stealing from him. "It's someone who combs through book-keeping records and financial accounts and finds the discrepancies. They find anything out of the ordi-nary or suspicious. Then they figure out the reason why the money went to a certain place."

"Ah. Well, I guess that could've been handy at the time, but like I said, I just wanted the divorce to be final so I could move on. It's been six years now, so it's definitely too late."

"I'm not sure of the legal side of this in the state of Texas, but this isn't about your marriage. It's about your business partnership."

"What good will it do? So I can find out if he be-trayed me one more time?" Her voice was thin and raw with pain like it hadn't been before. "I don't re-ally want to go there again."

"Don't you want the truth? Plus, we could sue him for the money if we can prove it."

"We?"

He cleared his throat. "I'm sorry. *You* could sue him. Or your business, more specifically. Or the dis-trict attorney might want to bring criminal charges. Embezzlement is a serious offense."

"I don't know, Colin. I wouldn't know the first thing about doing that. It sounds like a stressful pro-cess. The thought of it, especially since it has to do with numbers, is overwhelming."

"Let me help you." He was surprised by the readiness with which he'd uttered the words. It wasn't that he didn't like to assist others when they were in need. It was more that he didn't make a habit of pushing to make it happen.

"You'd do that for me?"

"Why do you sound so shocked?"

"Because I am. You're a highly successful work-aholic who knows how to maximize profits. I'm amazed that you would take the time to help some-one else with their business."

He wasn't sure why he felt so inclined to help her, other than she was a smart, hardworking, fascinat-ing woman who possessed rare talent and who'd also been through the wringer. He didn't want her to fail, especially because of someone else. "It helps me if you're successful. I want every business in Royal to do well. A strong community means a stronger business for me."

"It helps you if I'm successful, but you canceled Sheen's contract with my business?"

"Yeah. About that…" He stuffed his hands into his pockets as he recalled the words he'd uttered to her that day she'd marched into Sheen, full of fire and brimstone, ready to cut off his head and feed it to him for lunch. *My customers care about my food, not your flowers.* He'd been a real ass. "That was my mistake. And especially after watching you work to-night, I'd like to resume our partnership."

"Colin, I don't need your charity. Just because

we've gotten to know each other a little bit. Or because we slept together."

"It's not that." Although, to be fair, he would've been lying if he'd said he didn't want to have sex with her again. Because he did. More than he could put into words, or even wrap his head around. "It's just tonight. I got to see your work in action. And I realized that you're not simply snipping a bunch of flowers and stuffing them into a vase. I didn't realize how much artistry went into it. I didn't give you a chance. And I want to make up for that."

She studied his face. Like him, she had green eyes. Hers were lighter, but somehow more intense. "Okay. What do you want? And when?"

If only she knew the way he really wanted to answer that question. *You. Now.* "Can we resume our previous standing order? And can you bring something by tomorrow?"

She twisted her lips, seeming deep in thought. "I can make that work."

"Are you sure?"

"Yes. I don't want to give you the chance to go back on your word."

He laughed, which made her smile. "Not going to happen. I'm a man of honor."

"I sensed that about you, Colin. Despite you firing me months ago."

"Again. Sorry about that."

She held out her hand to shake his. "Apology accepted."

"Will you think about the forensic accountant?"

"I will." She started cleaning up her bench. "We also need to decide on when we can get together again. When I get to see you create and be brilliant."

"I thought about inviting you to the kitchen at Sheen, but if we are going to collaborate, we should work at my house. We won't have all of the distractions."

"Okay. When?"

"Saturday night?"

A look of surprise crossed her face. "Isn't that the biggest night of the week in the restaurant?"

"It is. But it's also the night when we have the most kitchen staff working. My sous-chef, Kristine, is excellent. Runs the kitchen with precision. I often just end up walking through the dining room and chatting up the customers. And believe me, I could use a break from that." *Especially if I get to spend it with you.*

"Saturday it is. I'll be ready to relax. That's wedding day, so it's always incredibly busy."

"Perfect. I'll be ready with a big glass of wine. And you won't have to do a thing other than sit back and tell me what you think of my food."

She grinned, which was its own reward. "And I want to hear more about you and your path to Sheen. And your family. Lots of money and prestige in the Reynolds family. I'd love to know more about how they influenced your journey to becoming a chef."

And to think, things had been going perfectly…

"I'll talk about Sheen, but don't care to talk about my family. No good comes of that."

"Oh. Okay. I'm sorry."

He swallowed hard, struggling to regain his composure. His temper was rearing its ugly head again, threatening to ruin what had been a lovely evening. "It's okay. You didn't know."

Four

Corryna was running on very little sleep, but between needing to design the arrangements for Sheen and the very cryptic thing Colin had said about his family, she simply hadn't been able to get any rest. She'd tossed and turned all night as she wondered how he could say that no good could come from discussing his family. From her bit of internet snooping, she'd learned that Colin's parents owned Reynolds Hospitality, a small but impressive group of four- and five-star restaurants across Ireland and the UK. His mother was a renowned pastry chef and cookbook author, and taught at a top-level culinary school. His father was also a chef, known for innovation, just like his son. The Reynolds family had a real empire. And since Colin had gone into the same line of work, she'd only assumed his mom and dad had played a key part in that. Perhaps they'd inspired and encouraged him.

It seemed like a logical conclusion to her, but there was clearly more to it, and she was curious to know why he had such disdain for them. Corryna adored her family, even though she didn't see them nearly enough, as her younger sister, Betsy, lived in Virginia and her parents were still back in Atlanta, where they'd grown up. College had brought Corryna to Texas—Austin, to be exact. Dan was the reason she'd remained in the state, but the charm and community of Royal was what was really telling her to stay put.

For now, she was finishing up the flowers for Sheen. She wanted them to be a "wow" moment, and not only because she wanted to impress Colin. Yes, she'd lost a chunk of income when Colin canceled his contract, but she'd also lost the exposure. Having her arrangements back in a top-notch restaurant like Sheen was a real feather in her cap, and a potential boost to her business. She'd take as many of those as she could get.

The chime on the back door rang. Corryna looked up at the clock on the wall. Ten minutes and the shop would be open, which also meant Jessica would soon be arriving for their hike.

"You haven't been here all night, have you?" Mike ambled into the workroom.

Hannah was right behind him. "Those are gorgeous, Corryna," she said, surveying Corryna's work, which was blanketing one of the longer benches that ran along the far wall. There were thirty small tabletop arrangements, a larger one for the host station, and two oversized ones for the bar area. They all coordinated and proudly featured the state flower, the bluebonnet.

"Thank you. And no, I haven't been here all night. I came in at five." She could admit to herself that it had been more than excitement over flowers and questions about Colin's family that had kept her up. Last night, he'd proven himself enticing in a different way from that night in his office or the day they'd met at the TCC. He was kind and thoughtful. That had been unexpected. She liked having people surprise her, especially when it contrasted with their public persona.

Hannah walked over to take a closer look at Corryna's creations. "Which client are these for? I don't remember this many arrangements in the orders for today."

"Sheen. We've been rehired."

Hannah turned to her. There was a knowing glint in her eye. For such a young woman, she was incredibly astute. "You must have really impressed him."

"You know, I think I did." It had felt so amazing to have Colin's admiration for her talent.

"Should I go ahead and load up the truck and take these over to the restaurant?" Mike asked.

Corryna looked at the flowers and decided it was better to make this first delivery herself. "I'll do it this time. If you can help me load up the back of my car, that would be great."

"No problem. I'll put them in plastic bins. Where are your keys?"

"On my desk."

"I'm on it." Mike went to work while Hannah and Corryna took care of opening up the shop.

Moments after Hannah flipped the sign to say Open, Jessica strolled in. "Good morning," she said. Her dark brown shoulder-length wavy hair was back in a high ponytail, and she was wearing black leggings that showed off her curves, along with a turquoise exercise top that brought out the blue-green of her eyes.

"Morning," Corryna said, giving her friend a quick hug. "Is it okay if we run an order over to Sheen before our hike?"

Deep creases formed between Jessica's eyes. "I thought you said that Colin Reynolds was a problem. Now you're bringing him flowers?"

"I don't think I called him a problem. I think I said that I needed to talk to you about him." Corryna glanced over at Hannah, who was clearly listening to their conversation. That one look was enough to make Hannah go back to bringing out the buckets of bulk flowers that went in the front displays.

"Got it. Subject matter for our hike. So let's hit it."

"We can take my car. It's out back." Corryna led

the way through the shop. Mike was just closing the back tailgate of her car when they arrived. "Thank you, Mike. I appreciate it."

He handed her the keys. "Of course. Anytime."

Corryna and Jessica climbed into her car and were on their way to Sheen. "How's school going?" Corryna asked. Jessica was finishing up graduate school and preparing to eventually be accredited as a music therapist. She was not only a gifted musician, but she also had a real affinity for kids, especially those with special needs. Her plan to build a career around her talent and passion was something Corryna identified with strongly.

"School is hard, but great. I love it so much. I'm just burning the candle from all ends if you know what I mean. Between working catering jobs and studying, I hardly have time to sleep. But it'll all be worth it. I know it." Jessica was a very hard worker— something Corryna readily admired and identified with as well.

"Well, I think you're kicking butt. And I'm very proud of you." A few minutes later, Corryna pulled into the parking lot at Sheen and parked near the back loading dock. "I'll run in and see if someone can help me with these."

Jessica glanced in the back of the car. "I think we can handle it if we do it together."

"Okay, then." Corryna hopped out, and they each took one of the three bins of flowers. "We're going to have to come back for the last one."

They climbed a short set of stairs next to the loading dock, and entered through a side door, which had been propped open with a cinder block. Inside, boxes of produce were piled high while several people in white chef's coats milled about. Corryna flashed back to the night she and Colin had loaded her flowers into the walk-in refrigerator. It was surreal to see this setting in the light of day, and the memory sent a current of electricity through her. Of course, she hadn't had the nerve to retrieve those flowers. She'd been too worried about seeing Colin, so she'd asked Mike to do it.

A woman with flame red hair emerged from what was likely the main kitchen door. "You must be from Royal Blooms. Colin told me to expect the delivery."

"Yes. Hi. I'm Corryna. Is there anywhere in particular you want these?"

"I'm Kristine Vargas. I'm the sous-chef. You can take the flowers into the dining room. Colin's in there right now, fixing the sink behind the bar."

"Okay." Corryna glanced at Jessica, then led the way through the back to the dining room. "Hello?" Corryna called. Other than the tables covered in white tablecloths, the room was empty.

"Oy. Is that you, Corryna?" Funnily enough, Colin's accent seemed even stronger than usual.

"It is. Where are you?" She set down her armful on one of the tables and, with a nod, suggested Jessica do the same.

"Under the bar," he answered.

Corryna wandered to the far side of the room, then peeked behind the bar. All she could see was a very long and tempting pair of denim-clad legs sticking out from under the sink. "Colin. What are you doing?"

"Restaurant ownership is very glamorous, in case you haven't heard." He shimmied out from under the sink with a wrench in one hand and a few beads of sweat on his forehead. His hair was a mess and he was wearing a Sheen T-shirt. He looked perfect.

"Can I help you up?" She offered her hand.

"This doesn't make me look very manly, but sure." He wrapped his fingers around hers as he got up from the floor. He didn't let go when he was standing. He simply held on, peering down at Corryna. "Are you making the delivery yourself? That's some exceptional service."

She couldn't disguise her smile, but she did pull her hand back. They were supposed to be keeping things businesslike and he was pushing the boundaries at every turn. "You're a very important client. I want to make sure you're happy."

Someone behind Corryna cleared their throat. She turned to see Jessica standing there. Staring. "Jessica, you know Colin." Turning back to him, she said, "Colin, Jess is my best friend."

Colin reached out to shake Jessica's hand. "Nice to see you again."

"You too," Jessica said with a *very* leading tone.

"Want to check out the flowers?" Corryna asked.

"Of course," Colin replied.

"I'll run out to the car and get the last few arrangements. We couldn't carry everything in one trip," Jessica said. Thank goodness she was thinking straight and had remembered that. Corryna certainly hadn't.

Corryna led Colin over to the table and picked up one of the small vases. "I kept them simple. The focus should be on the food. Of course. The roses I used are very low fragrance. And the bluebonnets are the state flower. They're one of my favorites. They bloom like crazy this time of year."

"They're perfect. And I recognize the bluebonnets. They're blooming out at my house. I can show you when you come over."

"That would be nice."

He was quiet for a moment, then cleared his throat. "I feel like I owe you an apology after last night." Colin folded his arms and a somber look crossed his face.

"Why?"

"Because I got defensive when you asked about my family. It was a knee-jerk reaction. I wasn't trying to be difficult. It's just a complicated situation."

She reached for his arm, wanting to comfort him. His voice had a melancholy tone to it that was so out of character. "Don't worry about it. I'm around to listen whenever you change your mind."

"Thanks. I appreciate that. Did you think about the forensic accountant?"

"Not yet." Something was making her hesitate, but she wasn't sure what it was. "I'll let you know."

"This is the last of everything," Jessica said, setting down the flowers.

"Thank you for helping," Corryna said.

"Of course."

"Are you going to invoice me for the flowers, Corryna?" Colin asked.

"I can bill you at the end of the month, if that works."

"You shouldn't extend your customers that much leeway. I'll pay you weekly," he replied.

Being around Colin made Corryna feel even more insecure about her business acumen. "Okay. If that works for you, it works for me. I'll see you on Saturday."

"Yes. See you then."

Corryna and Jessica wound their way back to the loading dock, then climbed into the car to start the quick drive to the old Royal quarry.

"Alright, Corryna. Spill the beans," Jessica said as they got underway.

"What's that supposed to mean?" Of course, Corryna knew exactly what her friend was asking. She just wanted to hear her say it.

"Oh, I don't know. Just picking up on the fact that you and Colin have some serious chemistry."

"You can't tell that from a few minutes of being around us."

"I'm shocked you two didn't start a fire in the dining room."

Corryna laughed quietly, then sighed. She was so attracted to Colin. That much was absolutely true. But getting involved was such a bad idea. "I need to tell you something."

"Yes. Go."

She sucked in a deep breath for courage. "Colin and I had sex. The night of the blackout."

"Oh, my God. Tell me everything."

She wasn't prepared to tell her friend everything. But she could share most of it. "I brought my flowers to his restaurant so I could store them in his fridge and I don't know. We were arguing, but then the next minute he was pouring me a glass of Irish whiskey and saying nice things to me. I completely lost my head." This was the first time she'd uttered a word about this to anyone. She'd expected to feel some measure of relief at confessing to what had happened, but it was only tying her stomach up in knots.

"Was it amazing?"

"It was hot. For sure. But it happened so fast. I mean, ten minutes. Fifteen minutes, tops. Then it was over and I was frantically searching for my clothes on his office floor so I could get out of there."

Jessica grasped Corryna's forearm. "Hold up. You did it in his office? On the floor?"

"And on the chair, sort of. I don't know. It was all a blur." It had been hot enough to sear the memory into her brain for all eternity, but she didn't like the fact that he'd made her behave in a manner that was so completely out of character. She thought of herself as a free spirit, but not *that* free, devoid of inhibition. What kind of mistakes would she make in a state like that?

"Do you like him? Could this be a relationship?"

Corryna nearly burst out laughing. "What? No."

"Don't say it like that. It's a reasonable question."

"Colin Reynolds? No way. I mean, he's smart and sexy." *And funny and clever and that accent makes me want to take off all of my clothes.* "But we're working together on the Noble-Ramos wedding. It's such an important job for both of us. So that's really not a good idea."

"I see your point about working on the wedding together, but there is going to be life after Xavier Noble and Ariana Ramos get married. I like Colin. He treats his catering staff with respect and pays us well. That's why everyone wants to work his events. And you and Colin will still be living in the same town. Don't shut that door completely."

Corryna hadn't thought about that, and it gave her a whole new perspective on her situation with Colin. Maybe she didn't have to work overtime to keep him at arm's length. She could keep him in the friend zone, then see where things went after the wedding. "It probably wouldn't go anywhere. Colin doesn't do serious. He's more focused on his career. But it could be fun." She pulled into the dirt parking area near the quarry. A thick rolling forested area surrounded it on three sides, and there were quite a lot of nature trails snaking through the woods.

"You've never really struck me as the sort of woman who would get involved with a man just for fun," Jessica said as they got out of the car.

"I'm not."

"So maybe think twice about that." Jessica reached out and cupped Corryna's shoulder. "I want you to have fun, but I also don't want you to get hurt."

"I don't exactly trust my judgment when it comes to men anyway. My track record isn't great." Corryna led the way up the main trail. It was dusty and arid along the upward incline, with outcroppings of rock, bits of vegetation and the occasional small lizard that would dart away when it saw them coming. The sun was already strong and fierce. It might be April, but summer was most definitely on the way. "So, Colin suggested one interesting thing to me last night when we were talking."

"Oh yeah?" Jessica asked. "What's that?"

"Remember when I told you that I had suspicions that Dan had stolen from the business? Well, I told Colin about it, and he said I should hire a forensic accountant." Corryna's words were coming out in choppy spurts now that they were walking up a steeper grade. But the woods were getting more dense, the greenery fuller and lusher, and she knew that soon they would reach the real payoff. "They would audit the books and figure out if money disappeared and possibly where it went."

"What would be the endgame with something like that?" Jessica asked.

"I guess I could sue Dan for the money."

"After what he did to you, I absolutely think you should do it. Can Colin guide you through it?"

"Yes. He offered to help me find someone." Corryna saw the trees opening up near the crest of the hill. There were wider swaths of light from the sun up ahead.

"That's great. I say go for it."

"I guess I just wonder why he would want to help me. That's my only sticking point. He even asked me about it again at the restaurant when you were out getting the last bin of arrangements." Corryna took a few more steps and reached the top of the hill. Jessica caught up a split second later. They stood and drank in the vision of the vast meadow on the other side of the slope. It was positively brimming with native Texas wildflowers—pink evening primrose, Texas bluebell, Indian paintbrush, white prickly poppy, brown-eyed Susan, and of course, bluebonnet.

"Wow," was all Corryna could think to say as she surveyed the stunning landscape, knowing how inadequate words were.

"It's gorgeous. And peaceful."

"I love to come here. I love seeing the flowers in the wild. It just reminds me how lucky I am to get to work all day with these beautiful things that nature creates. It's a little miracle."

Jessica wrapped one arm around Corryna's shoulder and tugged her closer. "You deserve a little miracle."

"So you think I should let Colin help me?"

"Yes. I do. And I also don't think you should rule out a romance. I'd just be careful. A guy like Colin Reynolds isn't easy to hold on to."

Five

Colin was the first to arrive at Sheen on Friday morning, before the sun was up, but that wasn't unusual. He worked more hours in the restaurant than anyone. As far as he was concerned, that was the only way it could be, because no one cared about the food and the experience of dining at his restaurant as much as he did. He went straight to work—not at his desk, where he would often spend hours analyzing the business's numbers. Today, he'd be starting in the kitchen.

He wanted to work out a few dishes before he had Corryna over tomorrow night. Although his kitchen at home was fully equipped, he had every ingredient he could ever want at Sheen. His plan was to cook and taste all morning, think on it for the rest of the day, then refine when he prepared a meal for Corryna tomorrow night. He wanted to impress her, but this wasn't about being flashy or even about pride. It was about trying to measure up. She'd truly bowled him over that night at Royal Blooms. It had taken his breath away to witness the moment when the world fell away for Corryna and she became immersed in her creativity, taking one thing and turning it into quite another. He knew that feeling. He'd been in that place before. But it had been a long time, and even then, he wasn't sure he'd ever been as uninhabited as she was. His approach had always been more cerebral and calculating. He formulated ideas in his head, tried them on his own, refined them over time, then presented the world with his creation when it was absolutely perfect.

He only had an hour or so to himself in the kitchen before his pastry chef, Elena Gutierrez, arrived at 7:00 a.m. "Wow. You're cooking this morning," she noted, looping her apron over her head and wrapping it around her waist to tie it. "Usually you're in your office." Elena was in her midthirties, with short deep brown hair and warm eyes. She was not only accomplished with pastries and desserts, she was a mom of three. Colin wasn't sure how she juggled it all, but he was extremely thankful to have her on his team. One of the original Sheen employees, she'd stayed on when Colin had bought the restaurant from Charlotte Jarrett Edmond.

"I'll be out of your way in a bit. Just wanted to give some ideas a lash."

"A lash?" she asked.

The staff, and for that matter, most Texans, struggled when he let his Irish slang loose. "Give it a lash. It means to give it a go."

"Ah. Got it." She wandered over and peered down at one of the dishes he'd composed—beef carpaccio with green garlic aioli and black truffle. "Looks amazing. May I?"

He wasn't sure it was perfect yet, but he wasn't afraid of Elena's honest appraisal. "Please." Colin stood back as she grabbed a fork and dug in.

Her eyes closed the instant she put the bite in her mouth. "Oh, my God. Colin," she said, holding her hand to her lips. "That is incredible. The flavors are sublime and the texture is perfect. It's like velvet." She licked the fork. "Is this going on the menu? Please say it is."

He really hoped he'd get that kind of response from Corryna, and eventually Xavier Noble and Ariana Ramos. "Probably. Possibly. It would first be for the Noble-Ramos wedding. The wedding planner was very specific. She wants dishes that are exclusive to their event. But we could do this at Sheen afterward."

"Well, you're a genius."

Colin had heard that word before, but he didn't believe it. He knew he was a damn good chef, but was he the absolute best he could be? Not yet.

Sheen's sous-chef, Kristine Vargas, burst into the kitchen with such enthusiasm that it left the stainless steel door swinging back and forth on its hinges. "Have you guys heard?"

"Heard what?" Colin asked.

Kristine strutted over to them, her chin held high. "The Jane Broad award nominees were just announced. And you were *both* nominated."

Elena shrieked so loudly that Colin recoiled. "Are you being serious right now?"

Kristine laughed and unleashed an enthusiastic smile. "I would not kid about this. You were nominated for pastry chef of the year, and Colin was nominated for chef of the year."

Colin reached for Kristine's arm. "Stall the ball. You mean best chef in Texas."

Kristine shot Colin an inquisitive look. "Stall the ball?"

"It means hold on," Colin said. Old reflexes, or colloquialisms, died hard.

"I do not mean best chef in Texas. I mean chef of the year. For the entire US," Kristine replied.

Colin needed to sit. His mind was reeling. He'd always dreamed that his hard work would pay off, but after spending day after day working his ass off for years, he hadn't had a chance to imagine that today might be the day. "I… I…can't believe it."

Kristine clapped him on the back. "Believe it. And congratulations."

He turned to Elena. "Our brilliant pastry chef. Finally, you get the acclaim you deserve."

Elena was frozen in shock, mouth agape and eyes glassy. "Am I dreaming?"

"No," Kristine said. "You are not dreaming."

"I never thought I would be nominated for something like this." Elena directed her vision to Colin. "And I owe it all to you. Charlotte got Sheen off to such an amazing start, but you were the one who really launched us into the stratosphere. You're the one who hired a publicist in New York and got important food writers to come eat at the restaurant. You're the one who's always inviting your famous chef friends. You got people outside of Texas to care about what we were doing."

"You got Oliver Shaw to come and dine here last month," Kristine said. "How amazing is that?"

Colin shrugged it off, even though Oliver Shaw's visit to Sheen had been a real coup. He was a highly respected British food writer, a discerning devotee of everything Colin's father had ever touched in the culinary world. Colin had only convinced him to make the trip to the US by promising to blow his mind. Colin and his entire team had worked their butts off for Oliver's visit, and it went incredibly well. But Colin wouldn't get his vindication until Oliver's review ran in the publication *Global Cuisine*. It could drop any day now.

"Everything Elena said is true, Colin," Kristine continued. "The food is only part of the puzzle. The publicity and playing the game is the other piece. So, thank you."

He was taken aback by their kind words, and it was his immediate reflex to deflect the attention. He appreciated it, but he wouldn't feel worthy unless he won the award. Up until that moment, he'd merely been following the plan he'd formulated as a young wannabe chef—prove to his family that he didn't need them, their money or their influence. "Just trying to do right by you all." In truth, these were skills he'd learned from watching his parents hustle in their own restaurants. He wondered when he would hear from them. Whenever Colin received an important piece of publicity or won a significant award, his father would reach out. It was never about offering congratulations. Instead, his dad weaponized his achievements against him. None of Colin's previous accolades came close to matching the Jane Broad nomination. It was only a matter of time before he got a call. "I'm going to check my email and do a few things in the office, but congratulations, Elena. You deserve it."

"You, too, Colin. You, too."

Colin hoped that was true. He wandered through the kitchen and back to his office. It was far too early for a drink, but he sure as hell thought about it. He was proud and more than a little in awe of what had just happened, but he found himself unwilling to take any real joy from it. He believed with every fiber of his being that being a chef and restaurateur was what he was meant to do, and it was magnificent to be acknowledged. But in his heart of hearts, he always felt as if he was falling short. He'd spent all forty-two years of his life fighting doubt. Pushing harder in order to measure up. But it was never enough in some people's eyes...

As if his father heard Colin's internal dialogue, Colin's phone rang. He sat in his desk chair, staring at the screen for a moment before finally taking a deep breath and resigning himself to his fate. "Da. How's the form?" he asked, slipping into the common phrases of his home country, as was his habit whenever he spoke to his parents.

"I saw the Jane Broad nominations. You finally did it. The nomination at least. It's a step. We'll see how things go when they give out the award. Later this month, right?"

Colin shook his head and leaned forward to rest his head in one hand, while holding on to the phone with the other. His father had conceded the tiniest possible sliver of positivity, but that was the way this always went. This was nothing new. He couldn't let it get to him. "That's usually how they do it. Announce the nominees a few weeks ahead of time. We'll have to wait and see."

"If you win, will you have proven your point? Will you come to work for me and your mam?"

"I'm not proving a point. I'm living my life on my own terms." He felt his fingers twitching, and he had to rub them together to make the sensation go away. They wanted to ball up into fists.

"I don't know how many times I have to say this. Can you not see that it's an embarrassment that I can't pull my own son in to work for me? If you win this award, it will only get worse. I look like I don't have my own house in order."

Colin would've laughed if it didn't make him so angry. Heat rose in his cheeks. How his father had managed to make the idea of Colin winning an award into a bad thing… Well, that was next-level martyrdom. "It's never my intention to make you look bad. Lest I remind you that I am still your son, and that you can stake your claim on me by simply boasting about me."

"You are my son in name only. You made that choice when you decided to stay in the US."

Colin remembered the choice very well. It was impossible to forget. It was the first time Colin had ever had the nerve to stand up to his dad. He was still proud of the things he'd said. Yes, he'd been young, idealistic and more than a little naive, but he grew a spine that day. "I had my reasons."

"You can't punish your mother and I forever, Colin. We didn't have a choice. You were impossible. And we had to focus on our business. So we sent you to boarding school in America. Some people would die to have an opportunity like that."

His dad always glossed over the fact that the school he'd been sent to was for boys with discipline problems. It was a rough militaristic place with a hidden hierarchy among the students, where being cruel and good at fighting was the only way to be at the top. At first, Colin was terrified of his new reality. He lost all hope and begged his parents to allow him to come home. But his dad believed in toughness. He thought Colin needed to tame his inner demons. Colin knew he'd been a handful, always getting into trouble at his private school in Ireland, which greatly embarrassed his parents. He had a wild streak, something burning deep inside him that longed to get out. But being sent away didn't cure him of it. It only made it stronger.

He could hardly believe he'd lived through those years at boarding school, but at least he'd learned one truth—love and family weren't to be counted on. He'd thought his parents would always love him. He'd thought they'd see the error of their ways and bring him home, but they didn't. And the damage was done. *Stop thinking about this. It doesn't help.* He took a deep breath and willfully banished these thoughts from his mind. It wasn't all bad—those hard times had made him the man he was today. It taught him the absolute heights of discipline. It brought him closer to the most coveted prize in his industry—a Jane Broad nomination. "Da, I need to get back to work."

"I see. Well, I need to do the same. Your mam sends her regards."

There was nothing left to say. "Thanks." Colin

hung up the phone and dropped the device onto his desk. His head was reeling, but he knew one thing to be true—he'd made the right decision when he decided to simply not be a part of his own family. To his dad, love and relationships were simply another form of currency.

His phone rang again, making him wish that he'd chucked it across the room. Or perhaps set the thing on fire. Tension gripped his shoulders like a vise. Each ring of the phone made his jaw tighter. Whoever was calling was being persistent. He couldn't ignore them forever. Reluctantly, he flipped it over and his heart jumped up into his throat. It was Corryna. "Corryna. Hello."

"Hey, you. I heard that congratulations are in order." Her voice was sweet and happy—a balm for his ragged nerves.

"You did?" He grinned and felt the strain on his body begin to wash away. He sat back in his chair. A split second ago, he'd been ready to explode. Now he felt like he was floating on air.

"I did. I ran over to The Royal Diner this morning for a cup of coffee and I heard people talking about your big award. Congratulations. I don't know much about the food world, but it sounds like a very big deal."

"It's just a nomination. Haven't won the thing yet."

"Still. Isn't it an honor to be nominated?"

"I won't lie. It absolutely is."

"I'm so proud of you. Your family must be thrilled."

And just like that, his elation was deflated yet again. "I did get a call from my dad." *He didn't actually wish me congratulations. Not like you.*

"Your voice sounds exactly like it did the other night in my shop when I asked about this subject. You don't have to talk about it if you don't want to."

"Let me put it this way. I'd rather talk to you about something fun. Like your flowers. They've been a big hit in the restaurant."

"They have not. You're just saying that to butter me up."

Good God, he wanted to butter her up. Quite literally. "I'm not. All of the servers said customers were commenting. They said it livened up the place. I believe the word they used was *cheery.*" It was an apt description for Corryna as well. She'd brought so much sunshine into his life.

"That's so nice. I love hearing that. Thank you."

"Of course. I'm happy to give credit where credit's due."

"It's almost like you shouldn't have canceled my contract in the first place."

"You're absolutely right. I should not have canceled it. I thought I was improving my bottom line, but if it creates a better guest experience, it's worth it. Every penny."

"Speaking of the bottom line, I wanted to tell you that I've thought about the forensic accountant and

I'd like to go through with it. I'm not sure I actually want to go after my ex, but it would at least give me some peace of mind to know definitively one way or the other."

Colin scrambled for a piece of paper and a pen, then scribbled down a note. "Absolutely. I will make a few calls and have someone reach out to you? They'll need your financial records, of course, but they can go through all of that with you. And feel free to ask me for help if you need it."

"I appreciate that. I don't totally understand why you're going so far out of your way to help, but I'm thankful."

"I told you. I want to see you be successful." He didn't mention that he also despised the idea that this wonderful woman had been married to such a monster. And if he'd stolen from her? Colin needed her to get justice.

"Do you need to cancel our plans to get together tomorrow night? I'm sure the restaurant will be even busier because of your nomination."

"We're fully booked for weeks out, so we can't really get more busy than we already are. And I made a plan with you, Corryna, and I intend to keep it." He tapped his pen on the desk, thinking about everything he needed to get done before she came over to his place tomorrow. There was a lot to prepare. He wanted it all to be perfect.

"Probably smart. This wedding is an important job for us both."

"The most important." Of course, that wasn't the full extent of Colin's reason for prioritizing time with Corryna. He greatly enjoyed her company. Still, she wasn't wrong about the importance of this wedding. Now that he'd been nominated for the Jane Broad award, the highest of expectations would be foisted upon him by everyone—the residents of Royal, Rylee Meadows, and most important, the bride and groom. He needed his role in the event to be a slam dunk—food that people raved about for weeks, months or years. "So I'll see you tomorrow?"

"I'll be there. Can't wait."

Six

Corryna's hair was done. So was her makeup. But try as she might, she could not decide what to wear to tonight's meeting at Colin's house. She'd put on at least ten different outfits, but none of them worked. Nothing seemed right. How was she supposed to strike a balance between looking nice and keeping things professional, while also not trying too hard? With only twenty minutes before she needed to leave for his house, she had to make a decision quickly. This required advice from the person she trusted most when it came to things like this. She sent Jessica a text.

What do I wear to this meeting at Colin's house?

Corryna's phone immediately started ringing. "You didn't have to call me," Corryna said when she answered.

"I'm in the car on my way to a catering job, so I couldn't text you back."

Corryna perched on the edge of her bed. "I'm sorry to bug you. I just can't figure out what I'm supposed to wear."

"You aren't bugging me. I want to help. Let's think about who, what, when, where and why."

"Okay." Corryna wasn't sure she was following this methodology, but she was prepared to try anything. "The 'who' is Colin."

"He's not just Colin. He's Colin Reynolds. One of the best chefs in the country, possibly in the world. And the 'what' is that he's cooking for you. Only you. On a Saturday night, which isn't like other nights."

Corryna was suddenly extremely nervous. "At his house, which I've heard is gorgeous."

"Honestly, the 'why' is unimportant at this point. I realize this is for a job you're working on together, but don't go over there looking like you're going to arrange flowers for the next three hours because you aren't. You're going to taste his food and you're going to feel awkward if you don't look the part. If it were me, I'd dress like I'm going to Sheen, but maybe pick something you'd wear if it was just you and I going out."

"I have a black dress. Knee-length and sleeveless."

"Perfect. You can't go wrong with that. Ever."

"Heels?"

"If they're comfortable."

"I can do that."

"Does that help?"

"Immensely. Thank you so much."

"I'm pulling into the parking lot at this event, so I have to go. But try to have fun tonight. This might be work, but you also deserve to enjoy yourself."

Corryna got up from the bed, pinning the phone to her shoulder with her ear. "Thank you. I'll try. You're the absolute best."

"Love you," Jessica said.

"Love you, too." Corryna returned to her closet and plucked the aforementioned dress from the hanger. It had some silver embroidery on it, but was otherwise a fairly simple design with a flattering neckline and full skirt that accentuated her waist. After slipping into a pair of black wedge sandals, she hopped in her car for the drive to Colin's house. Her nerves were getting the best of her again. Despite the fact that she'd been divorced for six years now, Colin was the only man she'd slept with during that time. The thought of being all alone with him again made her wonder about what might happen, even though she knew that the professional aspect of their evening had to remain at center stage.

Her car's navigation directed her to one of the newly developed areas on the outskirts of Royal, where luxurious fully custom homes were nestled on acres of rolling lush green landscape. A place like this was so far out of Corryna's budget it was nearly laughable. Her house was a modest one-bedroom bungalow about five minutes from downtown.

She pulled into the drive leading to Colin's house, which was situated quite far off the main road. She didn't care much about the trappings of wealth, but she couldn't help but be impressed as the home revealed itself to her as she drove closer. The sprawling ranch was creamy white, with a dark gray stone foundation for high contrast, dramatically lit from below. The multiple open gables of the roof were framed with exposed timbers, and the leaded black windows glowed from within with a warm light that made her feel welcome, rather than intimidated. It was stunning, just like Colin himself.

She parked her car to one side of the main entrance and made her way up wide stone steps to the double door, which was a rich dark-stained wood with inset multipaned windows. She rang the doorbell and drank in a deep breath of the sweet night air as she waited. It was peaceful out here. She already loved it.

Colin popped into sight, striding toward her down a wide central hall, wearing dark jeans that followed the temptingly long lines of his frame, and a black dress shirt with the sleeves rolled up to the elbows. Before he even reached the door, her heart was pulsing in her throat. He was too hot for words.

"Right on time," he said, opening the door for her.

"Of course. I've been looking forward to this."

"Yeah?" His question had a leading tone. He was already flirting with her.

"I'm ready to turn the tables on you," she replied, stepping into the foyer. What she could see of the house was gorgeous, with light-stained wood floors, an open layout and furnishings similar to those in his office at Sheen, with a calming earth-toned color palette. Most wonderfully, the house was full of heavenly aromas. "You've been busy. It smells amazing in here."

"Thanks. Most of the cooking is done."

That struck Corryna as odd. That wasn't what she'd expected. But she didn't want to make assumptions about his approach to their collaboration. She also didn't want to be rude. "I brought champagne. And it's already chilled," she said, offering the bottle.

"How nice."

"I thought we should celebrate your award nomination."

He tilted his head to the side. "Now that's even nicer. Thank you."

"You're welcome."

"Come on." He waved his hand, beckoning her ahead into the heart of the house. "Enough faffing about in the hall."

She walked alongside him, unable to ignore the way attraction pinged back and forth between them. He was so confident, so comfortable in his own skin, that it was impossible to not be drawn to him. Even if she was unsure about the idea of sleeping with him again, it would be impossible to resist him if he made an overture. One kiss and she'd be putty in his hands. "Faffing about?"

"It means messing around."

Maybe she just had sex on the brain, but nearly everything that came out of his mouth made her think about exactly that. The things Jessica had said to her—about having fun and not ruling out romance— echoed in her head. Her thoughts zeroed in on that night in his office at Sheen. She'd responded to his flirtatious ways with unbridled enthusiasm, and she hadn't even liked him then. She definitely liked him now. A lot.

As they strolled into the kitchen, Corryna was in awe of what a beautiful room it was, although it shouldn't have surprised her at all that a brilliant chef like Colin would invest so much into his home space for cooking. The cabinetry in the room was a warm gray, with glass insets in some of the doors of the upper units. Inside, dishes and barware were lined up neatly. A double Sub-Zero fridge sat to one side, while an eight-burner Viking range with a matching stainless steel hood took center stage. Despite what he'd said earlier, there was no sign that he'd actually been cooking. Everything was clean and straight as a pin. "Colin. This is absolutely gorgeous."

"Thanks. Have a seat." He pulled out one of the six barstools, which ran along one side of the long white marble island. "I'll pour the champagne."

As she sat, his hand remained at the back of the seat, then his fingertips grazed the small of her back as he stepped away, making goose bumps propagate along her arms. He pulled two stemmed flutes out of a cabinet, then turned back to her and removed the foil and wire cage beneath it. With the expertise of a master sommelier, he tilted the bottle with one hand, gripped the cork with the other and gently twisted. His forearm flexed, and the sight made her hold her breath as she was reminded of what it was like to be in his strong arms. The cork popped and Corryna jumped as a ribbon of excitement shot through her.

He poured the bubbly golden liquid into the glasses, then offered her one. "To our collaboration," he said.

"To your award," she countered.

He took a sip. "It's not mine yet. And the competition is stiff." His gaze connected with hers, and she felt as though she saw a glimpse of vulnerability in his expression. "Honestly, it might almost be better for me if I didn't win it. Even though it would be embarrassing."

"How in the world could that be better?"

He shrugged. "Keep my dad from bothering me."

Corryna could hardly believe he'd mentioned his family in front of her. He'd deflected the two times the subject had come up. "You mentioned that he called to congratulate you after your nomination. Doesn't he want you to win? I realize it's an American award, but from everything I've read, it's a very big deal in the culinary world. He must understand the importance of it."

"Have you been researching the Jane Broad awards, Corryna? You knew nothing about it when you called yesterday morning."

Heat flushed her cheeks. He'd caught her red-handed. "I was curious. I wanted to find out more."

He leaned against the kitchen counter, once again accentuating the long lean lines of his body. She had such a weakness for a tall man, and Colin was an exceptional example. How she longed to skim her hands over his firm shoulders, then trail them down his torso and abs. "Any time I get a major accolade, my dad expects me to go work for him. For his restaurant group." His face took on a decidedly more somber expression, which she hated seeing. She preferred happy Colin. "But it's not about wanting me. It's about his pride. Bragging rights. Whatever you want to call it. He's embarrassed that I had the gall to go out and build my own business."

"You've never worked for him, have you?" She'd done her research and seen no sign of it, which still didn't make sense to her.

"Not a day in my life."

"How does that happen? You're a chef. So are both of your parents. Why not work together?"

"They made that choice when they sent me off to boarding school. It forced me to make a life for myself, so that's what I did. Started culinary school when I was seventeen, then immediately went to work. As soon as I had enough experience, I bought my first restaurant."

"Sheen is your third restaurant, right?"

A wicked grin spread across his face, making his eyes light up. "You really did want to know more, didn't you?"

She dismissed it with a shrug of her shoulders. "Hey. Knowledge is power." Feeling flirtatious, she took a sip of her champagne while holding his gaze. His eyes were so mesmerizing she could've looked into them for hours, all in an attempt to unlock everything he kept tucked away inside his handsome head.

"I never planned to do what my father did, trying to build an empire. Always needing more." Colin straightened and downed the last of his drink. "I'd rather do one thing, make it all it can be, then move on to the next challenge."

"I could never do that. I like to feel settled."

"I've never felt settled a day in my life." He delivered a pointed glance, as if he needed to drive home his point. "There's too much desire pent up inside of me."

Corryna bit down on her lower lip. He was an absolute mystery with so many layers, and she deeply wanted to know more about him, but at the moment, what she wanted most was to be on the receiving end of his desire one more time. She'd never get to hold on to Colin for long. He'd essentially just told her that he wasn't that sort of man. But still, his raw appeal made her want to banish caution from her life entirely.

"Are you hungry?" he asked.

She nodded, recognizing that for her, the answer she was about to give had nothing to do with food. "Starving."

Colin felt as though his entire body was buzzing from one glass of champagne and fifteen minutes around Corryna. If he didn't pace himself, he was going to have a difficult time getting through their night together. *Focus.* "Let me get you fed, then." He already had absolutely everything in order. He didn't want to leave anything to chance. "I reworked all of the passed hors d'oeuvres for the wedding this week."

Corryna got up from her seat and rounded to his side of the island. "You did? I can't wait to see what you did."

"We'll start with the chilled dishes. That's four of the first seven menu items I'd like to present to Rylee at the end of the month." He opened up the fridge and removed the small plates and serving vessels he'd carefully chosen. "These just need a few final touches." He went to work, drizzling olive oil on some items, squeezing lemon on others and sprinkling sea salt on the rest.

Corryna placed her hand on his back while he finished the dishes. He could have sworn that the warmth of her hand nearly burned a hole through his shirt. He loved her presence, but he especially relished her touch. It made him feel alive. "It's fun to watch you work. Tell me what we're having."

"To start, we have a tuna crudo with charred Meyer lemon, capers and spring herbs." He continued down the line of dishes he'd prepared. "Then chilled blue crab with Thai basil, cucumber, lime and chile-miso aioli. After that, cold sweet onion and artichoke bisque served in a shot glass. Lastly, we have beef carpaccio with green garlic aioli and black truffle."

"Wow. I can't wait to try everything."

"The dining room table is set. Why don't you go in and pour us a glass of wine? There's a bottle on ice, but it's already open." With a nod, he directed her to the dining area, which was through a wide archway opposite the kitchen.

"I can't help?" she asked.

He wanted everything to be perfect for her. "Sorry. No."

As Corryna ambled into the other room, he loaded up a silver lacquer serving tray and walked the dishes in behind her. Corryna was getting settled before one of the two place settings. He'd worked hard at creating ambience in the room, with soft lighting, music and candles. As he set each dish before her, he couldn't ignore the fierce pounding of his heart. He cared what she thought. He wanted her to love every last bite.

"It's all so pretty. I'm almost afraid to eat anything. I might ruin it," Corryna said.

He took the seat next to her. "Please don't say that. Eating is the point."

She picked up her fork and glanced over at him, her eyes flickering with excitement as she took her first bite of the tuna. She moaned in ecstasy and licked her lips, prompting Colin to stare. "This is so good. It's amazing. It's so light and fresh and bright. Full of flavor."

He wasn't out of the woods, but her approval gave his shoulders the chance to relax slightly, which was a very good thing. The rest of his body felt as though it was on fire. "I'm glad you're enjoying it."

"So, I wanted to tell you that I talked to the forensic accountant today and gave her access to all of my records. She was really nice. That made me feel a lot better about everything." She finished the final bite of her tuna.

"Good. I'm glad."

"She said it won't take more than a week or two, which surprised me."

"All of your records are electronic. And your business is small and straightforward. It shouldn't take long."

"I guess you're right." Corryna took a bite of the crab dish, then reached out and grasped Colin's forearm. How he loved it when she touched him. "Colin. How is the crab even better than the tuna? This is the best thing I have ever put in my mouth."

Dammit. He fidgeted in his seat. Every flattering comment and appreciative sound she made was pointing his brain and body in only one direction—kissing her, leading her to his bedroom and taking off her clothes… "That's quite a review."

"I have a way with words, remember?"

"Oh. I do."

They finished the last of the dishes he'd served for the first round, each also receiving raves from Corryna. He was pleased that his hard work on refining his ideas was paying off. Frankly, the night was going perfectly. "Now we'll move on to the hot dishes if you're ready." He stood and began clearing plates.

"Do you need my help?"

He shook his head. "No. I've got it."

Corryna reached for the wine bottle and poured herself a bit more to drink. "For the record, I could get used to this."

"Good." Colin strode back into the kitchen, struggling to remember the last time he'd had a chance to cook for someone in his home like this. He hosted plenty of dinner parties, but that was usually more about staying in the good graces of the power players in Royal rather than any desire for social interaction. Or he was entertaining some VIP from the food world—giving them the royal treatment in the hopes that they would see him as his own force in the culinary arts and not merely the son of Killian Reynolds.

It only took him a few minutes to bring his remaining creations to Corryna. "Here we have a coffee-rubbed skirt steak with mint chimichurri and

Asian pears. Then a vegetarian option of homemade potato gnocchi with roasted garlic, parsley, sherry and parmesan. Lastly, Rylee asked for vegan as well, so we have cornmeal crusted fried mushrooms with herbs and a sweet chili sauce.

"You really outdid yourself," Corryna said when she was finished eating. She'd made countless glowing comments along the way. "I seriously want to lick this plate."

He cleared his throat, unsure of how to respond. If she did that, he might enjoy it a little too much. "I'll take that as a compliment."

"You should." She got up from the table. "You have to let me help you with cleanup. I won't take no for an answer this time."

He smiled and grabbed their bottle of wine. "I won't turn you down."

They filed into the kitchen with the last of the plates and silverware. "What can I do?" she asked.

"I can rinse if you want to load the dishwasher."

"Sounds like a plan."

He turned on the water, letting it glide over the plates before handing them to her. Their fingers brushed with every pass, and he tried to wrap his head around the fact that he and Corryna had managed to find such a comfortable rapport so quickly. Normally, when he was working with someone, he tended to hand down orders, but he couldn't do that with her. It was a nice change. And when he was interested in a woman romantically, he made a point of not getting close, but he couldn't do that, either. He and Corryna had to mesh. Those were the orders from Rylee and they both took them seriously.

"The meal was amazing, Colin. Truly," Corryna said as they finished up.

Finally, he felt as though he could take some respite. He'd done what he'd set out to do—he'd impressed the hell out of her. He poured them each a final glass of wine and leaned against the kitchen counter. "Not a single negative comment? "

"Actually. Yes. I do have one."

"Maybe I shouldn't have asked." He was surprised. She'd given no indication that she was unhappy with anything he'd served.

"You didn't play fair." She drifted closer to him until she was standing mere inches away. It wouldn't have taken much effort to reach out and tug her closer.

"I don't know what you're talking about."

"You made me stand in my workroom and design while you watched."

"I wanted to understand your process." Just thinking about it, he was still blown away by what it was like to see her shut out the rest of the world and give in to pure creativity. It was inspiring. "I've never arranged flowers, but surely you know how to cook. It's not the same thing."

She wagged a finger at him. "You can't call what you did tonight cooking. It was so much more than that. It was…" She looked deeply into his eyes, seeming to search for words. "It was a fully immersive art experience. All of these amazing sights and smells and tastes. I've never had anything like it."

"Really?"

"Yes. So, I don't think you can say that I know how to do what you did. I don't. And I'd be lying if I said that I didn't feel a little cheated by the fact that you didn't let me watch you create."

"You can't be serious."

"Of course I am. I felt naked when I was standing there working on that arrangement in front of you. And we did not know each other very well at that point. Don't you think that was hard for me?"

The mental image of Corryna naked popped into his consciousness and wasn't about to go anywhere. "I suppose."

"And I wanted to see you be vulnerable like I was. Instead, you went out of your way to show me the perfect side of your talent. But I want to understand how your brain and heart work together."

He took a deep breath while his body and brain waged a war against each other. She was right. He'd gone to great lengths to only present things that he'd known were perfect. But that was a reflex, one that was coded into his DNA, and he wasn't sure he could let go of it. It protected him. It made his life easier. "I'm sorry if you're disappointed."

"Colin. You couldn't disappoint me if you tried." Her eyes were misting with emotion. "I know this much about you. You have a lot of fire and desire inside of you. And I want to see it for myself. I want to experience it. Don't hide it from me."

"And what happens if I show it to you?"

"Well, I'll have no choice but to let down my guard and show you mine as well."

Seven

Colin didn't often succumb to flattery. Most of the time, he felt undeserving. But hearing it from Corryna's tempting mouth made him feel entirely different about it. Perhaps it was that her admiration was worth more than anyone else's because she knew what it meant to be creative. She understood how much it took to lay your heart and soul bare for all to see. "You see right through me, don't you? Because you're right. Absolutely right. I did try to hide from you tonight. It's the way I work. I try to make everything perfect. I work hard and I hone a dish until I see no faults in it. Then, and only then, I let the world see it. And taste it."

"You don't have to do that with me. Seriously.

You don't. I want to see and know everything that's locked up in that incredibly handsome head of yours."

He pushed forward from the spot where he'd been leaning against the counter. "I'm starting to feel like I can trust you." If only she knew what a consequential admission that was for him. He trusted very few people, and they all worked at Sheen.

"You can. You absolutely can."

He stepped closer to Corryna, drawn to her in a way that he felt on a molecular level. Every atom in his body wanted her and needed her. "I hope you know that you can trust me, too."

"I do think I know that."

"I want you, Corryna. One hundred times more than I wanted you that night at the restaurant, and I really, really wanted you that night."

Pink colored her cheeks, making her even more impossibly beautiful. "I'd be lying if I said I didn't want you too, but this wouldn't be like that night at Sheen. Neither of us had anything to lose then. Now we're working together, on a wedding that we've agreed is immensely important to our businesses. And you heard what Rylee said that day at the TCC. She wanted no drama. Sex will make everything more complicated."

He reached for a lock of her hair and twisted it in his fingers. "The last time I checked, Rylee Meadows isn't here. It's just you and me. And us, together in my bed, isn't complicated. It sounds bloody perfect to me."

"Why do I feel like you might be able to talk me into anything?"

"This has to be about free will, Corryna. I'm not trying to make a case. I'm simply poking holes in your argument."

Her tongue ran slowly across her lower lip. "No one can know."

"I'm excellent at keeping secrets." He pulled her into his arms and kissed her, amazed by how quickly and effortlessly they fell into sync. It felt like the logical next step after that night at Sheen, and just like then, he sensed that she was feeling as impatient and filled with urgency as he was. She arched into him, her belly hard against his. He threaded his hands into her hair as her supple lips made him lose all logical thought, which was absolutely for the best. He was always overthinking. It was his downfall. Kissing Corryna didn't require analysis or examination. They were acting on their attraction. It was nothing more than that.

"I really want to get you out of this dress," he said, breathless.

She peered up at him, her eyes half-closed and her mouth slack and beckoning. "You haven't even shown me your bedroom yet."

"How rude of me." He grabbed her hand and he wound his way through the kitchen, then down the hall and to his owner's suite, which took up nearly a quarter of the house. Just like his office at Sheen, this was a place he retreated to. He could let down his guard here, so it was only right that this was where he and Corryna would cast aside everything that was getting in the way, like their clothes and the preconceived ideas of professional behavior from people like Rylee Meadows.

"It's beautiful. Just like your whole house," Corryna said, stepping in a lazy circle as she looked around the room.

The space was lit only by a nearly full moon, still low in the night sky. He knew she couldn't see everything, but this wasn't the time for a full tour. That could wait until morning. "You're beautiful. Inside and out." He combed his fingers into her hair and brought her face to his, getting lost in the most magnificent kiss, her lips soft and supple, and for right now, all his. "The dress. It has to go."

"It is a little itchy."

"We can't have that."

Corryna turned her back to him, gathered her hair in her hand and pulled it to the side. Gazing over her shoulder at him, she extended an invitation with a single look that was born of pure passion and a bit of mischief. It was enough to make him give up everything that had ever been important to him. It was the look that had first made him want her.

He turned his attention to her zipper, drawing it down. Inch by inch, he got to see a little more of her creamy skin in the softly lit room, past a black bra, followed by more touchable skin, then down to black satin panties. Standing right behind her, he pressed his torso against her back, drinking in the reality that this was going to happen again. After last time, he'd truly thought that was it. That was the only taste of Corryna he would get. He was thankful to have been wrong.

He wanted his clothes off. He wanted hers gone, too. But he also wanted to savor this moment. He dipped his head lower and kissed her neck while he nudged the dress from her shoulders. The garment slid down her body to the floor, and he planted his hands on her naked waist, then slid them around to her belly and up to her full breasts. The lacy cups caressed his palms and he felt it as her nipples grew tight. He continued to skim his mouth along her neck, then brought his hands back to unhook her bra clasp. Corryna ruffled the straps from her shoulders, then cast it aside.

He turned her around, cupping her breasts again with his hands. Her skin was so warm and soft beneath his touch, but it was even better to taste as he lowered his head and drew one of her nipples between his lips. He swirled his tongue around the tight skin, loving the way it felt when her body reacted to his.

She frantically worked on his shirt while he focused on her incredible breasts, but she was quick with the buttons and he had to let go of her when she yanked his sleeves down his arms. He was just as eager to get rid of his shirt as she was. She grasped his shoulders and kissed him—fast and hot, then dropped to her knees and rubbed the front of his jeans, pressing forcefully against his erection. He'd thought he couldn't get any harder, and he'd been wrong. A rush of heat made him dizzy, or maybe he was simply drunk on Corryna.

She unbuttoned and unzipped his jeans, and then he shucked them before standing still and letting her decide where this went next. She slipped her fingers below the waistband of his boxer briefs and slowly pulled them down past his hips. She was taking her time, looking up at him with sheer desire on her face. She didn't have to work at all to seduce him, but he appreciated the way she was working her way into his psyche. Knowing how much she wanted him was as good as having her touch him. She wrapped her hand around his erection and it felt so good that he had to steady himself with a hand on her shoulder. She took long and firm strokes while their gazes connected. Her eyes were dark and surprisingly intense. Normally sweet and soft Corryna was showing him the side of her he'd seen that night in his office.

When she leaned closer and took him into her mouth, his mind went blank, then he experienced a flash of white. Nothing had ever felt so incredible. So luscious and hot. Again, she took things slow and careful, focused on him, and once his brain settled down, he opened his eyes to watch her lips on his body, the scene lit only by the soft blue light of the moon. He reached down and raked his fingers through her hair, curling them into her scalp and caressing. Having her mouth on him had him teetering on the brink, but he didn't want this to be all about him. He wanted to please her. He wanted her calling his name and quivering in his arms. He wanted to make her his own.

Corryna was surprised when Colin reached down and tugged on her arms. She hadn't been with many men in her life, but none had ever taken the initiative to shift gears like this. They'd always left it up to her. As she rose to stand, he was quick to kiss her, and with raw abandon—cupping the sides of her face while their tongues swirled in an endless circle. Corryna felt as though her entire body was about to go up in flames. She had to have him. Now. He steered them toward the bed, and they wound their way there by walking in circles and not dropping their kiss for even a split second. When he ran into the edge of the mattress, he made one more half-turn and used the gentle force of his strong hands to suggest she stretch out on the puffy duvet.

Corryna arched her back, skimming her skin against the silky bedding of Colin's bed. The only thing better than the sensory delight of touching the cool fabric was the view of Colin as he towered over her—all six feet and five inches of him—completely naked and all hers. Everything about his physical presence was perfect—he had a sculpted chest and muscular shoulders and a stomach that made her want to scrub her laundry on it, if only to test out the theory of washboard abs. Even so, he was about so much more than his appearance. Colin's inner confidence and self-assurance, the way he lived in his body, made him unlike any man she'd ever had the pleasure to look at. She craved him like the most decadent dessert she could imagine. He might not be hers, but for right now, she needed him like air and water.

He cocked an eyebrow at her and a corner of his mouth quirked up. He was satisfied with himself. And he deserved to feel that way. Despite the fact that she'd given him a hard time about his overpreparation for the meal he'd served tonight, he was still utterly brilliant. He was a rare talent and had an exceptional mind. She felt so damn lucky to spend any time at all with him.

"Get over here, Colin," she murmured, curling her finger in invitation.

"I could stand here forever and look at you."

"Something tells me you want a little more than the view."

"True." He reached down and shimmied her panties past her hips, then planted a knee on the bed and stretched out next to her.

She sucked in a deep breath, relishing this feeling of vulnerability with a man she trusted implicitly. She rolled to her side and he kissed her softly while he cupped her bottom with his strong hands and pulled her closer. "I need you, Colin." As soon as the words left her lips, she knew that this was about so much more than lust. That night at Sheen had been solely about satisfying an urge, but this was something more than that. He'd turned out to be so much more than she'd ever imagined. It was one more reason to believe she could never have more than a fling with him, but she was okay with that. She'd known what he was and who he was from the very beginning. "Please tell me you have a condom," she said. She hadn't had the presence of mind to ask for it the first time they'd had sex, which had been stupid of her. Luckily, there were no signs that there had been any serious repercussions of that misstep.

"Oh. Uh. Sure." He rolled to his side, opened the drawer of the bedside table and pulled out a box. A few moments later, he urged her to her back and positioned himself between her legs. She lifted her knees, inviting him inside. Inch by inch, he filled her so perfectly that it was difficult to know where one of them started and the other ended. He buried his face in her neck, blanketing the sensitive skin with wet and hot kisses, amping up the intensity of every sensation in her body.

They rocked together, Corryna tugging him closer with her legs, needing him to go as deep as possible. She closed her eyes and let her mind wander as the pleasure toyed with her, and the tension climbed, ever closer to a peak. His breaths grew shorter and he bore down a little harder with his body weight, applying the perfect amount of pressure with every thrust. Her peak was fast approaching now, like a runaway train. Colin simply had her too turned on. As soon as she felt the first rumbling, it went quickly, like a bolt of lightning that leaves the earth trembling beneath your feet. Colin followed, calling out with several forceful thrusts, then he collapsed next to her, gasping for breath.

"That was amazing," she said, feeling like she was floating several feet above the bed, but still wanting more of him.

"It was, Corryna. You're incredible." He held on to her tightly and tenderly kissed her forehead.

She pressed her face against his warm chest, wanting to soak up as much of Colin as humanly possible. She hadn't felt this content in a very long time. And she couldn't help but feel as though she deserved it.

There was no telling when she fell asleep, but Corryna woke to the sound of a rooster. For a moment, she didn't remember where she was, but then she drew in a deep breath through her nose and recognized Colin's incredible smell. She was in his room. And last night had been absolutely glorious. She opened her eyes, but the side of his bed where he'd slept was empty. "Huh," she muttered, finding it strange that he'd left, but guessing that if anyone was likely to be an early riser, it was Colin. She flipped to her other side and peered through the French doors she hadn't noticed last night. Outside was a rolling vista of bright green and what appeared to be a sizable garden. She was drawn to it in the same way that she was drawn to him—something deep inside her wanted to explore.

"Colin?" she called out into the room, wondering where he'd gone. There was no answer. She tossed back the covers to search for him, and that was when she saw his head poke up from the garden. She had to go. Right away. She scrambled out of bed, noticing that he'd neatly hung up her dress on a hook next to his closet. As much as logic said she should be wearing her own clothes, she hadn't been lying when she'd said her dress was itchy. Plus, she selfishly wanted to be wrapped up in anything that smelled like him. She grabbed his shirt from last night, threaded her arms into the sleeves, rolled up the cuffs and opened the door. The sweet morning air hit her nostrils. The rooster crowed again and the rising sun lit Colin from behind. It was as idyllic a setting as she ever could've imagined.

"Who knew you were a farmer?" she asked, padding across the dewy grass in her bare feet.

He looked up and smiled wide, his entire face lighting up. Damn, he was handsome. Especially so this morning. "I'm getting a few things for breakfast." He marched down one of the rows toward her with a basket in his hand, wearing jeans and a T-shirt.

"What a beautiful garden. Do you do all of this by yourself?"

He turned and surveyed the plot of vegetables and herbs. "I do. I picked up gardening when I lived in Santa Monica, California. That's where my first restaurant was. It's also where I met Charlotte, the original owner of Sheen." He returned his vision to Corryna and stepped closer. "That restaurant was tiny. Only twenty-four seats. And my concept was fully farm-to-table, but I didn't know the area well, so establishing relationships with farms took some time. The house I bought there had a large vegetable patch that hadn't been tended in years. I wanted the restaurant to be as much of me as it could be, and I also wanted to have the best of the best, so I taught myself how to garden."

"Does any of what you're growing now end up at Sheen?"

"I'd have to be a full-time farmer to keep up with that much demand. But I bring in herbs on an almost daily basis in the spring and I'll do a second planting in the fall. If I have a good crop of a vegetable like tomatoes or peppers, I'll compose an appetizer or an entrée around it."

How she admired his commitment to his craft. She'd given him a hard time last night about not being open with her about his creative process, but there was no question that he put a lot of heart and thought into it. "What did you harvest this morning?"

"Chives, flat-leaf parsley, spring onions, spinach and eggs. I was thinking I'd make you an omelet. I have a heavenly Irish cheddar in the fridge."

"Does this mean you're going to cook for me with no advance preparation?"

"It means exactly that." His eyes raked over her body. "You look great in my shirt."

"Thanks." *It smells good. It smells like you.* She grasped his shoulder, then popped up onto her tiptoes to kiss him. "Can we eat now? I'm starving."

"Of course." They filed back inside, this time through another set of French doors that led into a mudroom and the back entry into his kitchen. "Help yourself to coffee. I left out a mug for you and there's some cream in the pitcher on the counter."

"Perfect." He was the consummate host. Corryna poured herself a cup and added a splash of cream. She breathed in the intoxicating smell, then took a sip of the dark roast coffee. "I'm excited to actually watch you cook."

"I'm excited to prove to you that I don't hide."

Just thinking about their conversation last night prompted a question she wasn't sure she should ask. He'd said he trusted her, but to what extent? "How much of a perfectionist would you say you are?"

He unloaded the contents of his basket, avoiding eye contact, making her wonder if he was already feeling defensive. "I hate it when people answer a question like this with a number larger than one hundred, but I have to say I'm one thousand percent a perfectionist."

Just like that, she felt better about digging for the information. He seemed to be okay with opening up to her. "Does any of that have to do with your parents? Your upbringing?"

"Some of it's the restaurant business. If you want to be successful, you have to be consistent. And in consistency, lies perfectionism."

"But? I sense a 'but' coming here."

"I think the rest of it lies with my family."

She leaned against the counter and watched as he washed the vegetables and dried them with a white cotton tea towel. "Were they controlling?"

"My dad, especially." He pulled out a cutting board, then sharpened a chef's knife.

"You know, I understand that you aren't excited to talk about your parents, but just like you can't keep your creative process bottled up for no one to see, it's not healthy to keep your history with your family locked up inside, either."

He glanced at her, only in passing, as he pulled two sauté pans out of a pot drawer next to the stove. "It's pretty simple. I got in trouble a lot as a kid, and it drove my dad up a wall. He was embarrassed of me, and so was my mother, so they sent me away to a military school in Utah. It wasn't called that, but that's what it was. I was only twelve. No clue what was going on. And I felt like my parents didn't want me anymore."

The vision of a young Colin, banished to a country that wasn't home, materialized in her mind. Her heart squeezed tightly in her chest. He must have felt so vulnerable. So scared. "Oh, my God. I'm so sorry. How long did you have to stay there?"

"That's the thing. They sent me back every year for five years. I got to go home during the summers and I tried my best to earn my dad's approval, especially as I got more interested in food and cooking, but if I didn't do things exactly right, or if I made any sort of mistake, he wasn't impressed." Colin began chopping his bounty from the garden. "And of course, he sent me away again, hoping I'd learn some more discipline. He thought I lacked it and until I had some, he didn't want anything to do with me."

"What happened after the five years?"

"I didn't get on the plane to go back to Ireland at the end of the school year." He cracked eggs into a bowl and began whisking them furiously.

Meanwhile, Corryna was frozen. She hadn't expected him to say that he'd had such an extreme reaction. No wonder this was such a sore subject. "What did your parents say?"

"At the time? I'm not sure. I didn't call them for a month. I was too mad. I enrolled in culinary school and got a job as a dishwasher. I decided that I'd had enough."

"Colin. Your mom must have been worried sick."

"I guess she probably was. She was angry with

me when she tracked me down at my new school. I think one of my teachers tipped her off."

"Did you have your parents' money to help you live?"

He shook his head, seasoned the eggs with salt and pepper, then lit the flame under the first pan. "I did not."

Corryna took a long sip of her coffee. She'd always assumed that Colin had gotten his start in part because his parents had at least bankrolled it. "Wow. They could've helped you so much."

He stepped over to the fridge and pulled out a stick of butter, then dropped a knob of it into the pan. It quickly sizzled, and he rolled it around the edges with great confidence. This was what she'd wanted to see—the way he commanded the kitchen. Next to go into the pan was the spring onions, which he sautéed and tossed with a flick of his wrist. Last in the pan was the spinach. "To be fair, I had family money to open my first restaurant after I turned eighteen. But those were funds that had been placed in a trust by my grandparents. My dad didn't have a say over that."

"Still. You really had to go out of your way to prove your point."

Colin shrugged and lit the flame under the second pan. He poured the eggs into it, again tilting it with great dexterity, perfectly swirling the mixture to the edges. "It made me the chef I am today. I know that I've done it all on my own. There's something to be said for that."

But at what price? Corryna wanted to ask the question, but feared Colin's response. She'd already extracted far more information from him than she'd thought possible. "What's your relationship like now? You said your dad called you after you got your nomination, so it must be better."

"I haven't seen them in over twenty years."

Corryna's jaw dropped out of pure shock. "What? Not once?"

"Not once." He scooped the sautéed veggies from the first pan over the top of the cooking eggs, then sprinkled in the herbs. As it continued to cook, he walked over to the refrigerator and pulled out a block of cheese, which he quickly grated. "They've never come to see me. And I haven't gone back to see them. I've been to Ireland once, but visiting my family wasn't on my itinerary."

"And you're an only child, right?"

"I am."

All of this was hard for Corryna to wrap her head around, but she reminded herself that not every family was like hers. Colin might have grown up with all the money in the world, but that didn't make up for a lack of love, acceptance and encouragement. Still, she knew that he had to have suffered from not having that support system. "Maybe you can go see them some day."

He sprinkled the cheese over the omelet, then

turned off the heat and put a lid on the pan. "Maybe. But I'm not planning on it anytime soon, and I can't imagine what would make me want to go." He dropped four slices of rustic bread into the toaster and pushed down the plunger.

Corryna kept quiet, needing more time to think. No wonder Colin was known as a bit of a lone wolf. And perhaps his playboy ways were merely because he'd never felt attached to someone. Or loved. She didn't want to psychoanalyze him, but it made sense to her.

Colin pulled out some plates. "Breakfast is just about ready. We can eat here at the island if that's okay with you."

"Sure thing. It smells amazing, so I can't wait to try it."

"Go ahead. Take a seat. I'll bring it over."

Corryna perched in one of the barstools and patiently waited as he flipped the jumbo omelet, divided it into two portions and buttered the toast. He delivered it all with a smile, then sat next to her. However much he'd been defensive about his family before, he seemed to be in an okay mood after sharing the details.

Corryna took her first bite and nearly fell off her seat in ecstasy. The omelet was buttery, but light. Fluffy, but rich. And that Irish cheddar was creamy and sharp and so delicious she wanted to take a bath in it. "This is the best omelet I've ever had. The ingredients are so fresh. It's heavenly."

"Straight from the garden. It's not such a bad life I've carved out for myself here."

He was right, despite the fact that she felt he did have a few gaps in his fabulous life—namely, love and emotional support. "I'd say it's wonderful. I loved watching you cook. So much. I could do it every day."

He wiped his mouth with a napkin, then turned to her. "You know, Corryna, you make me excited to create. Seriously. You inspire me."

She was more than a little taken aback. Colin was brilliant. How could it be that she inspired him? "I do?"

"Yes. You're like a muse."

"I've never been anyone's muse before."

"Well, good. I don't want you to be anyone else's muse. Be mine. It'll make our collaboration for this wedding a magical thing."

Corryna loved hearing him express those things, but she couldn't ignore that he'd put a bookend on whatever it was that was going on between them. Again, she struggled with finding the real Colin. Was he what everyone, including Jessica, had said he was? A guy who wasn't easy to hold on to? She was starting to doubt the validity of that assertion. She felt as though there was a whole side of him that very few people got to see. He was more than endlessly hardworking and brilliant. He had a beautiful soul. He was a solid, dependable guy.

"Speaking of our collaboration, we need to talk

about when we're going to get together next to work on it," Corryna said.

He leaned closer and whispered in her ear, "I was hoping we could go collaborate in my room."

Tingles raced over the surface of her skin and she laughed. "That doesn't sound like work."

"It won't be. But it will definitely take both of us."

Eight

Time with Colin quickly became a given in Corryna's life. They did their best to keep the intimate aspect of their relationship very hush-hush, but there were no complete secrets in Royal. A few people had quickly figured it out. Hannah, Jessica and Mike all knew. As did Elena and Kristine at Sheen. They'd all promised to keep it to themselves, and Corryna and Colin trusted them all implicitly. Neither Corryna nor Colin could risk losing the Noble-Ramos wedding job. Corryna's reasons boiled down to finances and her future. For Colin, it was all to preserve his stature in the community and the food world at large. Especially with his recent award nomination, it would be absolutely humiliating if he and Sheen were dropped from the biggest, most lavish wedding to ever be held in Royal.

Despite the possibility of the news getting back to Rylee, Corryna and Colin could not stay away from each other. In fact, after that first night together at his house, and the fabulous breakfast he'd made for her the following morning, things had heated up very quickly. They'd been inseparable for more than two weeks now. Every night, they were together, mostly at his house, but sometimes at hers. To their credit, they always discussed their collaboration for the wedding. It was not only the thing that had brought them together, it was the thing they cared about most. But even though it started with work, it always led to sex. Always. Corryna couldn't get enough of Colin. He was so clued in to her needs. He was always unselfish, and his touch simply made her feel alive.

She knew that she was making up for lost time. She'd made love with no one since her divorce. Six years. At first, she'd been too crushed. Then she'd felt defeated, a feeling that took forever to go away, and only improved to a state of uncertainty. It was then that she'd gone on a few dates, but no one sparked any real interest. Many men didn't take her seriously. They saw that she was a florist, and assumed that was a wholly unchallenging career choice. Or they had no personality, wanting to talk about only themselves. Mostly, there was no chemistry. Corryna ultimately decided that it made the most sense to devote her energy to Royal Blooms and let love find her if it was meant to. After all, Royal Blooms was the one thing she could count on, and her track record with men was dismal. But then Colin waltzed into her life when she least expected it and turned everything upside down. Of course, she wasn't thinking super long-term. Colin simply wasn't that sort of guy. But what was between them already felt like more than a fling. He'd lit a fire inside her, and all she wanted was for him to continue stoking the flame, for as long as he felt like sticking around.

For now, Corryna was working her way through Monday morning, which was quiet enough that Hannah had no trouble handling the front of the shop on her own while Corryna devoted time to refining her designs for the Noble-Ramos wedding. Last week, she'd managed to place an order for the most prized bluebonnets in all of Texas—the patented Blue Darling, a hybrid developed by a botanist with ties to Royal. They were hard to come by, but she'd sweet-talked her way into a large order for the wedding, and a smaller sample order for her to work with now. She was so excited that she'd texted Rylee to tell her all about it. As luck would have it, Rylee replied right away that she wanted to stop by Royal Blooms to see them for herself. She was due to come by that afternoon with Ariana's maid of honor, Dionna.

Corryna was working with the Blue Darling flowers when the chime on the door into the workroom sounded. She expected it to be Mike, but when she glanced over her shoulder, she saw that it was Colin.

"What are you doing here?" she asked, setting down her scissors and wiping her hands on a towel. Funny how simply setting eyes on him made her entire body run about five degrees hotter.

He held up a pastry box and smiled as he strolled over to her. "Elena made croissants for you this morning." Leaning down, he planted a soft and sexy kiss on her lips.

"Aww. That's so nice. Although, I'm starting to think I should be romantically involved with Elena." She took the package from him and popped open the lid. The heavenly aroma of butter and chocolate wafted up to her nose. As she lifted one of the pastries from the box and took a bite, she caught him staring. There was something so electrifying about having his eyes on her. "Delicious. Perfect. As always."

"Good. I'm glad." He pulled up a stool, parking it next to her bench before he sat down. "What are you working on today?"

"These are the centerpieces for the reception."

He studied the arrangement, which had bold yellow roses named after Julia Child, striking white anemones with a dark purple eye, graceful lilies of the valley, and the bluebonnets, all accented with a delicate greenery similar to a willow. "I love it. It's very refined, but something about it is a bit wild. Unexpected."

"I need to make sure the colors are right. The theme is old Hollywood glamor, so I need black, cream, and gold. Not the easiest ask in the world of flowers. The roses might not be the right shade of gold, so I might have to pull them and find a closer match. But I'd really like to see them use the blue-bonnets. I mean, they're the state flower and the Noble family are Texas through and through. Plus, this variety is absolutely stunning and sturdy, which as a florist, is everything you could ever want in a flower."

He grinned at her again and reached out for her hip, tugging her closer by gripping the tie on her apron. "I love seeing you get excited about what you're designing. It's sexy."

It wasn't good for her to be this worked up in the morning, but this was what Colin did to her. A few kind words, a soft kiss and a possessive tug, and she was putty in his hands. "I love seeing you the same way. I feel like we understand each other when it comes to that. The creative part." It was her turn to drift into him as their gazes connected and they gave in to another kiss.

"We do understand each other. We absolutely do."

"Hey, uh, Corryna," Hannah's voice came from behind her.

Corryna jumped back from Colin's grasp and composed herself, then whipped around to face Hannah. "Hey, Hannah. What's up?"

"Rylee Meadows and Dionna Reed are here to see you. And Keely Tucker came with them, too."

"What? Now?" Corryna hated hearing the sheer

panic in her voice, but she couldn't help it. Rylee held her future in her hands and she'd been clear that she didn't want any problems between Corryna and Colin. There weren't any, thank goodness, but surely Rylee would not approve of them being personally involved. "They were supposed to come this afternoon." *And no one told me the dress designer was coming, too.*

Corryna turned back to Colin and straightened her apron. "You and I have been working on the wedding this morning, okay? You're here because you knew that I was busy with these centerpieces."

He popped up from the stool and stood at attention. "Yeah. Of course. Got it."

Corryna took a deep breath for strength and smoothed her hair, hoping it wasn't evident that she'd just been kissing Colin. "You can send them back, Hannah. Thank you."

Rylee, Dionna, and Keely marched into the back room, and Corryna witnessed the instant when Rylee spotted Colin and a look of surprise washed over her face. "Colin. You're here, too."

He stepped out from behind Corryna's workbench and shook Rylee's hand. "I am. Corryna and I are always working together on the wedding. She texted me and said she was working on arrangements this morning, and I had a few spare minutes, so I said I'd drop by to discuss where we're at with everything." He turned to Dionna and Keely and shook their hands as well. "Ladies. Morning."

"Good morning, Chef," Dionna said with a smile. Her long black twisted braids were pulled back, accentuating her enviable cheekbones.

"Yes. Good morning," Keely looked as impeccable and polished as any dress designer ever could, with a slim-fitting skirt and blouse and makeup on-point.

Rylee turned to Corryna, seeming impressed. "It's great that you and Colin are working so closely together."

"You told us to collaborate, so that's what we're doing. Collaborating," Corryna said.

Colin cleared his throat. "I brought croissants if anyone wants one."

"I'm good, but thank you. That's really quite considerate of you," Rylee said.

"No, thank you," Dionna and Keely said in near unison.

"Well, Corryna can't say no to them. I couldn't help but notice how much she loved them when we had our first meeting at the TCC. She just kept eating them and eating them. So now I bring them to her whenever I can," Colin said.

Corryna elbowed him in the ribs. A little less emphasis on how much he'd noticed that she loved the croissants would've been helpful. "I've been working on the centerpieces. I'd love for you all to see the bluebonnets I was able to bring in. These are a very special variety. They are quite difficult to get and not widely available." Corryna pulled one of the stems from the bucket to show to Rylee, Keely and Dionna. "They're called the Blue Darling. Prized for their brilliant color. I thought the bride and groom would appreciate that they're not only an exclusive choice, but are also grown here in Texas."

Rylee stepped closer and held the brilliant blue spire of the bluebonnet with her fingertips. "Fabulous. These are quite gorgeous."

"I think Xavier and Ariana will really like these," Dionna added.

"The color is perfect," Keely said. "Exactly what we talked about."

"The bluebonnets were a stroke of genius on your part, Keely," Corryna said. "Rylee, do you have thoughts about the rest of it?"

"I like that it's old Hollywood glamor and romantic at the same time." Rylee turned to Corryna. "I'd love to say that this is perfect, but maybe make it a little more bold? I mean, keep refining."

Dionna pulled out her phone. "If it's okay with you, I'll take a few photos and send them to Ariana. Then Rylee will get back to you with some feedback."

"Yes. Absolutely. Go right ahead." Corryna stood back and let Dionna take the pictures. She glanced over at Colin, who was grinning like a fool. He seemed to take great pleasure in seeing other people admire Corryna's work.

"Perfect." Dionna tucked her phone back inside her purse.

"And everything else is going well? With the food, too?" Rylee asked.

"Everything I've tasted so far is unbelievable," Corryna said.

"Yes." Colin nodded eagerly. "Corryna and I have followed each other's cues at every step. I think you'll find it's all seamless when we make our presentation to you at the end of the month."

"Great. If you could email me the menu as it stands right now, I'd like to look it over. But otherwise, I'm hoping we can get together a week from Wednesday to taste everything and take a look at the final flowers. That gives you about ten days."

"Have you thought about where you'd like us to do the presentation?" Colin asked. "We could do it at the TCC, but it will be a big undertaking to bring supplies into their kitchen. I'd like to do it at Sheen if possible."

"Maybe at lunchtime?" Rylee asked.

Colin regarded Corryna with a sideways glance. "Does that work for you, Corryna?"

"Of course."

"Perfect. I'll set aside the private dining room. Will Ariana and Xavier be joining us?" Colin asked.

"I'd love to say that they will, but it's hard to know," Rylee said.

"Their schedules are so unpredictable," Dionna added.

"I'll let you know," Rylee said.

"No problem. Just keep me updated so I can be sure that I have everything on hand," Colin replied.

"I will. Of course." Rylee's vision narrowed on Colin, then she turned to Corryna with the same skeptical expression. "I have to ask. What exactly happened between you two?"

Corryna's stomach lurched. Her hands became clammy. Could Rylee tell that there was something romantic going on between them? Was it that obvious? "Happened?" she asked, her voice faltering.

Colin fidgeted, folding his arms across his chest in one direction, then in the other—a dance of discomfort that wasn't like him at all. "Yes. Uh. Not sure what you mean by that."

"There was so much tension between you two when we met at the TCC. I was really worried about it, to be honest. That all seems to have evaporated. It's remarkable how that has all gone away."

Corryna couldn't help but remember that day, and Colin pointing out that sex was the best way to get rid of tension. They'd certainly put that theory to the test in the weeks since then. "I guess it's just been the process of working together. Even though our mediums are very different, we understand each other's creative mindset. That alone was enough to make a harmonious working relationship."

"Yes. Yes. That's right. We understand each other," Colin said.

Corryna glanced at Colin, and as their gazes connected, it felt as though they had their own silent conversation. What was going on between them *was* more than just sex. They'd built something. A bridge. A real connection. Was she falling for him? She'd told herself that she wouldn't, but he had become a constant in her life and she only wanted their romance to keep going. "It's as simple as that."

"Well, it's amazing to see. Really. Just keep it up." Rylee peered up at the clock on the wall. "We need to go. I have a million places I need to be today, and Dionna has a conference call this afternoon. I believe Keely has a fitting with another bride."

"That I do," Keely said. "Word is getting around in Royal."

"It was nice to see you both again," Dionna added.

"Thanks for dropping by," Corryna said. "We'll talk to you soon."

Rylee, Keely, and Dionna strode back out the way they came, disappearing into the front of the shop.

Corryna finally felt as though she could exhale. "Whoa. That was close."

"What are you talking about?" Colin asked.

"I mean, that was close. What if Rylee figured out that we're…you know…"

He arched one of his expressive eyebrows. "That we're what? Working well together? Getting along? Friends?"

She couldn't help but smile. He was right about all of that. They did get along. And they were friends. "I meant that we're sleeping together."

He dismissed it with a tut and a wave of his hand.

"I don't think she cares about that. She doesn't want tension between us. There's no tension. End of story."

Corryna hoped it really was as simple as that. One thing hadn't changed from that first meeting at the TCC—she and Colin both desperately needed and wanted this job. "I suppose that's true."

"Seriously, Corryna. Don't worry about it. You do what you're doing. I'll do what I'm doing." He gripped her elbow and pulled her closer, then wrapped her up in his embrace. "And we'll keep doing what we do together. Which I think is spectacular."

That familiar ribbon of excitement worked its way through her. If Hannah wasn't in the front room and Royal Blooms wasn't open for business, she would've started tearing off Colin's shirt right then and there.

"Corryna?" Hannah asked from behind Corryna. "I'm so sorry to interrupt again."

Corryna and Colin stepped back from each other again. Corryna was a bit mortified that she and Colin had been caught so wrapped up in each other twice that morning. "No problem. What's up?"

Hannah held up a large white envelope. "The mail was just delivered and I had to sign for this. I thought it might be important."

Corryna had an inkling about what that was and she'd been dreading its arrival. She walked up to Hannah and took the package from her. "Thank you."

"Of course," Hannah said, then returned to the front of the shop.

Corryna looked at the return address and her worst suspicions were confirmed. "It's the report from the forensic accountant," she said to Colin.

"Go ahead. Open it."

"Now?" She was terrified of what was inside that envelope. She'd been so betrayed by Dan. She didn't think she could endure learning that there was more.

"Yes, Corryna. It's best to face these things head-on."

Colin hated seeing that look on Corryna's face— the one that said she was overwhelmed and simply wanted everything to go away. He'd pushed her to do this investigation and he was devoted to the idea of helping her through it.

"Come on now. No time like the present."

"It's just going to be a bunch of numbers, and you know how I feel about that. None of it makes sense to me. I've tried."

He sensed that this was about far more than numbers, but he made a mental note to convince her to hire a real accountant once she could afford it. A woman as kind and talented as Corryna needed to be spending more time arranging flowers and interacting with customers, and less time bogged down by the financial side of her business. It wasn't that she was incapable. It was merely that Colin was a strong believer in playing to one's strengths. If a person was good at something, he believed they should lean into it and rely less on the things that frustrated or confused them. "I understand. Which is why I think you should open it now. I'll help you read it. If you want. I don't want to stick my nose into your business. But I do know my way around numbers."

"You've already done so much for me. And don't you need to get to the restaurant?"

He couldn't tell if she was reacting like this because she wanted him to stay out of it, or if she didn't want to talk about her ex, but they'd come this far and he wasn't about to back down yet. "This is simply about seeing this through. You deserve the truth. As for Sheen, I can show up whenever I want."

She sighed. "Okay. Fine. Let's go into my office."

"Sounds good." He followed her through the short corridor that led to her tiny workspace. He could hardly believe she was able to get anything done at all in here.

Corryna sat behind her desk while Colin took a seat in the only other chair available. She tore open the envelope, pulled out a thick stack of documents and began scanning the top page. Her face slowly drained of all color. Eventually, she thrust the stack of paper in his direction. "You do it. This is making me sick."

This was probably for the best. He could be objective. She couldn't. "Sure. Let's take a look." Colin took one glance at the cover page and knew that he'd never be able to read the report without a little help. He reached into the pocket of his shirt, pulled out his reading glasses and put them on. "Going to need these."

"Now, that is a sexy sight."

He laughed quietly. At least he'd been able to bring some comic relief to a tense situation. "I'm glad you're amused by the fact that I'm forty-two years old and my eyes are slowly failing me."

"They're still stunning."

He felt the heat rise in his cheeks. His immediate reaction to all flattery was to deflect. "Not as beautiful as yours." It was the truth. Her eyes always reflected so much heart. They often stole his breath away.

"That's sweet. Now, please read that thing so I can stop worrying about it."

Colin sat back in the chair and crossed his legs. As he began to flip through the pages and digest the content, a picture was forming and he didn't like it. Not one bit.

"Well?"

He removed his glasses and set them down on her desk. "I'm afraid that you're going to need to hire a lawyer. I can help you with that, too."

"No, Colin. No. Absolutely not. I didn't want this to turn into some big mess. I told you that."

"Your husband didn't merely skim money, Corryna. He fleeced your business. There's more than one hundred thousand dollars gone over the course of the two years that he was here in Royal and doing your books."

"That much? How is that possible?"

"He was methodical. He had one thousand dollars a week going into a money market account that was in the business's name. But he was the sole account holder. Did you know about that account?"

She shook her head. "No. He set up everything at the bank when we opened up. He did it all."

"This account was opened one month after the main business accounts. My guess is that the bank didn't question it since he'd been the one to open the initial accounts." He referred back to the report, flipping through the documents. "The money never stayed in there for long. He basically parked the money in what looked like a legitimate account, then he took it as he wanted it. I have to hand it to him. He was very disciplined. The amount always stayed the same, so it truly wouldn't raise any red flags with the bank. Usually, when someone does something like this, they get greedy when they realize no one is looking. He never did that."

"I'd say it was more like he was very good at being consistently sneaky over a long period of time."

"The question is what he was spending the money on that whole time." Colin scratched his chin, wondering what the answer might be. A man like Corryna's ex might have any number of vices requiring a bankroll.

"It all went to the other women. That's actually how I first confirmed that he was cheating. One day, I was getting some clothes together for the dry cleaner, and I found a receipt in his pocket for a fancy lingerie shop in Dallas. It was for a lace nightgown that cost almost five hundred dollars."

"I take it you never received an expensive nightgown as a gift?"

"Not only that, there was a business card from the store manager with a note that said…" Corryna's voice started to crack and she dropped her head, looking down and avoiding eye contact with him.

He reached across the desk for her arm, his heart breaking for what she'd gone through. She'd endured a betrayal he couldn't imagine. "You don't have to tell me if you don't want to."

"No. No. I need to prove to myself that I've moved beyond this." She composed herself with a deep breath and a straightening of her spine. She raised her head. "The note said that they had enjoyed meeting him and his wife. Whoever received that nightgown was pretending to be married to him. While I was here in Royal, actually married to the jerk and completely clueless."

"Don't say that. You can't blame yourself for not knowing." For a moment, Colin sat impossibly still. So many unpleasant thoughts rifled through his mind, none of them charitable toward Corryna's ex-husband. The man had never been worthy of Corryna. That was all there was to it. Unfortunately, he didn't think that sharing that thought with Corryna would help her. Frankly, there were no good words.

So he simply got up from his seat and stepped behind her desk. "Come on. Stand up. Come here."

She shook her head. "I'm fine."

"You're upset. Come here." He tugged on her arm and she immediately gave in, rising to a standing position.

"I don't want you to feel sorry for me," she murmured against his arm.

He stroked her hair, pulling her even tighter against his body. "I can't help it, Corryna. What happened to you is unforgivable. Seriously. No one should have to endure what you have."

"It all feels like a bizarre dream."

"It's only bizarre that someone would treat you that way. You are the most generous person I have ever met." *I'm falling in love with you.* As quickly as the words filtered into his consciousness, they were followed by one more thought—it was true. How had this happened? This had never been part of his plan. "I realize you're just now absorbing this information, but you need to think about your next steps."

"Honestly, I want to forget about the whole thing and move on."

He loosened his grip on her so he could look her in the eye. "You can't sweep it under the rug."

"Why not? It's in the past. I don't want to dig it up. I don't want to spend time thinking about him and the things that he did to me. It's just money. I'm doing fine without it."

"But you're not. You're barely scraping by." He

looked around. "I mean, your office is a broom closet."

"Hey. It's utilitarian. There's nothing wrong with my office. Just because it's not big enough for comfy leather chairs and a corner bar like yours doesn't mean that it doesn't do the job."

She was getting defensive. This conversation might be better left for another time. "Okay. Okay. I'm sorry. We can talk about it later."

She peered up at him, her eyes welling with emotion. "I don't want to waste my time living in the past. I want to look forward. I have a lot of good things going for me. I have an amazing staff. I love my job. I get to work on the Noble-Ramos wedding, which is an absolute coup for me."

Even though he was dumbfounded that she wanted to sweep aside the one-hundred-thousand-dollar loss, he couldn't help but admire that she preferred to focus on the positives. "You're absolutely right. Those are all very good things."

"And I have you on my side, which feels pretty amazing." Her eyes flickered with the optimism that was there almost every day. It was a big part of why he was falling for her.

"You do have me, Corryna." He ran his thumb across her cheek, where her tears had been mere moments ago. "Don't question that, okay?"

A smile bloomed on her face. "You have me, too."

Heat flooded his body. His pulse thumped in his ears. "Do you want to come over tonight?"

"Of course."

He loved that it was almost a foregone conclusion. He appreciated that he didn't have to try hard to make this work. He and Corryna were simply drawn to each other on a molecular level, and they'd fallen into a fun and simple routine as a result. This was the most emotionally involved he'd ever been with a woman, but it was also the least complicated relationship he'd experienced. Was this what it was like to fall in love? Could it really be that easy? "And tomorrow night? And the night after that?" He reached down and playfully squeezed her bottom.

Corryna laughed quietly. "I'd like it if we could stay at my house, too, if that's okay. I was actually going to ask if I could convince you to take a few hours off one morning this week and go on a hike with me. We're nearing the end of spring wildflowers and I really want to see them one more time."

He felt honored. This was an activity Corryna usually reserved for her best friend, Jessica. "I'd love to go. And your house is closest to the quarry, so it would work to stay there the night before."

"How about tonight and tomorrow at your place, then we'll stay at my house on Wednesday and hike on Thursday?"

That was a whole lot of planning ahead for a guy who didn't do serious, but making plans with Corryna didn't bother Colin. It felt right. "That works."

"Thank you for saying you'll go." She glanced at her desk. "And thanks for everything with the forensic accountant. I'm just not sure I want to act on any of it. I'd like to put it away for now if that's okay."

He sensed her discomfort with the topic and decided to leave it alone. "You need to make the choice yourself. But at least you know the truth now."

"It took me a long time to feel like I could look ahead. I don't want to stop doing that now." She smiled and pulled herself snug against him. "You make me feel like I can look ahead."

He kissed the top of her head. No one had ever said anything so sweet to him. With every word out of her mouth, he was falling a little harder. The only trouble was that he was worried this happy, euphoric feeling couldn't possibly last. Where and when would he have to come back down to earth? Just because he was willing to venture into more serious territory didn't mean that he was convinced he was equipped to make it work.

Nine

On the morning Corryna and Colin were set to go on their hike, she insisted they leave before dawn. "I know it's super early, but I've gone around this time with Jessica once or twice and it was totally worth it to see the sunrise. I promise it'll be amazing."

"More worth it than sleep?" Colin tied his sneakers, sitting on the bench in the entry of Corryna's house. Of course, the answer to his question didn't matter. He was prepared to do almost anything for her.

She stretched and yawned, looking so sexy in a sleeveless workout top and black leggings that followed her every curve. "I know. I'm tired, too."

He stood. "Who's driving?"

"Do you mind? My car is making a funny noise."

"Funny noise?"

"Yeah. It's like a whirring, but then there's a rattle when I accelerate."

"Hmm. Not sure what that is, but I'm happy to drive. Let's go. We wouldn't want the sun to come up while we're standing here talking." He grabbed his keys, Corryna took two flashlights she had stashed in a drawer, then they loaded into his car, and he began the drive to the quarry. Despite his complaints about the hour, he was thrilled that Corryna had invited him to hike with her. There was no question that Colin and Corryna had more than filled the friend role in each other's lives. They spent nearly every waking minute together. They texted off and on, all day long. They worked on their collaboration for the wedding, and of course, they made love. A lot. They were hot for each other all the time.

"When are you going to get your car fixed?" He glanced over to see her purse her lips.

"I don't know. Sometime soon."

"You need a working vehicle in Royal."

"I know. But I hate taking it in. I have no clue what they're talking about when they tell me what's wrong. I always worry that they're just lying to me and ripping me off."

Colin had heard both Kristine and Elena express a similar sentiment, and he felt for anyone who found themselves in that situation. He didn't know much about car repair, but he was just tall enough to be slightly intimidating. Very few people ever messed with him. "I tell you what. Let's drive into town this morning together. I'll follow you and we can drop your car off at Royal Auto. The guy who runs the service department comes into Sheen all the time. I'll make sure he takes care of you, and then I'll drop you off at work. I can pick you up whenever you want."

"Don't you need to get in to the restaurant?"

He caught the disbelief in her voice, and he understood what she was saying. His entire life revolved around Sheen. Well, now his life revolved at least partly around Corryna. "What if your car broke down in one of the rural parts of town? I can't let that happen. I'd never forgive myself."

"That's very thoughtful of you, Colin. Thank you."

He pulled into the dirt lot at the quarry, and parked his SUV. There wasn't another car to be seen. "I guess this is a best kept secret, huh?"

"I know you think this is silly, but you're just going to have to trust me." Corryna hopped out and turned on her flashlight while he locked up, then she started to lead the way. She started them along a winding and narrow trail. At first, the incline was gentle, but quickly became more and more steep. With every hundred yards or so, the foliage around them became more dense and the trees more frequent. "You doing okay back there?" she asked.

"Yep. Just enjoying the view."

"The trees and plants are beautiful out here, aren't they?"

"I was talking about the view of you. But the plants are nice, too."

She came to a stop and turned around to playfully smack his arm. "You're bad."

"What? It's true." He greatly enjoyed the chance to ogle her ass in those leggings, especially when the flashlight made it easier.

"Just keep walking. We're almost there."

They started up an even steeper and more winding incline, with a narrower, rockier path. It seemed like they were headed nowhere, but just when they reached the crest of the slope, the entire landscape opened up before them. As the trees fell away, nature revealed a vast meadow ahead, dotted with a rainbow of wildflowers. They both came to a stop, taking in the breathtaking view. The sun was just beginning to breach the horizon, casting soft golden light that turned the clouds overhead a brilliant mix of purple and pink. Colin had traveled all over the world, but this was one of the most stunning things he'd ever seen.

"Wow," he said, unable to think of anything to say that could fully capture the beauty.

Corryna flipped off her flashlight, then took his hand and leaned into him, resting her head against his shoulder. "I told you."

They soaked up the stunning vista, listening to

the birds and enjoying the peaceful solitude. "What do you love most about coming here?" he asked.

"It's hard to pick one thing, but I guess I'd have to say the flowers. I've just always loved them. Since I was little. They're happy and optimistic. I can be having the worst day in the world and they always make me feel better. It's impossible for me to be sad when I'm around them. And seeing them like this, in their natural habitat, just feels special."

He squeezed her hand and leaned down to kiss the top of her head. How he loved the way she looked at the world. She showed him the beauty all around him. Much of the time, he never stopped to smell the proverbial roses. He was too busy working his butt off, making money and worrying about proving his parents wrong. Corryna had not only inspired him to tap back into his creativity, she reminded him that he had quite a lot to be thankful for. "You know, this reminds me a little bit of Ireland. We have all sorts of lush green hills and flowers." For the first time in quite some time, he found himself almost feeling homesick.

"I'd love to go there someday."

"I'm sure you'd love it."

She turned to him and shielded her eyes with her hand to her forehead. "Have you thought about going back? I hate the thought of you being away from your family for so long."

He scanned her face, thinking how remarkable it was that she had become the only person he could talk about this with. Perhaps it was because she leveled very little judgment in his direction. She merely wanted to help. "I think about it every now and then. But you know, just like you told me that you don't want to live in the past, I don't want to, either. I like looking forward just like you do."

"I really don't think it's the same."

"What? Of course it is."

She shook her head. "But is it? My needing to move on from my divorce isn't the same as you trying to forget that you have a broken relationship with your parents. My divorce was closing a door. Forever. I had to leave it behind because it was over. I know that you think you shut yourself off from your parents when you decided to stay in the US, but you still talk to them, so there's still a line of communication there. The door is still open."

"I can't not talk to them. But I'm keeping them at bay. I'm establishing boundaries. I thought that was the healthy thing to do."

"It is. But I don't think you really came to terms with the pain in your past. I think that when you shut the door, it was just about trying to ignore the way you hurt each other. That's not good. And it's also not entirely fair to them. They made mistakes, but I think all parents do. I think you should at least give them the chance to explain themselves. And I think they should give you the chance to do the same."

Colin blew out a deep breath and looked off at the meadow again. In some ways, he'd come to peace with his relationship with his family. It wasn't what he ever would've wanted, but at least he knew exactly what it was. "I just don't know if I can do that."

"I know it won't be easy, but you're so much stronger than you give yourself credit for."

He shrugged. He *was* strong and he wanted to keep it that way.

She caressed his arm softly. "Just think about it. That's all I want you to do. Think about it."

"Why do you care about this?" He turned back to her. "You don't know my family at all."

She unleashed the soft smile that melted his heart every time she delivered it. "Because I know that you are the most incredible man I have ever met. Every time I think I've got you figured out, you surprise me."

"I feel the same way about you." *I love you.* The thought popped into his head and wouldn't let go.

"Aww. Thanks, Colin. That's sweet."

They stayed for a few more minutes, admiring the view before they started the trek back to the car. Meanwhile, Colin's head was a buzzing beehive between the things Corryna had said about his relationship with his parents, and the surprising conclusion he'd reached at the tail end of that conversation. Was what he was feeling really love? He wasn't sure, but oddly enough, it made sense.

When they got back to her house and inside, Colin was overcome by an overwhelming need to be closer to Corryna. Sex wasn't the answer to everything, but it was the answer to *some* things. "Shower?" he asked. "I'm sweaty after that."

"Of course. Go ahead and I'll hop in after you."

"I was hoping we could get each other clean." He placed one hand on her hip while the other slipped inside the back of her workout top.

"I don't have the biggest bathroom."

"And I don't care. I just want to get you wet." He nestled his face in the crook of her neck and kissed the soft skin.

Corryna moaned, then curled her fingers around the hem of his T-shirt, pulling the garment over his head. "Whatever you want."

Colin felt a rush of blood that went straight to the center of his body. The thought of Corryna wet and soapy was more than a little sexy. "I love it when you say that."

She leaned closer and flattened her palms against his abs, then pressed her lips against his shoulder. He needed her now and none of what he wanted to happen was going to take place in the front hall. Needing to take charge, he scooped her up into his arms.

Corryna let out a squeak, then wrapped her arms around his neck. Colin walked into the bedroom and then the attached bath. He set her on the floor, then took the liberty of reaching into the shower enclosure and turning on the water. He dropped his shorts and boxers while Corryna lifted her top over her head and wriggled out of her leggings. Colin wrapped his arms around her waist. He was already hard and ready for her. As he kissed her softly, his body flooded with warmth. He felt light-headed, grappling with the emotion that kept trying to bubble up inside of him. This was a very sexy scenario, but he found himself only thinking about things like love.

The air in the bathroom was getting warm and thick. "I think the shower is more than hot enough," she said. Corryna stepped in and Colin followed. Corryna immediately sought another kiss, lifting her arms to rest them on his shoulders and combing her fingers into his hair, which was slowly getting damp. The hot water pattered against her back and trickled over her shoulders, then down her chest and stomach. Colin's hands glided down Corryna's back and over the silky skin of her butt, gently squeezing and drawing her hips closer to his. Their tongues swirled in a kiss that he never wanted to end. In truth, he never wanted any of this to end.

Corryna moaned softly as Colin lowered his head and kissed her jaw, then down her neck and across her collarbone. The warm billowy air swirled around her. Being with him like this was sheer heaven. He dipped his head to one of her breasts and she watched his tongue circle her nipple as warm water cascaded across the side of his face and rolled over his jaw. He gripped Corryna's rib cage and dragged his tongue to her other breast, leaving a trail of heat as he went. She dropped her head to one side, eyes half-closed, as the sensations amped up her need for him.

Colin reached for the bar of soap and built lather with his hands. The look on his face was one of pure hunger. It made Corryna want him even more. His sudsy hands sank against her breasts, his palms against her nipples, spreading the silky bubbles in circles. His eyes grew darker as he studied her reaction to every touch, their gazes connecting while the temperature in the room continued to climb.

"Colin. We need to get clean or neither of us is going to make it to work this morning," she said.

"You're so sensible."

Corryna reached for the shampoo, pouring some into her hands, then handing him the bottle. They stood there together, each washing their hair, grinning at each other. She rinsed her hair out, then stepped aside to let Colin do his. That gave her the chance to spread soapy suds across his chest, then down his stomach and legs. Every inch of his chiseled physique was pure magic. And she couldn't wait to have all of him.

After a final rinse, Colin turned off the water and they both got out and toweled off. He leaned down and kissed her again. "I know you want to get going, but I need to make love to you."

She smiled. "Exactly what I was thinking."

He clutched his hands beneath her butt and hoisted her up. Corryna wrapped her legs around his waist and her arms around his shoulders as he maneuvered them into the bedroom. He laid her down gently on the bed, then reached for the box of condoms that was still sitting on Corryna's nightstand. He rolled it on while his eyes raked her body, his hair damp and a few stray beads of water still settled in his collarbone. Seeing the intensity on his face, she sensed that something had shifted between them. Had she gotten to him when she'd talked about his family? Was she finding a way into his heart?

He slid his hands beneath her hips, lifting them off the mattress and shifting her body until she was in the center of the bed. Then he climbed onto the mattress, in total control. He claimed her with one long thrust, and Corryna was quick to pull him in closer, locking her ankles around his waist. She needed his perfect being as close to her as possible. He pumped slow but hard, and Corryna felt as though her entire body was about to boil over. His breaths were heavy and short, and he muttered her name into her neck. She loved hearing that. She loved that right now, she seemed to be his only thought, just as he was hers. She tried to hang on for as long as possible, but the moment was too much, and she called out as the peak rocketed through her, just at the moment when he gave way as well.

He rolled to his side and reigned her in with his strong arms, kissing her forehead again and again. For the first time in a long time, she had zero desire to go to work, however much she loved it. Royal Blooms had long been her life, but it felt now like her life was right here in this bed. It felt like he had become her reason for being. The realization hit her hard, and she had to suck in a deep breath to get past it and keep it to herself. She'd already put him through the wringer with their conversation at the quarry. She didn't want to burden him with more. At least not now.

"I suppose we need to get dressed and get going, huh?" she asked.

He groaned. "Yeah. I think so."

They slowly got up off the bed, and Corryna wandered to the closet while Colin ducked into the bathroom. She wanted to look cute, so she put on a black-and-white sundress and sandals. Colin got dressed in the clean clothes he'd brought with him— his typical wardrobe on a workday of dark jeans, a white dress shirt, and today, a beautiful linen suit coat. Colin made coffee and toast for them while she put on her makeup and did her hair, then they each climbed into their cars for the drive to Royal Auto.

To Corryna's great relief, Colin handled everything when they arrived at the repair shop. She didn't enjoy the thought of giving in to too many gender stereotypes, but she'd forgotten how nice it was to have someone else around to take care of things like this.

Colin drove toward Royal Blooms. Town was busy that morning, with the only parking spot on the street nearly a block away from the shop. "Let me walk you to the door," he said.

"You don't need to do that."

"I want to. It doesn't feel right to do anything else."

Before she could argue the point any further, he was already out of the car and standing on the sidewalk. Corryna climbed out and joined him. Even though there were people everywhere, he took her hand. She thought twice about it, but decided that what was between her and Colin was more important than what anyone thought.

When they reached the front door at Royal Blooms, Colin came to a stop and took her other hand. "I just want to thank you for this morning," he said. "It felt really special. Thank you."

She peered up into his magical green eyes. Something had definitely shifted between them over the last few days, which both delighted her and scared her. She didn't have the best track record with men. But something told her that she was on the right path. It felt too good to be with him for it to not be going somewhere. "You're more than welcome."

Colin combed his fingers into her hair and brought his lips to hers. The world around her faded into the background and as he took the kiss deeper, he became the sole thing tethering her to the here and now.

"Corryna?" A woman's voice pierced the air.

For a split second, Corryna didn't react to hearing her own name. She was too caught up in the kiss. But then her mind managed to place the voice—Rylee. Corryna pushed away from Colin, and sure enough, Rylee was standing a few yards away, glaring at them. Even worse, dress designer Keely Tucker was with her. "Oh. Hi," Corryna sputtered.

Rylee's sights flew back and forth between Corryna and Colin, her voice and face colored with disbelief. "Is this… Are you two…romantically involved?"

Corryna looked to Colin for answers, as she wasn't sure what to say. What exactly *were* she and Colin doing? She had lots of thoughts tucked away in her head about the subject, but no one had asked them to put a label on anything. Dating? It was more than that. Sleeping together? Yes. But Corryna hated the thought of minimizing it like that. There was more between them. So much more. They had shared details of their pasts. Colin had helped her with the forensic accountant. They had spent so many nights up late, talking and making love.

Finally, Colin chose to answer. "Yes. Corryna and I are involved." He stepped closer to Rylee, holding his hands up as if he'd been found guilty of something and was making his confession. "But I want to tell you that it's not a problem. If anything, it's helped us get in sync. It's part of the reason our collaboration has gone so well." He turned back to Corryna and his eyes softened.

A wave of relief washed over Corryna. He felt the same way she did, or at least it seemed that way. She desperately wanted to reach out and take his hand, but this might not be the best time for public displays of affection. Rylee and Keely had already witnessed one hell of a kiss. "Yes. That's exactly right."

Rylee crossed her arms and grimaced. "So that's why you two were suddenly being so nice to each other the other day at Royal Blooms."

"That's part of it," Corryna said. "But to be fair, we've found that we simply work well together."

"But I asked you two what had made the difference and you gave me no indication that this—" Rylee fluttered her hands in the air "—was going on."

Corryna felt incredibly guilty. She never wanted to be dishonest with anyone. "I'm sorry. It's a very new thing. We've been trying hard to keep it quiet and private. You must know how much people gossip in Royal."

"Except that you were making out in the middle of the sidewalk in downtown Royal."

Neither Colin nor Corryna had an answer for that. Corryna's only defense was that she was on a high from their morning together. It had been so perfect.

"And what happens to the food and flowers for this wedding if you two have a falling out?" Rylee's voice was brimming with panic. Her eyebrows drew together tightly, forming a deep furrow in the center of her forehead. Meanwhile, Keely, who'd kept herself removed from the conversation, stepped closer.

Corryna and Colin made eye contact again. He seemed to be searching for an answer as hard as she was. "It won't be a problem," Colin said.

"Uh-huh. So says the guy who's dated half of the women in Royal." Rylee focused her attention on Corryna. "I'm sorry, but it's true. You *had* to know that."

Corryna swallowed hard. "I did."

"That's not fair," Colin interjected. "It's not half. It's not even one quarter. Or one tenth."

Corryna wanted to leap to Colin's defense, especially while he was only digging them a bigger hole. But Rylee wasn't wrong. Everyone knew that women all over Royal wanted Colin and that he was known for using that to his best advantage. Corryna didn't enjoy feeling insecure, but it did make her wonder whether she was deluding herself by getting wrapped up in Colin. Even Jessica, her ultimate supporter, had pointed out that Colin was not an easy guy to hold on to.

Rylee stepped even closer to them both. "I don't think you two have any concept of the pressure I'm under with this wedding. Every decision is in a state of flux. The bride and groom are all over the place. They're too busy to give me answers most of the time, but they want to approve every detail."

"She's not wrong," Keely interjected.

"In the meantime, I'm juggling one million bits of information—the guest list and accommodations for VIPs. Seating charts and music and flower girls, and meanwhile, the entire town of Royal is expecting the wedding of the century." She gripped Colin's arm, her eyes wide and frantic. "Of the century. If it's not absolutely perfect, who's everyone going to blame? Me. It's my butt on the line. My reputation. My business. I can't let whatever is going on between you two ruin that."

"I see your dilemma." Colin swallowed hard, but nodded eagerly as if he agreed with every word she'd just said.

Rylee sighed. "I'm sorry if I'm a little intense right now. I'm just under a lot of pressure."

"I think we all understand what you're saying. We all get it because we're living it, too," Keely said.

"Right. Corryna and I are also under pressure. This wedding is an important opportunity for Corryna. It will open so many doors for her in Royal. And for me, I can't afford to not be doing the food. It would damage my reputation, and frankly, it would be an embarrassment. So, I hope you know that we didn't get involved without thinking about it. We knew the ramifications, went into it with clear minds and hearts, and decided that it was worth it. That's how much we like each other."

Speaking of hearts, Corryna's was now beating like a hummingbird. Whatever doubts had creeped into her thinking earlier were now gone. He felt like she did. It was such a relief.

Rylee managed a thin smile. "I really hope that's true."

"You have to trust that Corryna and I have the

best intentions." Colin glanced at Corryna and smiled softly. "And the wedding is only a few months away. Whatever happens, we will hold it together."

Ten

Corryna was trying very hard not to obsess over what had happened with Rylee, but two days later, she was still on edge. She needed Royal Blooms to be successful, and Rylee Meadows was the last person who should have to question whether or not Corryna could pull off her part in the wedding of the century. And of course, it wasn't merely Rylee who was counting on Corryna. Hannah and Mike needed her, too. Hannah couldn't afford to pay for school on her own. And Mike had six-month-old Penelope to care for. In short, Corryna could not fail.

But that meant she and Colin needed to keep things on a perfectly even keel if they were going to be involved and continue to collaborate as Rylee wanted them to. On the surface, it was no problem. She woke up every morning, seeking his warmth and quick wit. She ended every day wrapped tightly in his arms. For the first time in a long time, she felt safe. She felt content and she believed that he did, too. But she still worried that he wasn't in as deep as she was. Maybe it was the remnants of her divorce and the way it had rattled her confidence in a way that went to the very core of her being. Or maybe it was simply because her time with Colin had not been long, and she knew from experience that oftentimes, love took time to take hold.

For today, she decided to spend less time thinking about Colin and more time focused on the nuts and bolts of running Royal Blooms. She placed her orders for next week, making sure she had everything she needed for her final presentation to Rylee next week. She worked on her website and caught up on the accounting. She'd even taken one more look at the report from the forensic accountant, but ultimately stuffed it in the filing cabinet. It wasn't really going to help her to pursue anything with Dan. It would only dredge up old pain. And despite her trepidation about her future with Colin, she was generally optimistic about what might be ahead for her. Things were mostly bright, and she'd ride that wave for as long as she could.

Hannah poked her head into Corryna's office. "Am I interrupting?"

Corryna looked up from her computer and shook her head. "Nope. What's up?"

"We need a few things for the break room and the bathroom. Do you want me to pick those up tomorrow morning before I come in?"

Corryna pulled out a piece of paper to write herself a note. "I can run out in a little bit. What's on the list?"

"Sugar and creamer for coffee. And we're out of hand soap and tampons in the bathroom."

Corryna scribbled down the list, then something struck her. She should have gotten her period more than a week ago. She glanced up at the calendar. Actually, scratch that—it was more like twelve days ago. But that didn't make any sense. She and Colin had been more than careful.

"You okay, Corryna?"

Corryna snapped out of it. "Yeah. Yeah. I'm good."

The chime on the shop's door sounded. "We have a customer. I gotta go." In a flash, Hannah was gone.

Corryna immediately pulled the calendar down from the wall and started counting. But numbers had never been her forte, so it quickly wound up frustrating her. "This doesn't make any sense," she muttered to herself. She officially needed advice. A second opinion. So she picked up her phone and called Jessica. "Do you have a minute? I need some help," she said when Jessica answered. For privacy, she got up and closed the door to her office.

"Of course. I'm working on a paper right now, but it's frying my brain. I could use the break."

Corryna swallowed hard. She wasn't exactly sure how to broach this subject. "How long after you miss a period until it's probably a good idea to take a pregnancy test?" A few moments of uncomfortable silence came from the other end of the line. "Jessica? Are you there?"

"Did you and Colin have unprotected sex?"

Corryna's stomach sank. She hated that she'd been so irresponsible, but she'd done several out of character things that night. "Unfortunately, yes. But it was only once. That was nearly two months ago now."

"So, the night at Sheen? Did you get your period after?"

"Sort of? I basically spotted for a few days. That was it."

"And how late are you now?"

"Twelve days. At least."

"I would take a test ASAP. A woman I work with had this exact same thing happen to her. She spotted even though she was pregnant."

Corryna could hardly believe she was having to confront this reality right now. Hopefully this was just her body acting up, possibly because of stress. "Okay. I'll go get one now. I need to get some things from the store anyway."

"Are you at Royal Blooms?"

"Yes."

"Get the test and go home. There's no sense in doing it at work. I'll meet you at your house."

Corryna was so relieved she wasn't going to have to do this on her own. "Thank you. It's probably nothing, but I appreciate you being there. I'll see you in a few." In a daze, Corryna grabbed her phone and let Hannah know she'd be gone for a few hours. Then she drove to the grocery store, where she bought the things the shop needed, as well as a two-pack of pregnancy tests. It felt so surreal to know that they were in the shopping bag as she loaded up her car. She'd dreamed of this moment when she was married, but Dan kept putting off the question of children. He'd say things like how he didn't want to bring kids into "this messed up world." Of course, he hadn't thought twice about messing up Corryna's world. Ultimately, it had been a good thing that they never conceived, but she still very much wanted to become a mom, and at thirty-six, the clock was ticking. She simply hadn't bargained on today being the day she'd find out if her dream was actually going to come true.

When she got to her house, Jessica pulled into the driveway right after Corryna. "This is silly," Corryna said as she opened the front door and they walked inside. "You have schoolwork to do. And a million other things. This is probably just a false alarm." She set the shopping bags on her small butcher-block kitchen island.

"It doesn't matter. I didn't want you to be alone

when you took the test." Jessica reached for Corryna's hand. "I know how much the question of kids weighed on you while you were married, and after your divorce. This is a big deal. And as your best friend, I felt like I needed to be here for it."

Corryna sighed and took the box from the counter. "Thank you for being so awesome. I'll be back in a few minutes."

"I'll be here waiting."

Corryna walked into the bathroom, read the instructions on the package, then followed them exactly. She didn't want to leave anything to chance. "Okay. Ten minutes," she called out to Jessica.

Her friend appeared in the bathroom doorway mere seconds later. She had the kitchen timer in her hand. "It's set. The countdown is on."

Corryna paced up and down the hall while Jessica stood sentry at the bathroom door. When the timer dinged, Corryna jumped. "Ten minutes is a lot shorter than I thought it would be."

Jessica waved her over. "Come on. Let's look."

Corryna stepped into the bathroom. She peered down at the plastic stick, which was sitting right there on the edge of the sink. The two blue lines were so dark and clear that Corryna's legs nearly went out from under her. She clamped her hand over her mouth. "Oh, my God. It's positive."

Jessica stepped behind her, placing her hands on Corryna's upper arms and peeking around her shoulder to view the test. "Whoa. So it is. Are you okay?"

Corryna turned and simply stared at Jessica. "I don't know. I'm in shock."

Jessica took her hand. "Come on. Let's go make some tea and talk." She led the way down the hall and into the kitchen. "Sit. I've got this."

Corryna plopped down in one of the chairs at her kitchen table. Her mind was such a torrent of thoughts that it was hard to make sense of any of it. She was pregnant. With Colin's baby. And as to how he was going to react, she had no clue. He had such a complicated relationship with his family. He'd had a traumatic childhood. And they'd hardly been together long enough to talk about things like children.

Jessica brought over two steaming mugs a few moments later, along with honey, spoons, and a small plate for the tea bags. "How are you doing?"

"I'm… I'm…" The first thing that popped into her head was Mike's baby girl, Penelope. The thought of having a little bundle like that to love and care for made her heart swell to twice its size. "Despite the uncertainty and the somewhat bad timing, I'm happy. Really happy."

"Understandable. You've wanted a baby for a long time."

"True. I have."

"And Colin is definitely the dad?"

Corryna shot her friend an incredulous look. "Yes. There's been no one else."

"I know we talk about everything, but I didn't want to assume." Jessica raised her mug to her lips and blew on the tea to cool it down, then took a sip. "Do you think it happened that first time in his office?"

"I don't see any other possibility. We've been very careful."

"The blackout was the beginning of March. It's almost the end of April. That would mean you're almost eight weeks along. Have you been feeling okay?"

Corryna shrugged. "Yeah. I mean, maybe a little tired, but I've been so busy." *And Colin's been wearing me out.*

"What do you think Colin is going to say?"

"I don't know. If I had found this out a month ago, I would have at least had a guess. But that was only because I had an idea of Colin in my head. Since then, he's surprised me so many times. I want to think that he'd be excited and happy. I mean, things are really good between us."

"Do you love him?"

Corryna had been wrestling with this question, but she'd always been posing it in the confines of her own head. Hearing it out loud and from someone else, there was only one answer. "Yes. I do."

Jessica's eyes widened and she smiled. "Well, good. Do you think he loves you?"

Corryna thought back on the last several weeks with him. He had been so exceptionally kind and wonderful. She didn't want to assume that he felt the same way she did, but he *had* to have feelings for her. There was no way there wasn't something of substance there. "I'm not sure. But I'd like to think there's a chance that he does."

"That's great." Jessica tilted her head to one side. "You know, I say that thinking positive is the best way to go. Talk to Colin and tell him how you feel."

As much as she wanted to be optimistic, the idea of the conversation that was ahead of her made her slightly queasy. If he took it badly, the whole notion of keeping things with Colin on an even keel would go right out the window. And then where would they be? They would have jeopardized their jobs with the wedding, and their fairy-tale relationship would crumble to nothing. But Corryna couldn't bring herself to look at the downside. Not now. Not when her dream of motherhood seemed to actually be coming true. "You're right. I need to stay upbeat and hope for the best."

"That's the spirit. When are you going to tell him?"

"Right after I finish this tea."

Colin was having a hell of a day, which was not good given that he was supposed to be working on finalizing the menu for the presentation to Rylee next week for the Noble-Ramos wedding. But unfortunately, the Oliver Shaw review in *Global Cuisine* magazine had finally come out, and although it was a rave on the surface, Colin saw a few too many details that made him deeply uncomfortable.

He sat in his office at Sheen, rereading the piece. Certain passages, surely meant to flatter, cut Colin to the core. *His brilliance is exactly like his father's, but it's been elevated for the modern palate.* And *Colin Reynolds and his dad seem to share the same brain and heart, but Colin stands alone on the forefront of something truly unique.* In some ways, these were things he'd longed to hear. They were going to get under his father's skin like nothing else could. But Colin wasn't sure he wanted to get back at his dad anymore. Or at least not in a vicious way. Corryna had gotten through to him on this very central issue in his life.

Even so, the comparisons did bother him. He'd always worried that he and his dad were exactly alike. It was part of the reason the distance between them brought some comfort. If he and his father weren't close, Colin didn't have to be confronted by their similarities. Colin could tell himself that he was different. But Oliver's review seemed to confirm what Colin had always feared—he and his dad were too much alike.

When he heard Corryna's voice outside of his office, it felt like someone had just thrown him a life preserver. He got up from his desk and rushed to the door. Outside the kitchen, she was chatting with Elena.

"I'm glad you like the croissants," Elena said.

"They are so good. Every time Colin brings them to me, I just want to keep them all for myself," Corryna replied. She glanced over at Colin and smiled. "Hey. Sorry I'm dropping by unannounced. I need to talk to you."

"Sure. Yeah. Of course. Come on in." He ushered her into his office, then closed the door. "It feels like a miracle that you're here. I'm having a terrible day and now it all feels better."

She looked at him with the most indecipherable look on her face. It was like she was both happy and confused. It made him wonder what in the hell was going on. "Oh. Well, maybe this isn't a good time to talk about important things."

"No. No. This is the perfect time. Important things will help keep my mind off everything else." He took her hand and led her to one of the chairs, then he sat on the edge of his desk.

"If it's okay with you, I'll stand."

That worried him. People with bad news always stood to deliver it. "Sure. Whatever works."

She sucked in a deep breath, as if she needed to give herself a dose of courage. "I'm pregnant."

For several moments, Colin was frozen. Neither words nor actions seemed appropriate. But that didn't mean his mind wasn't running. It was. Not smoothly, but it was whirring in stops and starts as he thought through what she'd said. "Pregnant. You're going to have a baby." He didn't want to be that guy, but he had to ask. "And it's definitely mine?"

"Yes, Colin. It is."

The shades of happiness that had been there on

her face earlier were slowly evaporating, but he didn't know what to say. He didn't want a child. He didn't want to be a parent. He never had. In fact, he'd sworn to himself that he would never do it. "Wow. This is big. Huge." He wandered over to the window and looked outside, hoping it might help to clear his mind.

"Is that all you're going to say? It would be nice if you told me how you're feeling."

He turned back to her. "I don't know what I'm supposed to say, Corryna. We're weeks into our relationship. And I never wanted to be a father. Plus, let me point out that I'm forty-two. Having a child was never part of my plan, but it really isn't now."

She nodded as if she agreed, but the hurt on her face was plain. "I get it. We never made any promises to each other." She looked around the room, seeming lost. "I'll just leave now."

Colin felt as though his heart was being ripped out of his chest. "Corryna. Please don't go. Will you give me a minute to wrap my head around this?" He couldn't imagine changing his opinion about this matter, but he cared deeply about Corryna. He didn't want to hurt her.

She blew out a breath. "Believe me. I understand. I haven't had much time to think about it, either."

He sensed her frustration and was eager to make it go away. Explaining his feelings and motivation seemed like the only path forward. "You know how I feel about my family. I never wanted to become a dad because to me, a father is someone who lets you down. It's not only someone who isn't there for you, it's someone who brings you heartache."

"You could take it as a lesson and decide to be nothing like your dad."

"But what if that's not possible? People are who they are. My dad and I are so much alike. People have always told me that. Hell, this food writer claimed we're practically the same person." He pointed to the open magazine on his desk. He didn't want to sound so stubborn about it, but he'd spent decades dealing with the aftermath of what had happened between himself and his parents. He couldn't magically un-spool it in the span of fifteen minutes.

"I understand what you're saying, Colin. To you, family represents betrayal. But you don't have to follow that script."

"What if I'm not capable? I'm not naturally lov-ing and nurturing like you are. This cold and calcu-lated focus on perfection is imprinted on my DNA. That's not going anywhere. Trust me."

She shook her head and blew out a breath. "I wish that you could see the things in you that I see. You are so much more than you think you are."

He wasn't convinced. "Well, I wish I could hear what you're saying and instantly change my mind, but I can't. Like I said before, this was not part of my plan."

"Okay. Fine." She stiffened her spine. "But I need you to understand that it has always been one of my dreams to become a mom. My ex-husband took that dream away from me. And I thought that dream was gone. But it turns out that it isn't, and no matter what you say, I'm happy about this."

"It's not my job to make amends for another man's mistakes."

"Of course it isn't." She scanned his face, her eyes sweeping back and forth in deliberate fashion. "But you took the time to care about the other thing he took from me. My money."

Damn. That one stopped him right in his tracks. "I did that because I care about you." Those words were zipping around in his head again. He'd never uttered them to a woman before, but maybe they could save him. "I did that because I love you."

Corryna blinked so many times that her eyelashes were fluttering. She let out a low and quiet laugh. "I hate to break this to you, but that only makes this worse."

He was so epically bad at relationships. He should have just kept his mouth shut. "You know I'll take responsibility for the baby. No matter what. Whatever you need."

"I don't want our baby to be seen as a responsibility, Colin. I can manage on my own. I'll find a way."

"How, exactly? Your shop barely breaks even. And you aren't willing to take the steps to go after the money you're rightfully owed."

Anger flared in her eyes and she stepped closer

and planted a finger in the center of his chest. "That was *my* choice to make. You said it yourself."

"Well, you can't keep me from helping you. I'll order flowers from you every day."

"Am I supposed to be impressed that you'd go to such extraordinary measures to give me money—the thing that you have more than enough of? The thing that you can afford to give away? Because I'm not." She took a step back, away from him. "I will find a way to make it work. I always do. I don't need you."

In some ways, he'd always expected to hear her say that to him. It was the truth. She didn't need him. She was a fully formed human being and he was a shell of a man. "I'm not trying to walk away from you, Corryna. I just need time."

She shook her head. "I can't stay here and listen to this anymore. I need to get on with my life. I need to look forward." She walked to the door, then turned back to him. "Apparently, I'm going to be doing that alone."

Eleven

It had been two days since Colin's conversation with Corryna, and every morning, he woke up feeling like he'd downed an entire bottle of his beloved Redbreast whiskey. He dreaded getting out of bed. He didn't want to go to the kitchen. It only reminded him of Corryna, although to be fair, his bed reminded him of her as well. As did the garden. And his restaurant. And his entire life. How in the hell did this happen?

But being a parent had never been part of his plan. From a very young age, as soon as he was able to recognize that the relationship he had with his parents was dysfunctional as hell, he'd vowed to never ever have kids. Because the truth was that he was otherwise exactly like his dad. He had laser-focus on the bottom line. He was a perfectionist at every turn. He expected the best out of everyone around him. He allowed for few mistakes, and when it came to himself, that number was zero.

For exactly that reason, he forced himself to get up and get going. It was Monday, the start of the workweek, which was always a busy day. He also only had two days until he and Corryna were due to make their final presentation to Rylee. There was much to do before then, including figuring out if Corryna would even speak to him. He wasn't sure she'd ever utter another word to him, which would make the next several months of working together an absolute nightmare.

He arrived at Sheen early and saw that Elena was already there. As soon as he walked in through the back door near the loading area, he smelled Elena's incredible chocolate croissants. *Dammit.* Everything was another reminder of Corryna. He wasn't sure he'd ever be able to eat Elena's incredible pastries. Every bite would be like scratching at an open wound.

"Good morning," Elena said when he dared to walk into the kitchen. "I don't know if you're working with Corryna Lawson today, but I baked her favorites."

"I know. I could smell them the minute I came inside. I'm sure they're delicious."

"Are you seeing her today?"

He shrugged. "I'm not sure." *She probably hates*

me. "Maybe. We have a few final things to talk about before the wedding presentation on Wednesday."

"Gotcha. Well, I'll box some up for her. Just in case."

"Thanks." Colin trailed back to his office, one of the most potent reminders of his past with Corryna. He'd thought about the night of the blackout countless times. He'd fantasized about what would have happened if he'd been able to convince her to stay longer that night or, even better, persuaded her to come to his place. They'd conceived a child that night. It was pretty miraculous considering how quickly the whole thing had happened.

He sat down at his desk and got to work, looking over last week's numbers, placing orders and making sure that the well-oiled machine that was Sheen continued to run. That much he could do. That much he wouldn't mess up. About an hour or so later, Kristine poked her head into his office. Elena was right behind her. They were both grinning like fools.

"What's going on?" he asked.

"You both won!" Kristine shrieked and started jumping up and down.

For an instant, Colin almost asked, *"Won what?"* But then he realized what had just happened. The Jane Broad awards. "We *both* won?" He rose from his desk, in utter disbelief. His first reaction was to give Elena the hug she so richly deserved. "Congratulations," he said. He felt genuine happiness for her. For himself? Nothing but disdain and disappointment.

"Congratulations to *you*," she said. "You made all of this possible."

"I didn't make your award possible. You did that."

"Well, I still think you're the best boss ever," Elena said.

"Huge congrats to both of you," Kristine said. "We should probably do a press release, don't you think?"

Funnily enough, that would normally be Colin's first thought—to find a way to capitalize on the award by drawing more attention to the restaurant. "Can you tackle that with our publicist? I don't think I have the bandwidth for it right now."

"Oh, sure. The Noble-Ramos wedding. I know that's front and center for you," Kristine said.

"It is." That was a lie. Corryna was first and last on his mind. Nothing else was getting through.

"I'm happy to do it." She smiled wide at both Colin and Elena. "I guess I'll get on that. I'll see you two winners later." Kristine patted Elena on the shoulder then exited the office in a flash.

"I should probably get back to work," Elena said. "Those mini pecan pies I need to prepare for dinner service tonight won't make themselves."

"Elena, hold on one second." Colin had something he wanted to ask her, although he realized this might not be appropriate for work. "Can I ask you a personal question? I mean, it's really more of a life question. I could use some advice."

"Of course. Anything at all." She perched on the arm of one of the upholstered chairs opposite his desk.

"Do you like being a mom?"

She delivered the most incredulous look—in a single glance she told him that he'd asked the most ridiculous question imaginable. "Like it? I love it. It is the hardest thing I've ever done. And the easiest thing I've ever done. It has transformed my life in ways I never could have imagined. There are days when it feels like my heart is going to explode from the rush of love that wants to come out of it."

"Wow. That's quite an answer." All Colin could think about was his childhood and the mistakes he had blamed his parents for. He wasn't sure he'd ever made any of it easy for them. Not that it was his job to do that, but he could appreciate that they weren't entirely to blame for everything that went wrong.

"I mean, there are also days when my head is the part of me that's going to explode. But that's life, isn't it? There are good days and bad. But there are also amazing days."

Colin nodded solemnly, taking in everything she was saying. He understood it on some level. The days since Corryna had come into his life had been remarkably full—of laughter and optimism and joy. "Did you ever doubt whether you could be a good parent?"

"Are you feeling okay? This seems like a weird conversation given the fact that you and I just won the highest accolade our industry awards."

"I know. I know. It's just that winning it has very suddenly put a lot of things into perspective." And of course, Corryna had been the force that brought so much clarity to his life. If only he'd been smart enough to notice it when she was doing it. If only she might be willing to forgive him for being such a stubborn ass.

"Well, I doubt my parenting every day, but I think that's normal. You do your best and you love them. In the end, that's what it takes. Nothing more and nothing less. Also, money. Kids cost a lot of money." She laughed, then narrowed her vision on Colin. "Are you thinking about kids?"

"Thinking about them? Yes. Why? Is that surprising to you?" *I have to start living my life. I have to get out there and grab it or the whole thing is going to pass me by.*

"That's amazing, Colin. I think you'd make an incredible dad. You're so generous. And kind."

He appreciated the vote of confidence, but he wasn't sure he deserved the praise. "Thank you, Elena. For everything."

She rose from her perch on the arm of the chair. "Anytime." She clapped him on the shoulder. "And way to go, Colin. You're a rock star."

If only I felt like one. Colin sat in his chair and turned to look out the window—the same view he'd had to the parking lot the night of the blackout, when Corryna had shown up in the Royal Blooms truck and turned his life upside down. He loved her, dammit. He did. And his life simply wasn't going to be right without her. But rebuilding the bridge he'd burned would take some doing. And then there was the elephant in the room—he'd told Corryna that he loved her and she'd said that only made things worse. For all he knew, she didn't love him back.

It didn't matter. He had to try to salvage some of this. He turned his chair back and stood. His phone rang, and he was sure it had to be his dad. Talk about needing to build a bridge… The one to his parents would need to be rebuilt, too. Corryna was right. She'd been right about everything.

But when he looked at the caller ID, he was taken by surprise. This call was from his mother. "Hello?" Colin answered.

"You won. I'm so proud of you."

The emotion of everything leading up to that moment hit him like a ton of bricks. Two tons. His history with his parents. The accolade he'd worked his ass off to get. And front and center in his mind, Corryna and the baby. It felt like everything was converging. It was scary and wonderful at the same time. He was teetering on the brink. One misstep and all could be lost. "Mam. Thank you." His voice trembled, but he refused to see it as weakness. This was what happened when you'd spent half of a lifetime or more squashing down your feelings.

"It's okay, darling. It's understandable that you'd be emotional."

"It's just a lot."

"Of course. You know, I always struggled when you were sad. It was always so painful to know you were hurting. It kept me up at night."

"It was?"

"Of course, son. I'm your mother."

His heart felt like it was about to explode as he realized what had always hurt the most during those years when he'd been away at school—he'd been left wondering if they cared. He couldn't allow anyone else to ever endure that pain. Certainly not a baby, a sweet and vulnerable, innocent child. More than anything, *his* baby. With *Corryna*, the woman he loved. He *did* care. He had an ocean of love churning inside of him and he'd spent too many years damming it up and holding it back, all because it was messy to let it out. Because it might reveal that he was imperfect.

"It's happy tears. I promise."

"Oh, good. I'm glad. What are you going to do to celebrate your big win?"

Big win. Despite the award, in his mind, there was no big win yet. "I'm going to go see a friend. We have a lot to talk about."

"That sounds nice. I'm sure your father would love to talk to you soon if you can. He'll probably give you that guilt trip about coming to work for him. You know, you can tell him to bugger off if you like. He only does it because he still wants you back in the fold."

He swallowed hard. What he was about to say was years late, but it was only weeks in the making. "I'd like to find a way back into the fold, Mam. But not like Da wants. Not business. I'm talking about family. Our family."

She gasped. And then she started to cry.

"Mam. Don't…" Colin said.

She sniffled. "You don't even have to ask. You can come back anytime and I'll squeeze you so hard that you won't be able to breathe."

She painted a lovely picture, but it still felt like a fantasy. Something so far off in the distance that it wasn't yet his. And that was because the real problem in his life, the one that meant even more, still needed fixing. "That sounds great. I want to talk some more, but I really need to go see that friend of mine. I mean, she's not simply a friend. Her name is Corryna. And I love her."

"You're in love?"

"I am. Is it okay if we speak about it later?"

"Well…well… Yes. Of course. Go."

My future is waiting. He wanted to say as much, but it would have to wait. "Thank you."

"I'm proud of you."

"Thank you. That means the world to me."

"I love you, son."

"I love you, too. Goodbye." Colin hung up the phone and collected himself for a heartbeat or two.

His mind had been like a tornado for the last several days, but now he felt as though he could see things clearly. The path ahead might not be easy, but he still had to take it. He grabbed his car keys. One quick stop in the kitchen and he'd be on his way to Royal Blooms. No, he didn't have a plan. He only had an aim. Everything else, he was just going to have to improvise.

It was an unusually busy morning at Royal Blooms, which meant Corryna was working the front of the shop alongside Hannah. She was just finishing ringing up a customer when Mike's wife, Serena, walked in, pushing her stroller.

"Serena. Hi." Corryna's heart leaped at the prospect of seeing Mike and Serena's baby girl, Penelope. She stepped out from behind the counter. "Mike's not here right now. He's out making deliveries."

"No problem." She leaned down, reached under the stroller and pulled out a small insulated bag. "He forgot his lunch. I thought I'd drive it over and take Penelope for a walk downtown. It's such a beautiful day."

"I'll take it." Hannah appeared from behind Corryna. "I can put it in the fridge for him."

Serena handed over the bag. "Thanks so much."

Corryna crouched down. Penelope was asleep, her head listing to one side, making her fine reddish hair, a brighter and lighter version of Mike's, fall across her cheek. "She's so beautiful, Serena."

Serena peered down at them. "She is. This is such a great age. She laughs and smiles. She sleeps a lot better. It's an awesome time to be a mom, I'll tell you that much."

Corryna started to do the math. It was never her strong suit, but this calculation was somehow easier to make. She'd conceived in early March. She hadn't been to the doctor yet—her appointment was next week—but she estimated her due date would be sometime in November. That meant that her baby would be a little younger than Penelope's age by this time next year. Thinking about the future was such a mixed bag right now. She was endlessly excited about the baby. But it was going to be hard to do it on her own. There was no doubt about that. Then again, she'd done so much on her own over the last six years. She'd kept her business alive despite her ex-husband's best attempts. She'd made it through. And she would make it through this as well.

"I'm pregnant," Corryna blurted, surprised at herself.

"You're what?" Hannah nearly shrieked from the back of the shop.

"Oh, my gosh," Serena said. "Congratulations."

Corryna straightened. "Sorry about that. It just sort of came out. I've been dying to tell someone. Jessica's the only one who knows." Along with Colin. But that was a different story. "I'm only about eight weeks along. It's still early. I haven't even told my family yet."

Hannah bopped over to Corryna and wrapped her up in a hug. "You are going to make the best mom."

Corryna wasn't sure about that, but she sure as hell was going to try her hardest. "Thank you."

"I should probably head out, but congratulations again," Serena said. "Mike will be so excited to hear the news."

"Thank you. And thanks for coming by." Corryna held the door so Serena could push out the stroller, but as soon as they were gone, Jessica was walking in. "Wow. It's like a parade in here today."

Jessica thrust a gift bag into Corryna's hand. It had the word Baby printed on it in pastel colors. "Sorry. I saw this cute little picture book about flowers. I couldn't resist."

"This is happening fast." Hannah turned to Jessica. "I just found out."

Jessica clasped her hand over her mouth. "Oh, my God. I'm sorry. I assumed that you would've told everyone right away."

"I just started. About five minutes before you got here." Corryna would've been lying if she'd said she wasn't a bit overwhelmed at the moment. "Hannah, can you watch the shop for a minute while Jessica and I go talk?"

"Of course."

"Do you have a minute?" Corryna asked Jessica.
"Always."

The pair walked into Corryna's office and sat. "Thank you for the gift. That's very kind of you."

"I figured you might need your spirits lifted. I'm sorry that your conversation with Colin went badly. I'm sure he'll come around."

Corryna wasn't so certain. He had a lot of hurdles to get past and she couldn't push him to do any of it. It wasn't her job to convince him that they could be great together. He had to reach that conclusion on his own. Of course she'd made one tragic mistake the other day when they'd had their big talk—he'd told her that he loved her and she hadn't returned the sentiment. She'd been angry. She wasn't proud of it. "It's okay. I figure that what's meant to happen will happen." She pressed her hand against her lower belly. "I have one thing I've always wanted. And I have you. I'll be fine."

Jessica scooted to the edge of her seat. "Remember when we went on our hike? And I said that you deserved a little miracle? Maybe the baby is that."

"We were talking about flowers, weren't we?"

"So I was a little bit off. I'm not psychic." Jessica spotted the folder on Corryna's desk. "Is this the report from the forensic accountant? What did you decide to do about it?"

Corryna had briefed Jessica on the results of the audit soon after she shared the information with Colin. "The lawyer called this morning so I got the report out again. He said there's no statute of limitations on embezzlement in the state of Texas. I can go after Dan any time if I decide to." She sighed. "But you know, for now, I think I'm going to let it go."

"Really? It's so much money. Won't you need that for the baby?"

Corryna nodded. She knew exactly how illogical her decision seemed. "It would certainly make life easier. But money doesn't make life *better*. It certainly doesn't help you raise children any better. Colin's parents had all the money in the world and they sure messed him up."

"Whatever you decide, I support you."

"I figure the evidence will always be sitting there. But ultimately, I don't have a vindictive bone in my body. Dan stole from me in more ways than one, but I've reclaimed my life for myself. He can't take that away from me."

Hannah appeared in the doorway to Corryna's office. Her face was flushed with pink. "I realize you're already having a bonkers day, but Colin Reynolds is here to see you."

"Plot twist!" Jessica exclaimed, then popped up out of her seat. "I'll clear out so you two can talk." Jessica leaned down until her face was near Corryna's belly. "Alright, baby. Be good to your mama."

Corryna peered down at her best friend. "Thank you so much. You're the absolute best. I love you."

"I love you, too." Jessica straightened, then planted a kiss on Corryna's forehead. "I hope your talk goes well."

"Thanks."

Jessica walked out and Corryna stood, preparing herself for another uncomfortable talk with Colin.

When he stepped into the doorway, taking up all of the space, he sucked the breath right out of her, which was so like him. He always managed to make her world tilt on its axis with his very presence. That was saying a lot because he looked like hell. She seriously doubted he'd been sleeping. And he held his arms awkwardly behind his body, seeming immensely uncomfortable.

"I've been an ass," he said. Except it sounded more like *arse* because of his accent.

"I won't argue the point."

"Can we talk?"

Corryna realized that she didn't want to have this conversation in her office. It was too cramped and it was full of things she hated, like spreadsheets and numbers. She needed to be close to things she loved right now. "Let's go in the back." She squeezed past him, trying to ignore his enticing scent, and led him down the short hall and into the back room. She grabbed a stool and dragged it to her main workbench. It was impossible to ignore her memories of being back here with him—the first time she'd arranged flowers for him and the times he'd stopped by to say hello—but she wasn't going to allow thoughts of those happy times be tarnished by the present state of affairs.

"You sit," Colin said. "I'll stand."

You're not staying, then. Got it. "Okay."

He stepped closer as she took the seat. "Here. I brought you this as part of my apology." He finally pulled his arm out from behind his back, revealing the reason he'd been standing like that—he had a bakery box in his hand. "Elena made them this morning."

Corryna couldn't help but smile, even though it didn't make up for everything that had happened between them. "Thank you. That was nice."

"I couldn't bring you flowers. I wouldn't want to give another florist the business. And well, no matter what someone else did, they would never match one of your designs."

"Thank you." She lifted the lid and saw the enticing pastries, but she wasn't going to take one yet. "So you were saying you've been an ass. I'd love to hear more about that."

He laughed quietly and inched even closer. "I figured I should start with the most obvious statement. It's absolutely true. And I would understand it if you wanted to tell me to get out of your life forever, but I really, really want a second chance." He took her hand. "I love you, Corryna. I meant that. You are the only thing I care about in my life."

A tear leaked out of the corner of her eye. Then another. How could *I love you* hold so much weight, and still hurt? "I love you, too, Colin. I know I didn't say it the other day. And I'm sorry for that, but I can't sit around and wait for the moment when you decide you're okay with becoming a dad."

He nodded solemnly. "I know. Which is the reason I came to talk to you. In person. I had a real moment of clarity an hour ago. I talked to my mom. And it went well. Really well."

"You did? That's so great." She couldn't help but be happy for him. This was a step that he'd needed to take for a long time. "Did she say something particularly profound?"

"No. She said the simplest thing in the world. She said that it had always made her sad when I was sad. And I realized that all those years when I was away at school, the one question I was stuck with was whether my parents cared. Now I know that she did. And as soon as that light bulb went off, the logical conclusion hit me. I can't leave a child with that question. Not even for a second." A tear rolled down his cheek. "Especially not a child that's one half the person my entire world revolves around. The one person I cannot live without."

Corryna found it nearly impossible to get past the lump in her throat. "Me?"

"Yes, you." He threaded his fingers into her hair and cupped the sides of her face, then lowered his head and kissed her cheek, allowing his lips to linger for a moment. The warmth from his skin washed over her, and he pressed his forehead against hers. "I love you, Corryna. And I love that you're having my baby. You were right. I can rewrite the script. I've been doing it for years. I'm not my dad. I'm my own person. But I didn't see that until you held a mirror up to my face and showed me what I really was. And what I really want to be. I want to be a dad. I want to be your partner. I love you, Corryna. More than I ever thought possible. I want us to be a family. The three of us. I want us to be together. Forever."

Corryna had cried an ocean of tears in her life, especially over the last six years, but they hadn't fallen as freely as they were right now. Her face was soaked, but it felt as though she was washing away the final remnants of her pain. She was wiping the slate clean so she could start a new life with the man she loved, and their child. "I love you, too, Colin. I want us to be together, too."

She stood and wrapped her arms around him. He did the same, holding on to her so tightly that she felt as though nothing could ever hurt her again. She raised her head and they tumbled into a kiss that was long and giving and more than a little hot. It spoke of nothing less than true love, and it was everything Corryna had ever wanted.

When she pulled back from it, she asked, "What prompted you to talk to your mom?"

"She called because I won the Jane Broad award."

"Colin. You did? Congratulations. I can't believe you didn't tell me that."

"It's just an award, Corryna. It's not what I really care about. What I care about is you and me standing in the back room of Royal Blooms confessing our love."

She smiled wide as she peered up into his handsome face. "I'm so proud of you. For everything."

"And that means the world."

Twelve

Colin was busy in the Sheen kitchen preparing for the final presentation to Rylee when his phone, which was sitting on the stainless steel prep table, lit up with a text. It was from his dad. For a moment, he hesitated to read the message. Call it a well-worn reflex, but he didn't want to be disappointed once more, just like he had been for most of his life. Fortunately, Corryna had taught him that no situation was one-sided. No one was purely good or purely bad. Most important, she'd shown him that the painful times in life only made the good times that much sweeter. It had only been two days since they made up in the back room at Royal Blooms, but life with Corryna was already exceptionally sweet.

Your mother and I looked at our schedules. August works, his dad's message said.

He smiled at his phone and was quick to tap out a response. Great. Looking forward to it. More soon. He sent that, but it didn't seem like enough. Now that he'd learned to let out his emotions, it was like a runaway train. Love you. He hit send.

The three dots that said his dad was typing appeared. We love you, too.

"Colin? Corryna is out back. Do you want to go help her with the flowers or should I?" Kristine asked.

Colin was already on his way out the door. "No. I've got it. Can you work on the garnish for the crab?"

"Yep. I'm on it."

He darted past the walk-in fridge and through the loading area to the side door. He thundered down the steps. He could see that she already had the back of the truck open. "Corryna Lawson, don't you dare carry those flowers. Let me do it."

She peeked out from behind one of the doors and smiled. "You're so bossy."

He was quick to pull her into an embrace and kiss her. These moments were too precious to waste. "And you're pregnant."

"The baby is the size of a peanut. I assure you that I'm fine."

The baby. He was still getting accustomed to the idea of what was ahead for Corryna and him, but he was more comfortable with it with every passing day.

And after his conversation with Elena, he suspected that parenthood was likely something that he'd never be fully prepared for. As little as two months ago, the perfectionist in him would have been sick over the idea of a major life change that required on-the-spot improvisation. Especially one where a tiny human's well-being was hanging in the balance. But he and Corryna made an amazing team, and she'd taught him to embrace a little uncertainty and trust that he had so much more in him than he'd ever thought possible. "Indulge me."

She rolled her eyes at him, but it was adorable, just like everything she did. "I'll take a little at a time. How about that?"

"Deal."

They ferried several loads of flowers into the restaurant and into the private dining room where they would be making their presentation to Rylee and Dionna. Kristine and several members of the waitstaff had already set up the entire space to mimic a reception, arranging each of the tables to seat ten people. Even though it would only be Rylee, Dionna, Colin and Corryna eating today, there was a place setting at every seat, complete with the dishes, linens and glassware the bride and groom had already chosen. It was a little over-the-top, but Corryna and Colin wanted Rylee and Dionna to be able to experience it all so they could report back to Xavier and Ariana. This wedding was the most important job of Corryna's life and right up there for Colin, but it was also the thing that had brought them together as a couple, so they both felt the need to knock this presentation out of the park.

Corryna orchestrated the placement of the centerpieces, smaller table arrangements and the other elements, like tiny bundles of blooms tucked into the napkins at each guest's seat and elaborate floral garlands adorning the backs of the bride's and groom's chairs. How he loved being around Corryna when she was in her creative zone, laser-focused on bringing her artistic vision to life. It reminded him of that first meeting at Royal Blooms. They were falling in love that night, even though there hadn't been a single kiss or embrace. They were finding their way to each other, even though they didn't know it. And she was sparking his creativity, while warming up his once frozen heart.

Eventually, everything seemed to be to Corryna's liking, and they stood back to survey the final product.

"I'm still not sure about those roses. I mean, I love them, but maybe they're too safe. Do you think they might not be bold enough?"

He put his arm around her shoulder and leaned over to kiss the top of her head. "It's all perfect. The bluebonnets in particular are stunning. And I really like the anemones. They're quite striking."

"I can't believe you know the names of flowers now. The first time I met you, you basically told me that you hated flowers."

He still regretted what had happened that first time she'd come into Sheen, after he'd canceled his contract with Royal Blooms. He'd really been an ass. "Actually, that wasn't the first time we met. Remember the night at The Silver Saddle? When I tried to buy you a drink?"

She stepped away from him and over to the main table, where she plucked a bit of greenery out of one of the arrangements. "I was in a pretty bad way that night. It's still for the best that I sent you packing."

He laughed quietly, although he didn't want to think about what his life would be like right now if he and Corryna hadn't found each other a second time. "It'll make a good story to tell our little one."

Corryna looked over her shoulder at him and smiled. Her gorgeous eyes glinted with life and happiness, which warmed his heart, as well as a few other parts of his body. "Yes it will." She stood back from the table again. "I really hope Rylee and Dionna are happy with this. There won't be much time to get things done if we have to start over. It's the last day of April and the wedding is in early June."

"I have every confidence in us, even if we have to make last-minute changes. Plus, how could they not be pleased with what we've put together?"

"So says the guy who had the first seven dishes he created for this wedding rejected."

Colin turned to her. "You know, I've pretty much resigned myself to the fact that things with this wedding are probably going to be in flux until Xavier

Noble and Ariana Ramos actually say 'I do.' So, I don't see the point in questioning what we've done so far. You and I know that we have left no stone unturned. We have pushed ourselves to the point of exceptionalism. I think we'll bowl over Rylee and Dionna today. Then we see what happens."

Corryna gripped his arm. "Who are you and what have you done with Colin Reynolds? It sounds like you're planning to go with the flow."

He laughed and leaned down to kiss her on the cheek. "What can I say? You've changed me for the better." His phone buzzed with a text and he pulled it out of his pocket. The message was from Rylee. "Alright, darling. It's time for me to get back in the kitchen. Rylee is on her way."

"Can I come into the kitchen and watch you work until Rylee arrives?" Corryna asked.

"Of course you can. Come on." Colin led her into Sheen's kitchen, where Kristine, Elena and a few line cooks were already busy working. "Here. This is a good spot for you." He carried a metal barstool to one of the far walls, which provided an excellent view of the line.

"Perfect. Thank you." She sat and watched as Colin went to work, taking over from Kristine and directing every member of the kitchen staff. It was like watching a conductor in charge of a symphony. The amount of multitasking involved was incredible—he knew the stage of preparation for every dish. He knew exactly what was right and what was missing. He tasted. He tweaked. And he guided his crew with a firm, but kind hand. Corryna marveled that they had found each other. He was such an exceptional person. She felt nothing short of lucky. And a little exhausted. Everything that had happened over the last month was difficult to wrap her head around—an assignment for a wedding, a red-hot collaboration, passion with a man she never imagined could be hers, and ultimately...love. It had taken *years* for her life to turn into something she hardly recognized, but it had only taken a month for it to turn around.

One of the Sheen servers poked her head into the kitchen. "Chef, Ms. Meadows has just pulled up."

"Thank you." Colin turned to Kristine. "Are we good with everything?"

"Absolutely," she answered. "We've got this. It's time for you to go turn on the charm."

Corryna couldn't have contained her smile. Colin managed to be charming always, even when he was being less than pleasant. It was his inexplicable superpower.

"Right." Colin turned to Corryna. "Ready? It's showtime."

She hopped down from her perch. "As ready as I'll ever be."

"We've got this," he muttered to her as they walked out of the kitchen.

After the talk they'd had in the private dining

room, Corryna felt like it didn't even matter if they didn't have this. They would sort it out. Just like they'd figured out everything else.

"Rylee," Colin said as they rounded into the main dining room. "How are you today?"

She tapped away at her phone, then kept it clutched in her hand. "Good. Busy. I'm sorry, Dionna can't come today. A last-minute meeting popped up and she had to fly to LA this morning. But I'm looking forward to this."

"We've been working really hard," Corryna said. "Hopefully it'll be everything Xavier and Ariana are looking for."

"I'm going to take a bunch of photos today if that's okay," Rylee said. "Including some video as I walk into the room for the first time. I not only promised the bride and groom, I promised Dionna. She's so sorry she couldn't be here."

"Of course. Go for it." Colin turned to Corryna. "Let's get a few steps ahead just to be sure the lighting is correct."

"Sounds good," Rylee said. "I'll wait a minute before I come in."

Colin and Corryna hustled into the private dining room. Indeed, everything was perfect. The overhead lights had been dimmed, and candles all over the room had been lit. Music from a playlist Rylee had provided was playing softly in the background. It was a sumptuous and romantic setting. If Rylee wasn't bowled over by this, nothing was going to impress her.

On cue, Rylee walked into the room, holding her phone and panning the room, shooting video. Colin and Corryna stood impossibly still and quiet as Rylee walked past them, but he did take Corryna's hand and squeeze it. She squeezed his back. This was their moment. And there was no turning back.

Rylee continued to film her full panoramic view of the room with her camera, turning in a circle, then she tapped at her phone and tucked it inside her bag. "Okay. Let's get started," she said.

Corryna glanced over to see that one of the servers had entered the room. "I'll notify the kitchen, Chef."

"Perfect. Thank you," Colin said. "Rylee, please make yourself comfortable." He directed Rylee to sit at one of the chairs at the center of the table, then he pulled out a chair for Corryna. He sat next to her. "You have the printed menu right in front of you for reference." On the table was a beautifully typeset card describing all of the dishes they were about to taste.

"Great." Rylee perused the card. "I'm ready to eat."

In a carefully coordinated procession, Colin's staff of servers brought in each dish, being careful to space them and give Rylee the chance to try each individually. Corryna was absolutely loving every bite, especially as it brought back memories of that first night she'd been over to Colin's house. But after the second course had been served and she'd been raving about how delicious everything was, she noticed that Rylee was being quiet. She did nod a few times, take pictures and write down some notes, but she was otherwise providing very little feedback. Nervousness started to take hold for Corryna. How would Colin handle it if she rejected his creations again? She wanted to think he could take it all in stride, but this was his pride on the line.

After the final bites of the final dish had been consumed, Rylee made a few more notes, then set aside her pen and tented her fingers in front of her with her elbows on the table. "So."

Corryna thought she might pass out from the tension.

"This was absolutely spectacular. Top to bottom." Rylee grinned from ear to ear. "I tried to find some criticisms, but I really don't have a single one. The food was exceptional. And the flowers are flawless."

Corryna finally felt like she could exhale.

"I look forward to telling Ariana and Xavier all about it," Rylee continued. "They'll want to taste everything for themselves, of course. Hopefully it won't be too much trouble for you to do all of this again."

Corryna and Colin glanced at each other, silently having one of their conversations. It was going to be a great deal of work to replicate this once more, then do it all over again for the wedding, but it was of little concern. They'd nailed the task for today. "Of course," Colin said. "It'll be absolutely no problem."

Rylee looked back and forth between Colin and Corryna. "And everything is still good between you two? Not anticipating any problems as we get closer to the wedding?"

"None," Corryna was quick to answer. "Things are great between us."

"Well, that's not exactly right," Colin said.

Corryna slugged his leg under the table.

He turned to her and grinned, then focused his attention on Rylee. "Honestly, Corryna and I need to thank you. You put us together. You asked us to collaborate. And that led to a change in my life that is so huge, I can't even fathom it. Corryna and I are deeply in love, Ms. Meadows." He reached for Corryna's hand under the table, and she held on to it like she might never let go as she listened to the raw honesty of his words and the sheer emotion with which he delivered them. "She is the most incredible person I have ever met. And we're excited to say that we're having a baby together. We're starting off on a life together."

Corryna had to fight back the tears. Even Rylee looked like she was getting choked up.

"Wow. That's not what I expected to hear today, but I'm happy if I got to play any role in this at all. It sounds to me like you've got the ultimate collaboration. In everything."

Corryna and Colin looked at each other. It was precisely that. Corryna's heart was thundering in her chest. She loved this man more than she'd ever thought was possible. "That's exactly what it is."

"Well, I won't keep you two from your day any longer. Plus, I have a full schedule." Rylee pushed back from her chair and stood. Colin and Corryna followed suit. "But thank you for today. For everything."

Colin and Corryna walked her to the dining room entrance. "Thank you," Colin said.

Rylee turned back one more time. "What are you going to do with all of these flowers?"

"I've already made arrangements to donate them," Corryna said. "My delivery driver will be here soon to take them to Royal Memorial Hospital."

"The maternity ward, perhaps?" Rylee asked.

"You know, I didn't designate exactly where they would go, but that's an excellent idea," Corryna replied.

"I hope you both have a great day," Rylee said as Colin's staff began filing into the room to start the cleanup.

"You too," Colin and Corryna said in near unison.

As Rylee walked away, Colin blew out a long breath and slung his arm over Corryna's shoulder. "I don't know about you, but I'm knackered. Let's go unwind for a bit."

"Knackered?" Corryna asked as they ambled their way into his office.

"Tired." Colin closed the door behind them.

"I have a feeling that's a word I'm going to become intimately acquainted with during this pregnancy." Corryna took a seat in one of the leather chairs as Colin took his usual spot, sitting on the front edge of his desk.

"Have you thought about hiring more staff? You're not going to be able to spend as much time on your feet as the pregnancy progresses."

"Hannah will graduate from her program soon, so I can promote her to full-time designer, and then I guess I'll just have to hire one or two more people to work the front of the shop. I'll need to work out the financial side, of course."

"What you really need to do is raise your prices."

She'd dug her heels in on this, but he was right. "Maybe you can help me with the final calculations."

"Of course." He cleared his throat. "But first, there are a few more things we need to discuss." He rose from his perch, then scooted the other chair closer to hers and sat. "I have a question to ask you."

"Of course. Anything."

"I've been thinking a lot about what you said about my family." His voice shook, but considering the subject matter, Corryna understood why. This was a pain point for him that was a mile wide. "Especially in light of us starting our own, I think you were absolutely right. I need to let go of the past and embrace the future. Our future."

A wide grin bloomed on her face. It had been a miraculous thing to witness this transformation in Colin's thinking. "That's so wonderful. Are you going to call them?"

"We've already talked. I'd like to go to Ireland and see them. They've said yes. But I don't want to go unless you'll come with me."

Corryna was absolutely thrilled. When she'd suggested that Colin reconnect with his family, she hadn't imagined herself as part of the scenario at that time, but so much had changed. "I would love to go to Ireland with you. Love to."

"Good. We'll have to go in August. After the wedding. But the weather is lovely there that time of year."

"I can't wait to see it. To have you show me around. And to spend time with your family."

"I'm looking forward to introducing them to the mother of their first grandchild." He slid forward to the edge of the desk, then stood and reached for her hand. "And more than anything, I'm looking forward to this next happy for our little family."

"Me too, Colin. We deserve it." A tear rolled down her cheek. Things were moving fast for them, but that was how elemental things were between her and Colin. Their love was as natural as the partnership that started it.

"You've made me so happy." He smiled wide, then leaned in for a soft and sexy kiss.

She felt light-headed, but needed to say one more thing to the man she loved more than anything. "And you've done the same for me."

* * * * *

Look for the final two books in the
Texas Cattleman's Club: The Wedding series.

Oh So Wrong with Mr. Right
by Nadine Gonzalez.

and

The Man She Loves to Hate
by Jessica Lemmon.

Both available May 2023!

USA TODAY bestselling author **Joanne Rock** credits her decision to write romance to a book she picked up during a flight delay that engrossed her so thoroughly, she didn't mind at all when her flight was delayed two more times. Giving her readers the chance to escape into another world has motivated her to write over one hundred books for a variety of Harlequin series.

Books by Joanne Rock

Harlequin Desire

Texas Cattleman's Club

The Rancher's Reckoning
Make Believe Match

Kingsland Ranch

Rodeo Rebel

Return to Catamount

Rocky Mountain Rivals
One Colorado Night
A Colorado Claim

Visit the Author Profile page at
Harlequin.com for more titles.

You can also find Joanne Rock on Facebook,
along with other Harlequin Desire authors,
at Facebook.com/HarlequinDesireAuthors!

Dear Reader,

It's always a treat to return to Royal, Texas, where there is always a new romance brewing—along with a scandal or two! This year is extra special in Royal because there's a big wedding coming to town and everyone is excited to host the couple when a hometown son brings his bride to tie the knot.

Enter overworked music therapy student Jessica Lewis, who is only working the prewedding party to pay her bills, and successful CEO Oliver Price, who attends out of obligation to his friend the groom. Neither one of them is ready for a relationship, but when their worlds collide, they can't resist the sizzling attraction.

They might have been able to walk away if it hadn't been wedding season in Royal. But everyone has marriage on the brain, and soon Jessica and Oliver are faking an engagement just to keep the peace. Will they keep their pact once wedding fever is over?

Happy reading,

Joanne Rock

MAKE BELIEVE MATCH

Joanne Rock

For my wonderful reader group, the Rockettes.
Thank you for sharing my journey!

One

Most nights, Jessica Lewis genuinely enjoyed her part-time gig as a server for a catering company. Even though she worked lavish parties as staff and not as a guest, she still soaked up the festive vibe of most shindigs around her hometown of Royal, Texas. It was her way of rubbing elbows, however briefly, with the rich and glamorous. Usually, while she delivered custom-ordered drinks to women dressed in clothes that could only be found on the pages of a fashion magazine or on a Milan runway, Jessica liked to imagine herself sipping a handcrafted cocktail while watching a sunset, a silk gown rustling around her bare legs.

Call her fanciful. But who could blame a woman for making the best of busting her hump to get ahead?

Tonight was not like any other work shift, however. Not with her family's bad news weighing down her every thought since she'd spotted the bank notice on her mother's bedroom dresser earlier in the day.

"Your order's up, Jess." One of her fellow servers, a senior at a local college who'd worked these kinds of jobs for as long as she had, nudged an elbow against hers to direct her attention toward the end of the bar.

The venue this evening was an elite golfing facility that integrated a technology experience into the game, providing air-conditioned bays for driving and putting. The private luxury suite and attached covered patio had been rented by Royal's well-known Noble family for the evening. The Nobles were sparing no expense for this pre-wedding party as their clan geared up for the marriage of their son, bestselling author Xavier Noble, to Ariana Ramos, a successful actress and producer with her own lifestyle brand. Neither Xavier nor Ariana—Ex and Ari, to close friends and family—were in attendance tonight, as the soon-to-be newlyweds were based in Los Angeles, but that hadn't stopped the Noble family from hosting events all over Royal as the big day neared.

Jessica had been following the local society news with interest. She'd even looked forward to working this party to put faces with the names of people she

Get up to 4
FREE FABULOUS BOOKS
You Love!

To thank you for being a loyal reader we'd like to send you up to 4 FREE BOOKS, absolutely free when you try the Harlequin Reader Service.

Just write "YES" on the Loyal Reader Voucher and we'll send you 2 free books from each series you choose and Free Mystery Gifts, altogether worth over $20.

Try **Harlequin® Desire** and get 2 books featuring the worlds of the American elite with juicy plot twists, delicious sensuality and intriguing scandal.

Try **Harlequin Presents® Larger-Print** and get 2 books featuring the glamourous lives of royals and billionaires in a world of exotic locations, where passion knows no bounds.

Or **TRY BOTH** and get 2 books from each series!

Your free books are completely free, even the shipping! If you continue with your subscription, you can look forward to curated monthly shipments of brand-new books from your selected series, always at a discount off the cover price! Plus you can cancel any time.

So don't miss out, return your Loyal Readers Voucher today to get your Free books.

Pam Powers

LOYAL READER
FREE BOOKS VOUCHER

YES! I Love Reading, please send me up to 4 FREE BOOKS and Free Mystery Gifts from the series I select.

Just write in "YES" on the dotted line below then return this card today and we'll send your free books & gifts asap!

➡ YES ⬅

Which do you prefer?

☐ **Harlequin Desire®**
225/326 HDL GRAG

☐ **Harlequin Presents® Larger-Print**
176/376 HDL GRAG

☐ **BOTH**
225/326 & 176/376
HDL GRAS

FIRST NAME	LAST NAME

ADDRESS	

APT. #	CITY

STATE/PROV.	ZIP/POSTAL CODE

EMAIL ☐ Please check this box if you would like to receive newsletters and promotional emails from Harlequin Enterprises ULC and its affiliates. You can unsubscribe anytime.

HD/HP-622-LR_LRV22

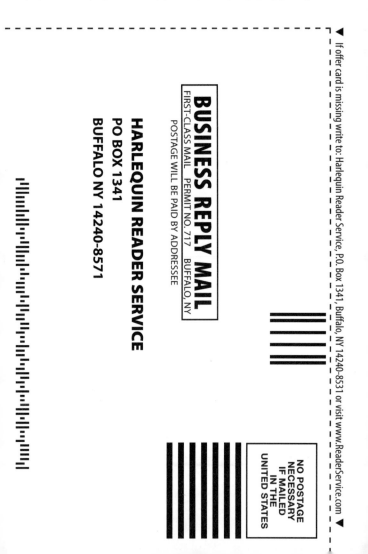

read about in the social columns. But after the blow that came from discovering the truth about her parents' finances, Jessica couldn't rouse any interest in the overprivileged crowd milling around the bar while their friends took turns with their golf clubs.

She tipped her face up toward an air-conditioning vent to help chill the sweat on her back, which had more to do with stress than the press of people all around.

"Sure thing," she murmured on autopilot to her colleague as she glanced at the tray of five drinks, trying to recall who'd ordered what. "I'll get them in a sec."

The other server, a hulking dude named Matt who could have doubled as a bouncer should the position have been required, frowned down at her. "You okay?"

She gripped an empty serving tray tighter, remembering the number of digits in the balloon payment amount of her parents' loan coming due in two months' time.

She was so far from fine it was ridiculous. Especially when she knew her folks had refinanced their home five years ago to help with her college expenses. Why hadn't they told her that they'd have to pay a criminal amount of money for that generosity during her undergraduate years? She'd been so proud of herself for working these catering jobs to afford her music therapy grad school degree on her own, but now she wished she'd been putting all of that money toward what her parents owed on their home.

How could she continue her expensive degree program when her folks were struggling financially? Her stomach cramped at the prospect of stalling everything she'd worked so hard for. But the idea of pursuing her own ends while her mom and dad lost their home was far, far more painful.

"I'm fine," she said brightly, momentarily forgetting what she was even doing as a group of men attired in expensive golf slacks and polos cheered over someone's shot. "Why do you ask?"

About half the crowd was garbed to play the game, while the other half wore suits or lightweight evening dresses. The evening was laid-back and elegant at the same time, with passed hors d'oeuvres from a top-tier chef and music from a celebrated deejay on the patio level.

Matt slid a tray of his own off the bar and lifted the well-balanced array of glassware over one burly shoulder, a white towel draped over his arm. "Because you said you'd grab those drinks the last time I told you they were ready—almost ten minutes ago."

"Crap. Thanks, Matt." Jessica edged around her coworker to get to the bar, racking her brain to remember where this set of beverages belonged. "I need to get moving."

Because losing this job now, when she needed funds more than ever, would be irresponsible in the extreme.

The sounds of crushed ice being scooped into a glass, a champagne cork popping and the swishing of a cocktail shaker mingled with light laughter and party music, which had gone from light rock to a pop-and-country mix as a few people took to a dance floor on the upper level. But Jessica tried to ignore everything else but getting her job done as she laid aside her empty tray and slid the new drink-laden one onto her carrying hand.

Where did they belong? She knew one of the beverages was something weird and herb-infused. A turmeric cordial. And, recalling that, she remembered the table she'd been remiss in serving. Pasting on her best smile, she served four of the five drinks in short order, all from the same party. None of them seemed to have noticed her tardy delivery, as they were engrossed in a lively discussion of the leaderboard for the golf competitors broadcast on a huge high-definition screen over the patio. Then, turning on her heel away from the group, she wound her way through the crowd, trying to recall who'd ordered the final beverage.

A lone glass of champagne.

Peering back and forth around the patrons congregating anywhere near her designated serving station, Jessica headed for the stairs to return to the bar on the lower level.

And slammed directly into a wall.

"Oof." The inelegant sound huffed from her as the air left her chest.

Her hand swiped fast through the air to try and right her tray, but it was too late for the champagne glass already tumbling down…then landing awkwardly in a stranger's hand.

Because of course the wall she'd run into was a party guest.

A very male, very solid party guest. In a black silk suit that surely cost more than her car.

And, just her luck today, his extremely costly-looking suit now wore the whole glass of spilled champagne. Panicking at her gaffe, she took in the rest of him now. From his light brown hair brushed off his forehead to his green eyes and stubbled jaw, he was handsome everywhere she looked. Striking, even, with a look of mischief in his eyes and a wry smile playing about his lips as he assessed the damage.

And, possibly, her breasts.

But then, she was still plastered to him.

"I'm so sorry," she blurted, backing up fast as her face flamed hot. The eyes of the whole party—the upstairs half of the crowd, at least—were still on them. "I've got some napkins."

Setting her tray aside on the floor against the brass railing that went around the patio deck, Jessica straightened again and reached into the pocket of her black apron to withdraw a wad of paper cocktail napkins. The rest of the partygoers seemed to resume their activities, the attention fading from their head-on crash.

"No need, miss." A smooth-as-butter baritone—maybe even a bass baritone—answered her, stopping her short as her hand hovered near his chest. "I can manage."

That timbre.

The musician in her swooned a little at the plush, velvety sound of him, the weight of his voice anchoring the fluttery panic she'd been feeling about running into a guest.

"No. Let me help," she insisted, needing to render aid when the collision had been all her fault. She'd been distracted ever since she'd arrived onsite. "Quick attention to a stain could be the difference between salvaging a garment or not."

"In that case, I'd better act promptly." Impossibly, he smiled at her as he set aside the now-empty champagne glass on a table recently vacated nearby. Then he withdrew a handkerchief from his pocket like a hero in a Regency novel.

Who carried handkerchiefs anymore?

This extremely handsome man with a bass-baritone voice that turned her inside out, apparently.

"That's actually a much better idea," she agreed, stuffing the cocktail napkins back into her apron before she took the white cotton handkerchief from him to better mop up the worst of the spill. "This won't dissolve into bits when it gets wet."

Wrapping the fabric around his lapel, she pressed the suit material gently with the cotton, her knuckles brushing the warmth of his chest beneath his gray button-down.

All the while, her words seemed to circle in the air between them, "getting wet" taking on new and interesting meanings. Making her self-conscious about touching him. Making her skin turn even hotter.

She stilled, feeling awkward all of a sudden.

Perhaps he sensed her sudden embarrassment, because he eased the cloth from her hands. "We wouldn't want to dissolve into bits prematurely."

Stepping back, she folded her arms, aware that her body was reacting in all kinds of ways to this man, and not just because of his sex-on-a-stick voice.

"Are you laughing at me?" She couldn't read his expression, that wry smile still teasing his mouth now and then.

"Not at all." He mopped at the fabric twice more and then pocketed the handkerchief, looking none the worse for wear. "Just smiling at the irony that the most entertaining part of my evening involved someone who is probably far too busy to accept an apology drink from me."

His gaze took in her server's uniform—a white shirt with a dorky black bow tie and a black skirt. Awareness made her skin tingle everywhere his gaze touched.

"You? Apologize?" She wondered if he really thought he was to blame or if he was just being polite. And what was this business about him finding their encounter "entertaining"? She couldn't help but be intrigued. "It's me who should be buying you the drink after I practically body-slammed you."

"Is that what happened?" One light brown eyebrow lifted as he rocked back on his heels. "In that case, I guess I'm fortunate I'm still standing."

He rubbed a hand along the front of his broad chest, presumably where she'd run into him. Did his body remember the feel of hers as keenly as hers recalled the shape and size of him?

They stood there for a beat too long. Smiling. Sharing something unexpected and unspoken.

A shout from the downstairs bartender—a call for more of a top-shelf vodka—shook her out of the preoccupation.

"I'd better go." Bending, she retrieved her tray and tucked it under her arm. "Sorry again, Mr...."

"Oliver Price. Just Oliver to you, Ms...."

"Jessica Lewis." She sounded breathless, but there was no help for it. Maybe he'd write it off as her having a busy shift. "Just Jessica to you, Oliver. And I finish up in less than two hours. I'll make good on that drink if you're still here."

Surprise jolted through her as the words tumbled out before she could think them through. Even more surprising? She had no wish to withdraw the offer even though she didn't have time for a relationship right now. She'd like to think her suggestion for a drink had been made strictly out of a desire to apologize, but she didn't think that was all there was to it. Her life was jam-packed between work and school, and she missed the company of a man. What would it hurt to indulge in just this one drink?

With a quick nod, she darted down the stairs before he could answer. She didn't want to know if he'd find an excuse to let her down easy. She simply wanted to make the offer because it was the right thing to do to apologize for spilling champagne all over someone.

Not because Oliver Price had a melted-chocolate bass baritone she could have listened to all night long. The fact that all her feminine senses were dancing didn't have a damned thing to do with it.

Besides, the possibility of a nightcap with a hot stranger at least helped her think about something besides the doomsday news in that bank notice on her mom's dresser. Although nothing would make her forget about what she needed to do tomorrow.

Because instead of paying her next semester's tuition for grad school, Jessica would be diverting every cent she had to help her parents save the family home. Her dream of her degree—and the music therapy certification that came with it—would have to wait.

Oliver Price followed the woman with his eyes all evening long.

Elbows resting on the rail of the patio overlooking an outdoor bar and firepit, he shook the last ice cubes in a glass that had been a Scotch on the rocks half an hour ago. He easily spotted Jessica Lewis in the crowd below as she sidled around a lighted fountain in the courtyard to deliver drinks to guests with a smile, her hips swaying subtly in a fitted black skirt. And damned if he couldn't pull his eyes away from her legs as she leaned forward to rest a brightly colored drink in front of a young woman seated with a rancher Oliver recognized from the Texas Cattleman's Club.

Jessica shared a laugh with the couple for a moment, her smile wide as she whisked away empty glasses and laid fresh napkins beneath the new beverages. With her thick dark hair pulled into a ponytail that bounced on one shoulder, Oliver could see her profile clearly, her expression kind and interested as she spoke with the couple. And even though there were at least twenty people he knew whom he hadn't spoken to yet at this party, he couldn't tear himself away from watching her. The band still played on the lower level, a fizzy pop song attracting a crowd on the small outdoor dance floor. The scent of toasted marshmallows drifted up from the s'mores station below, a handful of fire tables lit so that guests could roast their own dessert concoctions from the comfort of patio furniture.

But none of that distracted him from watching Jessica. Even when he'd been engaged in party small talk with friends earlier in the evening, he found his attention veering back to the curvy waitress with eyes that shifted between blue and green, the color of a summer sea.

Just thinking of a set of irises that way—a summer freaking sea?—told him how unwise his reactions seemed when it came to the sexy server. Getting worked up and distracted over someone had never been his style. As CEO of Nexus, a global marketing firm he'd established with partner Nikolai Williams, Oliver preferred brief, functional liaisons that allowed him to concentrate on his work first and foremost. He traveled between international offices frequently, and he wasn't in any position for a serious relationship. Normally, he sought companionship from like-minded ladies who were in similar positions—career focused and solely interested in an occasional good time.

So to have his head turned so thoroughly by any woman was more than just out of character—it was also a bad idea. Because he'd felt her rapid heartbeat when her body had been pressed to his. Seen her cheeks pinken with awareness. And nothing about the way she'd reacted to him suggested she shared his views about purely recreational, no-strings sex.

No. His gut told him Jessica was the sort of woman who waited to indulge herself until after the third date. Or quite possibly until the chemistry was too irresistible to ignore. And since when did that pique his curiosity so much? Or make him want to be the one to remind her how compelling a sizzling-hot attraction could be?

Cursing himself for thoughts he had no business thinking, he pivoted away from the railing, telling himself he ought to leave the party. He'd remained longer than he'd planned, not just because he wanted to support the Noble family since he was good friends with Tripp Noble—the best man for Ex and Ari's wedding—but also because he'd been seriously considering that drink with Jessica.

But it was a bad idea.

Setting his empty glass aside on a nearby catering tray, he headed to the stairs and descended to the lower level. He lifted his wrist to check the vintage Heuer Monza timepiece he wore. It'd been over an hour and a half since he'd run into Jessica, and she'd said she'd be done with her shift in less than two hours. He had a flight to the New York office early tomorrow, so he should thank his hosts now and call it a night.

Ten minutes later, he'd thanked Xavier Noble's parents for the evening and was on his way out of the venue. He gave the fountain and courtyard a wide berth, remembering that Jessica had served a couple of the tables downstairs as well as a small section on the upper level.

Now that he'd made up his mind to do the right thing and put her out of his head, he was determined to see it through. Right until he got waylaid by a whippet-thin blonde who stepped into his path in a swirly pale purple silk.

"If it isn't Oliver Price." Anabeth Ackerman pivoted on a pair of sky-high lavender-colored heels to face him, the floor-length ribbons of a huge shoulder bow on her short cocktail dress fluttering against her skin as she came to a halt.

His gut plummeted at the sight of her. Anabeth worked for a competing marketing company out of Dallas, so he hoped he wouldn't see her tonight even though she knew the Nobles. They'd had a brief relationship a year ago, but she'd been an anomaly in his dating history—a woman who'd signed on for a good time at first, but after a couple of dates, she'd done a one-eighty, suggesting they take things to the "next level." She hadn't been pleased when he'd declined, and he had the impression that men didn't say no to her often. Maybe never.

She'd ratcheted up the pressure on him by posting photo after photo of them together on social media, giving the world the impression they were a couple even after they weren't. Oliver's mother—hell, his whole family—had clocked it all, believing Oliver was finally ready to settle down. His mom in particular had been hurt to learn the truth.

"Hello, Anabeth." He forced his features into an expression of polite acknowledgment before giving a nod toward the exit. "I was just on my way out."

Her pale eyebrows lifted briefly in unison; then her fuchsia-painted mouth swelled into a pout.

"You can't possibly leave now, Oliver." She clamped a claiming hand on the arm of his jacket, her floral scent making his nostrils twitch. "I've just arrived."

Her elaborately painted nails decorated with sparkly gems hooked into him like claws, her platinum blond curls ducking toward him as if to impart a secret. Or plant a kiss on his cheek?

In the split second that he contemplated the unwelcome possibility, he spied Jessica Lewis. She was just shrugging into a faded jean jacket as she headed toward the exit he'd been trying to reach, her dark ponytail bobbing behind her like a lifeline he couldn't quite grab.

"Jessica, wait," he called to her now, not thinking through the ramifications so much as acting on the only potential out he could see for himself from the nightmare conversation that would be sure to come otherwise with Anabeth. Besides, he wasn't sure if he could speak to the woman without letting some of his anger at her antics show through.

Pausing in the middle of sliding an arm into one sleeve of her jacket, Jessica's sea-colored eyes darted between him and his companion. "Yes?" she asked tentatively.

Beside him, Anabeth's talons retracted a fraction.

Seizing the chance for freedom, Oliver withdrew his arm from her grasp as he held up a finger indicating for Jessica to give him a moment. He then turned back to the woman next to him. "Please excuse me, Anabeth. I don't want to keep my date waiting."

"Her?" Anabeth asked in a tone he didn't appreciate one bit when directed toward Jessica.

But he couldn't spare a moment to defend the server if he wanted to reach Jessica in time to thank her. Already, she was punching her fist the rest of the way through her jacket sleeve and marching away from him.

Oliver quickened his stride into the corridor leading to the parking area in front of the building, the night breeze stronger on this side of the structure. Ahead of him, Jessica's ponytail flapped against her neck, and he could see a few stray pieces wrapping around her cheek as he caught up with her.

"Seriously?" she asked him as he matched his step to hers.

The lights were brighter out front, old-fashioned streetlamps lining the sidewalk as valets ran to fetch vehicles for other guests beginning to depart. Oliver had already messaged his car service, so he knew his ride would be at the north end of the walkway, out of the congestion.

For now, however, he simply followed where she went in order to accompany her.

"What?" he asked, unsure what she meant. "I hope you don't mind that I flagged you down. I thought I'd walk you out."

Up close to her again, he noticed things he hadn't catalogued about her before. A smattering of pale freckles over her nose. The tiny silver earrings she wore in the shape of musical notes. Well, technically one was a G clef. He thought the other might be an eighth note, but it had been a long time since he'd read any music.

She stopped near one of the streetlamps to step

in front of him and fold her arms. A hint of challenge in her eyes, though a smile quirked the corner of her full lips.

"You wanted to walk me out?" she repeated playfully. "Or you needed any excuse to spring you free from the blonde ready to wrap around you like a boa constrictor?"

He threw his head back and laughed.

"I rest my case, Mr. Oliver Price." Her gaze fell to his lapel, the mischief fading from her voice as she plucked a windblown strand of dark hair from her cheek. "Sorry again for my clumsiness earlier. I really would have bought you that apology drink, but I noticed you winding down your evening a while ago."

In the parking area nearby, a departing Ferrari honked its horn at an antique Cadillac backing out of a space. The sounds of valets shouting to one another and waiting guests talking and laughing seemed far away from their end of the lot.

Recalling the way he'd attempted to leave early to avoid the temptation of the very woman beside him now, he couldn't help but feel that more time with her was inevitable. As if the night had conspired to put them together again.

"No further apology necessary," he assured her, remembering how many times his gaze had sought her out tonight. How he hadn't been able to look away. "But what do you say we get that drink anyhow? Just for fun?"

For a long moment, the look she gave him was inscrutable. Her eyes tracked his, as if searching for some answer there that he hadn't offered her in words. But finally, with one delectable nibble at her lower lip, she nodded.

"I'd like that, Oliver. Very much."

Two

Ten minutes later, seated inside the lobby bar of a luxury hotel across the street from the golfing facility, Jessica took a sip of the cabernet she'd ordered. Busied her hands to keep from touching the compelling man seated close to her.

"You've always lived in Royal?" Oliver asked her over the rim of his Scotch before he tested the amber liquid.

There weren't many patrons at this hour, and they'd taken a corner table in the back. They'd passed a piano on the way to their seats—an upright Kawai in the center of the establishment—though no one currently played the instrument. The chrome-and-concrete bar was minimalist and modern; the tables surrounding it were washed-out shades of pale gray, with white hydrangeas in crystal vases. Pink candles glowed warm on the tabletops, the only hints of color in the monochrome scheme. Their round booth allowed for privacy while also seating her close to the handsome man beside her.

A tingle shot through her, more from the proximity than from the full-bodied wine.

"No. My folks moved here from a ranch in El Paso in the hope of more secure work for my dad. He and my mom are both on staff at the Triple C." A way of life they fully embraced. Her parents had always been supportive of her need for an education and a world outside the ranch, but they'd also never pushed her in that direction. "They really enjoy caring for the land and living simply."

When her father returned home from his day driving cattle or tending horses, he shared stories about the animals or the men he worked with, and his contentment with his way of life fairly radiated from him. No matter what the bank statement said, her dad felt rich in the ways that counted. She admired his grounded values.

"What about you? Is that something you enjoy too?" He leaned forward slightly, the open collar of his gray button-down gaping in a way that made her attention flick briefly to his chest.

For a moment, she imagined herself touching him there, her palms running along the hard wall of muscle. What was it about him that attracted her so thoroughly? She'd never experienced this kind of pull with anyone before. On the plus side, thinking about how much she wanted Oliver was a welcome distraction from the financial disaster back home.

"I don't dislike it," she answered carefully, mindful of how she spoke about the lifestyle her family adored. "But music is my real calling."

"Now the notes makes sense." His gaze drifted to the side of her face as he reached one finger to trace the outside of her ear.

The touch was light. Barely there. And yet a shiver rolled through her so hard she thought he must surely see it.

"Notes?" She blinked through the heat of her reaction to him, trying to make sense of his words.

"Your earrings." His smile was warm and inviting. "I noticed them earlier."

Her heart pounded harder. Between the immediate draw she'd felt toward him and the easy rapport developing as they spoke, she feared she could get swept away if she wasn't careful. Fantasizing about it was one thing. Acting on it? Well, as much as this man tempted her, she needed to proceed with caution. She wasn't in the market for a relationship while she faced so much uncertainty.

The reminder that she needed to withdraw from next semester's classes was sobering, despite the cabernet she'd somehow already finished.

"I am pursuing a graduate degree in music therapy," she explained as she slid aside the empty glass.

Already, Oliver was signaling their server for another round. "Or at least, I will be pursuing it again soon."

Her schedule had kept her too busy to date even casually lately.

His brow furrowed as he studied her. "Are you taking a break from your studies?"

The interest in his eyes didn't seem faked. And in another moment, she found herself explaining the whole thing to him, the stress of the day unleashing into a torrent of words. The way her parents had helped her with her tuition as an undergraduate. How proud she'd felt to wait to further her degree until she could do it completely on her own. Then, the discovery of the balloon payment on their mortgage coming due and her need to contribute so they wouldn't lose their house.

When she finished the tale, she was surprised to have shared something so personal with a man she'd only just met. But the discovery of her parents' finances had been troubling her for hours, simmering just beneath the surface. Now it had just spilled out of her.

"You're not going to return to your program in the fall?" he asked, swiping at condensation on the water glass their server had brought along with the next round of drinks. "Even though music is your calling?"

She smiled sadly, the truth of what she had to do clear to her now that she'd had more time to think about it.

"Music will be there for me down the road. After I've helped my family." Maybe if she kept telling herself that, stepping away from her program would hurt less as time went on.

For a long moment, he seemed to weigh the words as he studied her. "That's very selfless, Jessica." He clinked his tumbler lightly against the rim of her wineglass in a toast. "Not everyone is willing to make sacrifices for the people they love."

The way he spoke—with a dark undertone to the words—made her wonder about the relationships of his past.

But no matter that she'd just confided something personal with him, she knew they weren't at the point in a relationship where she could ask him about past girlfriends. Instead, she shifted the conversation back toward him in another way.

"I bet you'd do the same for your family if they were struggling," she observed, even though she didn't know any such thing. But she'd talked more than her fair share of the evening, and it was Oliver's turn to speak. "Are you close with them?"

"Very." Leaning back in the booth, he extended his arm along the back of the gray leather bolster, which meant that it rested close to her back and shoulders. "We still do Sunday dinners with the extended clan most weekends. Considering all four of my siblings are married with kids, that means a huge crowd at multiple tables."

"You're Uncle Oliver, then." She tried to envision

this well-dressed man in his expensive clothes having a bunch of kids crawling on his lap and touching him with their sticky fingers.

The image tugged at her, making her ovaries stir to life even though she wasn't ready for anything like the vision that filled her brain.

She attempted to drown the images and her reaction with more wine, finishing her drink while a musician sat down in front of the piano and launched into a jazz tune. She nodded in appreciation of the music, even as she recognized that drowning her attraction wasn't a possibility. Then again, maybe the only reason she was having this fierce reaction to Oliver Price had to do with the alcohol. She hadn't eaten anything in hours, so the cabernet had gone straight to her head.

Resolutely, she slid her empty glass away from her, reminding herself she was a lightweight drinker.

"I am an uncle five times over." There was pride in his voice when he said it, something that only increased the fever in her womanly parts. "And I would do anything for my family too." His lips flattened into a thin line before he spoke again. "Except get married and settle down just like the rest of them."

She couldn't help the laugh that burst free at his admission. Perhaps because she could relate. She hadn't come close to achieving the things she wanted to before she got close to anyone.

"Are your nieces and nephews that terrifying?" she teased to keep the conversation light.

"Not at all. Even though the oldest niece attempted to drive my Jag last weekend and scared ten years off my life when she ran into the garage. Thankfully, she wasn't hurt."

"Thank goodness," she agreed as the pianist transitioned smoothly into "Take the A Train." Her fingers bounced along in time, playing phantom keys beneath the table, reminding her how much she was going to miss her music therapy program. She'd already researched a new internship for the fall where she could work at a local hospice facility, using her music to ease patients' final hours.

A place where she would have been making a real difference with her skills. She also could have shown her parents the concrete way her expensive degree had the power to do good things in the world.

Oliver spoke about his family a bit more; then she asked him about his work. She wasn't at all surprised to learn he was an entrepreneur—the owner of a marketing firm with offices around the world. Their lives were completely different.

And yet...

She couldn't remember a man ever having this effect on her before. So much so that she couldn't help wondering what if.

"Jessica?" The deep tone of Oliver's bass-baritone voice spoken close to her ear dragged her from her thoughts, making her realize she'd been lost in thought too long.

Now his voice acted like a knuckle grazing its

way up her spine, sending a shiver of pleasure
through her.

"I'm sorry. Just a little lost in thought for a minute." Shaking her head, she steadied herself with one
hand on the gray tabletop.

She wished she could blame the tingly feelings
on the wine, but his voice so close to her ear served
as a potent reminder that Oliver Price had a powerful effect on her at a time she deeply wished to push
aside a world of disappointments and worries. Now
his gaze dipped to her mouth and lingered there.

Her heart rate triple-timed.

"I should take you home," he said abruptly, raking his gaze upward once more before taking out his
phone and tapping the screen. "I didn't mean to keep
you so late, but I can have my driver meet us now. I
can give you a lift."

Was it late? She'd lost all track of time, cocooned
in the back booth with him, the warmth of his body
and his companionship making her crave the things
she rarely missed in her life.

The touch of a man. Sex.

Her mouth went dust dry as that truth rolled
through her. Her body hungered for more than just
a conversation tonight. And that jitteriness she was
feeling?

It stemmed from a long dry spell. She hadn't been
physical with anyone since her last serious relationship almost eighteen months ago. She'd quit dating
altogether after that, tired of meeting people who

were all wrong for her, who didn't seem interested in anything more than a hookup or who secretly remained on dating apps for months into a quasi-relationship. She'd told herself she didn't need a man in her life. And she'd been okay with that...

Until tonight. When her skin was tingling every time this man looked at her.

"I don't mind," she answered belatedly, her words slow even though her thoughts were sprinting forward now. "That is, it's been fun talking with you. But I'm ready to leave whenever you are."

In the bar area, the pianist slid into a bluesy rendition of "Moon River," adding a sultry backdrop to their conversation. But most of the tables were empty now save for a handful of hardcore fans finishing drinks near the musician. It had to be near closing time.

"We don't need to say good-night quite yet." Oliver slid one hand over hers where it rested on the table. His thumb stroked along her knuckles with slow deliberation. "I'm enjoying getting to know you."

Her heart hammered her rib cage so loudly she thought he might hear. Or see. The thumping felt that strong.

Was he propositioning her?

Would she even recognize a proposition from a man anymore?

"What are you suggesting?" she asked, reminding herself that one of the privileges of turning thirty had been recognizing that she could demand more for herself. Including, in this case, clear answers from sexy, enigmatic men.

"I haven't the slightest idea." He shook his head as if to clear it, a wry smile tugging one side of his lips. "Which either means you've gone straight to my head, Jessica, or I shouldn't have had that last drink. Probably a little of both. But I'm at least enough of a gentleman to have a safe ride home for you. My driver is out front."

"Thank you," she murmured as he let go of her hand to slide out of the booth. Her car was parked across the street, but she knew better than to drive home after drinking.

He reached out to help her from the opposite side of the curved bench seat.

Moments later, they stood outside in the Texas spring air, which had cooled a few degrees since they'd entered the hotel bar.

Jessica breathed deeply to help clear her thoughts and slow her pulse still beating erratically with Oliver's hand wrapped around hers. A black SUV pulled up to the curb, and a liveried driver jumped out of the driver's seat to open the back door for her.

"I'll settle her inside, Jason," her date told the driver, an older man with broad shoulders and a military bearing. "We'll need another minute."

"Sure thing, boss," the driver answered him while giving Jessica a friendly nod. Then he disappeared again on the other side of the SUV.

"Aren't you riding with me?" she asked, unsure why they hadn't already entered the vehicle.

The breeze ruffled her hair, making her aware of how many pieces had wriggled free of the ponytail she'd worn for work. Absently, she smoothed the strands behind one ear as she turned to face Oliver.

"I'd be glad to accompany you if you like, but I did book a room here tonight since this is closer to the airport and I have an early flight tomorrow." Resting his palm on the corner of the door, his body shielded her from another gust of wind that fluttered the leaves of an ash tree near the hotel entrance. "It's your choice what happens next."

The SUV engine rumbled quietly in the background while she stared up into Oliver's green eyes. The scent of his aftershave—cedar and sandalwood—teased her nostrils, making her want to lean into him and breathe deeply.

Saying good-night now meant she'd probably never see him again. Their lives wouldn't have any natural intersections, with him being a globe-hopping CEO and her being... What? A full-time waitress, now that she needed to help her parents with their finances?

The thought of the months ahead, working day and night without the bright incentive of her classes to engage her brain, weighed on her. Urging her to take one more moment of pleasure for herself before ending the evening.

"In that case," Jessica began, stepping nearer to him before she lowered her voice, "I choose this."

Trailing her fingertips along his stubbled jaw, she watched as his green eyes darkened, his focus narrowing to her while she closed the space between them. The reality of what she was about to do hit her in the solar plexus, robbing her of breath as she stood suspended in the moment full of possibilities and hunger.

Then, unwilling to back down from what she wanted, she arched up onto her toes and brushed her mouth over his, the way she'd been dreaming about for hours.

Oliver held himself still under the sweet slide of Jessica's lips only by exercising every ounce of his willpower.

More than anything, he wanted to wrap her in his arms and drag her body against his, feel every inch of her luscious curves for himself. He longed to have his hands all over, her hips pressed to the hard ache that had plagued him ever since she'd sat close to him in that damned restaurant booth. The light honeysuckle scent of her skin teased his nostrils, the berry flavor of wine sliding over his mouth as she kissed him.

His blood surged hot, need racing through him. And yet he remained still, knowing full well if he put his hands on her now, he would be tempted to lay her down on the SUV seat and cover her body with his while he peeled off all her clothes.

"Jessica." He managed the word with effort, the rasp in his voice surely revealing how much her kiss affected him. He took both her hands in his, wary of letting her fingers wander over his body when he was already hanging on by a thread. "If that's a good-bye kiss, I'm grateful for it, but I don't think I can return it without wanting more." He licked his dry lips, groaning inwardly at the way her gaze tracked the movement. "If, on the other hand, that kiss was the start of something more..."

He didn't trust himself to put into words all that it could mean. This woman was already a fire in his blood.

They stood so close her sharp inhale made her breasts graze his chest. The soft warmth of her curves damn near undid him.

"Is that an invitation?" Her head tipped to one side as she seemed to consider it.

A blatant flirtation that turned the fire to an inferno.

"Hell yes, it is." He feared his grip on her was manacle-like. But she was the one with all the power here, deciding his fate with one feminine tilt of her face. Still, he eased his hold on her, deliberately letting her go so that the only thing persuading her were his words and the invisible chemistry pulling them together. "Come upstairs with me. We can follow that kiss wherever it leads."

Behind her, the SUV waited with the partition up, so the driver heard nothing of their conversation. The scent of leather and lemon polish emanated from the vehicle while Jessica rubbed her hands over her arms like she'd just had a chill. They were alone out in front of the hotel except for a valet at his station fifty feet away.

Across the street, the golf-facility parking lot was still full, the stadium lights visible behind the building, along with the tall nets that prevented balls from flying off the property.

And Oliver allowed his gaze to take it all in, needing to focus on anything besides the sweetly sexy woman in front of him, her kissable lips parted and slightly wine-stained.

"Yes," she said finally, her jaw flexing with firm certainty. "Crazy as it sounds, I think I ran into you at the party for a reason." After dragging in a deep breath, she continued in a rush of words, "I never do things like this, but today hasn't been just any day. And I'm okay with turning my life in a brand-new direction tomorrow, but tonight, I'd like to…have a moment for me."

The idea of her turning to him for that kind of experience humbled him even as the ache for her tightened painfully. Then everything in him pushed him to execute her wish as fast as possible. Because the sooner he had her upstairs in his room, the more time he could devote to finding out what made her sigh and what made her scream with pleasure.

"I promise you'll have more than a moment," he vowed, taking her hand as he tugged her away from the SUV. Then he rapped on the passenger window to alert Jason that he needed to speak to him. Once the glass rolled partway down, Oliver dismissed the driver before returning his attention to Jessica. "This way."

He guided her through the main doors and into the hotel, bypassing the lobby bar that had emptied out even more since they'd left. He led her away from the central elevators, however, recalling he could reach his villa suite via a more private elevator on the western side of the luxury-hotel property. He hadn't been sure he'd need much space tonight since he wouldn't be staying long, but now he was grateful he'd requested the larger suite with a wraparound terrace, fireplace and generous-size living area. Jessica would be comfortable there after he left tomorrow morning.

But he didn't want to think about that now. Not when they had the night together still ahead of them.

A moment later, they were alone inside the elevator cabin, the piped-in classical music the only sound besides their breathing as they rode up ten floors to the penthouse level. He didn't touch her except where he still held her hand, knowing that once he started, it wouldn't be easy to stop. Instead, he cataloged the things he wanted to do as soon as they were behind closed doors.

Tug the tie from her hair to watch the dark strands

spill over her shoulders. Unfasten each button on the white shirt of her uniform, then taste every inch of skin he bared. But first, before anything else, he was going to return the tentative kiss she'd given him outside.

"You've gone quiet on me," she observed as the elevator chimed at their destination floor. "I hope you're not having second thoughts."

He hated that he'd given her any reason to question how much he wanted her.

"Quite the opposite." Pulling his room card from his jacket pocket, he led her toward the suite at the end of the corridor. "I've been working overtime to rein myself in and make sure you feel completely comfortable being here with me."

Her slow smile sent his pulse hammering harder— all the encouragement he needed to move faster.

At the end of the hallway, he scanned the key card and turned the handle to the suite, then held the door open for her to enter first. He'd left the lights in the living area on, and there were fresh yellow tulips on the dining table. More white tulips on a stand near the fireplace. The ivory-colored curtains to the terrace had been drawn, so the lights of the street below weren't visible. His laptop sat open on the contemporary walnut desk, the gray leather chair at an angle as if he'd left his work in a hurry.

She toyed with the end of her ponytail. "I texted my girlfriend while you were messaging the driver. I let her know where I am and who I'm with tonight, so I've taken the usual precautions. If I didn't feel comfortable with you, I wouldn't be here."

Tipping her chin at him, she stepped over the threshold and into the suite. Her black skirt hugged her hips, the fabric swishing softly against her skin as she moved. A sound he wouldn't have heard anywhere else tonight, but the suite was utterly quiet now that it was just the two of them. Alone.

Following her inside, Oliver allowed the door to close and lock behind them, the heavy thud and click almost as erotic as a woman's sigh, given what it meant.

"Excellent." He flipped the key card onto the desk before he shrugged off his jacket and laid it over the back of the chair. Then he headed toward his guest, who trailed a fingertip along a yellow tulip petal, tipped the flower toward her nose and leaned in to catch the fragrance. "Now that I've earned enough of your trust to have you here, I hope I can make you feel a lot better than just comfortable."

He waited while she straightened. Met his gaze.

He could see the moment when her pulse jumped in the pale skin of her neck. Feel the huff of her exhale as she gave a soft sigh. Smell the faintest hint of honeysuckle as he hovered closer to her.

"Yes, please," she whispered up at him since they were close enough to hear each other's breathing. "That's exactly what I'd like."

He reached out to tuck a finger into her hair tie, sliding it from the thick brown waves before he speared his hand into the silky mass, tilting her head just where he wanted her. With his other arm, he anchored her to him, pressing her softness against all the aching parts of him.

For a moment, he had an impression of those blue-green eyes again, blinking at him as he descended toward her. Then, losing himself in the heat burning him up inside and out, he dove in.

Three

Jessica knew two seconds into the kiss that she'd seriously underestimated her attraction to Oliver Price.

It was more than just potent.

The energy vibrating between them was red-hot and ready to combust.

Somehow she'd ended up backed against an oak bookcase in the luxury-hotel suite. Tulips scented the air, but this close to Oliver, she caught the hints of sandalwood from his aftershave. His lips moved over hers, claiming, exploring, possessing. Her knees went liquid, and she clutched at his shoulders to keep herself anchored to him.

I've been working overtime to rein myself in and make sure you feel completely comfortable...

His earlier words rang in her ears now, clarifying exactly what he meant. Because there was nothing *comfortable* about the searing heat racing through her now. His tongue in her mouth, stroking hers, made her skin feel too tight, like she'd burst right out of it if she couldn't get naked with him soon.

A moment later, he broke the kiss and they both pulled back for a shuddering breath. Taking each other's measure.

"You'd tell me if this is too much." He searched her eyes for the answer before she spoke.

"I would. But that's not what I'm saying." She had already decided this was a night unlike any other. That she could indulge herself with this man she'd never see again.

"No?"

Unclenching her fingers where she'd been fisting his shirt, she smoothed her way down the fabric to flick open a button. "No. I'm telling you there's no need to hold back now."

The hungry growl that rolled up his throat sent a thrill through her.

He lifted her in his arms and backed her toward the suite's lone bedroom. The air felt cooler against her overheated skin, a wrought iron ceiling fan spinning lazily above the white matelassé-covered king-size bed that dominated the space.

Then, returning her to her feet, he reached for the buttons on her work shirt. She mirrored his actions, unfastening the closures down the front placket that kept his body hidden from her.

She would have beaten him in the race to undress each other, except that he paused after each button to kiss what he'd unveiled. When he reached the V between her breasts and licked the sensitive flesh there, she forgot everything but the feel of his tongue.

Her fingers tunneled into his hair, holding him there while he laid her back on the mattress, his body following hers down. His hips such a welcome weight between hers that she groaned at the contact.

"How can you feel so perfect?" His question didn't seem to require an answer as he licked a path along the edge of her white lace bra, his fingers returning to work on the remaining buttons of her shirt.

"It's going to feel even better when we get these clothes off," she promised him, rocking her hips against the hard length of his erection and wishing she could wriggle her way out of the skirt.

For now, the material trapped her while he teased her nipple through the lace of her bra, sucking on the pebbled peak. She felt the echo of that kiss between her thighs and whimpered with the ache growing unbearable.

But just as he finished with her shirt buttons, he palmed her bare stomach in a way that allowed him to slide his hand beneath her skirt. Into her panties. Right where she needed him.

Oh, sweet relief.

She bucked against his hand, seeking more pressure, and he kissed his way up her chest to her collarbone. Lingering in the tender hollow below her ear while his fingers found the rhythm she liked between her thighs.

"Oliver." Rolling her head to the side, she gave him more access, her eyes fluttering closed while the tension built.

Waiting. Needing.

Then, sliding his finger inside her, he crooked it in a way that made everything stand still for a moment. Lights flashed behind her eyelids. Sensation swamped her. Squeezing. Releasing.

The orgasm rocked through her from head to toe, making her whole body undulate in a wave of fulfillment.

Moments later, as she floated back to awareness, his breath rasped harshly against her ear. Reminding her that he still balanced on the knife's edge between hunger and fulfillment. And that he deserved the same pleasure he'd just given her.

All without taking her skirt off.

"Your turn," she warned him, pushing lightly at his strong shoulders, warm beneath his shirt. "I need to touch more of you."

He rolled to his side, taking her with him so they faced one another on the bed, their legs still dangling off the edge of the mattress.

"I was thinking exactly the same thing about you." He withdrew his hand from her underwear, shifting to lower the zipper on her black work skirt. "I need more."

She swallowed hard, ignoring the fluttery feelings returning in her belly already. Even though she'd just found relief moments ago. Taking a deep breath, she redoubled her focus on him so she could finish unbuttoning his shirt. Then she shoved it off his shoulders, baring his chest to her avid gaze.

In a word? *Yum.*

His body was all ridges and rippling muscle, golden skin and hard everything. She ran her hand down the center line from his throat to the button of his fly, her mouth watering for a taste of him.

"You'd better not look at me that way for too long, Jessica. Not when I want you this badly." He unfastened her bra at the clasp between her breasts, the backs of his knuckles grazing her curves in a way that gave her goose bumps.

"I can't help it." She unfastened his pants, blood whooshing in her ears, making it the only thing she could hear for a moment. And then two. "I need to look at you so I can see where I'm going."

He stopped her then, holding the wrist of her free hand.

"I'm going to like whatever happens next," he assured her quietly, his voice serious as it brushed over her senses and gave her shivers. "I just want you."

The kindness of the sentiment tugged at her.

An indication this man wouldn't be so easy to forget after she walked away? Ruthlessly, she shoved that thought aside as she stood so she could wriggle out of the last of her clothes. Oliver did the same, withdrawing a condom packet from somewhere before his pants landed on a nearby chair.

She took the prophylactic from him, tearing open the package with her teeth while he watched her from his seat on the bed. A shiver stole over her, more from the thought of what was about to happen than the ceiling fan stirring the air. Her hair fluttered from the breeze of it, the silky strands teasing along her shoulders.

This was happening.

After a lifetime of playing it safe, she was about to straddle the hottest man she'd ever seen and welcome him into her body even though she'd just met him hours before. For reasons she refused to think about. Reasons she wouldn't allow to spoil this.

"Are you sure, Jessica?" he asked her now, his green eyes somehow divining her thoughts as he took her hand in his and pulled her between his thighs.

In answer, she rolled the condom into place before lowering herself to straddle him.

"Positive," she whispered as her bare breasts met the warmth of his chest. "I need this. Need you."

His breathing went shallow as she guided him inside her, seating herself fully on him. But then her focus fractured, the feel of him stretching her, filling her, too intense to allow for thoughts about anything else.

He took over then, his hands cupping her ass to

lift her and lower her, working his way deeper inside her. Giving no quarter. Not that she wanted any. She held on tight to him, fingernails digging, her teeth clenching on a moan. The need to cry out his name.

Because oh, did it feel so amazing.

She locked her heels around his waist, keeping him where she wanted him. He only paused the stroking rhythm to suck her nipples or take her lips in a devouring kiss. He left no part of her untouched as he built the tension inside her all over again. The need and hunger returned in full measure, even though he filled her again and again. She craved the completion he could give her—needed it.

"Oliver." When his name burst from her lips again, it was a plea. A request for everything he could give her.

He seemed to understand, because he lifted her in his arms as he stood. Then, pivoting so he faced the bed, he laid her in the center of the mattress and pumped his hips. Over and over. Faster. Harder.

The heat built and built until she couldn't hold back another moment. Her release unraveled, rolling through her with even more force than it had the first time. Tossing her in wave after wave of pleasure.

He followed a moment later, his hoarse shout mingling with her cry while his body went tense. She pried an eye open to watch him, to see his face as he found his own finish, his eyes closed and his mouth slack until his jaw snapped shut again. His throat closing on a long swallow before he lay beside her on the bed.

Spent. Heavy.

Jessica welcomed the weight of him holding her there. A reminder that it had been real, this impossible dreamlike night with a sexy, powerful man.

A man she'd never see again.

The thought chilled her even as she welcomed the reminder that she couldn't get too comfortable. She'd wanted pleasure. Distraction. An escape from the hardships that awaited her in the morning. And she'd found it in spades with Oliver tonight.

But she knew that was all she could have.

When he slid to one side of her, he reached for a spare fleece blanket folded at the end of the bed and draped it over her. She was just debating the etiquette of how long she should stay before making her exit when a loud boom sounded outside the hotel suite, followed by a series of whistles and pops.

Confused, she gripped the blanket tighter until Oliver grinned.

"That must be the fireworks display." He was already off the bed and dragging on navy blue cotton boxer briefs. "I bet we'll have a great view here."

"Fireworks?" She rewrapped the blanket shawl-style and got to her feet.

He pulled on his shirt but didn't bother to button it before parting the floor-length curtains on one side of the bedroom, revealing the doors to the terrace.

"The invitation for this evening's event promised a finale to end the after-party."

Already, crimson lights streaked through the sky before exploding into a flower shape. Behind it, more streaks of lights in blue and yellow repeated the flower pattern, each one brightening the night until the points of the petals dissolved into a rain of falling glitter.

Jessica followed him onto the private patio to take in the show, edging around the cushioned rattan chairs to stand at the railing.

"An after-party?" She shook her head, amazed to think there were still guests across the street at the golf facility. More explosions of color lit up the sky behind the huge golf nets that towered over the other building. "I can't believe they're still partying. Or that fireworks are even legal at this hour."

She peered around at the other hotel balconies to see if anyone else would notice them standing outside half-clothed, but the layout of the terraces made it impossible to see anyone else's patio. Relaxing into the show, she leaned on the railing, the evening breeze fluttering her hair around her shoulders.

"The Noble family is going all out on this wedding." His expression grew pensive as he watched a rocket burst into a white fountain, the light in the night sky illuminating his profile. "And Royal is always on board for an extravagant party."

"What about you?" She tried to gauge his tone, grateful for the distraction of the fireworks that had saved her from making an excuse for leaving the bed they'd shared, however briefly. "You don't sound enthused about that."

"Don't get me wrong, I'm really happy for Xavier Noble and his family." He turned toward her as one rocket after another whistled into the air before crackling into starbursts of color. "I just don't normally devote so much time to social events." He reached out to tuck a corner of the blanket under her forearm where she leaned into the railing.

The simple gesture made her heart give a little squeeze. It had been so long since she'd been in a relationship where someone looked out for her that way. But she stopped the thought short, reminding herself this wasn't a relationship.

"Will you be attending all of them?" She'd heard the gossip in the kitchen tonight during her shift at the party, with some of the staff comparing notes about who would be working which events. "I heard the couples' shower later this month at the Texas Cattleman's Club is going to be a huge deal."

Apparently, the bride and groom weren't doing separate bachelor and bachelorette parties, opting instead to fly into Royal a month ahead of the wedding for a joint shower.

"I need to make an appearance at all of them, including the couples' party." His gaze returned to the fireworks across the street, the speed of the next round growing more intense.

"Doesn't sound as if you've got wedding fever like the rest of Royal does."

Leaning back, he gave a wry laugh. "Did I mention my family is full of matchmakers who now live solely to see me settled down? They've got enough wedding fever to go around."

They watched the rest of the finale in silence, but Oliver's words bounced around her head afterward. He had a different kind of family pressure than she was feeling, but it was obvious the burden of expectation weighed on him. Reminding her she didn't want to be any kind of burden for him.

Their night had been fun, but she needed to say good-night and put an end to the surprise chemistry of her time with Oliver.

"I'll call my driver," Oliver insisted, wondering if he'd done anything to account for Jessica's sudden rush to be underway, "and accompany you home."

Their time together had been nothing short of incredible, and he was in no hurry for her to leave. But as soon as the fireworks had ended and they'd heard the sound of distant applause from the crowd remaining at the outdoor after-party across the street, Jessica had said she should be getting home.

Now he stepped into his pants and searched for his shoes so that he'd be dressed before she sprinted out the door. Logically, he knew this was supposed to be a one-night stand, but he wasn't ready to say goodbye to her yet…especially not when his head was still spinning from their off-the-charts chemistry.

"There's no need." She sidled into her skirt and pulled the zipper tab over her hip, leaving her white blouse untucked and the top button undone. "My car is parked right across the street."

"But we've both been drinking." He stepped closer to her, clutching the loose tails of her shirt in an effort to snag her attention without necessarily touching her again. He had the feeling if he put his hands on her body, they'd be raking their clothes right back off. "Whereas my driver will make sure you get home safely."

When she hesitated, nibbling her lower lip indecisively, he had a sudden recollection of her dragging that luscious fullness up his chest less than half an hour ago, setting him on fire.

"You can pick up your car tomorrow," he pressed his case to prevent himself from running his thumb over her mouth. Dipping a digit inside. "And if you're ready for some alone time, I don't need to go with you—"

She shook her head. "Sorry. You're right. And I'm not trying to ditch you. It's just that I feel clear-headed now, but I can see your point."

Relieved—too much so—he released her shirttails and glanced around the room for his phone. "Good. I'll text Jason to let him know we'll be downstairs shortly."

His gaze landed on it near the bathroom sink

where his shaving kit had been left open. As he went to snag the device, he accidentally brushed something off the countertop and onto the tile floor. A soft metallic ting made him wonder what it had been. It sounded too lightweight to be his razor or a blade.

"Here." Jessica had spoken up from behind him, and when he turned to see her, she was bending to retrieve something from under a small hallway stand. "I've got it."

Oliver shot the text to his driver and shoved the phone in his pants pocket before Jessica straightened. Between her thumb and forefinger, she held a golden band.

His stomach sank.

How close had he come to losing a precious family heirloom?

"Wow." Nearing her, he plucked the ring from her and stared down at it. "Thank goodness you spotted this when I dropped it."

After musing over the antique gold band with a rose-cut diamond and a halo of smaller diamonds around it, she glanced up at him again, her nose crinkling in confusion. "Looks like an engagement ring."

"Because it is. An heirloom ring given to me by my grandmother last year in an effort to speed along my process of finding a bride." Frustration knotted in his gut that his family had no shame in piling on the pressure for something that wasn't their business.

He hadn't wanted to accept the jewelry, but his grandmother had given it to him in front of the whole

Price clan during a Sunday meal, and she'd been adamant. And that had been before his mother joined
the clamor. Followed by his siblings. They'd taken
to clanging silverware against their drinking glasses
like they were already at a wedding.

Finally, he'd shoved the heirloom into his pocket
and then tucked the ring into his shaving kit and
promptly forgotten about it until now.

"You weren't kidding about them having wedding
fever," she murmured sympathetically. "That's a gorgeous piece, though."

"You like it?" He held the band out to her again,
presenting it with a flourish. "Then please know I
have my whole family's approval when I ask you for
your hand." He winked at her, sliding the ring into
place on her left hand before she could pull away. "If
only to keep this safe. I'm betting you would keep
track of my grandmother's engagement diamond better than I have."

"Clearly, I would," she agreed, tracing over the
halo diamonds with her opposite hand. "But I'm not
sure the Price family is interested in a placeholder
fiancée. Especially not a struggling waitress who
hasn't even gotten her real career off the ground yet."

Closing the sliding doors to the terrace where
they'd watched the fireworks earlier, Oliver picked
up his key card so they could leave the room and
meet the driver.

He hated that they were ending the evening so
early after discovering a chemistry he wouldn't be

able to forget anytime soon, but he needed to respect her wishes.

"My family isn't elitist," he assured her, surprised by her statement about the catering job after she'd made it clear that she enjoyed her parents' more down-to-earth values. "They would never begrudge someone doing honest labor."

He could only imagine his parents' joy if he brought home Jessica. She was kindhearted and hardworking. Independent. And, best of all, local. They would be thrilled if he would settle down in Royal instead of flying around the country on a regular basis to oversee his satellite offices.

"I didn't mean to imply they were elitist." She shook her head while she twisted the engagement band off her slim finger. "I'm speaking from my own shadows, I guess, because I wish I was able to leave behind the catering work and get started in my degree field. But that dream feels like it's still a ways off now."

As she held the ring out for him, he remembered what she'd said about delaying her degree program to help her parents and wished he could convince her to put herself first. But he understood how big the expectations of family could loom.

His gaze settling on the diamond band, he felt the weight of those demands all too well.

Maybe that's why he didn't take the band right away.

"Are you sure you won't keep it for a while? Just

until I return from my trip?" He hadn't planned on pushing her to see him again, but that had been before she'd rocked his world by coming back to his room and reminding him that dating had excellent benefits.

"I couldn't possibly," she protested, picking up his hand and pressing the jewelry into his palm. Just the feel of her touch sizzled through him.

"I'll be back as soon as my business concludes. In a day or maybe two." He closed his hand around both the ring and her fingers too. "If you keep this, you'd have to agree to a second date, right? And you have to admit, there was a definite spark between us."

Tugging her closer, he wrapped his free arm around her waist and gave in to the urge to kiss her. Slowly. Thoroughly.

When he broke the contact, her eyes remained closed for a long moment afterward. Almost making him think he stood a chance of seeing her again.

"There was a spark, all right." She gave him a half smile, but the heated look in her eyes had been shuttered, letting him know what her answer would be. "But I don't think we should see each other again."

He wanted to ask her why, but he also didn't want her to feel awkward about spelling it out that she didn't maintain casual relationships with guys. He'd guessed as much, and he thought that might be the root of the reason.

Either that or because she'd be working night and

day for the next year. A possibility that didn't sit well with him at all.

"I can't pretend I'm not disappointed." He let go of her hand, keeping hold of his grandmother's ring. Wishing they'd met at another time in their lives, when maybe… But that was foolish thinking. "But I won't forget you or the night we shared, Jessica. I hope you don't either."

After one more brief kiss, he stepped back, his gaze lingering on her for one long, last moment before he gathered his phone and his wallet. Palming her waist, he escorted her to the door of the suite and downstairs to where Jason was waiting for them. He would make sure she got home safely, and then they would return to their own lives. It should have been a good night, considering the sizzling encounter they'd had and how simple she'd made it for them to move on afterward.

Yet he couldn't help feeling like saying goodbye to Jessica was going to be a mistake he would regret.

Four

The next afternoon, Oliver tapped out notes on his phone from the back seat of a chauffeured Range Rover speeding up FDR Drive on Manhattan's east side. Earlier in the day, he'd had a successful meeting downtown with an important new client he'd personally signed. Now he was heading into Midtown to speak with Nexus's New York vice president to ensure things were going smoothly for a local merger with a smaller marketing firm.

It should have been a day of professional victory, capped with a view of the Brooklyn Bridge over a sparkling East River.

Instead, with every other breath, he found himself thinking of his night with Jessica Lewis. How she was feeling today. Whether or not she'd been able to retrieve her car from the golf-facility parking lot yet. If her thoughts were dominated by him half as much as his were of her.

And not just because of the hot attraction that played and replayed in his head, making him wonder if her lips had been as soft and juicy as he remembered them. He'd spotted a billboard for a new Broadway musical that morning and found himself wondering what Jessica would think of the production. Did she like that kind of thing? Or did her musical tastes veer in a different direction? He really wanted to know.

Which made no sense at all since he wasn't going to see her again. He didn't need to concern himself with how to woo her. How to win her. So debating whether she liked show tunes or opera, country or hip hop, didn't signify, damn it.

When his phone buzzed a moment later, he was grateful for the reprieve from the circling thoughts. Even if the contact on his screen came from his parents' video-calling account. Ever since his sister had encouraged them to FaceTime her toddler son, Oliver's folks had taken to contacting him that way too. So, after double-checking that the partition between him and his driver was raised, he connected a moment later.

Only to see his mom and dad standing arm in arm, a copy of a newspaper—was that the *Royal Gazette*?—held up between them. Timothy and Fiona

Price were both grinning widely, dressed in matching blue tracksuits that they often wore on afternoon walks, excitement barely contained. They'd been walking more this year, putting a bigger emphasis on their health after his dad's stroke.

"Congratulations!" they chorused together.

Confusing him.

"To who?" he asked, trying to maintain focus on his screen while enlarging the image enough to read the newspaper. "You're both wearing your 'new grandchild on the way' faces. Is someone expecting again?"

Oliver was already doing the math to figure out who it might be. His brother, Reid, and his wife had been trying for a few months. Although his sister, Kate, had also made it clear she wasn't going to wait long to have her next child.

"Congratulations to *you*, Oliver," his mother clarified, her dark ponytail swinging forward over her shoulder as she leaned closer to the camera—a tablet they kept on a stand on the mantel in the family room for just such occasions. "Your father and I couldn't be more thrilled to see you've found a special someone."

Special someone?

A sinking feeling in his gut told him this was going to be trouble. He recalled running into Anabeth Ackerman at the pre-wedding party the night before. She wouldn't have somehow planted a seed in the media that they were a couple again? She wouldn't dare, after all the grief she'd caused his family with her phony social media posts about them being a couple long after they'd stopped seeing one another. The need to see the newspaper redoubled as the Range Rover turned off FDR Drive and into an East Side neighborhood.

"I'm not sure what you mean—" he began, hating to disappoint his parents when they'd made no secret of their desire for him to settle down and start a family.

When they'd been so upset that his relationship with Anabeth hadn't been real.

"Oliver Price, don't be so coy," his mother teased good-humoredly, shaking a manicured finger at him while in the background his dad leafed through the paper—definitely the *Royal Gazette*—to find an inside page. "Timothy, show him the photo that made our day."

"Here it is," his father announced, straightening from where he worked over a leather-covered ottoman. Folding the newsprint in half, he flourished it toward the camera and held the copy steady so that Oliver could read.

"Wedding Fever Begins in Royal" stood out in bold letters above a black-and-white photo of him with… Jessica Lewis?

His heartbeat stuttered, the skyline outside the Range Rover window a blur in his stunned brain.

Whoever had snapped the picture had caught the moment that she'd mopped at his jacket with a cocktail napkin. They stood so close they looked like they were glued together. Her hand was on his chest as she gazed up at him with wide eyes and slightly parted lips that were every bit as full and juicy as he recalled. And she wasn't the only one who appeared hypnotized by the moment, since Oliver stared down into her eyes as if he wanted to devour her whole. No surprise to him, since that had been precisely what he'd been thinking at the time.

He could just imagine his parents' reactions that morning upon seeing the image. Anyone viewing the photo would believe Oliver and Jessica were intimately involved, so of course his parents now believed he'd found his "special someone." All of which was a struggle to process for him since the picture had his thoughts reeling again, reminding him that what happened last night had been no fluke.

There had been real chemistry between them. A connection. And even though Oliver had no interest in a relationship at this point in his life, he couldn't deny that he wanted the chance to see Jessica again. To kiss her. Touch her. Enjoy that connection and attraction for however long it lasted, relationship be damned.

"Will you bring her to dinner next week? We're all excited to meet her, and you can't possibly mean to keep her all to yourself now that she's been photographed with you." His mother's face loomed close to the camera before she apparently picked up the tablet and walked into another room with it, the image of her shaking in time with her steps. "You know how excited we are to see all you kids settled."

Placing her device on the kitchen island, she tilted the camera in a way that allowed Oliver to see her haul from a grocery store delivery. Black canvas bags covered the granite surface, while baguette loaves, a fresh floral arrangement and a roast were visible in the bags. Apparently, while he'd been hard at work closing his deal this morning, his mom had been discussing his love life with all his siblings and ordering the works for a special Sunday family meal that he would miss today while he was in New York.

Guilt pinched at the thought of disappointing her again next week. Especially after how upset they'd been with the Anabeth debacle. His father had experienced a stroke last fall, and ever since, both of Oliver's parents had been all the more insistent that they wanted the chance to spend time with grandchildren.

No matter that Oliver hadn't given them any yet.

"I know, Mom. But I don't even know if I'm in town next weekend," he hedged, trying to buy himself time to think of a way out. To let her down easy.

"You are," his mom insisted, moving around the kitchen with a new lightness in her step as she began to unload some of the shopping bag contents into her cabinets. "I already texted Lily, and she checked your schedule."

Of course she had. Since Oliver employed half his family at Nexus—Lily as his personal assistant and

Kate as his vice president—his schedule was easily accessible to the Price matriarch.

Unwilling to disappoint his parents—especially now that he'd seen with his own eyes how happy it made them to believe he was in a relationship—he racked his brain about what to tell them. While he was thinking, his vehicle turned north toward the Hudson Yards buildings and the site of the Manhattan Nexus office.

"I'll have to check Jessica's schedule too," he said finally, realizing he was stalling the inevitable in not telling them that he and Jessica weren't really a couple, but unable to stop himself.

Because already, he could see some benefits to letting his family's assumption play out for a bit longer. His guilt over not fulfilling his parents' wishes—his father's, in particular, given his health concerns—would be appeased. His parents would be thrilled if Oliver was in a committed long-term relationship.

Furthermore, having Jessica in his life would give him a plus-one for all of the upcoming pre-wedding events that he needed to attend. Xavier Noble and Ariana Ramos were planning the most extravagantly celebrated nuptials imaginable, and attending all of those events stag would only intensify the Price family's scrutiny of Oliver's nonexistent love life.

But attending the events with Jessica Lewis?

The thought sizzled over him, making him want to search the internet to download a copy of that image that had appeared in the *Royal Gazette*.

"Of course you do, darling. But I'm sure she'll be as eager to meet your family as we are to meet her." His mother turned back to her kitchen island and lifted a bag off the countertop before carrying it toward the refrigerator. "Your father and I are just so happy for you, Oliver. You have no idea."

He had an excellent idea, actually. He'd seen up close and personal their bitter disappointment when things hadn't worked out with Anabeth. After saying goodbye to his folks and disconnecting the call, he knew he needed a plan to address their misconception. Just not yet.

Because how helpful would it be if he could actually claim Jessica as his special someone? At least for a little while? His parents would be thrilled, to the point that maybe the added peace of mind would aid his father's health. Lowering his dad's stress could only be a good thing, when the threat of a second stroke remained high for a year after the first.

Stepping out of the Range Rover and onto the street in front of the Nexus building, he was already making plans to fly home early. He could wrap up his business by late afternoon and return to Royal. If his family had seen the *Royal Gazette* and had questions for him, how had Jessica reacted?

He wanted to know.

And yes, he also wanted to see her again. How well-timed that he had a convenient excuse.

The rush of adrenaline that shot through him at that thought made him aware of how much she had affected him. Would spending more time with her quench that fire so he wouldn't spend his days preoccupied with her?

He had a proposition for her that might help them find out.

The evening after her incredible night with Oliver, Jessica sat in the middle of a studio in a youth-recreation center, sharing her music with neurodiverse youth as part of her graduate internship.

Fingers strumming her guitar, Jessica lifted her voice in song, allowing the music to soothe her agitated soul even as she shared the calming effects of it with the room full of teens. She needed the de-stressing almost as much as they did today, her thoughts scattered and her emotions all over the map after seeing the photo of herself with Oliver in the *Royal Gazette* that morning. She'd been getting calls and texts about it all day long—from her parents, her friends, even a few classmates and colleagues. All wanting to know what was up with her and the CEO of Nexus Marketing, Oliver Price—a man well-known around Royal and beyond.

And she'd ignored each and every query, since she had no idea how to respond. What was up with her and Oliver? She had taken a temporary leave of her senses, apparently, sleeping with a man she'd only just met, but that didn't seem like the kind of thing to admit to anyone else. Her parents had a relationship based on shared values after meeting while working on the same ranch—her mom as a cook, her dad as a ranch hand. They had known one another for almost a year before they began dating, building a foundation for their relationship slowly—brick by solid brick—one that lasted through the years. And while she recognized that other people in her life would appreciate that Jessica could follow a different kind of dating path, she still couldn't help feeling like she'd jumped the gun. There was a big difference between knowing a guy for over six months versus knowing him less than six hours.

So she focused on her fingers playing over the strings instead, taking comfort from her instrument and the soft music it made, the sound rocking through her midsection where it rested near her belly. Music therapy wasn't just a professional interest for her; it was a passion. A belief. And it worked for her every time.

She was sad that her time with this group of teens was coming to an end. This had been the highlight of her week for months, driving north of Royal and into a South Dallas neighborhood where her work made a difference.

As she peered around the studio of the recreation center full of kids balancing homemade drums on their laps, each keeping time with the music in a way that made them active participants in their relaxation, she marveled at how far they'd come in the last fifteen weeks. She would miss each and every one of them so much. Before today, she'd believed that there would be other groups and individuals she would be helping in the future, and that had made winding down her time at the rec center easier to handle.

Now? She had no idea when she might be back in a situation like this, sharing music for stress management and healing. Sharing music to bring people together.

"Miss Jessica?" One of the boys in the back row raised his hand as the song came to a close.

She laid her hand over the guitar strings, holding the last vibrating notes in her palm. "Yes, Owen?"

"There's a guy at the door. Should I let him in?" Owen, a sweet and earnest seventeen-year-old who'd nearly walked out of her first session after telling her he had no sense of rhythm and wouldn't be able to participate in the activities, pointed his thumb at the windows to his left. He'd become one of Jessica's most vocal supporters over the course of their sessions together.

A few of the kids in the studio peered toward the window at Owen's comment, but others were already gathering up their personal belongings now that the session had ended. Most had more activities to attend elsewhere in the rec center, but a few had rides waiting outside for them.

Jessica could already see a hint of the tall figure dressed in dark jeans and a gray dress shirt, seated on a bench just outside the door leading to a back parking lot. Her heart rate tripped unsteadily, telling her exactly who was waiting for her.

Oliver.

Hadn't he been taking a business trip today? She remembered telling him about the internship on their ride home the night before, but she couldn't imagine what would be important enough to bring him to her place of work on a day when he was supposed to have been out of the state.

Curiosity mixed with the skin-tingling awareness she'd come to associate with being around Oliver.

"No need, Owen," Jessica assured the teen with a smile as she rested her guitar in a black metal stand beside the stool where she'd been playing. "I'll see him on my way out. Thank you all for sharing music with me these last few months. I hope you continue to play your drums and remember how calming it can be."

A few of the attendees approached her to say personal goodbyes or give her an elbow bump, but most filed out the door that led into the main rec center without looking back. When only Jessica and Owen remained, the teen shifted from foot to foot, eyes looking everywhere but in her direction before announcing, "I'll escort you. Just to be safe."

The young man's insistence brought a smile to her face, reminding her of the way Oliver had wanted to ensure she arrived home safely after their time together.

"That's kind of you." She stowed her guitar and the folding stand into a soft-sided carrying case before hoisting the strap over her shoulder. "Thank you."

A moment later, she followed her teen protector out of the rec center and into the spring evening. Oliver rose from the bench where he'd been waiting. Before she greeted him, Jessica thanked Owen again for accompanying her before watching him hop on a ten-speed bicycle, drum slung over his back, and pedal away along a dirt path and into the nearby woods.

Leaving her alone with Oliver on the sidewalk behind the rec center. The parking area was well lit, and a security officer patrolled the perimeter of the building at all hours to ensure the safety of the kids. A streetlamp hummed noisily overhead, but it meant that she could see nuances of Oliver's expression she might have otherwise missed now that the sun had set.

His green eyes were fastened on her, studying her as if looking for something he'd missed the night before. Or maybe she was projecting her own feelings on him. Because for her part, she couldn't have dragged her gaze away from him if she tried. Her body felt a magnetic pull from his, reminding her of the potent effect he still had over her.

More casually dressed in jeans and boots, he still radiated wealth and power, his ease in his skin evident in the way he moved. His gray shirt was open at the collar, the strong column of his throat snagging her gaze. Memories swamped her as she recalled what he'd tasted like there. How his stubble-roughened skin had abraded her tongue when she licked him.

"Looks like I have some competition for your attention," Oliver observed beside her as he lifted his hand to take her guitar bag from her, his deep voice filling the night air. "May I carry this for you?"

"Sure." Flustered at just the brush of his fingers along the shoulder of the simple knit T-shirt dress she wore, she shrugged off the strap so he could take the instrument from her. "But I haven't called for a ride yet, so I was just going to sit out here for a few minutes while I wait."

She pointed toward the bench where he'd been seated earlier. A rabbit hopped across a patch of nearby grass, its white tail zigzagging away into some bushes.

Hesitating, he frowned. "Were you able to retrieve your car from the golf facility today?"

She winced, remembering her attempts to do just that. "I tried to pick it up earlier today, but I think the battery was dead, because I couldn't start it. I didn't have time to call for a jump."

"Will you let me drive you home, then? I wanted to speak with you anyhow."

Agreeing, she followed him to a sporty gray BMW coupe and allowed him to help her into the passenger seat. She buckled her seat belt while he stowed her guitar case in the back and then slid into the driver's seat. She resisted the urge to trail a finger over the sleek silver logo for the M8 model on the black leather dash; everything about the vehicle was luxurious and elegant.

A world away from her hand-me-down and patched-together existence.

"I was surprised to see you tonight," she said a few minutes after he'd steered the vehicle onto the interstate heading south. "Did you cancel your trip today?"

"No. I was in New York City before nine this morning and finished my business by three. I flew home directly afterward." His thumbs drummed softly against the steering wheel.

"A quick trip." She tried to imagine the kind of life he led, hopping on planes twice in the same day, all in the course of business. His world was so different from hers.

"I felt compelled to return early after that photo of us in the paper caused a bit of an uproar in my family." He glanced her way briefly, and the eye contact was as compelling as any touch. "Would you mind if I made a quick stop on the way home? I hoped to show you something."

Surprised that he'd not only sought her out but also wanted to spend more time with her, Jessica reminded herself to proceed with caution. Still, she couldn't resist the pull of a surprise. "I don't mind an extra stop. And I've certainly had my share of responses from friends and family about that photo of us."

He pressed the accelerator harder as he passed a

slow-moving farm vehicle. Jessica's gaze moved to his thigh, where the muscles in his leg shifted the denim of his jeans.

She wanted to touch him. Skim her palm over his knee and up his leg. How had she gone so long without anyone so much as turning her head, and now that she'd met Oliver, she couldn't quit thinking about being with him again?

"I'm not surprised. That picture of us was…highly suggestive." He turned toward her as if waiting for her to acknowledge this. Her mouth went dry at the memory of the moment, and she nodded. Then he continued, "To my parents' eyes, the image was practically an engagement."

The hint of bitterness in his voice caught her off guard, reminding her how strongly he'd resisted his family's matchmaking attempts. She knew the resentment wasn't personal. But still, it stung a little.

"Did you tell them it was taken out of context? I can't believe someone just happened to capture those two seconds when we were standing so close." And looking for all the world like they were about to jump each other. Which they were.

Honestly, she'd had to fan herself anytime she pulled up the image on her phone today.

"It was difficult to get a word in edgewise when my parents were in full-court press mode to invite you to our next family meal." He downshifted as they reached the last exit before Royal, the traffic thinning out the farther they drove from the city.

"My father's health has been a question mark after he suffered a stroke nine months ago, and I've read that lowering stress in the year after a stroke significantly reduces the chance of a second one. Seeing how happy Dad was—how happy they both were today—made me think it would give them some peace of mind if I was in a steady relationship."

"I'm sorry to hear about your dad's health scare. I can understand why you'd want to consider dating for real." She empathized completely with wanting to do what was best for family. Even if she couldn't deny a twinge of disappointment that their picture together might be the catalyst to make him start seeing other people.

Then again, why wouldn't he date prolifically? He was young and successful. Handsome and ambitious. Anyone would be thrilled to be with him.

"Far from it," he corrected her, a wry smile curving his lips. "I decided I would prefer to maintain my fake dating life." Glancing her way as he slowed for a stoplight, he added, "With you."

Five

Switching on his turn signal to exit the highway, Oliver had a surprise destination in mind before returning to Royal tonight. He'd thought long and hard about how to pitch his idea to Jessica, and in the end, he decided to invest as much energy and effort into convincing her as he would use to sway any client into doing their marketing business with Nexus.

Which meant Oliver wouldn't just try to charm a yes out of her—he planned to outline in clear terms how his proposition would benefit her. Of course, while he was outlining, he also planned to make sure she was having a good time. Schmoozing was an important part of any business deal.

Hence a stop at a local county fair.

"Excuse me?" Jessica shifted against the leather passenger seat, turning toward him as much as her seat belt would allow. "Since when do we have a 'fake dating life'? The last I knew, we shared a moment. One night to indulge ourselves." She hesitated, her fingers spinning around a strand of dark brown hair, before she added, "And there was nothing false about it."

The challenging note in her voice told him he would need to utilize all his persuasive skills if he hoped to win her over on his plan. And he certainly didn't want her doubting anything about what they'd shared in bed.

He slowed the vehicle as he reached the signs for the county fair, the bright lights of the midway a beacon in the distance.

"Of course not," he backpedaled, regrouping his arguments as he followed a line of cars toward the fair entrance, a Ferris wheel visible above the tree-tops ahead. "Last night was one hundred percent authentic. I only meant to say that photo of us gives the impression of a deeper, ongoing relationship that we haven't established. Wouldn't you agree?"

While Jessica mulled that over, he parked the BMW at the end of a row in a grassy field, then exited quickly to help her from the car. The scent of fair food and livestock mingled in the evening air as he took her hand in his. Her pale blue dress hugged her curves, the hem grazing just above her knee. Silver sandals beaded with colored stones showed off a bright pink pedicure and a silver toe ring on her smallest toe. She still wore the musical-note-and-G-clef earrings, though they were less visible today since she'd worn her hair down.

All of which he took in quickly, doing his best not to stare. But she was even lovelier than he remembered, and he'd spent the whole damned day remembering.

He paused beside her, doing his best to keep his hands off her, wary of spooking her before he had his answer. "So? What do you think?"

"I'll grant you that," she answered before peering around, a strobing purple light from the nearest ride flashing over her face as she took in the surroundings. "What I can't figure out now is why you've brought me to the county fair to discuss your fake dating life."

She arched an eyebrow at him, but good humor danced in her blue-green eyes. He had to battle a fierce urge to kiss her, to run his hands over her curves and press her against him.

"You'll find out soon enough," he promised as he took her arm and led her toward the main gate, needing to stay focused on his goal for tonight.

Now that he'd formulated this plan, he had every intention of seeing it through.

The scents of popcorn and cotton candy grew stronger once he paid the admission and guided her through the games and exhibitions toward a tent in the back. He'd called ahead to pull some strings and request special seating for the evening musical act, although he hadn't known what to expect until he saw the small second tent off to one side of the big top, a white "Reserved" sign hanging from the gold rope that prevented people from entering. Inside the open tent flaps, a table for two was visible, a hurricane lamp beckoning a welcome.

The opening act on the main stage was just beginning, a husband and wife bluegrass duo of national acclaim. Even now, the fast tempo of the string melody swelled from the concert speakers.

Jessica halted outside the big top, squeezing his hand lightly as she lifted onto her toes to see beyond the crowd to the stage. "Can we listen for just a minute? These two have the most beautiful harmonies, and her flat-picking is amazing."

"We can listen for as long as you like from the comfort of your private table, just through here." He pointed toward the freestanding tent that resembled a repurposed fortune-teller booth, complete with gold fringe on the purple door flaps and a few gold stars painted on the canopy. Not quite what he'd been envisioning, but he was grateful someone at the front office had found a way to accommodate his request. "Welcome to your surprise."

By the way Jessica's eyes glowed with pleasure, he would have thought he'd secured VIP seating at the most sought-after show in town. Her hands clutched his arm and squeezed tight. "Really? That is incredibly thoughtful of you. Music is the best gift."

Every extra minute he'd spent on the phone during the flight back to Royal researching something fun for tonight paid off. Seeing her happiness filled him with a level of satisfaction he couldn't have possibly anticipated.

Moments later, seated in folding chairs under the fanciful canopy with a café table between them, Oliver waved over a nearby ticket taker who'd been keeping an eye out for them. The guy called for an extra hand from a nearby food vendor so that they could order a couple of waters plus funnel cake.

Jessica crossed her legs, her sandaled foot tapping in time with the music. While waiting for their food, Oliver asked her more about the instruments on stage. Even though there were only two performers on stage, the number of spare instruments spanning the stage behind them was nothing short of impressive.

"Cello, mandolin, fiddle, five-string banjo," Jessica said, naming them all in order for him and pointing to each in turn. "She plays them all."

"So you're familiar with this duo?" He hadn't been certain of her musical preferences, so he'd taken a chance when he'd read the bio of the critically acclaimed pair. "I didn't know if you'd enjoy bluegrass."

The crowd around them burst into applause as a song ended, and they followed suit. Once the next tune started—a slower number with a nostalgic sound—she answered, "I'm a fan of good music. Period. Particularly musicians who are elevating their art form or trying out new things. Whether it's rock or jazz, zydeco or opera, I'll take a listen to anyone testing boundaries."

"But if you're in your own backyard on the weekend, what's on the playlist?" He leaned closer, savoring the chance to be close to her, and—he hoped—her ultimate agreement to his plan.

"You can't take Texas out of the girl," she proclaimed, tilting her chin. "My personal taste skews country, of course. Although I have to admit, I'm one of those people who is just waiting for the guitar solo."

He laughed at her surprising answer; any more of a reply would have been interrupted by the arrival of their food and drinks. For another couple of songs, they enjoyed their funnel cake and the performance while Jessica pointed out the subtle differences in the artists' playing styles as they changed instruments. He slid his chair closer to hers to hear her better over the music. Also to breathe in the scent of her hair when she leaned over to explain percussive fingerstyle—a term that had his brain reeling in all sorts of sensual directions before he was able to tame his imagination.

It was all he could do not to slip his arm around her shoulders and pull her closer. Which meant he needed to get on with proposing his plan—the outcome feeling more important than it should.

"I owe you an explanation about tonight," he

began, sliding his empty paper plate aside. "About why I brought you here."

"It wasn't because you longed to hear my overly detailed explanations of guitar traditions?" she teased before taking the last bite of fried dough.

He followed the fall of powdered sugar from her lips, which left a narrow streak of white on her mouth before she swiped her paper napkin along the sweet spot. His own mouth went dry at the thought of tasting her there. Had it been less than twenty-four hours since the last time he'd had her beneath him? An ache with her name on it felt like it had been there for weeks. Months.

"I enjoyed every moment of that," he told her honestly. "I admire your passion for what you do."

His voice hit a deeper note that she must have noticed because her gaze dipped lower for a moment, skating around his shoulders and his chest before meeting his eyes again.

"Thank you." She cleared her throat, effectively banishing a husky rasp before she began again. "I forget sometimes that not everyone is as fascinated by string techniques and sculpting new sounds as I am."

"All the more reason why you shouldn't set aside your degree work next semester." He figured that was as good of a segue as any to his plan. "You deserve to continue your studies."

"Deserve or not, I can't afford to remain in the program now," she reminded him, swiveling in her chair to face him more directly even though they sat close together now. Her knees brushed his beneath the small table. "As I explained last night, I'll be working full-time—at least temporarily—to help my parents since they sacrificed for me to begin my studies in the first place."

"What if there was another way?" He withdrew his grandmother's ring from the back pocket of his jeans and placed it on the table between them. "What if we entered into a mutually beneficial arrangement for a few months that would help you pursue your studies and help me by buying some breathing room from family expectations?"

Her blue-green eyes zipped from the ring to him and back again. Her throat moved in a slow swallow.

"Is this where the fake dating that you mentioned earlier comes in?" She brushed off the remaining powdered sugar from her fingers before pushing her plate away.

"It is." He kept his focus trained on her face, trying to gauge every nuance of her expression.

"Ordinary people don't do things like that, Oliver. Fake romance only happens in the movies."

"So don't look at it as 'fake.' Consider it a relationship that meets very practical needs." He said it to appeal to her pragmatic side, but when her brows lifted, he realized how she'd interpreted his words. And his body reminded him that he would be very on board with meeting all her needs. Repeatedly. "I don't mean *those* kinds of practical needs," he hastened to explain in spite of where his mind went. "Although anything is negotiable."

"You want to negotiate a relationship of practical needs." She tucked a stray dark hair behind one ear. "I'm paraphrasing, of course."

He huffed out a long breath, realizing he was making a mess of things by treating the dating proposition as a business pitch. Jessica Lewis would be out of his life forever if he didn't find a way to appeal to her.

He picked up his grandmother's heirloom ring and rolled it between his thumb and forefinger.

"I want you to slide this diamond band on your finger and come to family dinner with me once to ease my family's concerns about me settling down. Give my father the peace of mind that will lower his stress level. Then I'd like you to attend the rest of the interminable Noble–Ramos wedding events with me to make a social obligation more enjoyable and to support the idea of us as a couple." He thought his outline had been succinct and accurate.

So maybe it still sounded like a negotiation. But at least he had Jessica's undivided attention now. Or maybe he'd just surprised her into silence.

"In exchange, I could help you stay in school until you finish." He'd turned this part over and over in his mind, trying to find a way to intrigue her into the bargain without sounding like an arrogant ass.

"How? It doesn't help me to have a fiancé," she explained bluntly. "I'll be working full-time now, so

if anything, I'd have less time to devote to dates—
real or otherwise."

"Which is why it will benefit both of us if you
stay in school instead. You could take on a role as
my fiancée as a better-paying alternative."

She was already shaking her head before he'd
finished the sentence. Even worse, she covered his
hand where he held Grandma Evie's ring and slid it
away from her.

"No. Taking money to date you? That is cringey.
It makes me sound like—"

"Someone who is passionate to finish her degree
and share her gift for musical therapy." He covered
her hand where it still rested on his. "And if we do
this together, I would be only delighted to make that
happen for you. In exchange, I get the satisfaction
of knowing I did my part to put my father's worries
about me to rest. I can have the chance to make my
parents truly happy with me for the first time in…a
long damn time."

For a moment, she said nothing. From the stage,
a lively version of "I'll Fly Away" floated over the
crowd, the music wrapping around the two of them
while he kept hold of Jessica's cool fingers in his,
the gold band now sandwiched between their palms.

He could feel her pulse there, a percussion all
its own, while she stared at him with thoughtful
eyes. He could sense her softening. Knew that he'd
tapped into something important to her when he'd
mentioned her music. Was it selfish of him to appeal

to her that way for something he wanted very much for himself? Especially now that he'd seen her again and recalled how much he really wanted to entice her back into his bed?

Pushing aside a guilty pang with the reminder that he would be helping her, too, he told himself to stay the course. He'd only act on the attraction if she wanted to, damn it. Their potential agreement had nothing to do with the way her every sigh made his skin sizzle.

"I'm listening," she said finally, giving him a level look. "If I agreed—and I'm not saying that I will— how exactly would this work?"

He released a breath that felt like he'd been holding all night long. She'd given him a green light to tell her more.

He wasn't about to waste the opportunity to win her over.

Jessica couldn't decide if this was the *most* romantic thing that had ever happened to her or the *least*.

An extremely attractive, sexy bachelor wanted to squire her around town so much that he'd arranged for a fun date at the county fair just to talk her into being his fake fiancée. She couldn't deny that was flattering, especially given how much thought he'd put into an evening she'd enjoy, complete with award-winning bluegrass artists. That seemed romantic in her eyes.

On the other hand?

Oliver Price was so anti-romance that he wanted a girlfriend in name only. Presumably one he could hire and fire at will like any other contract laborer. Which felt decidedly lacking in the romance department. But since she wasn't looking for a relationship either—she was committed to her dating hiatus after those hellish years on dating apps—what Oliver was offering was something different.

And she appreciated that he was up front about what he wanted.

Now he nodded his satisfaction with her answer. "Excellent. How about if I outline things while we wait in line for the Ferris wheel? Unless you'd like to see the end of their set?" He pointed to the blue-grass duo still on stage.

"The Ferris wheel sounds like as good a place as any for hammering out relationship details." It made sense for the surreal sort of evening it had turned into.

Minutes later, after crossing the fairgrounds to reach the midway, they stood in line behind a handful of people while the big wheel turned slowly. Nearby, a trio of women played country music standards on a much smaller stage, their matching fringed outfits and big hairdos fitting their playlist that leaned heavily on Loretta Lynn and Tammy Wynette. Jessica swayed to the music while she stood beside Oliver, waiting their turn to step into one of the colorfully painted cars.

A lanky young carnival worker with a lollipop

stick bobbing out of the corner of his mouth waved them over as a blue-and-red cart became available.

"Step right up, folks," he urged, readjusting the lollipop to the other corner of his mouth as he held the lap bar open for them. "Enjoy the ride."

Butterflies took flight in her belly as Jessica slid across the cool metal bench to sit beside Oliver and ended up closer than she'd intended. But the warmth of his body called to hers, as the evening temperature had dropped a few degrees. Just last night, they'd been naked together. And her every molecule seemed to remember that fact, straining to get near him again.

His arm stretched along the back of the cart, almost circling her but not fully touching. The heel of his hand brushed one of her shoulders while his biceps grazed the other when their car rocked on its axis. The scent of his aftershave made her nerve endings dance as memories of being entwined with him returned full blast.

She'd thought last night that the wine had affected her judgment when she'd decided to return to his hotel room with him. But this evening, she hadn't had a thing to drink besides water, and she could feel herself responding to him the exact same way. It was powerful. Potent. And a little unnerving since she needed to focus on his words and not the draw between them.

As the cart rose higher in the air, she shifted to

face him more fully. "So how do you envision this working?"

"I would ask that you attend the wedding events with me and the family dinner that I mentioned. Plus, whatever other family functions might crop up in the next few months." He hesitated, seeming to think for a moment. His fingers drummed lightly on the metal cart behind her back, the vibration humming along her spine. "Within reason, of course. I would never drag you to every niece and nephew birthday or kindergarten play. I'd respect your time and your studies."

"I've been on far worse dates than kindergarten plays, I'm sure." She shuddered at the thought of how many evenings she'd wasted meeting dates who kept one eye on their phone screen the whole time. Or who talked incessantly about themselves. And that was after taking her time to talk to prospective candidates for weeks first.

It had been disheartening.

Good humor lit his eyes. "Clearly, you've never witnessed kindergarten parents almost coming to blows over whose kid sang their part better in a school play."

"Seriously?" She would have laughed if his expression hadn't been so grim.

"I wish I wasn't. But we're going to circle back to those 'worse dates' of yours," he vowed as their cart jerked up another several feet.

They hadn't turned a full revolution yet while the

ride filled with new passengers, but she was enjoying the views from high over the fair, the big stage visible in the distance as well as the parking area and the darker ranches on the outskirts. Overhead, stars spilled across the sky with no moon in sight.

"My dating past definitely isn't worth discussing. Maybe that's why a goal-oriented partnership between us hasn't scared me off. I can see the merits of rules and an end date." Because it was that part that appealed to her and not just the feel of Oliver's arm grazing her back.

"I hadn't really thought about rules, per se." He frowned, as if he regretted the lack of foresight. "But as for a time limit, how about three months? I'd need you to commit to this through August."

"All doable," she agreed, hardly daring to believe she was actually considering this. An errant breeze stirred the hem of her knit dress, and she smoothed her hands over the fabric to keep it in place. "As long as I have enough time—"

"Right." He lifted his eyes to hers, making her suddenly aware that he'd been tracking the movement of her hem too. "I'll give you a copy of my schedule so you can plan out your work shifts. I realize that you wouldn't be able to work as much as you'd planned to this summer, so I could compensate you in whatever way you deem fair. You can keep the ring, perhaps, or—"

"I can't keep a family heirloom," she protested, remembering the elegant diamond sparkler he'd shown her. "It's irreplaceable."

For him to even suggest it made her more aware that this proposition of his definitely *wasn't* romantic from his point of view. How could any man entertain the idea of giving away his grandma's ring in a business deal? The realization helped her put things in perspective.

No more stargazing or fantasizing about licking her way along his stubbly jaw to breathe in his aftershave.

"Then how about something more practical...?" His lips flattened into a line as he seemed to think that over. Then he snapped his fingers. "Like a car."

She blinked. "Excuse me?"

"I saw your vehicle last night." He gave a half shrug as the Ferris wheel finally began to turn in earnest, the breeze lifting her hair from her neck and making gooseflesh shiver up her arms.

"And?" she prodded, confused.

"And you definitely could use an upgrade. I already have an extra vehicle, in fact, that would be perfect for you." He smiled, as if he hadn't just insulted the car that had been mostly dependable for her for nearly a decade. "We did some marketing for an American car manufacturer, and they sent us a couple for promotional purposes."

He just happened to have spare cars lying around?

She couldn't help but feel the gulf between them widen as she remembered how very different their lives were. He had brand-new automobiles to share while she worked nonstop to make ends meet for herself—and so did her parents. Would it be so wrong of her to accept a deal like that when—no doubt—whatever she got by reselling the car at the end of their time together would be more money than she could earn by working all summer?

While she worried over that, Oliver's hand landed on her shoulder, squeezing gently.

"Jessica, look." That gorgeous voice of his, low and conspiratorial, was close to her ear as he pointed to a spot high over the horizon. "A shooting star."

She welcomed the distraction. Her eyes found the glimmering trail at the last minute, a streak of white right before it faded to nothing. The bright flash seemed to imprint itself on the backs of her eyelids so that even when she blinked, she still saw the trail.

"How lovely." The words were a pale reflection of her real thoughts, which had more to do with the fact that she couldn't remember when she'd last spent any evening doing something that wasn't school or work.

Why was Oliver Price—an ambitious CEO with no time for dating—the person to point her eyes up to the sky to show her something borderline magical? The artist in her rebelled at the thought of devoting even more of her life to working just to make a small dent in that balloon payment her parents were facing.

She would take what he offered, as crazy as the whole idea sounded. Not just because she was attracted to him. In fact, the chemistry could be a problem since it was a major distraction. No, the reason she was going to say yes was because this might be her last chance to glimpse a glittering world beyond work. A world of shooting stars and reserved private tables at concerts. For a few months, she could live a life she'd only ever imagined before.

With his arm still around her, she turned to him, her throat dry from what she was about to say. Or maybe it was the heated look in his green eyes that made her tongue stick to the roof of her mouth.

Her stomach dropped as the Ferris wheel dipped, her world tilting. "It's a deal."

"Thank you, Jessica." Oliver lifted his palm to cup her cheek. He brushed his fingers lightly over her skin before he slipped his hand into his pocket and withdrew something. His grandmother's ring. Holding it up in the moonlight, he never took his eyes from her face. "You're going to need this after all. If not to keep, then just to wear for the summer."

She knew she should say something, but the whole moment defied words. She had no frame of reference for such an outlandish—and yes, exciting—arrangement. Mesmerized by the sight of him sliding the diamond band into place, Jessica reminded herself that it wasn't real. That the engagement ring was just a symbol of their agreement.

But the jeweled gold and the promises that it represented settled around her digit with more weight than she would have guessed. She stared down at it in place on her left hand, hoping she hadn't made a grave mistake.

Six

"So what happens next?" Jessica asked as Oliver pulled his car into the driveway of the small carriage house she'd been renting as an apartment for the last six months. They'd been quiet after the Ferris wheel ride, possibly because they'd needed time to process what they'd done. But now that he was dropping her off at her place, a hundred questions about their agreement spun through her mind. "I mean, how soon do you plan to tell your parents about this? We need to spend time synching up our stories before I meet them."

Light from the wrought iron streetlamp filled the car's interior as Oliver parked in the gravel driveway that wound past the main house on the property, a historic structure owned by one of Jessica's music professors. The house was dark now except for the porch light.

Likewise, the front light on the carriage house burned bright since it was on a timer. The arched wooden door was surrounded by whitewashed brick, the place small and snug. She'd been comfortable here, but she wondered what it looked like through Oliver's eyes. She'd bet he lived in something far grander.

Her thoughts were so distracted by those imaginings that she'd almost forgotten her question by the time he answered her.

"If it works for you, I would call my parents tomorrow to let them know the engagement news. Then we can attend the family meal next weekend so I can introduce you to everyone." Oliver switched off the ignition once he'd parked close to her door. "Let me walk you safely inside."

While she waited for him to open her door, she spun the gold-and-diamond ring around her finger. It would be a harmless deception, she hoped. She suspected there had to be more to Oliver's motives for the engagement than he let on, but how to ask probing and personal questions of the man you were only pretending to marry?

When he opened the passenger door, she took his hand automatically. As if they'd moved together as a couple a hundred times instead of just one unforgettable night. She let go of his fingers once she stood on the cobblestone walkway that led to her front door.

"That's fine with me. But will I see you before then?" She unlocked the door with her key but didn't open it. She wasn't sure how much she trusted herself in a small, enclosed space with a man who attracted her deeply.

The night before, she'd tossed all caution to the wind for a chance to be in his arms.

Tonight, she thought it better to breathe in the cool freshness of the night air while they sat in the side-by-side rocking chairs near the entrance. She gestured toward one of the rockers while lowering herself into the other.

"Of course. I'll clear my travel schedule, and we'll find a day to work out the logistics." He withdrew his phone and opened a screen before tapping something in and frowning. "Although time is always an issue for me—"

Stopping short, he glanced up to look directly at her, his green eyes assessing.

"What is it?" She wondered what she'd missed, not sure what he was thinking.

A dog barked in a yard nearby while on the street, someone's tires squealed as they drove off too fast. Her neighborhood was too far from Royal to be as safe as she would like, but the price was right.

"Are you locked into a lease here?" Oliver asked, shifting in his seat to peer back at the carriage house.

"No. I sometimes cover for my teacher, who gives

piano lessons at the main home, so she rents me the carriage house at a good rate." She knew she'd been lucky to find this, as real estate around Royal had been increasing in value for years.

"Would you consider moving in with me for the summer? Or for however long our arrangement works?" He made the suggestion in such an offhand way that she could almost forget he was asking her for a huge commitment. On top of an already-huge commitment. Perhaps he'd read the hesitation in her expression, however, because he seemed to change tactics then. "You could save on rent, and it would give me more flexibility to be able to see you. I won't have to rearrange or cancel my travel plans because I'll be able to see you every time I'm home."

She did the math in her head, calculating how much she would save not just on rent but also on the utilities and gas money she spent making a longer commute to school and to her parents' house from this place.

"It *is* convenient to be here when I teach lessons for her," she said, reminding herself as much as him, knowing it would still be far more favorable from a financial standpoint to give up the carriage house. "But I can't deny that saving on rent holds appeal."

"Just think about it. I can have a moving truck here later this week if it sounds workable for you, but I don't want to push." He clicked off the screen on his phone and pocketed it. "I've given you a lot to consider tonight. Perhaps it would be better if I call you tomorrow to make sure you're still on board before I scare you off completely."

He sat forward in the rocking chair, his knees close to hers as he seemed to search her eyes for answers she wasn't ready to give.

"Moving in together is a big decision," she agreed carefully, unwilling to be steamrolled into doing whatever was best for him. To deceive the world with a fake engagement was no small thing. Because this charade would affect her family too. "I'm not sure I would do that, but if I was to consider it, I'd need more information about the setup of your house." She hesitated before adding, "And I'd want to know what your expectations would be about…intimacy."

There was no sense dodging the issue, which seemed extremely relevant. Especially when her skin sizzled every time they got near each other. Even now, her heart rate sped fast, her body highly aware of his.

Actually, just the mention of the word *intimacy* ratcheted up the heat despite the cool spring evening.

"There are no expectations, Jessica. Zero." His gaze was level. Direct. "I would even go so far as to say that if you'd like to renew that facet of our relationship, the burden would be on you to say so. Explicitly." He let that word linger for a moment before continuing. "I am too aware that you're doing me a favor in the first place to mess it up by acting on attraction again."

While a distant part of her brain toyed with the

idea of what Oliver meant by her telling him "explic-itly" if she wished for intimacy, the rational part of her mind told her he was saying all the right things. That his suggestion was sound.

Sensible.

Even if just talking about *not* having sex made her remember every single sensation she'd experienced when they were together. Every touch. Every sigh. Every thrust of hips...

"All right, then." She blurted the words in an ef-fort to clear the sultry memories from the endless loop playing behind her eyes. "We agree on that much. As for the house, I'll think on it overnight."

"That's more than fair." Standing, he held out a hand to pull her to her feet. "I'll give you a call in the morning. But rest assured, you'd have more than enough room at my house. You'd have an upstairs suite, while I'd maintain my rooms on the main floor. And I'm not even home very often."

She listened attentively, but all the while, she thought about the way he'd touched her as a cour-tesy. A gentlemanly brush of fingers. And yet? That brief caress reminded her how often there would be incidental physical contact in the coming weeks—whether she opted to live with him or not.

Temptation would be a constant.

Five days after Jessica had agreed to take on the role of his fiancée for the summer, Oliver stood near her in his driveway as a moving van pulled away from his house.

Their house, temporarily, since he'd convinced her to move in with him for the duration of their arrangement. He hadn't been sure when he left her carriage house that night, but she'd surprised him the next day by agreeing to share his home. For the last two hours, she'd overseen the placement of her few furnishings into a suite he'd allotted on the second floor overlooking the pool. Now she turned toward him, ponytail swinging as she pushed a bright turquoise-colored bicycle a few feet forward. The touring bike had been the final item unpacked by the movers—an item he hadn't noticed at first, as he'd been tipping the driver for his team's efficient work.

"Where should I put this one last thing?" she asked, her sea-colored eyes roaming over his property and landing on the garage. "I probably should have stored things like this at my parents' place."

She looked incredible today in a pair of jean cutoffs and a white men's button-down that didn't begin to hide her curves. Gold hoop earrings winked in the sunlight while a yellow silk ribbon fluttered around her ponytail. He'd been thinking about untying that ribbon ever since she arrived that afternoon.

Such a simple thing to take down a woman's hair. Yet just the idea of it had kept him preoccupied all day.

Besides, he was better off fixating on that hair ribbon rather than thinking about the other essen-

tial item she'd worn today: the engagement ring he'd
slid into place on her left hand that night on the Ferris wheel. Seeing it there, a family heirloom meant
for the woman he was to marry, seemed a perpetual
reminder that their deal was no ordinary business
arrangement.

"I have plenty of room," he assured her, hurrying forward to take the handlebars from her. "You're
welcome to leave things here for as long as you like."

Their hands brushed as he eased the bike from
her grip, and he felt a jolt of electricity from her cool
skin against his.

He had appreciated her quick accommodation of
his preferences for the dating deal and wanted to
relieve any lingering concerns she might have. Together they walked toward the detached three-bay
garage that held his favorite vehicles.

And, as of last night, one for her.

He paused to key in the security code on the far-
thest bay from the house before the overhead door
retracted.

"You can check out the new car while I park the
bike." He nodded toward the bright blue crossover
SUV. "I took care of the paperwork yesterday, and
the keys are inside."

He'd done his damnedest to make all this easy for
her, but still she hesitated, as he'd worried she might.
She'd been clear about her reservations regarding
their deal, but he was determined to help her past any

leftover indecision. He'd planned a special evening in hopes of making her feel all the more welcome.

He wanted this to feel like her home too.

But as he watched her peek inside the windshield of the car without opening the door, he understood it might take some time.

"I'm guessing a music lover like you will appreciate the sound system in there. It's state of the art," he nudged, hoping the promise of high-quality acoustics would sway her.

She gave a reluctant laugh as she backed away from the car. "Of course it is. Seeing the way you live, Oliver, I would expect nothing less."

With a sweeping gesture of her arm, she indicated the rest of his property through the open garage door, and he tried to see it through her eyes. At just over four thousand square feet, the house wasn't as big of a home as some people in his position might have purchased. Yet he'd paid attention to the details, utilizing salvaged materials where possible and ensuring he only used native plants in the landscaping to stay resource efficient. Perhaps she'd rather explore that first.

"There's no rush to check out the car. Would you like to get settled in the house?" He looked forward to sharing the surprise he had waiting for her in the rooftop garden.

"Yes, please. I want to feel like more than an interloper in your life by the time we join your family for dinner tomorrow."

He recalled his parents' faces the last time they'd spoken about Jessica and felt a moment's pang at his deception. Yet he knew they'd be happy for a few months, and he needed to focus on that.

"Fair enough, then. There's an extra set of keys in the house, along with all the door codes." Another task he'd completed the day before—seeing to all the logistics of sharing his place with someone. "I messaged you a document as well."

"I looked it over this morning, and it seemed very thorough. You thought of everything." She followed him from the garage across the herringbone-patterned driveway pavers toward the two-story ultramodern residence he'd built three years before. "Do you mind me asking if you've cohabitated with anyone before?"

"Never. Well, not unless you count my stint in a college dorm." He led her through the front door and into the high-ceilinged foyer near a light-filled living area that looked out over a patio and lush backyard. "And I don't mind you asking at all. In fact, I hope we can spend the evening exchanging that kind of information since, as an engaged couple, we'd obviously know all those details about one another by now."

"Sounds good." Her gaze darted around the downstairs, lingering on the open patio doors leading outside before turning to the floating wood, glass and steel staircase that led to the second level. "I need a couple of hours to square away my space, but I'll have time after that."

Backing up a step, she reached for the staircase handrail with one hand while she scooped up her extra set of house keys from the foyer table. Her blouse gaped a little as she moved, the placket revealing a hint of lush curves that had him swallowing his tongue.

A vivid reminder that living with Jessica Lewis would be an ongoing temptation he needed to resist.

He'd been sincere about prioritizing her comfort in his home over the insistent attraction between them. He wouldn't act on it unless she approached him to initiate things. A scenario he would imagine often, even if it never happened.

"Perfect. If you meet me upstairs in the rooftop garden, I'll have dinner waiting." Along with the rest of his surprise. He hoped it wasn't too much, but they needed to fast-forward getting to know each other if they were going to ace the dinner with his siblings, who didn't know the meaning of personal boundaries.

With a brusque nod, she pivoted on her tennis shoe and disappeared up the stairs.

What to wear for a getting-to-know-you rooftop meal with a man you were pretending to marry?

Freshly showered, Jessica tucked a white Turkish bath towel around her as she stared into her newly arranged walk-in closet in the luxurious bedroom suite Oliver had given her. She could almost hear the zany musical track that would accompany her cartoon love life. "Flight of the Bumblebee," maybe? The "Sabre Dance"? Her moving in with a marketing tycoon and pretending to be his fiancée for the summer would almost be humorous if it wasn't driven by the bill that weighed down her conscience, if not her purse.

The cool dread that had dogged her ever since she'd seen the bill threatened to return, her stomach knotting.

Damn it.

A bead of water dripped from her hair to roll down her forehead, and she swiped it away before reaching for a navy-and-white polka-dotted sundress, a favorite consignment-shop find. The dress was pretty without being sexy, and she wanted to be careful about the message she sent in light of their combustible chemistry and their agreement not to act on it. For her own sake as much as his, because just being around him flipped a switch inside her.

And, crazy circumstances of her fake engagement aside, she really needed this arrangement to be successful. Which meant she wasn't about to blur the lines by initiating an intimate relationship with him again. No matter how attractive she found his toned muscles and thick, wavy hair. Or the voice that seemed to reach inside her and resonate on a frequency tuned precisely to her sex drive. Just listening to him made her knees weak.

Making quick work of drying her hair, she clipped half of it back and slicked on pink lip gloss.

Fresh-faced without trying too hard would be her new go-to.

And how strange was it to give herself a life pep talk in the mirror of this sleek, spa-like bathroom? She hadn't even needed to unpack her own shampoo since there were stainless steel dispensers for everything built into the gray-tiled shower wall. She now smelled like lavender and lilies of the valley, a scent that should have been relaxing; but in the hyperaware state she'd been in ever since arriving at Oliver's house, the fragrance seemed sensuous.

Glancing at the bedside clock that glowed softly in the gathering twilight shadows, Jessica turned her steps toward the door to meet Oliver on the rooftop. She wouldn't be late for their getting-to-know-you evening.

Yet as soon as she set foot on the stair landing, she heard voices in the foyer below.

Oliver. And a woman?

The fast twinge of jealousy surprised her.

Right away, Jessica recognized her mistake in standing there. Because the thing about Oliver's super-modern house with the floating wood, steel and glass staircase was that she was visible from the main floor now. She sensed movement below between the glass risers, and if she'd seen them, they'd surely spotted her as well.

Before she could think of her next move, Oliver called up the stairs to her.

"Jessica? Come down and meet my sister, Kate."

Relief that she wouldn't have to navigate the arrival of a potential rival for Oliver's affections was quickly replaced by a different kind of dismay. His *sister* was here. Ahead of the "Meet the Family" schedule set for tomorrow?

Her nerves jangled as she descended from the second floor, her gaze snagging on a tall blonde standing beside Oliver in the entryway. She wore a sleek blue suit, the pencil skirt ending just above her knee and showing off killer calves that looked like she ran long distance. Strappy nude-colored pumps gave the outfit a little edge with a row of small silver spikes up the back of the heels. Brown assessing eyes took Jessica in at the same time that Jessica was trying to get a handle on the visitor.

"Jessica, this is my sister, Kate, who is also the vice president for Nexus," Oliver offered by way of introduction. "Kate, meet Jessica, my fiancée."

Extending her right palm to the newcomer, Jessica shook Kate's hand. "It's really nice to meet you."

"You as well." Kate squeezed her fingers with a bit more force than strictly necessary, but her pleasant smile remained fixed. "I had to drop off some reports to Oliver anyhow, and I couldn't resist the chance to welcome you to the family."

Or to check up on me, Jessica silently guessed. She noticed that a new manila envelope sat on the foyer table, no doubt the object of the delivery.

"Thank you." Jessica took Oliver's elbow to steady

herself when she felt a bit unnerved. "I'm looking forward to meeting the whole family tomorrow."

Tugging her closer, Oliver curved an arm around her waist. A show of solidarity, perhaps. Jessica noticed that his sister's gaze followed the movement. Filed it away before she glanced back up to Jessica.

"Are you really looking forward to that kind of mayhem?" A mischievous light crept into Kate's eyes before she laughed. "Or are you mostly eager to get that part out of the way so you can start planning your wedding without the whole clan interfering?"

Good-natured teasing or deliberately provoking? Jessica tried to read the other woman but couldn't be sure. She had no context for Oliver's sister, no idea what his family was like. And right now, she felt woefully underprepared for tomorrow.

"Actually, I'm excited for any and all advice." She tried to envision planning her own wedding and failed, her brain drawing a massive blank.

Probably because real marriage wasn't anywhere on her radar.

"Honestly? Because I have some already." The smile held, frozen in place so long it had become awkward.

Uneasiness rolled through Jessica.

"By all means," she encouraged softly, bracing herself for whatever the woman might say.

"Kate." Oliver's voice sounded like a warning under his breath. "This could wait until tomorrow."

But the imposing sister merely squared her shoulders.

"Don't let Oliver hide you in the shadows." Her brown eyes locked on Jessica's, a steely glint visible in their depths. "His family is an important part of his life, so we want to be a part of yours too."

Oliver scoffed and made a half-hearted protest, but Kate's focus never veered from Jessica. Reminding her how big of an impostor she was in this family. Swallowing back her reservations, she mustered a small smile even though her conscience was stinging.

"Understood. I'm hoping tomorrow will go a long way toward forging new relationships." She made a point of standing tall and maintaining eye contact, but she felt the warning to her toes.

After exchanging pleasantries, Kate departed, high heels clicking determined steps out to her white sports convertible. When Oliver closed the door behind her, Jessica felt some of the starch in her spine dissolve.

"Do you think she saw right through us?" Untangling herself from Oliver's arm, she looked to him for answers while her skin hummed pleasantly where he'd touched her.

"Not a chance. Kate is fierce by nature, but it's mostly for show." He reached for her hand again, taking her fingers in his and stroking his thumb over the backs of her knuckles.

Just that simple touch enflamed her, making her want to forget everything but him and this magnetic connection. But it wasn't real, and she needed to remember that. Should she set more boundaries so she wouldn't lose herself in the addictive heat? Yet if they never touched each other in private, how would they convince his family they were a couple once they were all together?

"Then we need to turn our attention to shoring up our engagement story. Your family won't be able to take any pleasure from our relationship if they're worried it's not the real thing." Bad enough they would be disappointed in the long run when she and Oliver broke things off at the end of the summer.

"They're not worried. Kate just wants to make sure anyone in my life is part of hers too." Tugging her toward the stairs, he led her up to the second floor. "But to your point, why don't we go out into the garden for my surprise? We can work out the details of our whirlwind courtship there."

Curiosity stirred—and yes, anticipation too. No matter how much she wanted to tell herself this was strictly a business arrangement, there was a fantasy element threading through it all that lured her to enjoy the moment with this enticing man.

"I like surprises," she admitted, trying to recall the last time she'd had a happy one in her life that came from a source other than Oliver.

Because finding that bill for the balloon payment was a surprise, but it had been more like getting smacked in the chest by a two-by-four. Not the good kind.

"Then I hope you enjoy this one." When they reached the second-story common area—a sitting room with a pearl-gray leather couch and built-in white bookshelves decorated with plants and a few modernist sculptures—Oliver paused before a door leading outside.

Through the sidelights on either side of the door, she could see hints of greenery and the smudged violet sky from the last of a setting sun. The rooftop garden must be beyond.

With one hand, he pulled the door open for her. With the other, he waved her forward. Crossing the threshold in the simple gold sandals she'd worn with her dress, Jessica felt the springy give of a soft ground cover plant beneath her feet. Scents of thyme, basil and jasmine drifted on the breeze as she took in the scene in front of her. An elaborate rooftop garden, yes, complete with a couch covered in brightly printed cushions and a fire table already lit and lending an orange glimmer to the Moroccan-themed outdoor space.

Yet it was clear that part wasn't the surprise. Because arching over the other half of the garden stood a white canopy tent draped in greenery and white lights, its flaps held open with blue silk ribbons to show the wealth of blue and yellow pillows scattered over a straw mat on the floor. An elegant chandelier hung from the tent's center, the half dozen candelabra bulbs glowing on a low setting, the crystals dangling from each one magnifying the light.

The surprise stole her ability to speak for a moment.

Why was he pulling out all the stops for a fake engagement? How could a man so determined not to fall for anyone maintain such a romantic streak? Because how could she call this luminous rooftop hideaway anything but romantic?

"You think I went overboard, don't you?" He still stood beside her, and his eyes, she now realized, had missed nothing of her unguarded reaction.

"I think it's magical," she said simply, folding her arms across her midsection. As if she could erect a physical barrier to stop herself from ending up in his arms again. "And I'm trying my best to remember that this is just for fun and not the actions of a man trying to woo and win me."

"But if we were newly engaged, I would do everything in my power to make this time in our lives both magical and memorable." He gave an easy shrug before ducking into the tent and waving her to follow him inside. "I figured we could recreate some of our most important memories tonight so when we relate the story of our engagement, the details will be real."

A shiver jumped down her spine at the thought of him going to so much trouble for the woman in his life. She hid it by rubbing her hands up and down her arms, feigning a chill.

"If this is your level of commitment to your fake fiancée, I can only imagine what you'd do for the real thing. Either way, your dating game is about a thousand times more impressive than the men I've gone out with," she observed dryly as she lowered herself to take a seat on one of the floor cushions, recalling some of her Dates from Hell.

"Since I've never made the effort for any other woman, I guess I don't really know what I'd do for anyone else." He took the cushion next to her, then propped a second one behind them to lean against another stack of spare pillows.

His shoulder brushed hers as he made himself comfortable, teasing her senses and making her pulse speed faster.

Smoothing her polka-dot dress around her and tucking the hem so the wind wouldn't get beneath it, Jessica felt Oliver's eyes on her like a caress. Would she ever get used to this electric hum between them? She needed to find ways to steel herself against the draw of it before the chemistry wove another seductive spell around her. She could hardly blame her actions on wine when she hadn't had a sip to drink besides water all day. The reaction she had to his nearness was a different kind of potent.

"So tomorrow, when I meet the rest of your family, we're going to say you proposed on a night like this?" She realized that at some point, she'd started to spin the gold-and-diamond engagement ring around her finger.

Forcing herself to be still, she knit her fingers together instead.

"No. I vote we stick to the truth as much as possible, and I proposed on the Ferris wheel right as we saw a shooting star." His green eyes were a shade more emerald under the golden glow of the chandelier, drawing her in.

"That was definitely memorable," she agreed, resisting the urge to recall their other memories together. Kisses.

Much, much more.

"As for the tent on the roof, I thought that might have been one of our earlier dates this spring. From a night I knew I wanted things to be more serious."

Her speeding heartbeat thumped heavier, more loudly in the stillness inside the tent. She could hear the breeze flutter through vents in the canopy overhead, but here, they were more sheltered. Night birds began their evening cries now that the sun had fully disappeared.

"That makes sense." Her voice sounded thick with emotion, so she cleared her throat as she tried to clear her head. "How did we meet?"

"One of your catering jobs was for a marketing client?" He snapped his fingers. "The car company, maybe."

She recalled him saying that he'd ended up with

the extra vehicle because the automaker was a Nexus client. "That works. Did I spill a drink on you then too?"

"Of course." A lazy smile curved his lips on one side. "But it was a fortuitous accident that brought us together."

She resisted the urge to lick her suddenly dry lips.

"Did we know right away?" she ventured, wanting to have the details of this sort-of-fake history straight in her mind. "That we wanted to see each other again?"

He tipped his head back against the yellow cushion behind their heads, his gaze lifting to the stars visible just outside the tent. "I can only tell them what I felt on my side. I won't speak for what you thought at the time."

She pursed her lips in an effort to hold back the question she wanted to ask. Because of course she wanted to know how he'd felt. Even if it was only a partial truth about their first meeting. The ring felt heavy on her hand, the band somehow squeezing her finger.

"Do you want to know what I thought then? Right after we met?" Oliver reached over to take her left hand, laying it out over his as if he wished to admire the way the engagement jewelry looked in its place on her finger.

Don't ask. It shouldn't matter for the sake of their cover story. It shouldn't matter *period*, because all of this was just a kind of grown-up make believe.

Except parts of the story were true.

And she couldn't help but be intrigued by the facets that straddled the line between real and fiction.

"I will admit, I'm curious." She tried to say it lightly, as if it was all in good fun. But the words were thick with a longing she hoped he couldn't hear.

"I knew immediately that I wanted you." One hand still holding hers, he used his other to cup her face and turn her toward him. "That I needed to know your name and everything about you. That I would regret it forever if the evening passed without me tasting you."

His fingers trailed along her cheek and down to her mouth, as if underscoring his words somehow.

Fascinated by that trailing touch, she felt her blood surge hotter. Knew she wouldn't be able to resist the draw of his lips much longer.

Sure, he might not be the one to initiate things. But if he kept looking at her this way, she couldn't be sure she wouldn't *explicitly* ask him for more.

"It's a good story." Nodding, she acknowledged as much to herself and to him. Then, recognizing the time had come to start drawing her boundaries to protect herself, she took a deep breath before continuing. "But in the interest of making sure we don't blur the lines between us, I think it's important that from now on, we try to limit how much we touch one another when we're alone together. Just to help us keep our relationship strictly platonic."

His touch stilled, his fingers halting just below her lower lip before falling away.

"Of course." His jaw flexed as if he were chewing over the idea. Or perhaps he was grinding his teeth against the same frustration she felt—the ever-present desire that they didn't plan to indulge. "I didn't mean to overstep."

"Not at all. We'll need to touch one another when we're out in public. I just think when we are alone, it will be less…" She searched for the right word as she slid her hand free from his. "…confusing if we limit the physical contact."

The fire flickering in the nearby stone table didn't do anything to take the new chill from the evening as Oliver tucked his hands into the pockets of his jacket. She missed his touch immediately. The sense of loss she felt only emphasized how important these new boundaries would be in their live-in relationship.

It was crucial they understood each other. Respected each other's space.

Protected them both from a messy breakup when the fake engagement ended. They'd made a business deal, and she needed to keep things on a logical, objective plane.

"That makes sense." With a single clipped nod, he agreed to the terms. "We'll just have to let our imaginations fill in the blanks about what might have happened next after a night like this." His widespread arms seemed to indicate the tent, the fire, the cushions.

She swallowed hard at the visions that scrolled through her mind of them intertwined, her imagination all too willing to supply possibilities.

And she knew these next three months were going to be far more difficult than she'd first thought.

Seven

"I should say good night." Oliver rose to his feet, recognizing that he'd need to limit how much time he spent around his new roommate if he wanted to honor his promise to keep his hands to himself.

He would, of course.

But she was temptation personified, with her legs tucked under her on the cushion, her blue-and-white polka-dot dress spilling over her lap. The urge to haul her closer was fierce. Insistent.

"Me too," she agreed, standing a moment later. "What time will we leave tomorrow to go to your parents'?"

His cell phone vibrated in his pocket before he could reply.

Frowning, he reached for it. "I apologize, Jessica. I have my phone set not to disturb me, so if something's ringing through—"

"I understand," she said at the same time he saw Kate's number on his screen.

Tension knotted in his chest. His sister never bothered him with work outside of business hours. She was as protective of her own time as she was of his.

"Kate?" he answered without preamble. "Everything okay?"

"No. It's Dad." Her voice cracked. "He's at Royal Memorial. Mom just called me in hysterics…"

Dread rooted his feet to the floor as his sister's words trailed off. As if she couldn't continue. Had his worst fears about his father come true? His gaze found Jessica's. Locked and held. Needing that connection in order to ask his sister about Dad's condition.

"He's not—" His own voice failed him, and he had to clear his throat. "Is he still breathing?"

Jessica stepped toward him, concern scrawled across her features. Her hand landed on his shoulder while he waited the eternity of a second for his sister's reply.

"Yes. Sorry, I should have started with that." Kate took a deep breath and then spoke more slowly. "Mom said one of the ER docs is in with him now. Reid and Lily are already on their way, and I just pulled in the hospital parking lot, but we need you—"

"I'm leaving now," he promised her, already charging toward the exit from the rooftop garden. "I'll be there as fast as I can."

Behind him, Jessica followed close on his heels as he disconnected the call.

"What's wrong? Is it your father?" She kept pace with him down the stairs to the first floor.

His gut was in knots. His thoughts were all over the place. He only knew that he needed to be with his family now.

"Yes. I don't know how serious it is, but he's at Royal Memorial with my mother." He swiped a set of keys off the hook in the mudroom before stepping into the garage. "I'm sorry to race out on you, but I've got to be there with them."

"Of course you do." She hurried behind him toward the BMW sport coupe, her sandals slapping the concrete floor. "How can I best help? Would you like me there in case you need a nonfamily member to run errands? Or if your siblings need help with their kids?"

He had no idea what to expect at the hospital. Would any of his nieces or nephews be there? No doubt his brother and sisters would have left their homes in just as much of a rush as him. It was conceivable Jessica could be a welcome extra set of hands, especially since the hospital would limit the number of visitors no matter how worried they all were.

Or maybe he just really needed her sitting next to him on a tense ride.

"Yes, please. Come with me."

Two hours after arriving at the hospital, Oliver stood in the ICU waiting area of Royal Memorial, listening to his father's neurologist discuss next steps for treating Timothy Price's second stroke.

Logically, Oliver followed the woman's diagnosis of an ischemic stroke, and he understood the treatment plan of administering a thrombolytic drug that could break up potential blood clots. Yet the whole evening had been so scary and so surreal that he also now understood why people brought family members into medical offices with them to help retain and process what was said in that kind of setting.

Because the fear of losing his father had caused his thoughts to spiral and his concentration to fracture even when he'd told himself to pay close attention. Thank goodness his mother and siblings were all present to hear the same information as him—or at least, they were all present via video conference.

As for Jessica, she'd somehow become an integral part of the family without him ever making a formal introduction. Over the last two hours, he'd seen her set up video messaging with the family members who couldn't be present, ensuring a dedicated device went into any meeting between his mother and the medical team so that everyone could hear the news at once. At some point, she'd disappeared on a coffee run for the whole group.

Everyone had been distracted and scared but grateful for her help.

The neurologist wrapped up her overview of his dad's condition and asked if anyone had questions, careful to include all the concerned faces on the video conference screen. Oliver's mother spoke up.

"How long will he be on the medication?" Fiona Price was dressed in a pink tracksuit, her dark hair in a ponytail. Apparently, they'd been on a walk around the neighborhood when Timothy had noticed he couldn't lift his left arm.

"It depends on how he responds to the treatment," the physician replied, her concerned demeanor communicating that she was invested and caring—things Oliver appreciated on a day that had scared a decade off his life. "We'll want to monitor him closely for the next twenty-four hours."

"So he'll stay in ICU for that long?" asked Kate, still wearing the blue suit she'd had on when she stopped by Oliver's house hours ago.

"Yes. And as you know, he can't receive more than one visitor at a time, so you might want to take turns sitting with him so you all stay rested."

Oliver exchanged glances with Kate, knowing they should come up with a schedule now that—he prayed—his father seemed to be out of the woods. They'd all been on the internet, searching for answers, and what he'd gathered suggested that Fiona's quick reaction time had been crucial in getting Timothy on the drugs that would minimize damage.

As the doctor took her leave and the family took a collective breath, Oliver became aware of the scent of fresh coffee. Turning, he spotted Jessica holding a cardboard carrying tray with four cups.

Gratitude filled him, and it didn't have a damned thing to do with the coffee. He counted himself fortunate that he hadn't scared her off yet, considering the way she'd been thrown into the mix tonight. He moved toward her, but his mother beat him by a half step.

"Oh, you sweetheart," Fiona Price said with a smile, some of the worried lines on her face smoothing as she closed the distance between herself and Jessica. "That smells like heaven."

As Oliver watched his mother accept one of the drinks and Kate followed suit, he appreciated the way Jessica had been here for his family. For him. He would have never asked her to accompany him to the hospital tonight after that call came in from his sister. His thoughts had been all over the place; but even then he would have known better than to impose with something so personal.

Yet she'd not only volunteered—she'd made herself invaluable to all of them in a quiet, supportive way. Just having her in the car with him on the way to the hospital had been a relief.

All of which reminded him that the lines between them could blur too easily if they weren't careful.

While the engagement might be fake, there were real feelings involved, growing stronger by the day.

And as he observed the easy exchange between Jessica and his mom, heads bent close to each other in a private conversation while they sipped from their coffee cups, he reminded himself that it wasn't just his feelings or Jessica's at stake.

He couldn't allow this relationship to hurt his family. His mother and father, who would want to embrace a new daughter-in-law now more than ever. As the full impact of what he'd done rolled over him—the potential pain he could cause when he'd wanted to impart some happiness—Oliver steeled himself against it. Reminded himself that he'd had good reasons. Good intentions.

Still, he wasted no time in joining his mother and Jessica, feeling the need to intervene.

Looping his arm around Jessica, he was about to suggest they leave. But his mother's hopeful expression when she laid a hand on his shoulder stopped him.

"Oliver, wait until you hear Jessica's idea about music therapy for your father." Fiona's gaze darted to Jessica briefly before returning to Oliver. "Did you know they recommend music therapy for stroke victims to recover more quickly? Your father read a few case studies about the benefits after his first stroke, but we never pursued anything since he seemed fine." Her head bowed low for a moment before she added more unsteadily, "I really thought he would be okay."

Hating to see his mother racked with worry and guilt, Oliver released his hold on Jessica. He reached for Fiona, steadying her.

"And he will be," he assured her, hoping like hell it was true. "But let's leave his care in the hands of professionals, okay? They'll know what's best for Dad."

Over Fiona's head, he met Jessica's concerned eyes and shook his head, hoping she understood the message that she not bring up any more ideas right now. He didn't need for his mom to question herself about the right course of treatment when she was already dealing with too many fears.

A few moments later, when Kate joined them to share a digital calendar she'd made for the family to keep a schedule of who would sit with Timothy, Oliver realized that Jessica had slipped out of the waiting room at some point. Surprised that she was no longer there, he signed up for a slot to sit in the ICU the next day before bidding the rest of the family good-night.

When he found her seated on a bench near the elevators, she was looking out over the darkened city of Royal through a set of tall windows. With her shoulders slumped and her arms wrapped around herself, she looked as weary as he felt.

"Are you ready to head home?" he asked. The

corridor was vacant at this end of the hospital floor. They'd left the sound of beeping machines and busy staffers in the ICU. Here, they were surrounded by unused labs and doctor–patient consulting rooms gone silent for the night.

Jessica lifted her head, her eyes ringed with red. "Ready whenever you are."

Concern made him almost reach for her, but something in her expression—a flattening of her mouth, maybe—reminded him of her earlier request that they limit physical contact. Tonight, they'd both made exceptions in light of his dad's health scare, but he didn't want to overstep now that things had settled down.

"Is everything all right?" he asked instead, fisting his hands in his pockets to keep himself from offering any physical comfort.

Or taking any that he didn't deserve from a woman who was only here out of human kindness and not because he'd done anything to earn her caring and affection.

"Yes. Just tired," she assured him as she glanced away again. "I know it's been a long night for you too."

It had been. Relieved she wasn't upset, Oliver pressed the call button outside the elevator and the doors opened immediately.

He was sure they would both feel better after some sleep. Today had been rough. But in the weeks ahead, surely it would get easier to be around Jessica without the constant craving to touch her, to taste her again, all the time.

Alone in Oliver's house early the next morning, Jessica scowled at the high-tech coffee machine on Oliver's kitchen countertop, willing the thing to finish its brewing cycle.

What was it about having more money that made people decide they needed far more complicated machines? A perfectly ordinary coffee maker would have given her the required morning dose of caffeine ten minutes ago. When the oversize gadget finally flashed and beeped an excited tone, she tugged the stainless steel carafe from beneath it and set it on a tray, along with two gray stoneware mugs. She'd invited her best friend, Corryna Lawson, to stop by for coffee since Oliver had taken an early shift at the hospital to sit with his father. Corryna had been pressing her for answers about their sudden engagement and hadn't been satisfied with Jessica's answers. Should she cave and tell her the truth? That they were faking the whole thing? Anxiety balled in her stomach at the thought.

While she waited for her friend, Jessica planned to play her guitar in an effort to relax. Now she carried the tray outdoors to where she'd already carried her instrument.

At first, she'd considered practicing her finger work in the rooftop garden, knowing the tent would have provided good shade for her visit with Corryna. But after last night's exchange with Oliver in the hospital, she wasn't in the right frame of mind to see the tent again and remember one of his romantic gestures.

Let's leave his care in the hands of professionals...

The words had stung at the time and had been a mocking refrain in her dreams all night long. Jessica tried to shut them out now as she found a chair near the pool house and a glass-topped rattan table where she could set her coffee. The gray and white stones all around the pool maintained the modern, masculine look of the house, but the flower gardens surrounding the pool were full of scent and color, softening the effect. The morning air was cool enough for the old cardigan Jessica had worn over her shorts and T-shirt, but the clear blue sky suggested that by afternoon, the day would be hot. Breathing in the air scented with hyacinths, she swiveled the chair toward a view of the pink and burgundy ranunculus as she picked up her guitar, admiring the way their thin petals worked in harmony to form a stunning whole.

Recalling that she wasn't all that different from one paper-thin petal, at least not in Oliver's eyes. Her opinion didn't carry weight, because she wasn't certified; because she didn't have the endorsement of a professional community to back her up.

Yet.

Oliver hadn't wanted her suggestions about his father's treatment because she wasn't a paid music therapist. Logically, she understood his position. Respected that she might have overstepped in mentioning the idea to his mom at a time when the family was reeling.

And yet…

She *was* a professional musician. As her fingers worked the strings on her guitar, bending and pressing, tapping and picking, she ran through warm-up exercises that had been with her from girlhood. String skipping, descending slurs, ascending bursts, a little flamenco riff that strengthened the fingers— the work was rote but necessary, like a bridge between the regular world and the creative space needed to play really well.

The bridge period of her warm-up also helped her to forget about everything else. She had to leave behind the hurt Oliver had unthinkingly delivered about her therapy know-how. Only then could she coax beauty from her instrument. Only then could she be a part of her guitar, a vessel for sound to flow through.

When she transitioned into her first song, she found herself playing the Villa-Lobos "Prelude No. 1," an exquisite merger of a Brazilian folk melody with Western classical music. Only then did she relax fully, the music taking over. Rich sound filled the garden, the strings vibrating beneath her fingers, the guitar body a pleasant thrum near her belly.

After the last strains of the song faded, she paused long enough to pour a little of the coffee from the carafe into one of the mugs, just to test it. The molasses and chocolate notes came through for an excellent flavor despite her frustration with the brewing process. She leaned forward to set down her mug when a feminine voice called from the side yard.

"I didn't know there was going to be live music for our coffee date." Grinning widely, Corryna picked her way over a patch of grass in her tall leather boots until she reached the stone walkway that wrapped around the pool area.

Jessica's best friend was a crazy-talented florist who owned Royal Blooms, the local flower shop tapped to do the arrangements for Ari Ramos and Xavier Noble's wedding day. Corryna's workload had increased significantly due to the wedding business, but Jessica knew she was mindful of not overdoing it since Corryna had just found out she was expecting. Not that Jessica could see a hint of the pregnancy yet. Jessica had been with her best friend when Corryna took the pregnancy test. After the shock wore off, Jess had never seen her friend so happy. The baby's daddy was Colin Reynolds, owner and executive chef at one of Royal's best restaurants, Sheen.

Now Corryna walked closer, a pink pastry box in hand. Her long ombre-brown hair was still damp and wavy from a morning shower, but she managed to look like a fashion-magazine page in a fitted blue-floral dress with a high-low hem that showed off calf-hugging boots.

"And I didn't know there would be pastries, but you're a goddess of a best friend for thinking of it." Standing, Jessica set her guitar on a chaise longue nearby before wrapping Corryna in a hug. "You smell amazing."

"It's probably the scent of buttercream frosting," Corryna suggested as she dropped down into the cushioned rattan chair opposite from where Jessica had been sitting. "I've been salivating over it ever since I picked up the treats from Colin's pastry chef, and I may have hugged the box close at some point during the ride over here."

"Well, drool no more—let's dig in." Jessica filled their mugs from the carafe and passed the silver creamer jug to her friend.

"Fair warning, though," Corryna said, pointing at her with her spoon before using it to stir cream into her coffee. "I'll be initiating a formal inquisition about your whirlwind new romance as soon as you've had your sugar fix."

"I had the feeling you weren't here just for the live music," she admitted between bites of a flaky raspberry mille-feuille, recognizing that she couldn't possibly fake her way through this conversation about Oliver.

Especially not on a day when her feelings toward him were all over the place after the way he'd casually written off her abilities the night before. She needed Corryna's insights. Or, at the very least, her support as friend.

"I'm not even here for the gardens, and consider how gorgeous this all looks." Corryna swept one arm wide to indicate the nodding ranunculus, poppies and anemones spilling over the stone walkways. Corryna adored plants of all kinds, and whenever they hiked together she would spot some new and different greenery to admire, explain or sometimes propagate. There was an earthiness to her that resonated with Jessica after the way she'd been raised. "I could hear something off in your voice when you told me about the engagement, and it got me worried."

Setting aside her pastry, Jessica met Corryna's steady green gaze. "No need to worry," she assured her. "I know what I'm getting into—but if you heard anything amiss in my tone, it was only because Oliver and I agreed the engagement would be for mutual practical benefits."

Corryna set aside her chocolate croissant, too, and then reached for Jessica's left hand, where the heirloom diamond band rested. "You're saying this isn't real?"

Her friend turned her hand to the right and to the left, studying the vintage piece before releasing her fingers.

"The ring is very real," Jessica confessed softly, remembering her passionate first night with Oliver and his offhanded proposal with the family treasure. "But the engagement itself? Not so much. Please don't tell anyone else. Oliver's father is battling serious health issues, and he wanted to give his family some peace of mind about his future."

Corryna's eyes went wide, her expression sympathetic.

And then Jessica was spilling all of it. The bill for the balloon payment and accidental meeting with Oliver that same day. The sizzling chemistry neither one of them could resist, along with Oliver's surprise reappearance the next day with the ring and a proposal on the Ferris wheel. Once she was that far into the tale, she couldn't help but recap the incident at the hospital, too, since it still bothered her like a glass shard in her foot. Every step today was a reminder that Oliver might hunger for her physically, but he didn't respect her work.

"You could have called me," Corryna admonished when she'd finished her story. "At any point during all of this. Do you know you can always call me?"

The exasperation in her friend's tone reminded Jessica that her stubborn independent streak wasn't always a good quality. "I do know that. I promise. I just kept thinking I had a handle on things. Right up until last night at the hospital, when I offered my expertise to help his father, and Oliver shut me down as if I was trying to sell him a knife set at his front door."

Corryna pursed her lips. "I get why that stung, Jess, but I'm not sure it's fair to hold that against him when he was torn up about his dad and maybe not at his best. I'm more concerned about how you'll feel in a few months from now, after you've been living together all that time."

"Plenty of people have roommates without getting emotionally tangled up with them," Jessica argued as she reached for a second pastry, a layered strudel. She needed comfort food after unloading her worries. "We won't even be seeing that much of each other, between Oliver's travel schedule and my studies."

Because now that she didn't need to quit school, she'd been able to move her fall internship to the summer. The small amount she would be paid for the music therapy work at the hospice facility would be enough to pay for the college's internship credits.

"Yet you're attending the couples' shower together at the Texas Cattleman's Club. The wedding events are steeped in romance, and you'll spend those days pretending to be in love with one another." Corryna shook her head, her hands held upward as if pleading with the sky. "Do you not see how that might skew your perspective where Oliver is concerned? Especially when there is a lot of attraction beneath all your practical motivations?"

A prickle of warning danced across Jessica's shoulders, but she chose to ignore it. She could handle this. Maybe having Corryna over today had been Jessica's way of inviting in the opposing viewpoint so she could argue with it. Build up her resolve when she'd been feeling confused herself.

"So I keep my eye on the prize," Jessica reminded herself at the same time she explained it to Corryna. "I get to stay in school and help my parents with the balloon payment. Oliver gets to make his family happy. As long as we're very clear about our goals and how to achieve them, it will be fine."

For a long moment, Corryna chewed her lip, appearing deep in thought. Finally, she leaned back in her chair, took a slow sip from her coffee mug and then met Jessica's eyes straight on.

"All right, then. Call me anytime if things start getting confusing for you." She replaced her cup on the tray before reaching to pluck a single white anemone from the drooping stems that brushed against her whenever a breeze blew. Absently, she tucked the bloom behind one ear. "Speaking from experience, I can tell you that it doesn't matter how many plans you make about love in your life—losing your heart to someone is something you have zero control over."

Jessica knew her friend had fought hard for the happily-ever-after she was going to have with Colin Reynolds. She was thrilled for Corryna. But Jessica also understood that her circumstances with Oliver were very different. They'd only just met, whereas Corryna and Colin had a long history together, a professional relationship that had come before their romance. There'd been seeds for something deeper and lasting.

As for her and Oliver, they understood each other.

And Jessica felt a bit better about his easy dismissal of her skills now that she'd heard Corryna's take on it. She didn't need to get her ego caught up in Oliver's opinions about her; they were helping each other out, pure and simple. Once their agreement had come to an end, they'd both move on.

Alone.

So she absolutely did have some control over the situation. She just needed to remember that on all the lonely nights in her luxuriously appointed bedroom with Oliver just one floor away.

Eight

Swiping sweat from his forehead during a morning jog around Royal, Oliver waited for the runner's high to kick in. He craved that moment where his stride became fluid and his brain emptied of the thoughts that hounded him day and night. Ever since Jessica had moved into his house a week and a half ago, he'd needed these outings as much as oxygen in his lungs, the exercise burning off some of the hunger for her that never fully subsided.

Especially these last few days—now that his father was home from the hospital and recovering, it had been tougher and tougher to reach a place of mental clarity. Oliver had even added more miles to his workout. He rounded a man-made pond close to his development, the pounding of his stride startling a family of ducks to move closer to the water's edge. The sun had only just risen, and the neighborhood was still quiet except for a couple of riders on horseback he'd passed when he crossed an equestrian trail.

And how was it possible that he'd hit the eight-mile mark and his head was still wrecked with thoughts of his impossibly sexy roommate? By now, he was almost home and he still hadn't escaped the endless loop in his head from the night before, when he'd been working late in his home office only to cross paths with Jessica in the kitchen at midnight.

She'd been wearing a pair of too-short blue-and-white-striped boxers that would figure into his fantasies for years. And once he'd succeeded in dragging his eyes north, he'd only managed to reach chest-high when his attention snagged on the gentle sway of her braless curves in a T-shirt so thin and well-worn that it clung to her feminine shape.

Picking up his pace, he sprinted to make his lungs burn, to blast the memories out of his head since Jessica had made it clear that she was off-limits while they lived under the same roof. He would curse himself forever for agreeing.

A long chime pealed from his cell phone, which he'd secured to an armband made for that purpose.

Slowing his step since very few people or applications were allowed to notify him, Oliver tugged the phone from the memory foam sleeve.

The words "Back Door Alarm" flashed on the

screen of his device. An insistent vibration rattled the whole thing.

Jessica.

Fear for her shot through him. Chilling him.

He would never forgive himself if something happened to her while she was staying in his home. As his guest.

Already, his fingers tapped on the screen to open his surveillance-camera app while he answered a simultaneous call from the security agency.

"This is Oliver Price." He rattled off his address and confirmed his password. "I'm not at home right now, and I'm trying to access my cameras to see what's going on."

Even as he spoke, his phone vibrated with a second incoming call.

Jessica.

Everything inside him stilled.

He told the other caller, "My friend is at the house, and she's messaging me on the other line. I'm going to conference her in so we can both hear what's going on."

Breathing hard from his run and a fresh dose of fear, he hit the button to join the conversations as he answered Jessica's incoming call. "Jessica, are you all right? I've got the security company on the line with us."

"I'm fine." Her voice sounded steady. In the background of the call, he could hear the alarm system blaring. "I think the door codes changed last night,

and I forgot to make a note of the new one before I
went outside with my coffee."

Relief washed through him like a rogue wave,
so hard he steadied himself on a young maple tree
planted along the pond. His fingers clenched into the
bark. Thank God she was okay.

He issued the correct code into the phone for the
surveillance company to override the system and had
the satisfaction of hearing the alarm go silent in the
background of the call to Jessica. While the represen-
tative wrapped up that portion of the conversation,
Oliver noticed his device screen finally switched to
a live feed for the monitoring system.

There, in the backyard of his house less than a
half mile away, stood Jessica.

Dressed in the too-short striped boxers that had
played a starring role in his dreams the night before,
her curves on mouthwatering display. His breath
caught. Held fast in his chest like he'd just taken a
punch there.

Her voice in his ear caught him off guard. He'd
half forgotten they were still on a call together.

"So I can go inside now and the alarm won't go
off again, right?" she asked, her tone wary.

He knew that seeing her now was an invasion of
privacy. He'd told her about the cameras, though,
hadn't he? Remembering that conversation was the
only reason his finger hovered a half second too long
over the button to shut down the live feed from the
back entrance of the house. She must know he could

see her. That the home-security company could have seen her if they chose to access the footage.

"It's safe to enter," he assured her, his gaze traveling over her with a hunger he couldn't deny. He hadn't managed to subdue the craving after miles of running. How the hell could he expect to stuff down what he was feeling for her now when the sight of her turned him inside out? "And sorry about changing the door codes. I have an app that changes everything on a weekly basis for safety, but I can limit how often we change the codes."

"No. It's fine. I won't forget next time." She tipped her head against the side of the house, not entering the door yet. "See you soon."

She disconnected the call and he did the same. Telling himself to shut down the surveillance feed too.

In just one more moment.

One more second to remember how it had felt to kiss her right where her fingers tucked her wavy dark hair behind her ear. To recall how those lush hips had cradled his when he'd buried himself deep inside her. How her breasts had molded to fit his palm, the perfect handful.

A few seconds later, she stepped into the house, taking herself out of his view, and Oliver cursed himself for not shutting down the feed sooner. He needed to be more disciplined around her. Had to find a way to live with her without wanting her every second of every day.

Seeing her this morning had made one thing crystal clear to him, at least:

He would be in the best shape of his life by the time this fake engagement came to an end.

On the evening of the couples' shower for Ari Ramos and Xavier Noble, the scene outside the Texas Cattleman's Club was a crush. Jessica arrived alone in the back seat of a private car, the service arranged by Oliver, who had been out of town for the past three days. Ever since the day she'd locked herself out of his house.

"Miss Lewis?" The driver spoke to her from the speaker built into the console tucked between two of the leather bucket seats in the rear of the black SUV. "I'm going to take another lap around the parking area to give some of the traffic at the entrance time to clear."

"That's fine, Jason," she answered the driver—the same man who'd been chauffeuring Oliver around the night she'd met him. "Will you let me know if you see Oliver?"

"Of course, ma'am," he replied before clicking off the two-way speaker.

Peering out at the red-carpet style entry into the TCC clubhouse that had been specially arranged as part of the old Hollywood–glamor wedding theme, Jessica could see how entering the event would take a little time with the photographers set up outside the venue. No doubt some of the "paparazzi" had been hired by the event planner to set the scene and capture pictures of the guests, but she was certain there were a few real entertainment reporters in the mix as well. There was a short backup of guests waiting for their turn on the carpet.

She'd been looking forward to this glitzy party from the moment she'd agreed to the fake engagement, so she didn't want to spoil the night by thinking about how much Oliver had retreated from her over the past weeks. There'd been a wall between them, to her way of thinking, from the day she'd moved into his house. To a certain extent, she believed that had been of her making since she'd needed strict boundaries in their relationship to prevent herself from getting confused about what was real in their relationship and what wasn't.

Yet some of the gulf that yawned between them was definitely of Oliver's making. He'd barely met her eyes the day she'd locked herself out of his house, then announced abruptly that he had forgotten about a meeting he needed to attend at the Los Angeles office. He didn't seem like the type of guy to get out of sorts about minor things, such as her setting off an alarm to wake his whole neighborhood. Yet his demeanor had been strange that day, as if he'd urgently needed distance from her.

Remembering it now still stung.

The two-way speaker crackled to life again as the SUV pulled up to the front curb. "Miss Lewis, Mr. Price just emerged from a vehicle two cars in front of us. He'll be opening your door in a moment to escort you inside."

Anticipation bubbled up, making it hard to sit still. She edged forward on her seat, gathering the beaded gold purse that she'd chosen to go with a green silk wrap dress she'd scored at a consignment shop in her quest for something elegant for the party. The hem was floor length, but the bodice was a deep V in front and in back, with a knot to hold the pieces together just above the base of her spine. The fabric felt like a sensual caress against her skin, the moss green color bringing out some emerald in her eyes. A stack of thin gold bangles and strappy-heeled sandals rounded out the ensemble.

Would Oliver approve, she wondered?

She couldn't deny that she'd dressed with him in mind, taking more time on her hair and makeup than she normally expended. All of those minutes she'd spent primping had made her hyperaware, her blood heating as she now glanced out the window and caught her first glimpse of him as he walked toward her SUV.

He had taken care with his appearance today, too, it seemed, his black suit custom fitted to his broad shoulders and tapered to his waist. The crisp white shirt and black bow tie highlighted a clean-shaven jaw and deeply tanned skin. But it was the heat in his green eyes that most held her attention as he strode toward the vehicle and opened the door, offering her his hand.

Her pulse pounded harder.

The sounds of laughter and country music greeted her as her mouth went dry even before she laid her fingers in Oliver's palm. She knew full well how much that simple touch would affect her.

"I'm glad you made it." She tried to say it with a breezy air as their hands met, unwilling to let him see how much she'd missed him these last few days that he'd been out of town.

Actually, she'd felt his absence for longer than that. Because even before he'd left town, she had experienced a sense of loss with the end of their intimacy. Living with him and not being able to touch him—not having him reach for her either—had been a unique strain after the way they'd combusted from the moment they met. A loss that had caught her by surprise, so powerful, more each day.

His hand enveloped hers, squeezing gently as he helped her from the SUV in her long dress. She noted everything about that simple touch, from the warmth of his skin to the slight abrasion of hands that were more work-roughened than her own.

"I wouldn't have missed it for anything," he assured her as he drew her closer to brush a kiss on her cheek. He held her a moment longer than strictly necessary, speaking against her ear. "My first real opportunity to enjoy showing off my fiancée in public."

The words were low and intimate, his voice lighting up her insides with that tone perfectly tuned to her desires. She closed her eyes for a moment, drinking in the feel of him.

Of them together.

Her heart beat a rapid tattoo against her rib cage. Until there was a discreet feminine throat clearing nearby.

"Excuse me, Mr. Price?" A gorgeous, slightly flushed blonde in an ivory-colored sheath dress stood nearby, her hair in an updo adorned with pale pink roses, a digital tablet in her hand. "Are you and Miss Lewis ready for your turn on the red carpet?"

Jessica recognized Rylee Meadows, the high profile wedding planner hired by Ari and Ex to handle every aspect of their nuptials, from a photo she'd seen of her online. Before Jessica had worked the pre-wedding golfing event, she'd shamelessly researched all the players in the soon-to-be marriage that all of Royal seemed to champion.

Rylee was even lovelier in person, her blue eyes missing nothing as she assessed the traffic on the red carpet.

"We're ready," Oliver assured the wedding planner, moving his hand to the small of Jessica's back. His fingers brushed a bare spot between the top of her skirt and the silk knot where she'd tied the wrap dress closed.

Desire thickened in her veins, scattering all other thoughts but the feel of his touch on her skin.

"Excellent," Rylee murmured, indicating with one hand that they should come toward her. "I'll have you stand right here. As soon as the best man and maid of honor are finished having their picture taken, you will take their places in the center of the red carpet."

Jessica glanced ahead of them to see Dionna Reed and Tripp Noble gazing into each other's eyes before locking lips in a kiss that would have had Jessica fanning herself if she hadn't been so close to camera scrutiny.

Her skin heated at the thought of kissing Oliver that way. Like it was her right. Like she had all the time in the world to savor it. Cameras clicked and flashes of white light flooded the couple before they broke apart, all smiles as they looked into each other's eyes. Jessica had heard they'd fallen in love through some gossip among the waitstaff at a catering event last month, but she hadn't seen the pair together until tonight.

"Are you ready for your close-up?" Oliver's voice was in her ear again, his strong arm hugging her to his side. "You'll be photographed for all of Royal to see with my ring on your finger."

She wanted to lean into him. Kiss her way methodically along his jaw. And then his words sank into her brain, even as they stirred her senses: tonight was a very public declaration of their engagement.

Her stomach clenched a little at the thought of revealing the news on a wider scale, but it was far too late for second thoughts. She watched Tripp and Dionna continue their walk down the red carpet toward the main entrance of the Texas Cattleman's Club, the two of them glowing with love for each other. At the same time, Rylee announced their names to the gathered crowd, and Oliver led her into the spotlight.

Camera lenses zoomed and retracted as photographers on the other side of a velvet rope called to one or both of them, trying to get them to look toward one camera or another. The old Hollywood–glamor feel was so realistic she could almost believe their red carpet was on the other side of the country at a movie premiere instead of a posh Texas wedding party.

The thought made her miss a step. She hesitated a moment, her heart slamming with the first signs of prickly panic at the thought of being publicly photographed while posing as a fake fiancée. Was it wrong of her to mislead people? Would the assembled guests inside the Texas Cattleman's Club view her as an impostor in her consignment-shop dress and shoes that had seen better days?

Before her worries could spiral, however, Oliver's lips settled near her temple, and he spoke for her ears alone.

"You look stunning in that gown," he murmured softly, that rich voice of his wrapping her in a sound that soothed and tantalized all at once. "I'm the envy of many other men right now."

His flattery was lavish, and yet the warm words eased the anxiety, helping her to feel less nervous and more grounded. His arm around her waist anchored her, a steadying presence. She peered up at him, wondering how he'd managed the trick of helping her to relax when she felt like an interloper in this wealthy, elite world. She still didn't understand why he'd left Royal so abruptly earlier that week—but she had to admit, he seemed fully committed to their roles as a couple in love.

When his gaze met hers, she heard another round of cameras clicking. Flashes lit up the atmosphere all around them, casting them in a haze of white light. She couldn't help but picture a Cinderella moment and the wave of a magic wand transforming the heroine for the evening.

"I think we can go in now," Oliver told her a moment later, his hand at the base of her spine to steer her gently forward. "Let's find our table and settle in."

Heat seared its way up her back from the place where he touched her. To distract herself, she focused on the transformed Texas Cattleman's Club main dining room, decorated to look like a series of movie sets with backdrops relating to periods of Ariana and Xavier's relationship.

"Wow." She stifled an appreciative gasp at the scale of a giant book cover behind the book-themed area that must connect to Xavier Noble's status as a best-selling author. There were throne-style seats for the bride- and groom-to-be made out of stacks and stacks of books. "I would never even recognize the Texas Cattleman's Club tonight."

"Neither would I," Oliver confessed as he pointed to the movie set that recreated the offices of Ari Ramos's production company, the bride's name on a prop-style doorway with a big gold star beneath it. In that corner of the dining room, a wall of miniature television screens looked like they were each running a different one of her films. "Have you been here before?"

"Only to work catering jobs." She'd seen the kitchens and food-prep areas more than the guest spaces, in fact. She couldn't begin to guess what a membership cost at this prestigious club—yet another reminder of how they came from two very different worlds. "I've always admired the dark wood and stone, especially in the older parts of the building."

She couldn't help but marvel at how lovely the space looked tonight. Not just the elaborate decor that made her feel like she'd stepped into a Hollywood sound stage but also the historic building that had been the site of so many important Royal meetings, deals and weddings. Her gaze followed the line of one of the original old beams still visible in the high ceiling.

"I'm glad you're my date tonight instead of my drink server." Oliver stopped near a table overflowing with wrapped shower gifts for Ari and Ex. He removed a silver envelope from his breast pocket and laid it on a pewter platter with a stack of others. "I didn't see nearly enough of you the night we met."

Her cheeks heated at his intent gaze. The memory of that evening passed between them.

"That's a surprise since I seem to remember you

saw quite a bit of me." She didn't know where the flirtatious words came from, since she'd told herself she was not going to succumb to the potent attraction. But it was tougher to remember the boundaries when they were actively pretending to be in love.

When his hands were on her. His green gaze eating her up.

For a moment, the rest of the room fell away as she swayed a little under his hot perusal. Her throat went dry as dust.

"I remember." He spoke the words slowly. With emphasis. Significance. In a way that only stirred more memories of their time together. "And while recalling that night will ensure we do a convincing job in our roles as an engaged couple while we're here, it might not be easy to shake off the chemistry when we have to head back home afterward."

"You're right." She broke the eye contact to glance around the room again, needing a moment to collect the runaway thoughts growing more heated with every breath. "We're walking a bit of a tightrope to live together and keep our distance at the same time."

The party was filling up now, the room growing more crowded as friends and relatives arrived after their turns on the red carpet outside. A fiddle-and-accordion duo played some country standards from a stage in the back of the room, the acoustics of the mostly wood structure making a warm, welcoming sound despite the crowd noise and laughter.

Jessica hadn't spotted the bride and groom yet,

but over near the bar, she thought she recognized Sasha Ramos, the bride's sister, from Ariana's lifestyle blog. Corryna and Colin were supposed to attend the event as well, but Jessica hadn't spotted her friend yet. And she could scan the party with her eyes ten more times and it still wouldn't lower her spiked temperature from this conversation with Oliver.

Before he could respond, however, a tall man dressed in all black with a huge Nikon around his neck came to a stop in front of them. Jessica recognized local photographer Seth Grayson from other parties and events where she'd served on the catering staff.

"Excuse me? I'm trying to capture some photos for the bride and groom's Love Story album in front of our flower wall." Seth pointed toward a spill of red roses in an alcove nearby. A big white light on a rolling dolly pointed to a spot in front of the floral display. "Would you mind being one of my couples in love?"

"Of course," Oliver answered, at the same time Jessica asked, "What's a Love Story album?"

"I'll show you." Seth led them toward the alcove, where a whiteboard lay on a display table, showing the outline of an intricate mandala. Except each segment of the mandala was a photo image. Several in the middle were already full of candid shots of Ari and Ex. Around the perimeter, lotus-petal shapes curled toward the center with pictures of the bride's parents and friends, a few of the groom's friends. But many more spaces were blank. "We're designing a custom piece of art for the bride and groom's home with images from their wedding and the events leading up to it."

"This will be a beautiful way for them to remember their wedding." Jessica's fingers trailed over the sample board, ringing a picture of the elder Nobles kissing in front of the flower wall. "It's so special and romantic."

And it made her feel like a fraud for her fake engagement.

"Then I hope you'll be my next couple," the photographer wheedled, taking Jessica's hand and leading her to a mark on the floor in front of the roses. "Just try to forget I'm even here and give your fiancé a kiss."

Nine

Oliver steeled himself for having his restraint tested to its limits by the photographer's directive. Kiss Jessica in public after he'd spent the last three days running from their sensual chemistry in another city?

Sweet, sweet torment.

Even now, his body moved toward her of its own volition. Hell yes he wanted to wrap his arms around this woman and pull her against him. He craved the taste of her on his tongue, the feel of her soft breasts pressed to his chest. The way she looked in that silky wrap dress had been wrecking his head ever since she stepped out of the SUV in front of the venue. The thing looked ready to slide off her body at the slightest provocation.

And he yearned to be the man who unfastened the ribbon that would send the fabric on its downward trajectory. He'd spent three days on the road for Nexus, desperate to outrun the hunger for the woman in front of him. Yet no matter where he'd traveled, the memory of her walking around his house in a pair of too-short boxers chased him.

"Are we really doing this?" Jessica asked, her voice husky and low enough that only Oliver could hear her while the photographer twisted the lens on his camera and adjusted settings a few feet away from them.

"Are we really doing what?" he questioned her, settling his hands in the notch of her waist, just above the flare of her perfectly formed hips. "Teasing ourselves with all the pent-up longing we've been pretending doesn't exist?"

Her eyes locked on him, pupils dilating while the blue-green rims turned a deeper shade of azure. His blood thickened with hot need for her.

"No." She shook her head. Licked her lips in a fast sweep of her tongue he wished he could capture in his mouth. "I meant, are we really going to pose as an engaged couple for someone's memory album when we know perfectly well this won't last beyond the summer?"

He couldn't answer her, however, since the photographer chose that moment to call to them. The man—Seth, according to the literature on the display table—held up his camera and waggled it in the air as if to draw attention to it. Beyond him, the couples' shower grew louder as people began pairing up for some sort of party game.

A scavenger hunt, perhaps, since each pair of guests received a printed card and small pencil.

"All right, folks. I'm ready when you are," Seth alerted Oliver and Jessica. "No need to pay me any mind. Just act natural and lean into a kiss anytime."

Act natural?

The guy couldn't possibly know what kinds of visions that stirred because for Oliver, what felt most instinctive would be to sweep Jessica off her feet. Carry her to the nearest storage room or coat closet so he could have enough privacy to peel off her clothes and feel every inch of her nakedness against his.

Kiss her until she forgot her own name. Forgot everything but *him* and the insane chemistry that threatened to burn them both.

So yeah, he wasn't about to behave according to his genuine desires. Seeing the concern in Jessica's eyes, he recalled her question. Were they really going to have their fake engagement memorialized in Ari and Xavier's wedding album?

"Yes, we're really doing this," he answered her at last, skimming his hands a fraction lower, sliding over the slick dress fabric so that more of his hands rested on the swell of her hips. His fingers grazing the luscious curve of her ass.

The sounds of the band faded away. The laughter

and noise of the crowd became a distant backdrop for his pounding heartbeat while he angled his head and lowered his mouth over hers. For a moment, he simply breathed in her minty breath and fruity lip gloss, drinking her in. But then he heard the slightest hungry hitch in her otherwise-even pattern of inhales and exhales.

A sign that she was not immune to the same fierce appetites that plagued him.

The leash on his restraint felt taut. Frayed.

But he clung to it like a lifeline as his lips swept over hers. Once. Twice.

The third time, he licked into her, dizzy from the effort of holding back. Her mouth molded to his, her hands fluttering lightly against his shoulders before landing there more firmly.

He might have stood a chance against the sensual onslaught if her head hadn't tipped backward, her lush curves grazing his body and setting him on fire with need. But she melted into him like she'd just been waiting for the moment that they would reconnect. Like she'd been yearning for all the same things he had been these last few days.

Oliver's fingers flexed, gripping her tighter even as he kept his kisses soft. If she wanted more from him, he'd made it plain that she would have to articulate her preferences. He stood by that.

But his promise to respect her boundaries in private didn't apply right now, when they were in public and in front of someone who believed in their engagement. They were only acting to make it all look real.

Weren't they?

A voice in his head shouted at him that he didn't have the first clue how to separate real from pretend when it came to Jessica Lewis.

Another voice shouted too.

"I said, I've got it," Seth called loudly to them.

Making Oliver realize it wasn't the first time he'd said as much. Breaking the kiss, he edged a step away from Jessica, only to realize her eyes were still closed, her lips slightly parted and still glistening.

The sounds of the party returned to his ears— fiddle music and laughter, the pop of a champagne cork by the bar. Reality returned, making him aware that he still clutched her hips, the silken dress wrinkling beneath his grip.

What was it about this woman that turned him into someone he barely recognized? Cursing inwardly at his lapse of control, he relaxed his fingers and stepped away from her so fast she swayed a bit in the aftermath. Another time, he might have enjoyed the brief acknowledgment that their attraction was definitely not one-sided. But right now, when his sole purpose for their fake engagement was to ease his parents' worries about his future and to make the Noble wedding season more bearable, Oliver could hardly celebrate the fact that Jessica felt as off-kilter about their relationship as he did.

"Let's go find something to eat." Taking her

hand—if only to keep her steady, he told himself—
Oliver steered her toward the food offerings piled
high on tables in the back of the room.

"Do you really think that will help?" Jessica murmured beside him, keeping pace with his quick steps.
"I'm pretty sure the hunger we just stirred isn't going
to be appeased with pot stickers or bacon-wrapped
sea scallops."

Although he was pleased that she owned her part
of the attraction, he gritted his teeth to keep from
telling her that it made no sense to deny themselves
what they both wanted. With an effort, he unclenched
his jaw to answer her more politely as they arrived
at one end of a platter-laden table.

"But since food is the only thing on the menu for
at least a couple more hours, I suggest we use it to
sate what we can." He passed her an appetizer-sized
plate from the warmer, then took one for himself,
grateful the rest of the party guests were still looking over their player cards for the scavenger hunt.
At least this way, they could have their conversation without worrying anyone else would overhear.

"You say that as if you think it was a bad idea for
me to have suggested we keep things platonic," she
said softly, using a pair of tongs to transfer a couple
of prosciutto-wrapped persimmons with goat cheese
to her plate.

"Not at all. I understand your reasoning, and I
respect it." He started to reach for the oysters until,
recalling their reputation as aphrodisiacs, he thought

better of it. He served himself some croquetas from the tapas section of the appetizer buffet instead. "But you have to admit, it feels like we're fighting the forces of gravity sometimes, don't you think?"

Her laughter eased some of the tension in his neck, helping him remember he wasn't alone in his feelings. He took some comfort in that—and maybe a spark of hope that she could still change her mind.

"Maybe so." She added a vegetarian summer roll to her plate and a mini–chicken slider. "But I stand behind my rationale that our relationship will become confusing in a hurry if we start mixing personal desires with a mutually beneficial business agreement."

His brain stuck on the "personal desires" bit for a long moment, wishing he could hear her say it again and again. Preferably while acting them out for him so he could see firsthand exactly what shape her personal cravings took.

By the time he'd blinked his way through that mental inferno, he realized his plate was full and Jessica was waiting for him to accompany her to the seating area so they could eat. Doing his damnedest to refocus, he slipped a hand onto the small of her back and guided her toward an empty table near one of the fireplaces.

Lowering his head to speak quietly in her ear, he confided his take on the situation. "On the contrary, I would suggest what we're doing now is far more confusing. We're spending all our time running from an attraction that's not going away."

She missed a step, or maybe just halted in the middle of their trek to the tables. One moment, they were walking side by side; the next, she stood perfectly still, peering up at him with worried eyes that tracked his. "You really think that's what we're doing?"

He glanced around the main dining room of the Texas Cattleman's Club, careful about who might overhear them. They were close to a pillar roped with greenery and intertwined with white lights and gold columbine flowers; so for the moment, they had a small amount of privacy. Across the room, he spotted Jessica's friend Corryna Lawson making her way toward them.

So he was running out of time to make his case.

"I guess I can only speak for myself. But I boarded a plane after the security-alarm incident rather than wrestle hourly with the need to touch and taste you. Living together while pretending not to want you feels like a bigger facade than any make believe scenario we play out in public." He hoped like hell he hadn't overstepped their agreement by admitting it, but he had never guessed that keeping a lid on the simmering attraction would prove so difficult.

Her jaw dropped for a moment before she snapped it shut again. Then, giving herself a shake, she asked, "That's why you left so suddenly?"

"It is." He recalled vividly the way she looked when she'd been locked out of his home. The boxer shorts showing off her delectable thighs. The thin fabric of her shirt providing a visual he'd never forget. "When you locked yourself out of the house that day, I made the mistake of turning on the cameras to see what was happening for myself."

Understanding dawned. He could see it in her eyes. In the spots of hectic color blooming on her cheeks.

"I knew you were out of the house that day, so I didn't think—"

"It's your home too," he reminded her gently, unwilling to give her any reason to feel less comfortable there. "You did me a tremendous kindness to move in—"

"That you're already paying me for—" she began sharply.

Just as Corryna stepped around the pillar at Jessica's back to join them. Frustration stabbed through him.

"There you are!" Corryna exclaimed a moment later, her uncertain expression revealing she'd probably overheard at least some portion of their conversation. Oliver had done business with Corryna's floral shop, Royal Blooms, before, so he had a passing acquaintance with her.

A moment later, she was hugging Jessica tightly. "Sorry to interrupt. I just wanted to say hello and make sure you were having fun."

"I am," Jessica returned, her polite smile revealing nothing. "Oliver and I were just sitting down to eat."

"I won't keep you, then." Corryna turned toward him, her green eyes taking his measure and not making any pretense about it. "It's good to see you again, Oliver. And congratulations on your engagement. Jessica is one of my favorite people in the world."

He heard the warning in her words and regretted that she'd caught them during an awkward conversation. "Mine too." Taking Jessica's free hand in his, he lifted it to his lips and kissed the backs of her knuckles. "And thank you."

Excusing themselves, they slid into seats at a vacant table in the back of the room while the music and games continued around them.

No sooner had Jessica unfurled a white linen napkin across her lap than she rounded on him, a flare of vexation in her eyes.

"If you can't be comfortable in your own home, Oliver, I can't stay with you any longer."

Jessica could have never guessed how difficult it would be to live with Oliver throughout this pretense of an engagement.

They hadn't been at the couples' shower for even an hour yet, and her nerves were stretched near the breaking point from being around him. Or, more accurately, because of the kiss that had made her lose all her senses until she forgot everything but him. That brief locking of lips had reminded her how futile it was to fight the attraction that existed whether she ignored it or not. Her skin felt raw and exposed, like she'd scrubbed too hard in the shower and now everything that brushed past her made the oversensitized flesh tingle. She felt Oliver studying her now. Weighing her words and his response before he spoke. The silence stretched and tension thickened.

Digging into the appetizers on her plate, she hoped to hide her agitation from her dining companion. But sitting next to Oliver, in his perfectly fitted custom tuxedo, only made her want to rake her fingers through his hair and muss him up. She had visions of straddling his lap in her gown and rocking against him just so she could see his cool composure erupt into fiery passion.

And he thought he had fantasized about *her* in a pair of old boxers? He really had no idea how detailed her own imaginings grew the longer she kept apart from him.

Now, as she tore into her food with all the grace of a ravenous she-wolf, Jessica felt the heat of his gaze like a laser searing everywhere it touched.

"You can't move out now." Pinning her with his stare, Oliver used his broad shoulders to block out the rest of the room from her view. "You only just arrived."

"Nevertheless, I've been there long enough to make you want to leave." She chased an errant scallop around her plate with her fork. "I can't feel good about staying with you when it keeps you from being comfortable in your own residence."

Oliver laid a hand on her wrist, his thumb stroking the soft underside.

"So we rethink how to make it work, but let's not scrap the whole plan yet. As you pointed out, the arrangement is mutually beneficial." He stared down at where his fingers rested on her forearm, making her hyperaware of that connection. "And to be clear, it's not that I want to leave you. Far from it. I only wish to respect your boundaries."

His gaze lifted to hers, and for a moment she could feel the fire they'd both been trying to ignore. It smoked through her now, heating her from the outside in. The silk dress she wore teased her skin everywhere it skimmed over her body.

Even the fiddle music had swapped to a sultry number.

"I appreciate that," she said slowly, recognizing when she had backed herself into a corner. "Maybe it was a mistake to tie our hands where the attraction is concerned."

His nostrils flared, his eyes narrowing while the shade of green deepened. His fingers flexed lightly into her skin as he gripped her wrist.

"In other words, you might reconsider?" The bass-baritone voice that made everything he said sound like sex only served to incite a shiver now.

"I think that kiss we shared in front of Seth Grayson already did my reconsidering for me." How hypocritical would it be to deny something they both wanted when she melted into his arms like hot candle wax?

Corryna's voice returned to her mind, how her friend had warned her about the wedding events being steeped in romance. That all those romantic events might skew her perspective when there was a lot of attraction beneath all the practical motivation for their fake engagement.

And here Jessica was at her first wedding event as Oliver's date, already succumbing to the romance and the attraction.

To her surprise, his hand slid away from her arm now, his attention returning to his plate. "You should give it some thought first," he cautioned. "We can't let wedding fever make all our decisions for us."

A look passed between them. She could have sworn they were both thinking about their night together. They'd talked about wedding fever then. A shiver skated over her skin, but she hid it, forcing her attention back to the appetizers on her plate. She took another bite of a bruschetta just as a tall man in a blue suit approached their table, grinning at Oliver.

"I hear congratulations are in order," the man announced, his dark eyes full of good humor. "My partner is really getting married?"

Rising from the table, Oliver's grin matched his friend's.

"Nikolai. Glad you're back in town." Rounding the table to greet him, Oliver clapped his friend on the shoulder. "Jessica, allow me to introduce my business partner and the Nexus CFO, Nikolai Williams. Nik, this is Jessica Lewis, my extremely talented musician fiancée."

Nik leaned closer to shake her hand. "I'm thrilled for you both. Truly. Oliver deserves happiness as much as anyone I know."

Wiping the corners of her mouth with the linen napkin, she swallowed past the guilt at the lie they were caught in, feeling like an impostor more than ever in front of this nice man with kind eyes.

"Thank you so much. It's great meeting you too." She rose from her seat to speak to him, aware the party venue was filling up now, the volume louder, the noise slightly more raucous as the crowd settled in. "If you'll excuse me for a minute, I'll let you two catch up while I touch base with my friend."

She'd felt awkward about the way she'd left things with Corryna and wanted to check in with her. Excusing herself, Jessica was halfway across the room when one of the servers—her frequent waitstaff companion when Jessica worked catering jobs—flagged her down.

Big, burly Matt Sampson was carrying a tray of empty champagne flutes in one hand and a bag of ice in the other. She'd been working with him the night she'd met Oliver at the golfing event.

"Hey, Jess." Matt gave a nod hello, as both hands were full. His face was red from the heat of the job, his forehead dotted with sweat. He must have backbar duties tonight. "I just saw your mom in the kitchen, if you have a minute to say hello. She asked me to let you know she's here."

"Mom is here? At the TCC?" Self-conscious of her ultra-feminine dress in front of someone she usually worked with, Jessica realized her words might have come out the wrong way. Uppity, maybe. "That is, her ranching work doesn't usually bring her over here."

She tried to imagine what business would have brought her mom to the Texas Cattleman's Club tonight. She really owed her a visit—another thing to feel guilty about. Jessica had phoned her parents with the engagement news, but between moving, getting registered for summer courses and getting set up with a new internship, she hadn't made time to show off the ring yet. Although, maybe some of her reticence had been rooted in the fact that the engagement wasn't real.

Matt shrugged and backed up a step. "I didn't ask. They've got me running tonight."

He hastened his step toward one of the doors leading into the back.

Toward the kitchen. A place Jessica had not anticipated visiting while wearing her silk consignment-store find that she would hate to ruin.

But what kind of daughter ignored a request from her mom to say hello?

Steeling herself for the heat and frantic pace of the kitchen, Jessica pushed on the swinging door between the glittering world of a Hollywood couple's love story and the hardworking people behind the scenes that made the glitzy stuff possible. Normally, she was firmly in the second camp, so she was comfortable in that world. But tonight? Dressed like Cinderella at the ball, she felt every inch the intruder as steam from a nearby dishwasher belched out the open appliance door.

Her silk dress went from skimming her body to shrink-wrapping her skin. And the hair she'd worn loose tonight probably retreated an inch or two as it snaked itself into frizzy corkscrews.

Servers blasted through the walkway at hyperspeed, never sparing Jessica a glance.

"Jessica!" A familiar voice called to her from deeper in the prep area—a section of the kitchen with a big worktable in the center and three sous-chefs at work assembling dishes.

One of them looked up from his task to frown at her.

"Mom?" Jessica searched the crowded, busy scene until a small figure emerged from the store room near the refrigerated section.

Dark-haired and petite, Raquel Lewis wore two long braids for work every day. Now a weathered cowboy hat rested on her head, and she wore a chambray shirt embroidered with the Triple C logo. Jeans and boots completed the outfit that had varied little from day to day for as long as Jessica could remember. Even her scent was the same, the White Linen a distinctive choice that always made Jessica think of home.

"Baby girl, look at you!" her mother exclaimed, taking Jessica's hands and holding her arms wide to admire her dress, ignoring the soft curses of a sommelier rushing past with a bottle of wine tucked in his arm. "So sophisticated! Although this humidity isn't doing your dress any favors, is it?" She frowned a moment and then shook off the expression to smile once more. "But let me see this ring you wear. It is the whole reason I am here."

Jessica attempted to shuffle back a step to avoid the worst of the kitchen traffic while her mother brought her left hand forward to inspect the heirloom diamond band Oliver had given her.

"I'm sorry I haven't been over to the house before now," she apologized, keenly feeling the wrongness of showing off the special ring in the middle of a busy workplace. "I was surprised to find out you were here tonight."

"The band is beautiful, Jessica. Just gorgeous." Her mom pulled her in for a tight hug. "I knew the TCC was hosting the Noble and Ramos family's couples' shower and figured you would be here. So when the Triple C got an order for more steaks tonight, I traded kitchen duties with the driver who would have normally delivered them."

Another guilty pang shot through her at the lengths her mom had gone to in order to see something that Jessica should have shared with her within the first few days of receiving. Would her mom guess that something was off about the engagement?

"Thank you, Mom. I'm going to bring Oliver over for dinner. He's been out of town a lot—"

From deeper in the kitchen, a clanging bang sounded, like someone had dropped a pan. Two voices cursed in unison.

"It is fine, sweetheart," Raquel assured her, her dark eyes warm with a happy light. "We will meet in good time. There's no need to rush when we will be family for a lifetime."

Jessica gave a wooden nod in return, grateful for her mother's easy acceptance while the shame from lying clogged her throat in a cold lump. Her mom encouraged her to return to her party, and Jessica pivoted to exit the hustle and bustle of the prep area.

She caught sight of herself in the reflective glass of the swinging doors that led back to the party. Her hair was wild. Her dress clinging. Just a few minutes back in the real life of the kitchen and it seemed like all her attempts to be a part of Oliver's wealthy world had collapsed.

But the way she felt inside was far worse than how she looked on the outside. Not bothering to find Oliver, Jessica made a beeline for the exit. She needed to find the fastest way to escape before her longing for the man led her to add to the pile of regrets.

Ten

Oliver kept one eye out for Jessica's return as his business partner, Nikolai Williams, brought him up to speed on a few deals in progress with Nexus's West Coast offices. Nik seemed to have things in hand, as usual.

Leaving Oliver free to wonder what was taking Jessica so long to return to the table. Even now, he could see Corynna in conversation with the bride-to-be near the gift display, but Jessica wasn't with them. Where had she disappeared to?

"Oliver, are you listening anymore?" Nik asked suddenly, swiveling around to glance about the crowded Texas Cattleman's Club dining room. Then he turned back to Oliver, grinning. "It's going to be a new era at Nexus when business doesn't monopolize your thoughts 24-7." He shot a knowing glance Oliver's way. "But it looks like I can't compete for your attention with your new fiancée."

Realizing there was more than a little truth to the teasing accusation, Oliver questioned how Jessica had become so important to him so quickly. He tried to convince himself he only felt responsible for her because they were attending the event as a couple. It wouldn't look right for him to just abandon his fiancée midway through the evening.

"Sorry, man. I'm not used to having a significant other, so I'm not always sure of the protocol. I don't want to make a wrong step." His conscience stung at the idea of lying to his partner—his closest friend. Frankly, he couldn't go through with it. Not when he'd already deceived his own family. He clapped a hand on Nikolai's shoulder and drew closer to confide, "Actually, just between you and me, the engagement is more of a…business arrangement."

The musicians playing on a small dais at the far corner of the room switched to a lively jig, making a handful of the bride's friends take to the floor to show off their newly learned square dance–style moves.

Nik's dark eyebrows shot up as they watched the women twirl and spin. "As in, you're faking it?"

Oliver scowled, his hand sliding away from his friend's shoulder. "For good reasons. You know about my dad's health issues. I thought giving my family a fiancée like they've been lobbying for would ease his mind so he could recover. And Jessica has her own reasons for agreeing to the plan."

Nik gave a low whistle, the sound somehow implying Oliver was in over his head. Then again, maybe Oliver was reading into it since he was beginning to worry that he'd underestimated how tough it would be to deceive family and friends with a fake engagement.

Or, more accurately, he'd underestimated the toll the deception would take on him. And on Jessica too.

"You think that's a mistake?" Oliver asked, sincerely wanting to know his friend's thoughts.

"Honestly?" Nik spread his arms wide as if to show he was powerless to give anything but an honest opinion. "I think you're deceiving yourself a little bit about faking it. Because the sizzle was evident when you two looked at each other."

Oliver opened his mouth to argue, but his partner held up both hands to stop the flow of words before they began.

"Hey. You know what you're doing. But I've got to call it like I see it." Excusing himself, Nikolai left to speak to Tripp Noble, after assuring Oliver he would be attending the Nexus party to celebrate the new merger the following weekend.

Leaving Oliver to brood over the fact that he had visible sizzle with his fake fiancée. The same one who had pulled a disappearing act in the middle of a couples' shower that she knew was important to him.

Half the reason he'd wanted the engagement was to make the pre-wedding parties easier to handle. Had something upset her?

Before Nik had arrived at their table, Jessica had confided that she was reconsidering their former agreement to keep things platonic between them. The possibility had been circling around his brain ever since, tantalizing him with what might happen when they left the party tonight, even though he'd done his level best to advise Jessica to proceed with caution.

Caution was the last thing he wanted with her, but he also cared about her enough that it mattered to him a great deal if she made a decision that she would later regret. The depth of that concern for her should be a warning to him. Yet he could only think about finding her right now. Making sure she was okay.

After circling the interior of the dining room, Oliver pushed through a side exit to the revamped gardens and pool area of the club.

He spotted her immediately. A lone feminine figure pacing in front of a wooden bench, her green silk dress hugging her body in the light spring breeze. She looked incredible to him, like a garden sprite with her hair loose, the dark waves dancing around her head. But something about her posture—her folded arms, the set to her jaw—alerted him that she was distressed.

"Jessica." Shading his eyes from the sun so he

could better see the nuances of her expression, he walked toward her. "Is everything okay?"

As he reached her side, he could see a few curls around her face, the natural state of her hair reasserting itself. His fingers itched to stroke through the silky mass, but the wariness in her blue-green eyes warned him that they needed to talk first. The sounds of the party were muted out here, but the strains of a country love song were audible, along with the chirping song of a few sparrows and chickadees in a nearby live oak.

"No." She shook her head, meeting his eyes for the first time. "Things are not okay. I saw my mom just now, in the kitchen." She paused a moment, as if to let that sink in, her emphasis on "kitchen" subtle but telling. "That's where my own mother got see the ring for the first time, surrounded by swearing chefs and a waitstaff moving at the speed of light. I never felt like such a fraud in my whole life."

Ignoring any former sense of caution, Oliver opened his arms to her, and she walked into them without hesitation. It was wrong to feel a small sense of victory in that, the fact that she would accept comfort from him at a time when she felt unnerved. He wasn't worthy of that trust if he couldn't focus solely on Jessica's happiness, so he did that now, shutting down all his body's reactions to having her in his arms.

"You're not a fraud," he told her softly, stroking one hand over the back of her sun-warmed, silky head. "It was me who talked you into this scheme, Jessica, and I'm sorry it's causing you hurt."

"That's not true." She shook her head, her forehead moving back and forth against his shoulder while her words remained muffled from his jacket. "I own my role in this arrangement. I wanted to help my mom and dad, the same way you wanted to give your parents peace of mind. It seemed so simple then. I should have known how complicated this could become."

His hand stilled on the back of her head. "Those intentions aren't all bad, are they? People marry— genuinely marry—for worse reasons, and half of them wind up splitting up anyhow."

The light fragrance of her skin teased his nose while he waited for her answer. Her hair had fallen away from the back of her neck, revealing the tattoo he had spotted the night they'd met.

Blue letters spelled out "When words fail, music speaks." He traced the curve of the W, where green ivy wound through it. He felt the shiver his touch caused, and she straightened a moment later, edging back a step from him.

"That's true, I suppose." She hugged her arms around herself. "Although it seems a pessimistic outlook for a man surrounded by a family of happy marriages."

"I prefer to think of myself as a realist." He'd never met a woman who'd made him think marriage would be preferable to building his business. "And for what it's worth, our fake relationship has been more rewarding than the so-called real dates I've been on over the last few years."

Inside the TCC clubhouse, a cheer went up as the musicians launched into a popular country dance tune. Outside, the sun was setting and the lights in the garden turned on, spotlighting trees and specialty plants. The pool lights came on as well, the water illuminated from below the surface, the color changing every minute or two.

"I would agree with you there," she mused, pivoting on her heel to take in the garden. Night birds called from tree to tree.

"You never did tell me about your dating days." He extended one arm to indicate the wooden bench nearby, tucked under a rose arbor, then led her in that direction. "Remember when I tried to outdo you with my stories of aggressive kindergarten parents? I told you we'd circle back to those bad dates of yours."

Lowering herself to take a seat on the bench, she smiled ruefully.

"They are hardly worth the telling." She smoothed her palms over the wrap dress, preventing the silky fabric from catching too much breeze.

Not before he'd caught a glimpse of curvy thigh. Enough of a view to make him recount all the reasons he needed to focus on her feelings right now instead of how badly he wanted to touch and taste her again.

Out in front of the club, a pair of headlights swung

wide, casting a brief swath of brightness across their faces before the shadows returned.

"Still, I'm curious," he pressed, joining her on the bench, letting himself breathe in her sweet scent even if he couldn't risk touching her. They should probably return to the party soon, but he hadn't seen Jessica in three days. Talking to her tonight reminded him how easy it was to converse with her. The night they'd met had been about more than sex. He'd enjoyed getting to know her. "How bad was dating that you chose a fake relationship over the possibility of a real one this summer?"

She lifted a shoulder as if at a loss to explain. Then, shaking her head, she said, "I'm probably going about it all wrong. But who has time to meet people the old-fashioned way? I end up on dating apps, where everyone is lying about themselves and what they're looking for."

He hated the idea of anyone lying to her, but he didn't want to shut down her confidence when she was finally talking about herself. Picking up her hand, he threaded his fingers between hers, telling himself he wasn't touching her for seduction. He touched her to reassure her. Because he was a friend.

"I understand about being too busy." He'd often told his parents the same thing—that he didn't have time to date because work filled his evenings and weekends.

She shifted on the bench, crossing her legs in a way that drew his attention despite all his good intentions toward her. "Mostly, I'm just tired of dating men who are more interested in checking their phones than they are in having a conversation. I don't want to be someone to fill their time until something better comes along."

Anger heated his chest at the thought of anyone using her that way.

Until he remembered how their relationship was one of convenience as well. But it wasn't the same thing, damn it. They'd set up rules and boundaries. The agreement was mutually beneficial.

"Now that I know about your dating experiences, I stand by what I said before. Our relationship is better than plenty of others." He lifted their joined hands and kissed the back of hers. He kept her hand there for a long moment, breathing in the scent of her skin.

Knowing damned well what he felt for her was more than just friendly, but unable to pull away yet.

Earlier, she'd suggested she was ready to resume a physical relationship with him, but he wouldn't push. She deserved to know how special she was, and he was confident he could prove to her that he wasn't interested in anything else when she was around. For that matter, she'd been all he thought about even when they weren't together.

She studied him over their united hands, the sound of crickets beginning to overtake the song of birds as the twilight deepened.

"Really? Because sometimes I wonder if love and romance is all a myth and everyone else is faking it too. My parents have a great relationship, but it seems like it's about respect and shared goals. Maybe that's the most real kind of relationship there is."

To hear her dismiss romantic unions caused a twist of hurt inside him. Not for himself, of course. But for her. He regretted that she'd been involved with people who'd caused her to be so jaded.

He'd regret it even more if their relationship contributed to those feelings.

"Now who is being a pessimist? I'm sure those things exist. My family is full of wildly-in-love couples." Weren't they? He didn't believe his siblings had all chosen practical partners for the sake of expediency. "Look at your friend Corryna. I saw her inside with Colin Reynolds just now. There's no way you can believe their relationship is anything but a love match."

The two of them had been unable to keep their hands off each other, always touching somehow, even if it was just standing so that their shoulders brushed. What would it be like to be able to kiss and touch Jessica whenever he wished?

She chewed her lower lip while her gaze shifted back to the clubhouse, every window glowing with light from the party within. Country music and laughter spilled out onto the gardens and grounds, but they were the only ones who'd sought the fresh air.

"What if that's just passion?" she asked, her voice thoughtful. "A connection that fades with time?"

He paused for a beat before answering, recognizing that he didn't want to share any of the immediate responses that blasted through his brain. He wasn't about to contribute to the negative view she already held about romance and dating.

"Why is it a given that passion diminishes?" he asked instead, stretching one arm behind her on the bench. Not touching her, but almost.

Aside from how much he wanted her, he was also curious to learn more about her. He realized he'd rather spend the evening out here talking to her than return to the party. Just like that first night they'd met, she captured his full attention. Fascinated him.

Even when he couldn't have her in his bed.

"Maybe it doesn't. I'm just not sure I believe that something so…" Hesitating, she seemed to search for a word. "…*momentous* could last."

Flames licked up his spine at her choice of words.

Was she recalling the passion they'd shared? He sure hoped so. Because it had felt that way for him too.

"I would think the opposite is true." His voice was pure gravel, given the way her words had unleashed all his hottest thoughts. "The more intense the passion, the more likely it will last."

Where their hands were still bound together, he could feel her pulse thump harder. Or maybe it was his. Because he knew for sure his heart rate had kicked up. They stared at one another for several long, uneven breaths.

"Unlike romance, at least passion is something concrete. Something I can feel." She listed closer to him, her eyelids falling to half-mast.

He was pretty sure sweat broke out along his brow at the direction of their conversation, and he didn't trust himself to speak. Hell, he didn't even breathe.

"Oliver?" She whispered his name over his lips, her mouth near enough to taste. "I won't deny either one of us something we both crave. Not anymore."

Hunger for her surged, the need he'd suppressed for two weeks redoubling now. "I can't tell you how pleased I am to hear that. But if I start kissing you now, I'm not sure I could stop."

She affected him the way no other woman ever had, messing with his control. Infiltrating all his thoughts.

Her eyes went wide. Then she nodded once, as if satisfied with his response. "Then I suggest you take me home as fast as humanly possible."

His hunger for her kicked him into gear. Rising from the bench, he pulled her to her feet with one hand while he withdrew his phone with the other. "I'm texting the driver to meet us out front."

Jessica wanted to be with him now?

He would set a new land-speed record to make it happen.

Passion, Jessica understood.

Heart beating fast as the black SUV sped them toward Oliver's home, Jessica reminded herself that she could indulge in the heat of attraction tonight. Because while romance might not exist the way she'd once imagined it, passion was genuine. Quantifiable. It was a conflagration of the senses. Not unlike music, where she could get lost in the emotions, experience the dramatic highs and lows.

All while standing a little outside it at the same time. When she finished an ethereal piece of music, she could separate herself from it by setting down the guitar and walking away.

This chemistry with Oliver was the same. Momentous and consuming, yes. But she would still walk away when it was over at the end of the summer.

And if she was going to feel guilty for deceiving her family and his, didn't she deserve to experience the joys that intimacy could bring? She'd thought about their night together every single day since it had happened. She dreamed about it when she went to sleep too.

Tonight, there would be no more dreaming and wishing. She risked a glance over at Oliver in the back seat beside her. He looked out the window, jaw set, his whole body tense. But at least she understood why since the same tension gripped her.

If I start kissing you now, I'm not sure I could stop.

A sentiment she understood all too well.

A moment later, the SUV turned into the long driveway that led to Oliver's modern home, the gray-stone facade illuminated with a wealth of landscape lights and a few interior fixtures that were on daily timers. Ever since she'd been locked out of the place by the high-tech security alarm, she had been more careful about taking note of the house's "smart" features.

When the SUV rolled to a stop, Oliver didn't wait for the driver to come around. He shoved the rear door open himself and helped her from the vehicle. Then, taking her hand, he led her up the front steps and through the front entrance that he'd already unlocked from his phone.

As the weighted door locked behind them, they turned to one another. One moment, their eyes met. The next, their mouths were fused.

Jessica couldn't have said who moved first. They seemed to come together in unison, their heads tilting for better access, hands roaming arms and shoulders, as if being closer, closer, closer still was an imperative need.

"I've missed you." Oliver spoke the words over her lips while he backed her through the living room.

She moved with him as easily as if they'd choreographed the dance. Stepping out of their shoes. Feet tracking toward his bedroom on the main floor. Hands unfastening buttons and zippers so that his shirt and jacket were gone and her dress drooped to her waist by the time they reached the threshold of the darkened suite.

Her breath came in heavy pants, her heart pounding wildly. If it had been a symphony, the whole percussion section would have been involved. She almost laughed at the image in her mind, but she was too consumed with the need to feel more of Oliver's warmth. His strength.

"I've been dreaming about this," she admitted between kisses, her fingers hooking into his belt as she worked free the clasp.

"I haven't dreamed about anything else," he countered, untying the ribbon that held the dress closed at her waist. "Not one damned thing except this. You. Us together."

She closed her eyes for a long moment, savoring that idea. That this powerful, compelling man had been thinking of her with that kind of single-minded focus. Her silk gown fell away in a slow flutter to the floor, the cooler air meeting her skin and giving her goose bumps.

Or perhaps it was a reaction to Oliver's hot stare as his gaze raked over her simple white strapless bra and matching thong. The dress might have been a consignment find, but she'd splurged on the underthings, knowing full well that she intended for him to see them. Touch her while she wore them.

The fire in his green eyes was worth every hard-earned cent she'd spent.

"In that case, I hope you take your fill tonight." Freeing the belt, she laid her palm over his abs, feeling the ripple of muscle there.

He gripped her wrist, stilling her wandering hand.

"It's going to take more than one night to quench this thirst."

Beneath her palm she could feel a shiver pass over him, and it felt like the reaction leaped from him to her, a tremble quivering over her flesh. She'd never craved a man this way.

"Then it's a good thing I live here too."

If she'd thought his gaze was hot before, it turned positively molten now. He lifted her in his arms, dragging her body against his as he hoisted her in a way that wrenched a soft, hungry moan from her throat. Her breath raced between her lips. She wrapped her legs around his waist, her core pressed to the hot, hard length of his erection.

If not for the clothes that remained between them, he would be inside her now.

His hands cupped her ass, holding her tightly against him, raising and lowering her by slow degrees in a way that made her breath catch. Tension coiled inside her already, her orgasm so close. All her nerve endings were attuned to his touch. His taste and scent.

She threaded her fingers into his hair, holding on to him to anchor herself while he slid his palms along her thighs, his thumbs circling her knees. Who knew knees could be an erogenous zone?

Yet with Oliver, the touch made her legs shake. She whispered a litany of encouragement in broken words and sighs since she couldn't keep a coherent thought in her head. She only knew she wanted him. Now.

So, with unsteady fingers, she flicked open the fastening on his pants. Stroked him through his boxers while she wriggled against him, trying to increase the friction. Or at least edge her panties sideways.

With a soft oath, Oliver backed her against a mirrored door—a closet or bath, maybe. The cool glass felt good against her overheated skin, though not nearly as good as the man who pinned her to the reflective surface.

Their gazes collided as she locked her ankles behind him. He leaned to one side, reaching into the drawer of a nearby bureau. Emerging with a foil packet.

Grateful he'd kept his reason since all her focus had been on him, Jessica took the packet while he juggled her in his arms, making room between them so he could roll the protection into place. His pants still clung to his hips, but he'd freed his erection and she'd slid her underwear aside enough to make room for him.

When he nudged his way inside her, deeper and deeper, her head fell back against the door as sensations assailed her. Heat. Fullness. A perfect, delectable union.

Her fingernails dug into his shoulders, her knees hugging his hips as he seated himself as far as he could go. The needy sounds she made were noises she didn't even recognize, but somehow Oliver seemed to interpret them because everything he did felt better than the moment before.

His tongue stroked a path up her neck while his fingers tugged down the satin cups of her bra. When his lips closed around one taut nipple, the pleasure was exquisite. She held him there, desperate for his touch. His kiss. For the fulfillment that only he could give her.

Because no touch she'd ever experienced—her own included—could compare to the way his fingers played over her skin. Like a skilled musician, he coaxed new notes from the instrument of her body.

"Please, please, please," she chanted, her hands restless on his upper arms, where hard muscle shifted and flexed as he moved her body on his.

Then his lips tightened on her nipple, drawing hard on her as he moved inside her. Release cascaded through her in a sweet, rippling rush, making her forget everything but how good he made her feel. Moments later, when the aftershocks subsided and she returned to her senses, Oliver was moving them toward the king-size bed on the opposite wall of the room. She had a moment to register the earthy-colored plush cushioning that served as a headboard and stretched across the entire back wall of the room. The dark gray coverlet was folded back halfway, exposing lighter gray pillows.

She landed in the center of the mattress with Oliver on top of her. He was careful to keep his full weight from her, using his arms to lever himself above her. His green eyes met hers for a moment before he moved inside her again, his strokes long and deep.

Rhythmic.

Her eyes fell shut again with the need to simply feel all the things he made her feel. *Momentous. Overwhelming.*

Her memory of their chemistry had been accurate. She wanted to make him feel every bit as fulfilled and satiated as she did, but she could feel the tension building in him already. His fingers gripped the softness of her curves, holding her steady while he sank into her.

Over and over.

Propelling them both headlong toward bliss. Jessica felt the orgasm coming, stronger this time, racking her body as her muscles squeezed and shook. Oliver was right there with her, finding his peak and hurtling over the edge while he called her name.

She heard the hoarse shout, but she was so lost in her own sensations she could only cling to him for long moments afterward.

Later, she couldn't have said how much time passed as they lay side by side together, sated and spent. Breathing one another's air. Waiting for their heart rates to return to normal. She stroked her fingernails over his back. He smoothed her hair from her face.

Had it only been minutes? An hour? She only knew the room had grown much cooler by the time Oliver dragged the covers over them and tucked her against him so that her head rested on his chest. Had he done that to avoid the awkwardness of talking about what had just happened? Because she was pretty sure the earth had moved. Possibly mountains too.

More likely, it had only been her heart that had shifted.

She was afraid if she looked at it too closely, she'd see that it had cracked wide open. And despite all her best intentions, she'd allowed Oliver to take up residence there.

Tonight, her feelings were too raw to examine, however. How could she have fallen for someone when she didn't believe in love and romance? That would be a grave mistake. So she flung her arm across Oliver's broad chest and allowed the sweet exhaustion of lovemaking to lull her for one night at least. She had deserved this night of heat and passion. They both did.

Tomorrow, they'd need to discuss the consequences of their fake engagement. She knew that it was taking a toll on her heart. But she wasn't about to share that with Oliver when he'd been adamant that this was a business arrangement. Instead, she'd remind him of the cost to both of their families in the long run. Because even if she could put aside her own new feelings for Oliver, Jessica knew they couldn't keep on lying to people they loved.

Eleven

Oliver flipped pancakes on the griddle built into the center of his cooktop, a cool kitchen feature he'd never used before.

But then, he'd never felt compelled to make a beautiful woman breakfast after a night of hot sex. Probably because Jessica was more than just any beautiful woman, and their time together had been about more than physical intimacy. Details he wasn't ready to dwell on yet when they had the whole day together ahead of them.

And he wasn't going to waste a single moment of this pocket of time they'd been granted.

He'd cleared his schedule, ensuring he didn't have any work commitments for the weekend. In fact, his schedule was light right up until the Nexus party he was hosting at his home next weekend to celebrate the successful merger that almost doubled the Nexus New York branch's client list. Oliver had wanted the new executive team to feel welcome under the larger company's umbrella and had found events with a personal approach helped accomplish that. Next Friday, a catering-and-event company would take over his rooftop garden to entertain a group of fifty people—executives and their significant others flown in from New York City—for drinks and dancing under the stars. He reminded himself to ask Jessica if she was familiar with the musician they'd booked for the event.

Turning the heat off on the griddle, Oliver plated the pancakes and slid them into the warming drawer before he started on the eggs. The shower in the primary suite had just shut off, so he guessed Jessica would emerge soon to join him.

He didn't dare think about Jessica still wet and naked in the other room, or he would never finish making her breakfast.

While cracking the first egg into a frying pan, Oliver heard the front door chime. He couldn't imagine who would be awake and ready to visit before nine in the morning on a Saturday. He checked the doorbell app on his phone, hoping it was someone he could ignore. Instead, he saw his mother standing on the front step. Definitely not someone he would avoid. He might have worried that she had news about his father, except that Fiona Price carried a plastic container almost certainly filled with baked goods in her arms.

If she'd been baking, she must not be here to deliver bad news about his dad. She was dressed up more than usual, too, wearing a floral shirtdress and pink cashmere cardigan that suggested to him that she was probably meeting with her book club or heading to the farmer's market with a friend— both things she liked to do on her free Saturdays. He heaved a frustrated sigh, determined to send her on her way as soon as possible.

Switching off the heat under the frying pan, Oliver walked out of the kitchen and into the front room to open the door, grateful he'd taken time to pull on a pair of joggers and a clean T-shirt before making breakfast. Briefly, he considered texting Jessica to give her a heads-up about their guest, but he assumed she would realize they had company soon enough.

"Mom." Holding the door open for her, Oliver stepped back so she could enter. "Come on in. I was just making breakfast for Jessica and me, if you'd like to join us."

"Good morning." Stepping into the foyer, she greeted him with a hug and a kiss on the cheek while he closed the door. "I'm on my way to Jeannie's house for book club. I just wanted to bring over some fresh apple fritters." She slid the plastic container onto the hall table next to a vase of fresh white tulips. The scent of apple wafted from the box as she lowered her voice to add, "And I had a question for you."

Her tone would have alerted him that it was something important, even if she hadn't made a special trip to his house. Her friend Jeannie lived close to her on the other side of Royal.

"I'll do what I can." He thought she seemed a little edgy. So much for a speedy chat. "Do you want to have a seat?"

She twisted a diamond-stud earring between her thumb and forefinger.

"No, thank you. I just wanted to check with you if you had an issue with me asking Jessica to guide your father and I through some music therapy?" Crossing her arms, she faced him head-on, her expression serious. "I thought I detected some reticence on your part when she mentioned it at the hospital, and I definitely don't want to cause any relationship issues for you."

Oliver became aware of the fact that Jessica could join them at any moment. He didn't hear any sounds from the bedroom. But this wasn't a discussion he was ready to have with her yet. Not when their future remained up in the air.

Or rather, when their future was a very different one from what he'd led his family to believe.

"It's not that it would be a problem for me—"

She interrupted him, capturing both his hands in hers. "And yet it's obvious you don't want her to be involved in it, although for the life of me, I can't understand why. I've thought about it often ever since she talked to me at the hospital, and I can't see why you would object to having someone you love and trust lead your father through a program."

Her expression was so earnest that his guilt threatened to swallow him whole. How could he have foreseen his parents wanting to pull Jessica deeper into the Price-family world this way so quickly? He'd hoped there would be time to break things off before they formed an attachment to her. Yet should it surprise him when his family was as close-knit as they were?

His heart rate notched higher from being put on the spot. He knew Jessica meant well when she'd broached the idea with his mom, but blurring the lines between their worlds even more would make it that much tougher to disentangle them when the summer ended.

"It's not that I would object, Mom. I just think Dad would be better off with someone more experienced." He felt disloyal as hell saying it, since he had every faith in Jessica's musical ability and her instincts as a therapist. He remembered the way one of her student's had walked her out of the building where her group music therapy session had taken placed.

It had been obvious to him she made a difference in at least one kid's life. And he would bet she made a big difference in many more.

"But it would be a way for us to get to know her," his mother pressed, her forehead wrinkled with confusion. "You can hardly blame us for wanting your future wife to be a part of our lives too—"

Jessica's cool voice sounded behind him. "I can refer you to someone more experienced, Mrs. Price."

His gut dropped. The ice in her tone let him know how she felt about his dismissal of her abilities. He turned to see her stride forward, her hair damp from her shower and combed away from her pretty face. She wore a pink long-sleeved T-shirt with a pair of well-worn jeans, and despite the awkwardness of the moment, he couldn't help a wave of feelings for her. About her.

Their night together had been special, and he hadn't meant for it to end this way.

"Jessica," he began, hoping she would see beyond his words to the obvious concerns he had about her spending too much time with his family, "I didn't mean to suggest you aren't excellent at what you do—"

"Didn't you?" She gave him a brittle smile as she stepped around him to pick up a pen and paper from the hall drawer. She wrote something on the paper before passing it to his mother. Then her expression softened along with her tone as she met his mother's eyes. "This is the name of one of my professors who specializes in music therapy for stroke patients. She can walk you through your options for Mr. Price. I didn't mean to overstep that night at the hospital. I only wanted to help."

"Of course you did," his mother murmured, her

anxious eyes darting from Jessica to him briefly, then back again. "And Timothy and I are both grateful to you for mentioning it. We're going to pursue this for him."

Oliver watched, unsure what else to say to smooth things over, as his mother took her leave. He knew she was confused about the exchange—and his reluctance to have Jessica more involved in their lives—but he was counting on Jessica understanding once he could explain himself.

As soon as the door closed, he pivoted toward her, his heart beating fast with his unease.

"You must know the only reason I put her off was so that you wouldn't wind up feeling obligated to them after the summer ends. I know you didn't sign on for being my dad's therapist—"

Her lips flattened into a thin line. "I forgot how you were keeping your eye on the ticking clock of our limited time together. But trust me, I wouldn't have mentioned it to your mother if I didn't feel comfortable with it in the first place."

Another wave of guilt hit him over the fact that she thought he was focused on the expiration date for their relationship.

"And that was very thoughtful of you, but you have a lot on your plate already with school and the new internship." He didn't know how she fit in catering jobs, but she'd worked every night she wasn't in school that he was aware of. She'd kept her schedule clear just for the couples' shower.

"It's kind of you to monitor my schedule," she said evenly, her sea-colored eyes turning stormy. "But are you sure you aren't simply holding out for a more sought-after therapist with multiple degrees and years of scholarly publishing behind them? I've come to realize how much stock you place in having the best of everything, from your coffee maker to your alarm system."

He reared back at the accusation. "My *coffee maker*? You're angry at me over a kitchen appliance?"

She huffed out a sigh as she paced away from him with agitated steps. "What I can't understand is why you wanted to bring me into your life in the first place when nothing but the best will do for you. From your five cars—not counting the expendable Jaguar your niece dented—to the way you wrangled a private box at the county fair, for crying out loud. You must admit, you are used to the finest of everything." Reaching the floating staircase, she did a one-eighty so that she faced him again.

His head spun with the unexpected direction of her thoughts. The anger he hadn't anticipated. She had a right to be angry with him, but her reaction was off the charts, like there was something else driving her frustrationthat he couldn't seem to pinpoint. "Jessica, listen—"

"Except for fiancées," she continued, as if he hadn't spoken. She held out her hand where the engagement band rested. It winked in the light streaming through the sidelights around the front door. "In that category, you were willing to compromise your standards. But I guess that's what happens when you order up a fake."

Tugging the ring from her finger, she laid it on the hall table next to the box of apple fritters.

Panic started to roil in his gut. Too much. Especially given they'd entered this arrangement on a temporary basis.

"You're not being fair." He kept his voice steady even though it rocked the hell out of him to see her set aside that ring. Oliver racked his brain to understand how the morning had gone so wrong. How had he been blind to her frustrations with him? With his way of life? What else might he be missing? "I think the work that you do is noble and important. I just didn't want to make things more awkward for you with my family."

"You're right," she acknowledged more quietly. She tucked a damp strand of her hair behind her ear as she faced him once more, her eyes troubled. "It wasn't fair of me to bring up a lifestyle you worked hard for. I lashed out because it hurts to be constantly reminded that this relationship has an end date. Especially after last night."

Her honesty slashed through all the confusion, clarifying the murky argument and cutting to the heart of the problem. This frustration, he understood. How could he blame her for feeling slighted when he'd done exactly as she'd charged?

But it's not like they hadn't hammered out the arrangement ahead of time. They'd agreed on the terms that would help them both. Still, he felt the ground falling away from his feet and wasn't sure how to shore it up again. He just knew he wasn't ready for her to walk out the door—or out of his life.

"I thought I was helping you by keeping some boundaries with my family," he explained, the sting of her rejection burning his chest. She couldn't walk away from him now, could she? Not after what they'd shared. "I have every intention of honoring our agreement, and I hope you will too. I started to make us breakfast—"

She shook her head, her motions stiff. Her shoulders tense. "I can't keep lying to the people in our lives. I've been lied to enough times that I know how much it hurts."

Too late, he recalled the bad dates she'd mentioned. Men who'd deceived her. His throat burned at the possibility that he'd hurt her that way.

"We're being fully honest with one another, though." He prided himself on that. The terms had been clear. "Our arrangement has been transparent—"

"I can't honor the arrangement any longer, Oliver." Her voice rasped over the words, but her eyes were clear as she looked at him. "I'm sorry."

Something about her tone told him she wasn't changing her mind. A chill had descended on the day that had begun with so much promise. He wanted to ask her why, to understand how she could turn her back on him when their connection was unlike anything he'd ever experienced. But hearing her talk now, seeing her stony expression, made her seem like a stranger in spite of everything that had passed between them the night before.

And perhaps she mistook his silence for agreement because she cleared her throat a moment later before adding, "I can borrow my dad's truck to collect my things later this week. But for today, I think I'd better leave."

She padded away from him on bare feet while Oliver wondered why, after just a few weeks together, watching her go made him feel like his whole world was falling apart.

Not sure where else to go, Jessica found herself sitting on the sunporch of her parents' house later that afternoon.

Unwilling to take the vehicle Oliver had offered her as part of the bargain, she'd used a rideshare app to visit the mechanic who had changed her car's battery. Now she had a working vehicle of her own again. Too bad her heart was broken and she was no closer to helping her parents save their home.

But hearing Oliver's dismissive words about her to his mother? That made her realize she had to end things now. Loving him changed everything. She couldn't harbor those feeling and pretend they were a couple. It would destroy her already-aching heart.

She sipped from the steaming mug of chamomile and lemongrass tea her mother had brewed for her after Jessica had unloaded the whole messy saga, from her finding the notice about the balloon payment to meeting Oliver and the terms of their agreement, to the way she'd fallen for him while he was committed to ending things once summer was over. Her father was working at the Triple C all weekend, so he hadn't been subjected to the tear-filled tale. Jessica might have been able to remain dry-eyed with Oliver, her wounded pride kicking in. But as soon as she'd begun the retelling for her mom, the pain of walking away from Oliver had overwhelmed her.

Raquel Lewis dropped a kiss on Jessica's shoulder. "My darling girl," she said with a sigh, flipping one of her long braids behind her back as she swiveled on the cushioned rattan patio sofa to face her daughter. "You should have come to me when you saw the bank notice about the balloon payment."

"I felt terrible that you'd taken out the loan in the first place since I knew it had paid for my undergraduate degree." Jessica settled the hot mug with a butterfly-shaped handle on the tile-topped patio table.

Plants and flowers grew in pots all around the perimeter of the sunporch, green offshoots snaking between the windows overlooking the small backyard. Her mom was a green thumb, and everything she planted thrived. Potted sunflowers dominated one corner of the room, while a simple African violet decorated the coffee table near her tea mug. Hanging baskets of ferns dangled from the exposed wood beams of the enclosure.

"But that was our choice." Raquel spread her hands wide as if in disbelief. "You paid for your books and things, and we were proud to help pay for the tuition not covered by scholarships."

"At what cost, though, Mom?" Panic bubbled inside her, along with guilt and helplessness that she couldn't be there for them the way they'd always supported her. "You're going to lose the house if we can't make that payment—"

"'We'?" Raquel sat up straighter. "*We* are not doing anything, Jessica. The bill is the responsibility of your father and me, and we decided long ago that when the payment came due, we would simply put the house on the market."

"Sell the house?" Agitated at the very idea, Jessica rose from the sofa. "You can't just give up your home, a place you've loved for years."

Her mother laughed dismissively. "'Loved'? Jessica, this is a nice house, but it is just that. Walls and a roof that have sheltered what is far more important—my family. And now that you are older, we don't need the extra bedroom or a lot on a cul-de-sac close to other children."

Stunned her mom could write off all the memories they'd made in the place, Jessica studied her parent's face, trying to figure out her angle. "You can't be serious. Mom. Don't try to make me feel better about this—"

Raquel rose and took Jessica's hands in her own. "Sweetheart, I love you, but this decision doesn't have anything to do with you. Your father and I loved the time we spent raising you—but now that you are grown and pursuing your own life, we have the time and freedom to follow other paths."

"What other paths?" She regretted having to ask the question that revealed how little she knew her own family. "Have I been that self-absorbed that I closed my eyes to dreams you've deferred to be here for me?"

"Of course not." Her mother tugged her toward the sofa again, lightly guiding her onto a cushion again before taking the seat beside her. "It's just that we are content to live on the ranch, the way lots of our colleagues do. We spend much of our time there anyway, and the animals and staff are our extended family now."

"You won't miss having a place of your own?" Jessica searched her mother's face, looking for clues that all of this was an act to make Jessica feel better about them selling their home to avoid the big loan payment due soon.

But she saw only honesty. Contentment. Certainty.

"I won't miss having appliances to fix and roofs to replace. When you own a home, there's always something to repair. Now we can save our money for vacations so we can travel in our free time." The excitement in her voice convinced Jessica that she really didn't mind giving up her house.

Relieved for her parents' sake, she would have felt happy if she didn't have the new wound that her breakup with Oliver had left behind. How ironic that the fake engagement would have ended soon anyway since her parents didn't need her help.

"In that case, I'm happy for you, Mom." Jessica laid her head onto the backrest of the sofa, grief for what she'd lost weighing her whole body down. "And I wish I'd come to you about the bank notice too. Then I would have never been tempted to make this crazy bargain with Oliver—"

"But you would have found one way or another to see each other again after that first electric meeting," her mother interjected gently, sitting up to examine the African violet. She turned the clay pot in her hands, plucking a few dead leaves from the base. "From what I can tell, the two of you share a passionate connection. I would bet you would have found your way back together after the night you met, even if it hadn't been for the fake-engagement idea."

Jessica remembered the night on the Ferris wheel, when she'd been so dazzled that he'd found the place where she interned and made a special surprise of the seats at the county fair. Part of the reason she'd agreed to be his fake fiancée had been a wish to walk in his world for a change. It had been unfair of her to fling his wealth in his face when she'd enjoyed plenty of facets of his lifestyle.

"Perhaps. But either way, I would have had to face the truth that Oliver doesn't want the kind of relationship with me that I crave with him." She couldn't forget the way he'd emphasized the expiration date of their arrangement. The fact that he didn't want her spending too much time with his parents for fear she would develop a bond that would be difficult to break when the engagement ended.

"Does he know the sort of relationship you want?" Her mom settled the newly pruned violet back on the table.

Jessica wondered if she had the emotional fortitude to prune her own life as ruthlessly as her mother was willing to shape and pare down hers. But maybe she would never reap the reward of a thriving life and love if she didn't put in more effort to mold the future she yearned for.

But how big of a risk would it be to put her heart on the line again? What if she spelled out exactly what she craved from him, and he still only wanted a casual friends-with-benefits plan?

Just the thought hurt.

"He doesn't know," she admitted, longing for some of her mother's clear-eyed wisdom. "But I think I'm still officially on the guest list for a party he's hosting Friday."

An idea began to form. A way to see him again but still have the safety net of a public event that would remind her to keep her composure, no matter the outcome.

"So you waltz in there one more time and tell him how you really feel. If he doesn't reciprocate, then it's his loss. But at least you put it all on the line."

Imagining the gut punch it would be—if she made a fool of herself for no reason, only to have him continue to host his friends at his exclusive party— nearly made her want to forget the whole thing. But she'd been hiding from love and romance for too long. She was already hurting. She had nothing to lose, and potentially, everything to gain.

She hadn't thought they were even real until she fell for Oliver Price. Now the weight of what she felt crowded out everything else inside her, threatening to topple her. And it was very, very real.

"I'll do it," she vowed, wrapping her mother in a hug and holding on tight, heart full of wary hope. "But I'm going to need a new dress."

Twelve

The party on his rooftop to celebrate the new merger should have been one of the highlights of Oliver's year. He tried to tell himself that it was as he stood at the railing off his rooftop garden, overlooking the backyard and pool.

The May weather was ideal. The gardens were in perfect form, with the flowers scenting the air and keeping the whole event colorful. Invitations to the party had been sought-after enough that there were at least fifteen more people than he'd accounted for ahead of time. Even Xavier Noble had stopped by since the celebrity groom's publisher was repped by the Manhattan marketing firm Nexus had acquired.

Yet, as Oliver finished off his glass of a top-shelf

Scotch he'd stocked for the open bar service, he could no longer deny that tonight's party was far from a highlight in his year. It blended with a hundred other business events he'd attended, one after the other, in his quest to make the Nexus name a formidable contender in the global marketing world.

Without Jessica by his side, the whole thing felt empty. Just the same way his house did this past week without her in it. Had he done anything else all week besides think about her? Ever since she'd left, he'd been carrying around the engagement band she'd returned to him. His fingers found the diamond ring now, tucked into the pocket of his suit jacket, where he traced the lines of the heirloom like some kind of talisman.

"Looks like you need a refill." Xavier Noble— Ex—settled his forearms on the railing next to Oliver and clinked his champagne glass against Oliver's empty crystal snifter. "You've got a lot to celebrate tonight."

Reminding himself to smile, Oliver tried to arrange his features in the correct order as he let go of the ring in his pocket. With the merger, Ex Noble had become more than just a friend. He was also a premier part of their client base.

"Thank you. And thanks for stopping by the party tonight. I know you must have a lot going on to prepare for the wedding." Oliver could see a few party guests outside by the pool and hoped Nikolai was down there with them. He hadn't intended to make his whole house available to his guests, but maybe Nik had wanted to talk to some of the guests privately.

Mostly, Oliver was scanning the grounds in the hope of seeing Jessica. Which was foolish. He hadn't heard a word from her all week, but he'd held out a little hope she'd make an appearance tonight since she'd agreed to attend the event with him. But that had been back when they were a couple.

A fake couple, he supposed. But in many ways, it had felt more real to him than any relationship he'd ever been in.

"The wedding is under control as long as the wedding crasher stays away," Ex assured him, downing the last of the champagne and setting his flute aside on the concrete base of the steel railing where they stood. Urbane and well-spoken, the author turned celebrity might be one of Royal's most famous residents, but Oliver remembered him as a rancher's son and an all-around good guy. "Ari and her event planner have heard reports from some of the vendors that the crasher is in town."

Oliver frowned. His work in marketing had made him familiar with how much damage a prankster could do at any event. "Seriously? What kind of person crashes a wedding?"

"Ari's fame is a double-edged sword," Ex told him seriously. "If this guy is looking to cash in on her name by making trouble—" He shook his head as if to ward off the bad thoughts. "Needless to say, we're on the lookout for any problems"

"You're in the right town for people to watch your back," Oliver assured him, still staring out over the pool house and the spot where Jessica had played her guitar in the mornings. "I can't imagine anyone trying to stir trouble for you in Royal, where we're all rooting for you and Ari."

"Thanks, man." Ex clapped him on the shoulder as he turned as if to rejoin the party. Then he paused. "But I should be asking you about your significant other. The photos of you and Jessica from the couples' shower turned out really well." He withdrew his phone. "I'll have Seth Grayson send them to you."

Oliver could only imagine how he'd feel looking at the photos of him and Jessica kissing that day. "Thanks. But, ah, we're not together anymore."

Admitting it aloud felt like a failure—and more. He couldn't find the words to articulate the sense of loss over a woman who was never really his.

"Really?" Ex asked, before leaning closer to confide, "Because she just walked into the party."

Everything in him stilled for a moment.

Then he whipped around to see for himself, half-convinced Ex was pranking him.

But there, close to the door that led to the second floor of the house, stood the most beautiful woman he'd ever seen dressed in a pale blue gown. Her dark brown hair was loose, the waves rippling in the breeze the same way her hem fluttered around her legs, a high slit revealing one thigh.

Had he missed her so much this week that he'd conjured her there, looking like a slow-motion dream sequence in a movie? And if he missed her this much in such a short time, how was he going to face forever without her?

Short answer? He couldn't lose even one more second with her.

"Will you excuse me?" he said to Ex, unable to drag his eyes away from Jessica for a moment in case she vanished.

He thought Xavier might have chuckled in response, but it didn't matter. Nothing mattered except closing the distance between him and Jessica. In his periphery vision, he noted that Nik was back in the rooftop garden, circulating with some of the executives from the Royal office. Oliver passed by him close enough to inform him he was in charge of the party for the next little while.

Nik's gaze followed where Oliver's was still transfixed, then—like the stand-up friend he'd always been—he told Oliver he had things in hand.

Freeing Oliver to pursue the woman he couldn't stop thinking about. The woman he'd missed more than he could have imagined.

Her eyes met his when he was a few yards away. She tracked his progress toward her, her hands smoothing down the satiny blue ruffle that crossed her body in a diagonal sweep from her neck to the sexy thigh slit.

"Jessica." He stopped a foot in front of her. Too close, perhaps. But he needed to breathe her in after the days away from her. And he was rewarded with the softest hint of honeysuckle.

"Hello, Oliver." Her lips quirked in a half smile as her gaze darted from his to glance around the party. "The rooftop looks beautiful."

He didn't have the wherewithal to make small talk. Not when he realized that having her here with him was the only thing good that had happened to him since she'd left. The only right thing.

He didn't just miss Jessica. He needed her.

Loved her.

The simple truth was staring him in the face with blue-green eyes the color of a faraway sea. It might be too dim on the rooftop to see the exact shade to-night, but he knew from memory. From his dreams.

"Can we talk?" The words burst out of his mouth too quickly, a new urgency compelling him now that he'd figured out why his life had felt like walking through a barren desert all week. "Somewhere qui-eter?"

Her brows knit together briefly. "It's okay with me, but won't your guests wonder where you went?"

"They'll be fine." There'd been a time when he would have simply taken her hand to lead the way, but he'd lost that right, hadn't he? Grinding his teeth together, he nodded toward the outdoor staircase that led to a balcony off the second floor. "We'll just be down here."

They were halfway down the steps when Oliver realized he hadn't even offered her a drink or anything. But then, he'd been so surprised to see her after the way she'd called things off he wasn't thinking clearly.

At the base of the steps, he pointed toward two wide cushioned chairs flanking a cocktail table. The seats overlooked the side yard, where his landscaper had convinced him to install a flagstone path leading to a white marble fountain surrounded by purple flowers and gray stones. A few flowering trees were outlined with spotlights, and the fountain was illuminated from within.

"I'm too nervous to sit." Jessica walked to the railing instead of the chairs he'd shown her. "I won't stay long, Oliver. Maybe it wasn't a good idea for me to show up unannounced—"

"No." He took her hand then. Just for a moment. Just long enough to squeeze lightly in the hope of pressing home the point. He let it go again. "You're the best thing that's happened all evening."

Jessica's fingers tingled where Oliver had touched her.

That electric connection hadn't changed in the week they'd been apart, that was for certain. But she was having the toughest time reading his expression. Ever since their gazes had met on the rooftop, she'd been trying to gauge his reception of her surprise appearance.

Yet Oliver looked at her in a new way, a different glint in his eyes than she'd seen in the past. That look made her heart flutter against her ribs in a way that was about more than sex.

At first, she'd been self-conscious of her appearance, convinced she must be having a wardrobe malfunction or something. But now, as their stilted conversation stalled again, her racing thoughts circled back to the words he'd just said. Really hearing them this time.

She was the best thing that had happened tonight?

"Is the party going that badly?" she asked, only half joking since she was struggling to read his reaction.

Oliver looked so handsome tonight in a black suit. The crisp white shirt collar and gray tie made her fingers itch to smooth over them, even though both garments already lay perfectly on his broad chest. Instead, she settled her palms on the smooth steel balcony railing.

Beside her, Oliver did the same. Their hands rested just inches apart. The guitar music from upstairs—a soloist doing an instrumental version of a David Bowie tune—mingled with laughter and conversation from the party above them. But here, tucked behind the staircase and overlooking the empty garden below, they were all alone.

"On the contrary," he answered in the bass baritone that she'd missed so much. "The party has gone off flawlessly. And I couldn't pinpoint why I hated every minute of it until you walked into the garden tonight."

Her heartbeat sped up faster at the words that gave her hope. Words that recalibrated her understanding of the way he looked at her now.

Hope gathered so fast she had to caution herself to wait. To listen. And to share what she'd come here tonight to say. She'd been nervous about it all week long.

"I've missed you." She blurted the simple truth, scraping together all her courage to continue. She couldn't expect honesty from anyone else if she didn't give it freely herself. "I wasn't sure when I could see you again to tell you, so I've been waiting for tonight, when I knew you'd be here and I still had an invitation. But I need you to know that I only broke our arrangement because I was—"

"Wait. Please." His hand slid closer to hers on the railing, their pinkies touching. "You had every reason to end it because I was expecting you to live a lie. And that was wrong of me."

He stood close enough now that she could breathe in the scent of his aftershave, the familiar notes reminding her of times they'd been wrapped around each other.

"But I knew that when I agreed to it." She didn't want to make excuses for herself. "I just didn't realize how difficult that would be in the execution."

"It was a plan doomed to fail." A shadow fell over his features as he scowled. "And I'm so damned sorry that I gave you any reason to think I doubted your abilities as a professional. I had no business trying to run interference with my mother when you could help my dad. Please know I was only trying to keep everyone from growing more attached, to save you and them from getting hurt because of me."

His words soothed a hurt that had festered ever since that night in the emergency room. "Thank you, Oliver. That means a lot to me." Relieved of that concern, she allowed herself to focus on the rest of what he'd said. "And for what it's worth, I didn't think the engagement plan was all bad."

"Definitely not," he rushed to add, his warm hand covering hers. Finally. "In hindsight, I think I came up with the fake-engagement idea just to keep you close to me—my subconscious helping me along. You were nothing like anyone else I'd ever been with, and I was at a loss to see you for as long as I wanted since you were as wary of dating as I've been."

"You really think so?" Blinking in surprise as the hope she'd been feeling swelled faster, Jessica flipped her palm over to face his, missing the feel of him.

"How else to account for an otherwise-rational guy upending his whole life to see you as often as possible?" Gripping her hand more tightly in his, he turned to face her, tugging her with him so they stood inches apart on the balcony.

The sincerity in his voice matched the honesty in his green eyes, and she wanted nothing so much as to stand here forever with him this way, feeling the connection between them grow again. And his admission made her wonder if she'd accepted the ring because, on some level, she'd already been falling for him.

"It sounded practical at the time." Her pulse sped up faster, her voice breathless.

"But it would be far more practical if I gave this to you for real." He produced the engagement ring from his pocket, the diamonds of the band winking in the moonlight. "Because this time, when I offer you this ring, it comes with all of my love and a promise that if you give me another chance, I will never give you any reason to second-guess how much I respect and care for you."

Happy tears stung her eyes at the tender words her heart had longed to hear. She didn't bother trying to hide them, needing to be completely honest with everything she was feeling for this amazing man.

A watery laugh bubbled up her throat as she took in the ring with surprise and a whole lot of happiness. She laid her hands on his chest, her fingers stroking over the lapels of his jacket as she absorbed the warmth and strength of the man beneath the clothes. She needed to tell him why she'd come tonight.

"Oliver, I've been psyching myself up all week long to see you tonight just so that I could confess that I love you. So very much. More than I'd imagined possible. I kept telling myself I needed you to know, even if you didn't feel the same way." She bit her lip, her heart full to overflowing.

His forehead tipped to hers for a long moment, a sigh of relief shuddering through him before he kissed her cheeks. Her eyes.

"Nothing was right without you. And the work that seemed so important to me didn't matter when you weren't here." He edged back to look into her eyes, his thumb stroking her cheek as he cradled her face in his hand. "So I'm not going to worry about traveling the globe anymore to keep up with a business that doesn't need me to babysit it every second. I want to spend time here. With you."

"I'd love that." Happiness filled her up inside. And it seemed only fitting that the guitar soloist had just begun the opening of Etta James's "At Last." The music swirled around them, but it was her love for Oliver that made her heart dance.

"So is that a yes to wearing my ring again?" He wrapped an arm around her waist, pulling her close. "For real and forever?"

She gave him her left hand, more than ready to commit herself to a man she loved and trusted. A man who made her believe in romance again.

"That's a yes." She watched as he slid the heirloom engagement band back on her finger, where she knew it would always remain. "For real. Forever."

* * * * *

Look for the next stories in the
Texas Cattleman's Club: The Wedding series.

Oh So Right with Mr. Wrong
by Nadine Gonzalez.

and

The Man She Loves to Hate
by Jessica Lemmon.

Available May 2023!

SECOND CHANCE RANCHER & FAKE DATING, TWIN STYLE

SECOND CHANCE RANCHER

Heirs of Hardwell Ranch • by J. Margot Critch

After a Vegas wedding, billionaire black sheep Wes Hardwell returns to Texas intent on divorce. But his brief "honeymoon" to get Daisy Thorne out of his system makes him question if Texas *and* Daisy are the happily-ever-after he's been yearning for.

FAKE DATING, TWIN STYLE

The Hartmann Heirs • by Katie Frey

After her latest fender bender, serial bad driver Amelia Hartmann needs a solution—fast. Pretending to be her celebrity twin is the best solution. Except the other driver is former NFL star Antone Williams. And he's determined to find—and seduce—the Hartmann sister who crashed into his life!

JUST A LITTLE JILTED & THEIR TEMPORARY ARRANGEMENT

JUST A LITTLE JILTED

Dynasties: Calcott Manor • by Joss Wood

Jilted by her boss *and* her famous, superficial fiancé, model Eliot Gamble needs a life reset. But an unexpected, steamy weekend in Soren Grantham's bed works, too! The competitive swimmer is stunned by Eliot's depth and passion. Is love the next step they've both yearned for?

THEIR TEMPORARY ARRANGEMENT

Dynasties: Calcott Manor • by Joss Wood

Personal assistant Ru Osman is tired of people trying to control her—including her new boss! But the notoriously difficult Fox Grantham is more consumed with seducing the feisty beauty than replacing her. Will passion and purpose collide for these professional opposites?

BLUE BLOOD MEETS BLUE COLLAR & ONE STORMY NIGHT

BLUE BLOOD MEETS BLUE COLLAR

The Renaud Brothers • by Cynthia St. Aubin

Single dad Remy Renaud doesn't remember his one night with television producer Cosima Lowell. Which is fine by Cosima, because filming his family for a reality show is the professional break she needs...if the embers of their connection don't set both their worlds ablaze.

ONE STORMY NIGHT

Business and Babies • by Jules Bennett

When a storm strands Mila Hale with her potential new boss, she plans to keep things all business. But playboy Cruz Westbrook is too reckless, too wild and too damn sexy—and determined to indulge in unbridled passion until he finds the one...

You can find more information on upcoming Harlequin titles, free excerpts and more at Harlequin.com.

Get 4 FREE REWARDS!

We'll send you 2 FREE Books plus 2 FREE Mystery Gifts.

FREE Value Over **$20**

Both the **Harlequin® Desire** and **Harlequin Presents®** series feature compelling novels filled with passion, sensuality and intriguing scandals.

YES! Please send me 2 FREE novels from the Harlequin Desire or Harlequin Presents series and my 2 FREE gifts (gifts are worth about $10 retail). After receiving them, if I don't wish to receive any more books, I can return the shipping statement marked "cancel." If I don't cancel, I will receive 6 brand-new Harlequin Presents Larger-Print books every month and be billed just $6.30 each in the U.S. or $6.49 each in Canada, a savings of at least 10% off the cover price, or 6 Harlequin Desire books every month and be billed just $5.05 each in the U.S. or $5.74 each in Canada, a savings of at least 12% off the cover price. It's quite a bargain! Shipping and handling is just 50¢ per book in the U.S. and $1.25 per book in Canada.* I understand that accepting the 2 free books and gifts places me under no obligation to buy anything. I can always return a shipment and cancel at any time by calling the number below. The free books and gifts are mine to keep no matter what I decide.

Choose one: ☐ **Harlequin Desire**
(225/326 HDN GRJ7)

☐ **Harlequin Presents Larger-Print**
(176/376 HDN GRJ7)

Name (please print)

Address   Apt. #

City   State/Province   Zip/Postal Code

Email: Please check this box ☐ if you would like to receive newsletters and promotional emails from Harlequin Enterprises ULC and its affiliates. You can unsubscribe anytime.

Mail to the **Harlequin Reader Service:**
IN U.S.A.: P.O. Box 1341, Buffalo, NY 14240-8531
IN CANADA: P.O. Box 603, Fort Erie, Ontario L2A 5X3

Want to try 2 free books from another series! Call 1-800-873-8635 or visit www.ReaderService.com.

---

*Terms and prices subject to change without notice. Prices do not include sales taxes, which will be charged (if applicable) based on your state or country of residence. Canadian residents will be charged applicable taxes. Offer not valid in Quebec. This offer is limited to one order per household. Books received may not be as shown. Not valid for current subscribers to the Harlequin Presents or Harlequin Desire series. All orders subject to approval. Credit or debit balances in a customer's account(s) may be offset by any other outstanding balance owed by or to the customer. Please allow 4 to 6 weeks for delivery. Offer available while quantities last.

Your Privacy—Your information is being collected by Harlequin Enterprises ULC, operating as Harlequin Reader Service. For a complete summary of the information we collect, how we use this information and to whom it is disclosed, please visit our privacy notice located at corporate.harlequin.com/privacy-notice. From time to time we may also exchange your personal information with reputable third parties. If you wish to opt out of this sharing of your personal information, please visit readerservice.com/consumerschoice or call 1-800-873-8635. **Notice to California Residents**—Under California law, you have specific rights to control and access your data. For more information on these rights and how to exercise them, visit corporate.harlequin.com/california-privacy.

HDHP22R3

HARLEQUIN
PLUS

Try the best multimedia subscription service for romance readers like you!

Read, Watch and Play.

Experience the easiest way to get the romance content you crave.

Start your **FREE TRIAL** at
www.harlequinplus.com/freetrial.